James Maidment, John Crown, William H. Logan

The Dramatic Works of John Crowne

Volume 1

James Maidment, John Crown, William H. Logan

The Dramatic Works of John Crowne
Volume 1

ISBN/EAN: 9783337267803

Printed in Europe, USA, Canada, Australia, Japan

Cover: Foto ©Andreas Hilbeck / pixelio.de

More available books at **www.hansebooks.com**

THE DRAMATIC WORKS OF JOHN CROWNE.

WITH PREFATORY MEMOIR AND NOTES.

VOLUME THE FIRST.

MDCCCLXXIII.

EDINBURGH: WILLIAM PATERSON.
LONDON: H. SOTHERAN & CO.

CONTENTS.

LANGBAINE, in his account of the English Dramatic Poets, Oxon. 1691, 12mo, although a contemporary, mentions Crowne as " a person, now living, who has attempted all sorts of Dramatick poetry with different success. . . . If I may be allowed to speak my sentiments," he continues, " I think his genius seems fittest for Comedy, though possibly his Tragedies are no ways contemptible, of all which, in my weak judgment, his Destruction of Jerusalem seems the best." Then follows a list of his plays to the above date, with some notes as to the sources whence their plots have been derived.

Subsequent biographers have for the most part derived what little information they are pleased to offer from the account of this poet given by John Dennis in his Letters.* Following in the wake of one another they simply indorse without enquiry, as seems usual with book-makers, the statements made by the original writer, copying even his very words. In this way, they unite in saying, as Dennis himself has it, that "John Crowne was the son of an independent minister in that part of America which is called Nova Scotia. The vivacity of his genius made him soon grow

* Letters, vol. i., p. 18.

impatient of that sullen and gloomy education, and soon oblig'd him to get loose from it, and seek his fortune in England; but it was his fate at his first arrival here, to happen on an employment more formal, if possible, than his American education."   Oldys has these notes in MS. on his annotated copy of Langbaine, in the British Museum :—" John Crowne was the son of William Crowne, gent., who travelled under the Earl of Arundel to Vienna, and published a relation of the remarkable places and passages in the said Earl's said Embassy to the Emperor Ferdinand II., 1637, but full of imperfections and errors. This William, afterwards succeeded H. Lilly as Rouge Dragon in the Herald's office, and was continued in 1660; but, selling to Mr Sandford,* went over with his family to one of the plantations and there died." "There is some order or paper of instructions I once saw in the Harleian Library, from Charles II., as I remember, either to the Lord Baltimore or some other possessors, or Governors in one of the American settlements, to enquire into, recover, or restore for or on behalf of Mr John Crowne or his father."

On Crowne's arrival in England, his urgent

---

* The following notice of Mr Sandford is from a MS. of Dr Farmer's :—" Francis Sandford, a younger brother of the Sandfords of Sandford, in Shropshire, a gentleman of good education, and a lover of antiquities and mathematics. He was first made Rouge Dragon, *circa* 1662, on the death [?] of Mr Crown, and second, 1675, on the death of Mr Chaloner, was made Lancaster Herald. He published many treatises in the way of Heraldry of his own translation and composition, the principal whereof was, his Genealogical History of the Kings of England, and the History of the Coronation of King James II. ; in which last he was jointly assisted by Mr King, Rouge Dragon. He resigned his place of Lancaster in the beginning of William and Mary to King William aforesaid, and died in low circumstances, a prisoner to the Fleet, 16th Jan. 1693."—*Sepultus in Cœmiterio S. Brigitta, Fleet Street, London.*

necessities obliged him to become gentleman-usher to an old Independent lady of quality, but, so soon as he was able to exist otherwise, he quitted this most uncongenial employment, and launched into the world of letters, for which he had evinced an aptitude. His taste lay in favour of dramatic literature, which was the readier path to favour and distinction, though not to power or fortune. His writings ere long made him known to the Court and the town, and the Earl of Rochester, in order, as it is said, to mortify Dryden, at whom he had taken umbrage, prevailed on the king or his brother to lay commands on Crowne, in preference to the Poet-Laureate, to write a masque for performance at Court, which he duly executed under the title of Calisto. The circumstance of Crowne being set up in opposition to Dryden is noticed by St. Evremond in a letter to the Duchess of Mazarine.

That the favour extended to our poet by Lord Rochester was not owing, it has been asserted, to any peculiar personal regard, for, in the short space of two years, he incurred the envy and subsequent enmity of that nobleman, in consequence of the great success of his two-part tragedy—the Destruction of Jerusalem—and the Earl went so far as to endeavour to injure him at Court; but in this he was unsuccessful, Crowne standing high in the favour of the King, as all those usually did who contributed to his amusement. However this may be, Crowne dedicated his tragedy of Charles VIII. of France (1680) to Rochester, who in return thus lampooned the author, in an imitation of Boileau's Third Satire, which will be found in the collected edition of his remains :—

" Kickum for Crown declared ; said, in Romance.
He had out-done the very wits of France.

Witness Pandion and his Charles the Eight ;
Where a young monarch, careless of his fate,
Tho' foreign troops and rebels shock his state,
Complains another sight afflicts him more.
(*Viz.*) 'The Queen's galleys rowing from the shore,
Fitting their oars and tackling to be gone,
Whilst sportive waves smil'd on the rising sun.'
Waves smiling on the sun ! I'm sure that's new,
And 'twas well thought on, give the devil his due."

Rochester wrote some other verses upon Crowne in which he characterized him as "Starch Johnny Crowne." "Many a cup of metheglin have I drank with little starch Johnny Crowne," says the author of a letter on the celebrated poets and actors in King Charles II.'s time, in the "Gentleman's Magazine," vol. xv., 1745. "We called him so from the stiff unalterable primness of his long cravat."

After the discovery of what was called the Popish plot, and the consequent antagonism of the two parties, Crowne, from the favour he was held in by the King, and the natural gaiety of his temper, sided with the Tory party, and wrote a comedy called the City Politiques, in ridicule of the Whigs, the wit and merit of which even many of his opponents acknowledged. When written, he found much difficulty in getting it performed. Bennet, Lord Arlington, the then Lord Chamberlain, exerted all his authority to suppress it. It would seem that Lord Arlington, in order to support himself against the power of the Earl of Danby, the Lord Treasurer, his declared enemy, was secretly a supporter of the Whigs, who were at that time potent in Parliament. The reasons for prohibiting the performance of the play were various; at one time it was dangerous, at another it was flat and insipid, and exception would have been taken to it at every turn, had not Crowne exerted his influence with the King to cause the Lord Chamberlain not to delay it longer. This command the King was pleased to impose in person.

Crowne, though attached to his Majesty, disliked the insincerity of the Court, and seldom made his appearance there excepting when he went to receive such sums of money as were from time to time accorded him.

Towards the end of King Charles' reign, Crowne, desirous to escape from the tedium of writing combined with the uncertainty of theatrical success, and at the same time to shelter himself from the resentment of numerous enemies he had made by the production of his City Politiques, applied to his Majesty for an appointment to some permanent office. The King assured him he should be provided for, but he must first produce another comedy. Crowne begged to be excused in this, stating that he was slow and awkward in devising a plot. His objections were overruled by his Majesty saying he would help him to a plot, and immediately placed in his hands a Spanish comedy called "No puede ser." He set at once to work upon this, and was far advanced in his adaptation, when he discovered that the piece had been previously translated by Thomas St Serfe, a Scotchman,* under the title of "Tarugo's Wiles, or, the Coffee House," and acted at the Duke's Theatre without success.

Pepys has the following entry in his diary,

---

* He was son of the Bishop of Galloway, the only surviving prelate, at the Restoration, of those removed at the famous, or rather infamous, Assembly of 1638. *See* A Book of Scotish Pasquils, 1568-1715, Edin. 1868, p. 25, *crown 8vo.* The Bishop, though a very old man upon the restoration of Episcopacy, was translated to the richer benefice of Orkney, which he held until his death in 1663.

from which it is evident that, before recommending the play to Crowne, the King had previously seen the performance of the adaptation by Sidserff—or St Serfe, as his name was spelt—and had not been satisfied with it:—*15th October* 1667. "My wife and I, and Willet to the Duke of York's house, where, after long stay, the King and Duke of York came, and there saw the Coffee House, the most ridiculous, insipid play that ever I saw in my life, and glad we were that Betterton had no part in it." It appears that Mrs Pepys suspected her husband of paying too much attention to Willet, and began to knag about it, a circumstance which would not tend to put the worthy Secretary in a proper humour for considering a performance, which was specially recommended by so competent a judge as the Earl of Dorset, in verses addressed to the author on its publication, in which he is styled Sir Thomas St Serfe, " whence we may gather that he had been honoured with a Knight Hood, though in the title page of his play he is called Thomas St Serfe, Gent."*

Encouraged by the King, to whom he had read his piece scene by scene, in so far as it had gone, he completed it, taking for its title " Sir Courtly Nice ; or, It cannot be," but, alas ! for his hopes of gratifying the King, and obtaining the provision for life which had been promised him. The very morning of the last rehearsal of the play, his Majesty was seized with a fit, caused, as has been

* Jones' Biographia Dramatica, vol. ii., p. 624. The following is a correct copy of the title page:—Tarugo's Wiles, or the Coffee House. A Comedy as it was acted at his Highness's the Duke of York's Theater. Written by Thos. St. Serffe, Gent. London. Printed for Henry Herringman, at the Sign of the Anchor, on the lower-walk of the New-Exchange. 1668. 4to

hinted, by some mysterious agency, which eventuated in his death in three days thereafter.

The comedy of "Sir Courtly Nice" was, however, produced some short time after the King's death, and was well received. It continued to be a stock piece at many theatres for upwards of a century.

Dennis, although he promises in his letter to give further particulars of Crowne on another occasion, does not appear to have done so. His subsequent career is therefore uncertain, as well as the period of his decease. It has been conjectured that his writings were his only means of support, for, after Sir Courtly Nice, he wrote other six plays, which were pretty generally successful. From Mr Coxeter's notes we learn that Crowne was alive in 1703, and, being then advanced in years, it is probable he did not thereafter long survive. Jacob tells us that he was buried in St Giles's-in-the-Fields.

The following are his Dramatic works :—

1. Juliana. A Tragi-Comedy . 1671
2. Charles VIII. of France . . 1672
3. The Country Wit. Comedy . 1675
4. Andromache. Tragedy . . 1675

This was merely a translation from Racine, which he edited for a friend.

5. Calisto. A Masque . . . 1675
6. City Politiques. Comedy . 1675
7. The Destruction of Jerusalem.
     Tragedy—2 parts . . . 1677
8. The Ambitious Statesman. Tragedy 1679
9. Henry the Sixth. Tragedy—2 parts 1681

The first part is called Henry the Sixth ; or, the Misery of Civil War, under which latter title it was acted and printed in 1680.

10. Thyestes.   Tragedy   .   1681
11. Sir Courtly Nice.   Comedy   1685
12. Darius.   Tragedy   .   .   1688
13. The English Friar.   Comedy   .   1690
14. Regulus.   Tragedy .   .   .   1694
15. The Married Beau.   Comedy   .   1694
16. Caligula.   Tragedy   .   .   1698
17. Justice Busy.   A Comedy (not printed).

In addition to these dramatic pieces, Crowne wrote :—

Pandion and Amphigenia ; or, the History of the Coy Lady of Thessalia.   Adorned with Sculpture.   London 1665, 8vo.

Dæneids ; or, the Noble Labours of the great Dean of Notre Dame in Paris, for erecting in his quire a throne for his glory, and the eclipsing the pride of an imperious usurping chanter.   An heroic poem in four cantos, containing a true history, and shews the folly, foppery, luxury, laziness, pride, ambition, and contention of the Romish clergy, 1692, 4to.   This is a burlesque poem partly translated from the Lutrin of N. Boileau Despréaux.   It was subsequently reprinted by Dryden under the title of " The Church Scuffle," in the third part of Miscellany Poems, p. 352, 1716, 12mo.

A Poem on the lamented death of our late gratious Sovereign, King Charles the II., of ever blessed memory.   With a congratulation to the Happy succession of King James the II.   London, printed for John Smith, bookseller in Russel Street, near Covent Garden, 1685, 4to.

In this " Poem " Charles is depicted, according to the adulation of the day, as possessing every virtue under the sun, and as being greater than divinity itself.

Crowne also contributed a song or two, set to music by Henry Purcell, to the "Gentleman's Journal, or Monthly Miscellany," edited by Motteux, 1691-2.

Of Crowne and his merits as a dramatist, the "Biographia Dramatica" advances this opinion, of which our own is confirmatory:—"As a man, he seems to have possessed many amiable and social virtues, mingled with great vivacity and easiness of disposition. As a writer, his numerous works bear sufficient testimony of his merit. His chief excellence lay in comedy, yet his tragedies are far from contemptible. His plots are for the most part his own invention; his characters are in general strongly coloured and highly finished; and his dialogue lively and spirited, attentively diversified, and well adapted to the several speakers."

As a writer of Comedies, he is the superior of Dryden, who in no one instance has produced anything to be compared to Sir Courtly Nice.

Warton, in a note upon a passage in one of Pope's prologues to his Satires relative to the public starving Dryden when alive, and burying him munificently after his decease,* gives an account of the Laureate's emoluments, so far as Tonson was concerned, and instances the receipt upon the publication of his Fables of two hundred and sixty-eight pounds, "for ten thousand verses, and to complete the full number of lines stipulated for, he gave the bookseller the Epistle to his cousin and the celebrated Music Ode." It cannot be said that this was an overpayment. It leads to a somewhat interesting disclosure: "Old Jacob used to say,

* Bowles Pope, vol. iv., p. 47.

that Dryden was a little jealous of rivals. He would compliment Crowne when a play of his failed, but was very cold to him if he met with success. He used to say that Crowne had some genius, but then he added always that his father and Crowne's mother were very well acquainted."

If this anecdote is true, which it probably is, the explanation is not difficult. Born a poet, and conscious of the *divinus afflatus*, what pain Dryden must have endured at the indignity of having such a miserable poetaster as Elkanah Settle set up as a rival, and patronised by parties in power who preferred, or seemed to do so, such wretched tragedies as the Empress of Morocco, and the Illustrious Bassa to his All for Love and Don Sebastian, in both of which are passages worthy of the older dramatists. Nor could the insult in transferring Calisto to Crowne be pardoned. No doubt the latter, in his address to the reader, yields the palm to Dryden with a delicacy and propriety exceedingly to be commended, but still the insult by Rochester would not be forgotten, and when it is recollected that neither an ancient pedigree, a titled wife, nor noble relatives could supply the wants of a family or exclude the presence of poverty, we are surely entitled to overlook such ebullitions of temper as Old Jacob has been the means of preserving for the edification of posterity.

It has not been deemed essential to reprint Crowne's Dramatic pieces · in the exact chronological order in which they were first presented to the public, or to include such as cannot properly be described as his own composition.

JAMES MAIDMENT.
W. H. LOGAN.

JULIANA.

I

JULIANA, or the *Princess of Poland*. *A Tragi-Comedy.
As it acted at his Royal Highness the Duke of York's
Theatre. By J. Crowne, Gent. Presto, e bene, di rado
riesce bene. Licenced Sept. 8, 1671. Roger L'Estrange.
London, printed for Will. Cademan, at the Pope's Head, in
the lower Walk in the New Exchange, and Will Birch, at
the lower end of Cheapside. 1671.*

In his dedication to the Earl of Orrery the author laments that his "first-born" had, in the absence of the Court, been left to the mercy of a common audience, " in which unguarded condition" it might well be expected to receive some wounds, and so it did though much fewer than " I expected, yet such as it deserved";—admissions which shew that the drama had only been partially successful. It is not surprising that such had been its reception, for the plot is somewhat confused, and, without the explanations added to the names of the dramatis personæ, not very intelligible to spectators.

Although the events are represented as occurring at Warsaw, before the meeting of the Diet for election of a King, they have no foundation in reality, there never having been a Princess called Juliana, and no Duke of Curland, or Courland, bearing the Christian name of Ladislaus, who was elected King of Poland upon his marriage with the Princess of that kingdom. At no period in the history either of that country or of the Duchy of Curland was there a King or Duke called Ladislaus. The list of Polish monarchs, and Dukes of Courland, given in 1696 by Dr Connor* in his interesting letters from Poland, have been carefully gone over to discover if any information could be procured relative either to the parties or incidents in this Tragicomedy, but without success.

Why a Duke of Courland was selected as the hero may have arisen from the fact that, in the early part of the reign of Charles II., the ruler of that Duchy, a fief of

* " The History of Poland, in several Letters to Persons of Quality, giving an account of the ancient and present state of that Kingdom. London, 1696, 2 vols. 8vo." Published by the care and assistance of Mr Savage.

This must have been the " J. Savage " who is represented in the Biographia Dramatica as the "translator of Celestina." Fc. 8vo, 1707.

Poland, became known to the people of England from a
contention in relation to the occupancy by the Dutch of
the Island of Tobago, which had been discovered by
James, the fourth Duke—a godson of James I. of
England—and named after his Majesty. The Duke
placed a colony there, and built a fort called James' Fort.

For a series of years the colony prospered, so much so
that it attracted the notice of a rich Dutchman of the
name of Lambson, who, getting permission to settle on
a corner of the Island upon condition of paying a
yearly tribute, took the opportunity of the imprisonment of the owner by the Swedes, to dispossess him
of the Island, and refused, after his Highness had recovered his liberty, to restore it to him. After ineffec-
tually endeavouring to induce Lambson and the States
of Holland to give back what had been so unfairly
taken from him, the Duke applied to Charles II. for
assistance, and offered to hold the Island off the Crown
of England. Accordingly, an agreement, dated 17th of
November 1664, was entered into between Charles and
the Duke, by which the former gave and granted " to
the said Duke of Curland, his heirs, and successors, all
and every that Island called Tobago, to be held and en-
joyed under the King's protection."

Their High Mightinesses the States of Holland were by
no means pleased with the interference of Charles in
endeavouring to procure restoration of a colony so un-
warrantably taken from the godson of his grandfather, and
by various artifices contrived to hold possession, so that
it was not until the year 1681, or about that time, that
Duke James, by compulsion, got back his Island, which,
during the occupation of the Dutch, had been held by
them as convenient for the ready pillaging of their neighbours—its remote position and its accessible harbours
rendering it a suitable place for depositing the spoil
which they had obtained either by their own acts or
through the pirates whom they patronized. At this
date, the Amboyna massacres had not been forgotten in
England, and the Dutch were still unpopular. Thus the
name of this ill-used Prince would naturally find favour
with the London citizens, and Crowne, alive to this
impression, conferred the honours of Courland on the

hero of his drama as a means of drawing attention to it.

As a first production this drama is entitled to more credit than is accorded to it either in the Biographia Dramatica, or by Geneste in his history of the English stage. The plot is apparently original, and not taken from any of the Italian novelists, upon whom our old dramatists were accustomed so frequently to draw. No doubt the story is somewhat perplexing, and the marriage in the dark of the supposed Ladislaus to the Muscovite Princess Paulina rather improbable,—still, with judicious pruning and curtailment, Juliana might yet be converted into an attractive play—infinitely superior to the great mass of modern sensational dramas of ephemeral existence which appear for a season or two and then vanish and are seen no more.

The character of the landlord is admitted by Geneste to be an amusing one. He must have contributed materially to such success as attended the original representation.

But Paulina in her male costume is infinitely more calculated to please an audience than the Polish Princess. The interest of the piece rests with her rather than with Juliana; and her wild goose chase after an imaginary husband is more interesting than the bold defiance of the Cardinal by Juliana, or her grief for the supposed infidelity of Ladislaus.

The piece was well cast. Mrs Saunderson, better known subsequently as Mrs Betterton, a performer of great merit, acted the Princess of Poland, and Mrs Long, esteemed " a fine actress," was the representative of Paulina.* She assumed the part of the Justice in Betterton's comedy of " The Woman made a Justice " —a play so successful as to be acted fourteen days running. She afterwards appeared as Mrs Brittle in " the Amorous Widow or the Wanton Wife," a character in which she was succeeded by Mrs Bracegirdle. In Lord Orrery's Henry V., 1688, she took the character of the Queen of France. Geneste says the name of Mrs Long does not appear after 1673. Downes commends

* See History of the English Stage. London. Curll, 1741, 8vo.

her greatly in Widow Rich, as well as in the characters above mentioned.

Mrs Shadwell is named as Cleora the Queen of Hungary's woman in Lord Orrery's tragedy of Mustapha, 1668. She must have been a vocalist, as, in her character of Joanna, the attendant of Paulina, she is discovered, upon the rising of the curtain, singing beside her mistress, who is sleeping under a tree.

Geneste says:—"Mrs Shadwell's name does not occur after the union of the two companies in 1682. She was certainly the wife of [Thomas] Shadwell the poet, and perhaps Mrs Williams before her marriage. The name of Mrs Williams stands to the parts of Leandra in the Slighted Maid, and Pontia in the Stepmother in 1663, after which we hear no more of her. Mrs Shadwell's name first appears in 1664." She survived her husband, who died suddenly in 1692 in the fifty-second year of his age at Chelsea, and was interred in the church there. In the Apotheosis of Milton, printed in the *Gentleman's Magazine*, vol. 8, p. 235, a singular picture of Shadwell's personal appearance will be found, which may be presumed to be correct, as many persons then alive must have seen him often.* Mrs Shadwell was living in 1693, as she dedicated to Queen Mary her husband's posthumous comedy of the Volunteers, or the Stock-jobbers. The late Sir Launcelot Shadwell, the vice-Chancellor, is understood to have been a descendant of the Dramatist.

Of the male performers, the important part of the Jesuitical Cardinal was assigned to Joseph Harris, originally a seal cutter, a calling he abandoned for the stage where he met with great success. Pepys was a great friend of his, and makes mention of his agreeable society. His portrait was painted as Henry V. by Hales, and the Secretary of the Admiralty saw it in his studio but " did not think the picture near so good as any yet he has made for me." This was not Shakspeare's Henry V., but a rhyming tragedy by the Earl of Orrery, first published by Herringham in folio at London 1668, with the tragedy of Mustapha by the same noble Earl, in which Harris is entered amongst the Dramatis

* See D'Avenant's Dramatic Works, vol. i. p. liv., Prefatory Memoir. Edinburgh, Paterson, 1872.

Personæ as Mustapha, the son of Solyman the magnificent. He was so successful in the Cardinal Wolsey of Shakespeare that a mezzotint engraving was taken of him in the character—now of extra-rarity—but of which an impression is preserved in the Pepysian Library at Cambridge.

In 1793 a print of him was published, probably from the painting by Hales just mentioned, then in possession of Horace Walpole at Strawberry Hill—but whither it has gone since the dispersion of the treasures, once there preserved, has not been ascertained.

Of Betterton, the representative of Ladislaus, so much is known that, respecting his extraordinary talents as a performer, it is unnecessary to say more than that he has never been excelled either as an actor on the stage, or as a gentleman off it.*

"Among the many fine players of this age," it is remarked in "Betterton's History of the English Stage," "Mr Sandford must be remembered, and sorry we are that we can obtain no other notices of him than what we find among the Dramatis Personæ prefixed to the plays in which he acted." Sandford excelled "in such characters as Creon, Malignii, Iago, and Machiavel."† Necessity more than choice forced him into this line of acting, his stature being low and his person crooked. Cibber "had often lamented that Sandford's masterly performance was not rewarded with that applause which inferior actors met with, merely because they stood in more amiable characters." This gentleman's name appears in the list of Dramatis Personæ appended to the present play, set against two characters, "Count Palatines of the Cardinal's faction." Which of the two he performed is not apparent, but, from the fact of both of them being on the stage at the same time, it is evident he did not "double" the parts, as one might be induced to think.

Young, the Demetrius of the piece, took the part of the Cardinal of Veradium in Lord Orrery's Mustapha, and the Dauphine in his Lordship's Henry V. Of his history or his histrionic merits the writers on the stage have thrown no light.

* See D'Avenant. Life. lviii., lxviii., *et seq.*
† Geneste, vol. i. p. 493.

William Smith, who played the part of Sharnosky the friend of Ladislaus, was a barrister of Gray's Inn. After Sir William Davenant's decease he became a partner in the Duke's Theatre, and, as such, appears as a party to a memorandum of agreement between Dr Charles Davenant, the eldest son of Sir William, Thomas Betterton and himself, on the one part ; and Charles Hart and Edward Kynaston, players of eminence, on the other, dated 14th October 1681. The document was reprinted from the life of Betterton, by Geneste, in his useful and generally accurate " Account of the English Stage from the period of the Restoration in 1660 to 1830." Smith performed Zanger in Mustapha, and the Duke of Burgundy in Orrery's Henry V.

That facetious personage, the Landlord of the inn, on whose clever acting so much depended, was allotted to Mr Angel, who originally played female parts, but subsequently resumed his male habiliments, and became a popular performer. His name does not appear after 1673. These lines, in which he is mentioned, occur in the Prologue to the Amorous Prince, by Mrs Behn :—

> " Now for the rest,
> Who swear they'd rather hear a smutty jest
> Spoken by Nokes or Angel, than a scene
> Of the admired and well-penned Catiline."

Angel's name is among the Dramatis Personæ in Mustapha, where he is set down for Viche (a Hungarian Lord), and in Henry the Fifth he represents the Earl of Warwick. Both characters are short.

Crowne was self-interestedly judicious in his selection of a patron who had the means and power to benefit him. Roger Boyle, the fifth son of Richard, usually known as " the great Earl of Cork," obtained the Irish Barony of Broghill when only seven years of age. He was educated at the University of Dublin, where he distinguished himself as a man of genius and ability. During the Rebellion he was entrusted with the defence of his father's castle of Lismore, where he behaved with the courage and sagacity of a veteran soldier. After the murder of Charles, he was inclined to leave his native land, but was induced by Cromwell to remain, who not only received him with kindness, but took him into his confidence, and placed implicit reliance on his fidelity and sincerity. The Protector had a good knowledge of mankind, and was no doubt much influenced by the gallant and honourable conduct of Lord Broghill when espousing the cause of the Crown against the Roundheads. It has been said that Broghill suggested to Cromwell a marriage between one of his daughters and the exiled monarch, which was met with this answer,—that it was not possible Charles could forgive the death of his father, and, if he could, he was unworthy of his daughter. After the death of Cromwell he continued firm to the interests of his son, whose gentle disposition was unable to contend with the ambitious republicans around him. When Richard abandoned his high office, Broghill saw that the restoration of the exiled family was the only way to save his country from a new civil war and years of anarchy and bloodshed. He then exerted himself to effect Charles' return, and, upon the consequent restoration of a monarchical government, he was created Earl of Orrery.

Walpole, in his character of this noble Lord observes, " He was a man who never made a bad figure but as an author. As a soldier, his bravery was distinguished, his stratagems remarkable. As a statesman, it is sufficient to say that, he had the confidence of Cromwell. As a man, he was grateful and would have supported the son of his friend. Like Cicero and Richelieu, he could not be content without being a poet."

A complete catalogue of the works of Lord Orrery is given in the last edition of Walpole's royal and noble Authors, by Thomas Park, Esq.. F.S.A. His plays, with the exception of a comedy called Mr Anthony, ascribed to him, were collected in two volumes, 8vo. 1739. A reprint of the omitted drama was published by T. Wilkins at the end of the last century, London, 1794, 8vo. Lord Orrery died on the 18th of October 1679.

In Lawes' "Ayres and Dialogues," 1663, the following song by his Lordship occurs :—

THE EXCELLENCY OF WINE.

'Tis wine that inspires,
And quencheth Love's fires,
Teaches fools how to govern a State.
Maids ne'er did approve it,
Because those that love it
Despise and laugh at their hate.

The drinker of beer
Did ne'er yet appear
In matters of any great weight.
'Tis he whose design
Is quicken'd by wine,
That raises all wit to its height.

We then should it prize,
For never black eyes
Made wounds that good wine could not heal.
Who then doth refuse
To drink of the juice,
Is a foe to our good commonweal.

Cromwell loved music, of which fact there is good
evidence, and had no dislike to wine, as his enemies say.
Might not Lord Broghill have composed this spirited
song for the gratification of the Protector?

Evelyn mentions in his diary, that he saw Mustapha
performed on the 6th of March 1665-6—but gives no
opinion of its merits in his entry of that date, but the next
time he witnessed its representation he remarks that it
was " exceedingly well written." This was on the evening of the 18th October—there having been on the 16th
of the same month a general fast on account of the great
fire—the war—and the plague. The entry is so very
striking,* that we cannot refrain from bringing it under the
notice of our readers. " This night was acted my Lord
Broghill's tragedy called Mustapha before their Majesties
at Court, at which I was present, very seldom going to
the public theatres for many reasons now, as they were
abused to an atheistical liberty, foul and undecent women

* Evelyn's Diary. Lond. 1850, vol. ii. p 18.

now, and never till now, permitted to appear and act, who inflaming several young noblemen and gallants became their misses and to some their wives; witness the Earl of Oxford, Sir R. Howard, Prince Rupert, the Earl of Dorset, and another greater person than any of them, who fell into their snares to the reproach of their noble families, and ruin of both body and soul. I was invited by my Lord Chamberlain to see this tragedy, exceedingly well written, though in my mind I did not approve of any such pastime in a time of such judgments and calamities." To explain Evelyn's statement respecting the actresses of the time:—Peg Hughes became the mistress of Prince Rupert, by whom he had a daughter christened Ruperta. The Prince died on the 29th of November 1682, having, two days before, executed a settlement, by which he amply provided for " Mrs Margaret Hewes " and his and her daughter Ruperta, appointing the Earl of Craven their trustee. The young lady became the wife of Emanuel Scrope Howe, Esquire; from them descended Sir George Bromley of East Stoke, Nottingham, Baronet, who in 1787 published a volume of Original Royal Letters which had come into his possession in right of Ruperta, with a very good engraving of the lady and her husband, Prince Rupert and the Queen of Bohemia, from original paintings,—with a plate of autograph and seals. Ruperta, judging from the engraving, must have been a very beautiful woman.

Dorset, for a consideration, was so obliging as to hand over Nell Gwyn to the King, who, by her, founded the Ducal house of St Albans.

Moll Davis attracted the notice of Charles by singing the ballad of " my Lodging is on the cold ground."*

* It is said that being a very obliging person she successfully negotiated with Lord Buckhurst (Dorset) for a transfer of Nell Gwyn to the King, upon Charles paying the expenses his Lordship had been put to by her whilst under his protection, besides creating him Earl of Middlesex. Pepys has this characteristic anecdote of Nell. Becky Marshall, a well-known actress, falling out with her, called her Lord Buckhurst's mistress. Nell's reply is excellent, " I am but one man's mistress though I was brought up in a brothel to fill strong water to the gentlemen, and you are mistress to four though a Presbyterian's praying daughter." Vol. iv., p. 216. By Moll Davis

Aubrey, Earl of Oxford, the last of the historical race of De Vere, with whom the title became extinct in 1702, deluded by a false marriage Elizabeth Davenport, a virtuous young actress. She had obtained great popularity for her performance of Roxalana. Evelyn's Note which follows is not exactly correct— "9th January 1661-2, I saw acted the third part of the siege of Rhodes. In this acted the fair and famous comedian called Roxalana from the part she performed,—and I think it was the last. She being taken to be the Earl of Oxford's miss—as at this time they began to call lewd women. It was in recitative music." The Lady was deceived by Lord Oxford, who had attired one of his servants as a clergyman and induced him to perform the marriage ceremony. When the cheat was discovered, Charles II., by no means very fastidious himself, was exceedingly irate, and compelled Oxford to settle upon the lady an annual income of £300 per annum. She had a sister, who, after she left the stage, was an unsuccessful performer of Roxalana—according to Pepys.

Mrs Uphill the actress was the lady patronized by Sir Robert Howard, the author of the once popular Comedy of the Committee. He afterwards married her.

Lord Orrery's poetical merits have been unjustly underrated by Walpole. The chief defect of his Mustapha is its having been written in verse, which, however well adapted for French Tragedy, never became popular in this country. Even Dryden's Plays, when written in

Charles had a daughter Mary Tudor, who, becoming the wife of Francis Ratcliffe, was the means of having the Earldom of Derwentwater conferred upon her husband by her uncle James II. in 1687. Their grandsons James and Charles suffered for rising against government in 1715 and 1746. The latter married Charlotte Livingstone, in her own right Countess of Newburgh, by whom he had issue. She obtained £150 per annum from Government, and died in August 1755. She was succeeded by their son James in the Scotish Earldom ; he died 3d January 1786 leaving an only son, who died in 1814 without issue, thus the male representation of the Earls of Derwentwater failed. By this failure her Highness Cecilia, Princess Giustiniani, as heiress of Charles Ratcliffe, the great grandson of Charles II. and Mary Davis, and who married Charlotte, Countess of Newburgh, was adjudged to have right to that Peerage on the 30th July 1858.

rhyme. did not suit the taste of the public. Orrery seems to have been more successful, for his tragedy, from its frequent repetitions, must have proved attractive, and excepting for the unceasing jingle, contains passages of considerable power. Evelyn, although no great patron of the stage, not unfrequently visited the Theatre, and as previously mentioned had a very favourable opinion of Mustapha. The drinking song we have ventured to quote is a fair specimen of Orrery's lyrical powers, and is equal, if not superior, to most of the convivial songs of the reign of Charles the Second.

The character of the Earl, as depicted by Crowne in his Dedication, is in all the essentials substantially correct.

His lordship's eldest son and successor, Roger, did not long survive his father. He died 29th March 1682,* leaving his son Lionel a minor. In a letter 25th October 1690, from Mr Henry Bemde to Evelyn, he informs him that the " Duke of Berwick, with 1500 horse, was upon the march with a design to relieve it [Kinsale], but Lieutenant-General Ginkel† having notice, had like to have been in the rear of them with 3000 horse, and 1000 dragoons, but of this they had notice, and did return to Limerick, burning many villages, and the Lord Orrery's house, which cost but lately £40,000. The building was the noblest palace in Ireland. The Duke of Berwick sent twice to Maxwell not to fire it, but could not prevail." Lodge says that the Duke after dining there ordered the castle to be set on fire. But the above extract shows it was burnt against, and not by, the order of his Grace.

The honours of Orrery are now merged in that of Cork, the elder branch of the Boyles having failed in the male line.

* Lodge's Peerage of Ireland, Lon. 1789, vol. i. p. 193.

† Created Earl of Athlone by William and Mary, 4th of March 1691-2. He had a grant of the forfeited estates of Limerick from William, but Parliament revoking the grant, the Earl returned to Holland where his descendants continued to reside, until his great grandson was deprived of his estates by the French in 1793. He came to Ireland and took his seat in the Irish House of Lords, 10th March 1795. Subsequently the De Ginkel family returned to the continent, and the Peerage came to an end in 1844 upon the death of George Godart Henry, the ninth Earl.

TO

THE RIGHT HONOURABLE

ROGER, EARL OF ORRERY, &c.[*]

MY LORD.—What hath introduced the custom, I cannot tell, whether the extraordinary favour and indulgence that dramatic poetry hath found amongst persons of the greatest wit and honour; or the over-much confidence of those of our scribbling tribe, who are willing to assume to ourselves the utmost liberty any will give us, or we can with any modesty pretend to : but so it is, that of late, nothing of this kind, though never so inconsiderable, appears in public, without some great and illustrious name fixt before it; like a gigantic statue at the portal of some trifling building. Whether they design by it, that the mighty name to whom their little follies are consecrated, should, like the relics of saints, work miracles on the unbelieving critics of our age, make them distrust their own understandings, and have an implicit faith in every little priest of Apollo, I cannot resolve; but since it is grown a custom, I shall not be so much a fanatick as not to conform to it ; or rather shall approve myself one, in conforming to a custom against my judgment, for interest sake. None of my fraternity ever having more occasion to creep under the shelter of some noble patronage than myself. For first, my Lord, this unworthy poem, which I humbly prostrate here at your Lordship's feet, was the off-spring of many confused, raw, indigested, and immature thoughts, pen'd in a crowd, and hurry of business and travel ; interrupted and disorder'd by many importunate, not to say insolent affairs, of a quite different nature, and lastly, the first-born of this kind that my thoughts ever laboured with to perfection. And though I will not

[*] In the old quarto the Earl is called in the dedication "of Orrory."

undertake here to reflect anything upon elder brothers,
whose usual misfortune is, if the observation of some be
true, not to inherit all the wit, as well as all the estate,
but leave that as a thread-bare portion to the cadets:* yet
I will be bold to affirm it true in these matters : and I
think the experience of all that ever attempted anything
in this kind, will second me. The first-born of some
most florid, and after most successful wits, having been
so rude and unshapen, as that they have been kept like
witless elder brothers, out of company, for fear of
shaming their parents. And though others have been
more fortunate in their early productions, yet few but
have had those slips from their prune, which their riper
thoughts either were, or at least had reason to be ashamed
of. And now, my Lord, I have told you the faults of
this Play, give me leave also to tell you the misfortunes
of it, for those two commonly go together. It had the
misfortune to be brought into the world in a time, when
the dog-star was near his reign, and my judges sat in a
hot bath, rather than a theatre, and were doubly per-
secuted by the heat of the weather, and the impertinence
of the poet; and which was the worst mishap, when the
most candid, as well as the most illustrious Judges, I
mean the Court, were absent, and, excepting the presence
of some great and noble persons, this unhappy Poem left,
for the most part, to the mercy of a common audience:
in which unguarded condition it might well expect to
receive some wounds, and so it did ; though much fewer
than either I expected, yet such as it deserved ; whether
it will survive or no, I know not, nor am concerned at ;
if it will not, then it gives me good occasion to apologise
for this dedication, and to tell your Lordship, that it
receiving its first life and being in the world from your
Lordship's favour, and now dying in the corporeal part
of it, I mean the action, the spiritual and surviving
part of it, ought like its parent, the soul, to return to
him that gave it. And if I may have leave from our
rigid religionists, to prosecute the metaphor, as in that
abstracted state the soul is infinitely more happy than
in any it could attain to, whilst immersed in flesh and
blood ; so, my Lord, to have any the least residence in

* Cadets?

your Lordship's thoughts, will be a state of more felicity and honour, than any this Poem, whilst embodied in action, could arrive to by the private or general applause of the wits of the world. But now I am fallen upon the consideration of your Lordship, I am plunged, methinks, into a vast ocean, where I have nothing to determinate my sight, but a bright and serene sky full of light, at a vast distance from me, and as vast a height above me, and no shore but that from whence I came, and to which I must retire again, to take a safe and pleasant prospect of that which I can neither fathom nor describe. It is, indeed, the common practice of dedications, to stuff their epistles full of panegyricks, not perhaps so much to describe their patrons, who sometimes are as obscure as themselves, as to shew their own skill in writing characters and essays. But the case is not the same with me; and what may be tolerable enough with them, would be absurd in me, and I should fall into the impertinence of those that would write large encomiums on the sun, who certainly commends himself to us by his own light and influence, much better than any man can do by his wit. Not to say anything, my Lord, of the soldier, and statesman in you, which have rendered you both known and famous to all the valiant and politic part of mankind; that of your poetry is a large theme, in which, perhaps, I could expatiate with more success than on any of the former; yet I shall not dare to do it for want of art; and if I could make your Lordship's heighth, I should but discover the vast distance I am situate in from so bright an orb; as navigators that take the heighth of the sun, only to find what degree of latitude themselves are in. If there be any part of the world so obscure as not to have heard your Lordship's fame in that, as well as other respects, I shall refer them to a character of your Lordship: not to the praises and applauses of the world in general, nor the panegyricks of lesser pens, which have always waited on the triumphs of your's, as the common soldiers in the Roman triumphs did on their generals, but to the incomparable issues of your own thoughts, wherein they will see not only a character of your Lordship, but of the present improv'd genius of England, which, by the assistance of your

1 2

Lordship, and many sublime wits in other arts, begins
to be as famous in arts, as formerly it was in arms;
witness those new academies and societies erected
amongst us for Philosophical commerce, and the im-
provement of language, wit, and arts ; commodities which
forreign virtuosoes would have engrossed to themselves, and till of late denied to be the native growth of
this, now in all respects, most happy, and most fertile
Island.   It is from your Lordship's pen, that Solyman
may be truly stiled Magnificent, and you have made him
succeed to the civility and gallantry of the Greeks, as
well as to their Empire ; nor was Mustapha ever so
much the hopes of his barbarous nation, as in his image
and the generous character you have given him, he is
the delight of England, who weep the fate, not of
Mustapha, but of murder'd virtue.   And, indeed, what
pen but your Lordship's could have refined and softened
a story so barbarous, and made a people so remote from
friendship, honour, and religion, walk disguised in the
highest characters of them all?   It is your Lordship's
pen that hath assisted Henry the fifth in a second conquest of France, and in the noblest characters of valour,
love, and friendship, hath made the English wit and
language as triumphant as their arms : nor could a story
acted with so much glory and success, be attempted by
any pen beneath your Lordship's.   In fine, it is your
Lordship that hath charmed up the ghosts of many
noble heroes, who otherwise would have lain unlamented
in their tombs ; and they have walked on the stage in
brighter shapes than ever they lived, and have been
conducted to their fates, with more sorrow of the
spectators than perhaps they had when they died.
And all this your Lordship hath done, not in the pleasure
of shade, ease, and retirement, and with the advantages
and assistances that meaner spirits are forced to make
use of for their compositions : but they are only the
sallies of your pen, and that during the uneasy intervals
which pain sometimes borrows from State affairs ; and
what a fit of the gout snatches from the use and benefit,
your Lordship takes care to employ to the delight and
pleasure of the world ; and if your Lordship can do all
this, upon the rack of pain, and with some glances of

your thoughts, whil'st the rest like scattered rays of light, are dispersed on various objects; what would you do with all the freedom and ease of other men, and with the united force of your soul? But, I am sinking again out of my depth, and must retreat once more to that shore from whence I am insensibly wandering; I mean, my Lord, to the consideration of myself, and of this worthless present which I make to your Lordship. Which, my Lord, I cannot but look with much contempt upon, as being conscious to myself in what haste and confusion it was composed, and of what *ex-tempore* thoughts the greatest part of it consists. Nor should I have presumed to have usher'd it into the world, under so great a patronage, had not I first obtained your leave. And now I hope, your Lordship, that at the hearing of it whil'st it was in loose sheets was pleased to forgive the faults of the poem, will now in this address pardon those of the author, whose chief design is not to gain the name of poet, author, wit, or critic, but that of

My Lord,

Your Lordship's most humble

and most obedient Servant,

JOHN CROWNE.

Oct. 4, 1671.

CARDINAL, *Governor of Poland, ex officio, during the Interregnum.* — MR. HARRIS.

LADISLAUS, *Duke of Curland, a Sovereign Prince, Feudatory to the Crown of Poland, oft General of their Armies, contracted to Juliana in her father's life-time; and in an expedition against the Muscovite was taken prisoner, and carried to Moscow.* — MR. BETTERTON.

DEMETRIUS, *a young Prince of the Imperial house of Muscovy, in love with Paulina, and privately married to her by deceit, she supposing him the Duke.* — MR. YOUNG.

SHARNOFSKY, *a Count Palatine, friend to the Duke.* — MR. SMITH.

OSSOLINSKY, *Lord Grand Marshal of Poland, and of the Cardinal's faction.* — MR. BAMFIELD.

CASSONOFSKY, LUBOMIRSKY, *Count Palatines of the Cardinal's faction.* — MR. SANDFORD.

COLIMSKY, *a Count Palatine, friend to Sharnofsky, and of the Princess's faction.* — MR. NORRIS.

LANDLORD *of the house in Warsaw, where the Duke lay concealed.* — MR. ANGEL.

THEODORE, *servant to the Duke.* — MR. METBURN.

ALEXEY, *A Russian Lord that assists and accompanies Paulina in her flight.* } MR. CROSBY.

BATTISTA, *[Servant] to Demetrius.* } MR. WESTWOOD.

JULIANA, *Daughter of the deceased King of Poland, in love with the Duke of Curland, and contracted to him before her Father's death.* } MRS. BETTERTON.

PAULINA, *Daughter of the great Czar of Muscovy, in love with the Duke; and, upon a supposed marriage with him, assists him in his escape, and pursues him to Poland, in the habit of a man.* } MRS. LONG.

JOANNA, *Maid of Honour to Paulina.* } MRS. SHADWELL.

FRANCISCA,
EMILIA, } *Maids of Honour to Juliana.*

SOLDIERS, SERVANTS, GUARDS, &c.

THE SCENE:

Warsaw in Poland, at the meeting of the Ban, and Arrier Ban, arm'd in the field for the Election of a King.

THE PROLOGUE.

You judges, critics, wits, and poets too,
And whatsoever titles are your due;
As pretty features, each in proper place,
Put altogether make a pretty face,
So you good wits, and you that would be so,
You all together make a pretty show;
And when you thus in general council sit,
You are the body politic of wit:
Unto you all our poet bids me say,
Good faith! you're kindly welcome to his play.
'Tis a plain compliment, to speak the truth,
But you must know he is a modest youth;
Like country gallant just, whom courtier brings
To see fine dainty Miss—— who plays and sings;
Approaching to'r, poor gallant falls a mumping,
Scraping o' legs, and feign he would say something
And round about the room he flings and skips,
Whil'st tongue lies still i'th' scabbard of his lips.
Just so our poet usher'd to the door,
To court coy wits he'd never seen before,
Wits that have all the sparkish gallants known,
And tried th' abilities of all the town;
Poor bashful poet, faith, h'ad got his play
Under his arm, and had run quite away,
Had not we promis'd him to use our skill
And in'trest we've to gain him your good will:
Then, faith, for once, since he's so eager for't,
Seem kind and coming, though it be for sport;
Then like some cully on his wedding night,
Thinking his bride lies ravisht with delight,
Bestirs his simple self whil'st she lies still,
Laughs at the fool, and lets him work his will.
So will our poet to't, and work his brain
To try to entertain you once again;
And if he mends, you that delight to range
With every youth, may use him then for change:
If not, e'en huff the fool, and give him o'er,
Then he perhaps will trouble you no more.

JULIANA;

OR, THE PRINCESS OF POLAND.

ACT THE FIRST.

The Scene a GROVE *and* GARDENS.
PAULINA *sleeping under a tree,* JOANNA *sitting by
and singing.*

THE SONG.

Lo, behind a scene of seas,
Under a canopy of trees,
   The fair new golden world was laid,
   Sleeping like a naked maid,
   Till alas! she was betray'd:
In such shades Urania lay,
Till love discover'd out a way:
And now she cries, "some power above,
Save me from this tyrant love!"

Her poor heart had no defence,
But its maiden innocence;
   In each sweet retiring eye,
   You might easily descry
   Troops of yielding beauties fly,
Leaving rare unguarded treasure
To the conqueror's will and pleasure;
And now she cries,—&c.

Now and then a straggling frown,
Through the shades skipt up and down:

Shooting such a piercing dart,
As would make the tyrant smart,
And preserve her lips, and heart.
But, alas! her Empire's gone,
Thrones and temples all undone:
And now she cries,—&c.

Charm aloft the stormy winds,
That may keep the golden mines,
    And let Spaniard love be tore
    On some cruel rocky shore,
    Where he'll put to sea no more;
Lest poor conquer'd beauty cry,
Oh! I'm wounded! oh! I die!
And there is no power above
Saves me from this tyrant love.

Jo. Oh! cursed Duke! Africa ne'er bred
A monster like thee, to forsake my Princess
After th' a'dst married her, and thus entic'd her
From all the glories of her father's court,
To follow thee, vanquisht, wandering exile;
Unhappy victory, that brought thee captive
To Muscovy, and more unhappy she
To sacrifice her heart, her life, her honour,
To one so false.   But I shall wake her, see!
She starts!——
Her soul is walking in a grove of dreams,
And there some mournful vision entertains
Her sad despairing thoughts. See! see! a ponyard;
How came she by that fatal instrument?
She stabs at something: oh! she makes me tremble:
I'll snatch it from her!
    Paul. Oh! ungrateful man!
And dost thou then deride at my misfortunes?
Is this the recompense of my too fond
Unfortunate love? die in thy mistress' arms!
Bleed! fall! Ha! gone! whither? where am I?

Was it a dream?

Jo. She's had some frightful dream
I see.

Paul. Joanna, did nothing pass that way?
Yes, sure there did; 'twas Curland and his mistress!
They embrac't, and smiled at me, and then they
    vanisht;
See! there he stands all wrapt in white, that, that!

Jo. Oh! the good heavens, she is grown dis-
    traught.
Madam, what is't you see?

Paul. Look there! there!
Is not that he, that tall and shining thing?
He's dead, and I have wrongfully accused him.

Jo. That! that's the moonshine, nothing else
    indeed,
A stream of light that glances through the trees.

Paul. See, now it vanishes!

Jo. And now a cloud
Covers the moon; it is no more. Come, Madam,
The dewy vapours of the night are cold;
The shade is melancholy, and the air unwholesome;
Pray to your chamber, Madam.

Paul. Ah! never, never
Was any so unfortunate as I.   [*weeps.*
What shall I do? and whither shall I go?

Jo. Oh! do not weep thus, you will break my
    heart;
I hope the Duke will prove a man of honour yet;
You do not know what accidents have happened.

Paul. No, no, he's hid in his fair princess' arms:
But, perjur'd man, I'll chase thee from thy bowers
Of love. I'll steep thy joys in blood. Thy heart
    I'll stab
Until the poisonous serpentine dew
Drops weeping at my feet.
Ah me! unfortunate, what shall I do?   [*weeps.*

Enter ALEXEY *running.*

Jo. Poor lady——

Alex. Madam ;

Jo. Who's that ?

Alex. 'Tis I ! the Princess—is she there ?

Jo. The Princess, blunderheaded old soldier !
Thou wilt betray us.

Paul. Who, Count Alexey ?

Alex. Oh ! Madam, I'm out of breath with
 running ;
The Duke's come !

Paul. What is't thou say'st? the Duke !

Alex. Madam, for certain he was seen, this
 evening,
To fling a letter in Count Sharnofsky's coach,
And upon this the troops are all alarmed ;
The Cardinal sits close in his cabal.
Orders are issued out to secure his friends,
Chiefly, Count Sharnofsky, and the Princess ;
The guards are drawing up about the palace :
In the interim, five thousand crowns are proffer'd
To any one that will discover him.

Paul. Did I not say that I should hear some
 news ?
I thought my dream was a forerunner of him.
This news congeals my blood. What shall we do ?

Jo. Had we not best go in ?

Alex. No, no, the guards
Are searching every house, and we being strangers
Perhaps may meet with incivility.

Enter GUARDS *with lights, and drawn swords,
followed by* LANDLORD.

Hark, they're i'th' house already ! see, they come
To search the gardens. Madam, take no notice.

Guar. Come, sir, now we must catechise your
 garden.

Land. Ay, ay, do sir, my garden's a good boy, he can say his catechise.

Guar. Nay, ben't so jocular, sir : we have power
To carry you before the Cardinal if we please.

Land. Carry me and my house too afore the Cardinal if you please, sir; set us but here again where you found us, and I am contented.

Guar. Here are people! who are you, sir ?[*To Paul.*

Paul. A stranger, sir.

Guar. A stranger, sir; what stranger, sir ?

Paul. A Russian, sir! a pristaffe's son of Arch-
angelo.

Guar. Your name, sir !

Paul. Basiliwich.

Jo. I see, my Princess hath a quick invention.

Guar. And who are these?

Paul. My servants, sir.

Guar. 'Tis well ! keep in your lodgings, sir ; there must be account given of you. Come to the next house.   [*Ex. Guards.*

Land. Go, and a good riddance on you. Here's a pudder, ho! see if none of my cups, or silver spoons be missing.

Paul. Now all's over, I'll retire to my chamber.
Revenge appears to me in shapes so horrid,
It frights my soul. Call for a light !

Jo. A light for my master's Landlord !

Land. Ho, there ! a light for the gentleman !
                                   [*Ex. Paul, Jo., Alex.*
Well, how bravely were I made now, could I but light upon the Duke ! five thousand crowns ! that is to say, five times ten hundred crowns ! most monstrous, prodigious, gigantique, pedantique, un-arithmetical sum ; why, this would make me a Duke. Well, I'll go to a conjurer to find him ; but hold then, the rogue will find him for himself.

But then I'll make him believe I am a conjurer
as well as himself, and make him be glad to go
half shares.   But hark ! I hear talking.

Enter DEMETRIUS *and* BATTISTA, *a porter with
a cloakbag.*

Dem. Never was any thing so fortunate,
To hear of him just at my arrival.
I'll into the town and search for him immediately.
     Bat. Hold, my lord, are ye mad ? whither do
          you go ?
To rush into a town throng'd with arm'd men
So late at night, and all the guards about,
And you a stranger too ? Come sir, 'tis time
We rather went somewhere to seek a lodging:
All inns and public houses are taken up,
And for ought I see we're like to lie i' th' streets
To-night.
     Dem. I care not where I lie,
For I cannot rest in body or in soul,
Until I find this most ungrateful Duke.
     Land. What do these people babbling in my
          garden
All this while, and say never a word to me ?
This 'tis to let it lye unfenc't.
     Dem. Look, I see a man !
And I am got into a garden here :   Who's there ?
     Land. Nay, who's there, an' you go to that ?
Here's one that hath authority to be here.
     Bat. The master of the house I do perceive.
And by his tone a kind of letter of lodgings :
I'll ask the question.
Sir, we are strangers, newly come to town,
Could you afford us any room in your house ?
     Land. I cannot tell, sir, whether I can or no :
According as I like you. Bring a light, here !

Dem. Nay then w'are well enough. Take up
  my rooms,
Ne'er stand agreeing with him, give him twenty
Thirty, forty, a hundred crowns a week,
What he hath a mind to.
I'll into town—I grow impatient.   [*Exit.*
  Bat. Oh! heavens, sir, whither do you go
To rush in armed crowds so late, a stranger?
Curse on all rashness, I must follow him,
For fear some mischief happens to him.
Landlord, look to the things! provide our rooms!
We'll return within this half hour, or never.
  Land. Ha! gone and left their cloak-bags with me;
What kind of fellows are these? some high-way men
I know by their haste;
But sure I'm in a dream; is this a cloak-bag?
Let's see what weather 'tis; it doth not rain cloak-
    bags!
Come I'll go see what's in it.   A light there!

Enter a SERVANT *with a candle.*

  Ser. Here, sir:—
  Land. Nay here, sir.
Here's a cloakbag dropt i' my mouth:
Come let's see the entrails of this beast.
A rich chesticore * with diamond buttons;
Enough, enough, I'm satisfied
These are stolen goods as sure as I am here.
And now what shall I do with this cloakbag?
Shall I keep the cloakbag? or shall I cry the
cloakbag? or shall I sell the cloakbag? nay, then
I may chance to stretch for the cloakbag; so I may
if I should keep the cloakbag, if the right owner
should come with an officer, and find the cloakbag;
why then the devil take the cloakbag, for never
was any one so plagued with a cloakbag. Well, if

* Waistcoat.

nobody comes to claim the cloakbag, I'll sell the
cloakbag, buy land, and marry a lady with the
cloakbag, and then be dub'd a knight of the order
of the cloakbag.   [Ex

Enter LADISLAUS *and* THEODORE.
The Scene continues.

Lad. Ungrateful men! and do they thus re-
        ward me,
For all the blood I've shed in their defence?
To set my head to sale,
That head which once these flatt'ring Poles would
        cry
Their state could live no more without than I.
    The. I wish your highness had not flung that
        letter,
It seems you were discover'd—I'm amaz'd
Which way.
    Lad. Sharnofsky hath betrayed me!
Thus had he done had I expos'd my person
Instead of a trifling paper, or had sent thee,
He would have wrackt thee to discover me.
    The. But I'd have been torn limb from limb first.
    Lad. I doubt not thy fidelity, good Theodore;
I've ever found thee generous and faithful:
More generous than those, whose birth and
        grandeur
Obliges them to higher pretence of honour.
Good heavens, what's this world! I should have
        sooner
Suspected angels than the Count or Princess.
    The. Good sir, do not discompose your soul
With these suspicions of your noble friends
Till you know more.
    Lad. My noble friends! ah, Theodore,
I have no friends. My fortune, fame, and honour,
Heaven, and earth, and she whom I adore

Above 'um all deserts me; nothing adheres to me
But my own courage. I see the Count and she
Convert the news of my escape from Moscow,
By the generous kindness of the Russian princess,
Into pretences to disguise their falsehood,
To ruin my interests, and unite their own,
To marry, and to aspire to the crown.
All Poland sees it: and the Card'nal dreads 'um
Much more than me. And all this great alarm,
You'll find, aims at their lives, as well as mine.
   The. Ah! do not credit, sir, the common vogue.
   Lad. Come, Theodore, 'tis true. But that I've
     learnt
How to command my passions as well as armies;
And owe more reverence to my own memory,
Than after death to have my head plac'd aloft
On some old tower, to feed the greedy eyes
Of my proud enemies, this very instant
Sharnofsky's soul or mine should fleet in air.
   The. Well sir, I say no more; I only beg you
Take into some house. You see what danger
You're in; the guards are searching all about,
And here we wander up and down i' th' dark,
Only what sickly light the moon will lend us.
But sir, I think we're got into a garden.
   Lad. On the backside of a house: knock!
    Theodore.   [*Knocks, and*
           Enter LANDLORD *with a light.*
   Land. Who's there? well, this is not to be
     endur'd.
Every one gets into my backside:
If my landlord will not fence it, I'll promise him
I'll do't, and stop it in his rent. Well, what's the
Business with you, now? more cloakbags?
   The. Sir, we are strangers—newly come to town
And are in great want of lodgings.
If you could furnish us, name your own price.

By this gold we'll not refuse it you. [*Gives him money.*
   Land. Let's look on you, according as I like you :
By this gold you have good honest faces.
I have a room for you.
   The. Thank you sir! pray, what other lodgers
      have you?
We ask you, 'cause we would be very private.
   Land. I have none at present but some fiddling
women, that come from Cracow to see the choosing
of the new king, a young gentleman and a cloak-bag.
   Lud. What doth this fellow mean by this cloak-
      bag?
   The. Your highness hath hap'ned very fortu-
      nately.   [*Aside to Lud.*
   Land. Well, but how did you pass the guard so
      late?
For here's a heavy pudder about the Duke of
      Curland.
He's come to town it seems in disguise ;
And here's five thousand crowns bid for his head.
Happy man be his dole that catches him ;
For my part, I don't expect so good luck,
Five thousand crowns and a cloakbag are too much
      for one night.
   The. I perceive this fellow's none of the
      honestest.   [*Aside.*
Ay! here's a great alarm, what's the matter?
   Land. Why sir, the Duke of Curland, look ye.
      you must know,
Was a great favourite of the last King's,
And he contracted him to his daughter,
And intended to marry him to her, but then it
      hap'ned
The Muscoviters invaded us with a great army ;
The Duke, sir, upon a simple quibble of honour,
Goes general of our army against 'um.
I was a corporal under him at the same time.

The. D'ye hear, my lord? pray, keep your disguise close.

Land. And thought forsooth to have come back in triumph,
And married the lady, and he was taken prisoner,
And ne'er comes back at all.

Lad. That was unfortunate.

Land. Now, sir, it seems he hath given 'um the slip out of Muscovy, by the help o' the Russian Princess, and they are run away together, and here he lies lurking in Poland to fit his business ; and now all the Ban and Arrierban are met armed in the field, to choose a King, he's come to town in disguise, and so there's a heavy bustle, the Cardinal on one side, and the Princess on the t'other, and between 'um both he's got into Lobb's pound,* and I am very glad on't ; he's but a kind of a pitiful whiffling small-beer Duke ; I ne'er was drunk thrice in his house, all the time he was here. I can go into the Cardinal's cellar and tie my nose to one barrel, and my horse to another, and tope who shall tope most for a wager ; and he, a sneaking hide bound Duke of a Duke, hates the sight of us true spaniels, that will take water at any time, dive o'er head and ears in liquor, and he would smell a red nose as far as a teal would gunpowder.

Lad. How am I tormented with this fellow !

[*Aside.*

The. He's not to be endured.

Land. And now he's come to town, to be King ! yes, he shall be King, when I am Emperor of Morocco, or Muster-master general of Bantam ; we'll ha' no such thin-gut Kings, that shall in half a year die o' the gripes, and, whilst he lives, shall

* Jocularly, a prison or place of confinement. The phrase is still used, and applied to the prison made for a child between the feet of a grown-up person.

1   3

starve the English beer-merchants, set a tax upon
the tap, and an excise upon rednoses : and there's
one Count Sharnofsky, too, such another ambitious
dry-chops, he hath not the grace to love good drink,
and yet he hath the impudence to aim at the
Crown. 'Tis 'true, he doth not goggle at it so
plain as Mr Mumpsimus o' Curland doth ; but he
doth as I do now, he squints at it fearfully, and he
hath an itch at the Princess too ; (*Landlord squints,
and makes grim-faces,*) but I hope the Cardinal will
feage* 'um all. I hate such ambitious tantalizing
rascals ; a loyal boy I have been from my cradle.

The. This villain, I could kill him.   [*Aside.*

Lad. Shall I be for ever tortur'd with this
     fellow ?   [*Aside.*
You're not at leisure then to show us our chambers,
Landlord.

Land. Yes, yes ; come, come !

Enter a SERVANT.

Ser. Sir! here's the gentleman about the Cloakbag.

Enter DEMETRIUS, *and* BATTISTA.

Land. Oh ! Mr Cloakbag, you're welcome, sir.

Bat. Come, Landlord ! will you show us our
     chambers ?

Lad. One of my fellow lodgers ! See if you know
     him Theodore.

Dem. No news.   [*Theo. looks upon Dem.*

Bat. What news can you expect, sir ?

Dem. That heaven would be so just to direct me
     to him.

The. I do not know him, sir,   [*Aside to Lad.*
And yet methinks I've seen a face like his
In Muscovy.

Lad. Come, let us to our chambers.

* " Whip" or " beat."

Landlord, we'll follow you.
   Land. Stay behind, somebody!
And light the cloakbag. [*Ex. Land., Lud., and Theo.*
   Bat. Come, good sir, conquer your impatience!
You'll find him soon enough, perhaps on a throne;
And speedily, he who in passion now
Is proclaimed traitor, shall shortly with applause
Be proclaimed King; this is a feverish fit
Of the state-sick Cardinal; nor doth the Duke
Come hither in disguise, on no design.
   Dem. But hark thee; when they make him King
     of Poland,
They will not make him God of Poland,
And immortal; will they?
   Bat. No sir, he'll be mortal
No doubt.
   Dem. If he'll be mortal, I am satisfied.
Go, I am weary, light me to my chamber!
I shall dream o' the Duke.   [*Exeunt.*

The Scene a ROOM IN THE PALACE.

Enter FRANCISCA.

   Fran. Treason! treason! the Princess will be
     murder'd!

Enter EMILIA.

   Em. Oh, Francisca, what's the matter?
Here's a noise of soldiers about the palace,
And every one runs shrieking up and down.
Oh! my heart aches.
   Fran. Oh! there's the strangest news.
The Duke's come, and sent a letter to the Princess
By Count Sharnofsky, and all the town's alarm'd;
The guards they say are come to search the palace,
And we're afraid the wicked Cardinal
Designs the Princess' death.
   Em. Oh, horrid tyrant! But see, she comes.

Enter JULIANA *in her nightgear, with a flaming taper
in her hand, followed by* HYPOLITA, *and*
SHARNOFSKY *with his sword drawn.*

Jul. Ha ! must I die, for being abus'd, affronted
By that false man ? hath he betray'd my honour,
And doth he now throw in his hand granadoes
To blow my life up too ? thus in the flames
Thy scrawl shall die ; and, as it pines to ashes,
Then wanders in the wind, so dies for ever
Thy memory in my soul ; and if thy image
Appear but to my thoughts but in a dream,
I'll hate that dream, and I will stab that thought
As I'll do thee, if e'er thou dost approach me.
Now call up all my servants ! bid 'um arm.
   Sh. Ha ! fling a letter and disguise himself !
                                    [*Aside.*
What means this mighty caution of the Duke's ?
Dost thou mistrust my honour ? if thou dost,
I may in just revenge distrust thine ;
And let me tell thee, if thou dost design
To wrong the Princess and surprise the crown,
I in this tempest will not fall alone,
Thou shalt destroy my fortunes and thy own.

Enter a GENTLEMAN *running.*

   Gent. Madam, the guards are broken into the
palace, the common hall glitters with naked swords,
and hither they are running in confusion. Escape !
or you'll be murder'd ! hark ! they're come, they've
overtaken me. Madam, you're lost!
   Jul. And let 'um come, I'll look the villains
     dead.
And let me see who dares assassinate
The yet surviving majesty of their dead King.
   Sh. Who dares, shall fall as victims to his shade.
But see, the Count Colimsky : ha ! our friends
Betray us.

Enter COLIMSKY *with his sword drawn.*

Col. Madam, for heaven's sake retire
With all the speed you can, your life's designed :
My lord grand marshall hath orders from the
    council
To seize you both ; the troops are drawing up ;
News of the Duke's arrival haunts each ear,
Just like a frightful spectre ; letters
Are intercepted by the Cardinal
Written by you, my lord, of horrid consequence.
    Sh. By me !
    Col. By you, to Dorosensko General of the
        Tartars
To assist you with fifty thousand men,
Ten thousand cassacques should be sure to second
    him,
That y'ad decreed upon a time perfixt
To fire the city, kill the Cardinal,
Dissolve the general diet in the tumult,
Seize the crown.
    Sh. Monster of villany !
Thou scarlet prodigy, Poland's glaring comet,
Barbarous idol, not content with blood
But must have kingdoms victim'd at thy altars !
Almighty powers, I kneel, I kneel !   If ever,
Ever one thought——
    Col. No more, I do believe your innocence,
And therefore stole away from the cabal
To give you intelligence, what horrid spells
Are made, what spirits conjur'd up
Against you, in our magician's grotto,
And here I've brought a hundred resolute
Young gentlemen, whose swords shall cut the
    charm,
And yet secure the Princess's retreat
And yours ; if you'll accept their generous kindness.

Then, Madam, hasten! let us lose no time.
Each minute now is precious as the Indies.
　Jul. Pious Cardinal, my guardian angel,
Heavenly tyrant, little thinks my royal father
How he hath left me to the guardianship
Of dragons that devour me.
　Col. Oh undone!
We have lost time! all, all, to arms!
　　　　　　　　　　　　[Noise of arms without.
　Sh. Call up the Princess's servants! Arm, arm!

Enter OSSOLINSKY, CASSONOSKY, *and* LUBOMIRSKY,
　　　　　　and GUARD.

　Wom. Murder, murder!
　Casso. Now the long wish't for time o' my re-
　　venge
On the old tyrant that affronted me
Is come.　But ha! Colimsky here?
　Osso. Are you there, traitor?
　Col. Are you here, cheated bubbles?
　Casso. This too honest fellow hath prevented
　　us:　　　　　　　　　　　　　　　*[Aside.*
You'll answer for this treason to the general diet.
　Col. With my sword in hand in th' interim
My Princess shall not fall an Indian martyr
Under the chariot wheels of your great pagod;
Your idol shall not have such noble victims.
　Sh. Let us not stand disputing.
　Osso.　
　　　　　} Seize the traitors!
　Lub.　
　Casso. Ay, you may say, seize the traitors. Long
enough you might have had the wit to have come
with a stronger party. [*All fight, Osso., Casso., Lub.
retreat pursued by Sharnofsky, and Colimsky.*
　Wom. Murder, murder!
　Jul. Oh! bloody Cardinal.　Royal shade

Of my great father, hide thy glorious head,
And see not my oppressions.

Enter COLIMSKY and SHARNOFSKY as
from victory.

Col. Now, all's clear,
My lord convey the Princess by a private way
To the monastery of Sancta Clara; there's a vault
Where you may lie perdu for an hour or two.
In th' interim I'll go place a guard in my house
And then conduct you thither: my gardens
Lie just opposite to the monastery,
And there's a private way, where you may pass
    secure;
And then for our greater preparations.   [*Exit.*
   Sh. Come, Madam,
The tempest is begun, let's bravely through.
   Jul. Lead on, my lord!
I'm none of those, who when the storm prevails,
Creep to the winds, and humbly strike the sails.

THE SECOND ACT.

Enter CARDINAL, OSSOLINSKY, CASSONOSKY,
LUBOMIRSKY.

Card. Escap't! ·
Osso. All betray'd by Count Colimsky.
Card. I fear'd as much.
Casso. My lord, you may remember
He gave us warning with mysterious words
He dropt at council; I might have had the wit
To have seen it, but I am grown both fool and
    knave

With keeping knaves' and fools' company. [*Aside.*
　　Lub. With mysterious words ?
In plain terms he talk't both saucily
And like a traitor.
　　Casso. Well said, wisdom.   [*Aside.*
　　Card. I observed him ;
And do repent we did not then secure him :
But I was unwilling to create
Too many enemies. Well, this news is bad,
The Duke arriv'd, the Count and Princess fled
To arms, Colimsky turn'd a partizan.
I now foresee a dreadful storm o' blood.
　　Casso. A storm of thy own creating ; but yet I
　　　　love thee,
Because thou lov'st mischief, 'though these simple
　　　　lords
Have not the wit to see't.   [*Aside.*
　　Osso. My lord, all places shall be strictly searcht,
Houses, vaults, churches, monasteries,
And then by break o' day we'll be ready
To bring our slaves arm'd into the field.
Then let the tempest blow, this storm o' fate
Shall overset the pirates of the state. [*Ex. Osso., Lub.*
　　Card. Brave patriots ! may heaven succeed your
　　　　loyalty.
　　Casso. Oh ! most noble Cardinal ; I am almost
　　　　as cunning
A knave as thy self, and I have one knack more ;
　　　　　　　　　　　　　　　　　[*Aside.*
To appear, what I am not, one of thy bubbles. [*Exit.*
　　CARD. Good men, how easily they swallow down
The bait ; such honest men are the soft moulds
Wherein wise men do cast their great designs.*
Still crost ! what ill-natur'd star envies my glory ?
Oft have I built my great designs so high,

　　* " Honest men are the soft, easy cushions on which knaves
repose and fatten." *Otway.*

That they have dazzled each spectator's eye ;
When to the highest storey I should come,
Even just to have a prospect into Rome,
To view the conclave, and o'ertop them all,
And catch the golden fruit, when it should fall,
Then some unhappy ball, at one rebound,
Hath thrown down all my projects to the ground.
And now, as all my policies were ripe,
And each thing fitted as I had design'd,
The Duke a captive, and his friends confin'd ;
And I had stole an interest in the state,
Enough to sell the crown at my own rate ;
Just on the sudden they are all got free,
And the whole storm is like to fall on me :
Such things as these would puzzle human sense,
And make one half believe a Providence ;
And I confess it staggers me, to find
My engines broke by one that stands behind.
But all this shall not my designs defeat,
It is a wise man's duty to be great
To save the helpless world.
For they above affect to show their powers,
And haughty wisdom, by confounding ours.
Then, heaven, we bow ; but if that will not do,
The sword shall give what I demand from you.
When beads and altars no relief afford,
The best devotion then is in the sword.   [*Exit.*

The Scene THE TOWN. *A noise within of
breaking doors.*

Break down the doors, I care not for ne'er a city
    cuckold of 'em all.   [*Within.*
Murder, murder ! call up all our neighbours.
                                           [*Within.*
  Gu. Hold your babbling or I'll set a pellet in the
    throat of you.

I've authority to search your house for the Princess.
[Within.

Land. A Princess, sir! I'd have you to know I keep no such house, I keep no Princesses, and so get you from my doors.   *[Woman within.*

Do I pay tax and contribution, and the devil and all, to have my doors broken open at midnight to search for Princesses? I'll complain to the council.
[Man within.
Some scalding water there!   *[Woman within.*
How! do you threaten? fire upon 'um! *[Officer within.*
Murder, murder!   *[Within.*

The scene the COMMON HALL *in* LANDLORD'S *house.*
Enter LANDLORD *striking fire with a steel.*

Land. Murder! murder! there's murder cried in the streets, we shall be all kill'd in our beds. Ho! where are you all? light a candle; call up all our lodgers; ho, murder!

Enter PAULINA *and* JOANNA.

Paul. Oh! we shall be murder'd.
Land. Here's a steel hath as much fire in't as is in my tooth.

Enter ALEXEY.

Alex. Oh! Madam, madam! I have seen the Duke; [*softly to Paul,*] he lies in this very house. Coming by a chamber that had a light burning in't, I had a curiosity to look through the key-hole, and I saw the Duke walking without any disguise, and talking to a gentleman, his servant I suppose; and instantly hearing a noise, slips on a disguise, took his sword, and here he's coming.
Paul. Oh! thou ha'st surpris'd me; I faint!
Jo. Strange, what a fortune's this?

Alex. See! this is he.

Enter at one door LADISLAUS *and* THEODORE,
at another DEMETRIUS *and* BATTISTA,
with drawn swords.

Land. Why, ho! will you a bring a light here?
Sleepy rascals, are you all dead?

Om. Where is this murder?

Land. Nay, what know I? All the guards are
about, horse and foot. This is about the Duke of
Curland; I would I had him by the nose with a
pox to him, I'd hold him as strong as mustard;
he might smell to a crust long enough I' faith, nor
should it be four thousand nine hundred ninety-
nine crowns should excuse his head.

Theo. D'ye hear my lord? This fellow's a rogue.
[*Aside to Lad.*

Lad. I hear him.

Paul. A damp strikes to my heart at sight of
him. [*Aside.*

Dem. Where are these murders done?

Bat. In the landlord's pate.
No other we shall meet withall to-night.

Enter a SERVANT.

Ser. Master!

Land. Master, you rogue! where's a light? Shall
we all be killed in the dark here?

Ser. All's over, sir!

Land. Over or under, I'll have a light, sir. I
won't lose my life in the dark. A light I say! whil'st
I go call up all my people. [*Exit.*

Dem. What an impertinent cowardly fellow is
this!

Bat. Fear, sir, is natural to vulgar spirits.

Dem. What people are those in the room here?

Bat. Your fellow lodgers, sir!

Lad. I do suppose the guards are searching for
me ;   [*Aside to Theo.*
Perhaps they may break into the house.
'Tis safer being abroad. Call for the key of the
garden door ; I'll go walk in the grove.   [*Exit.*

Alex. Follow, follow, madam ! he is going out.

Bal. Come, my lord, y'ave slept but little: will
you to your chamber, or walk abroad ?

Dem. 'Tis too early yet, hardly day, and I feel
my eyes a little heavy: I care not if I take the
t'other slumber, and finish the remainder of my
dream.

Bal. Had you a dream ? I thought you slept so
little, you had no time to dream.

Dem. 'Twas a confus'd one of the Duke, and
my Princess. Methoughts I met 'um in a grove ;
and in a house I wounded him ; she fainted,
and they both vanisht: and a thousand such wild
things.

Bal. This busy soul of ours cannot be idle ;
It must be doing, and doth, it knows not what.

Dem. Come ! I'll to my chamber, take t'other
slumber, and then in chase of the Duke ; and I'll
find him if all the arts of hell can discover him.

SCENE, THE GARDENS.

Enter LADISLAUS, THEODORE, *and* LANDLORD,
followed by PAULINA, JOANNA, *and* ALEXEY.

Land. Now, you may venture to walk in the
garden, all's over; beshrew me, I tremble like a
quaking pudding.

Lad. How comes your grove and gardens to lie
open ?

Land. How comes a wench to lie open, and
common, when nobody will fence her ? Your
grandfather: you wonder to hear me say, your

grandfather, I warrant. You must know, I call all my lodgers my sons; and so I being your father, my landlord is your grandfather. Now, sir, your grandfather is in law about it with the monastery of Santa Clara! And did you never see a couple of hectors fight for a wench? here I tickle thee, and there I tickle thee, so, sa, sa! Co' your grandfather, a homethrust! Co' the monastery! and so they fetch one another with whiscum, whascums, and I know not what; and neither of 'um will suffer it to be fenc'd, and so my garden lies stark naked, without ever a rag to her back; but I keep the poor jade as private as I can, and suffer none to pass, but those that go between the Count's gardens and the monasteries.

Paul. There is no speaking whil'st this fellow's here.   [*Aside.*

Lad. What gardens are those, yonder?

Land. One Count Colimsky's gardens; a very brave man, he hath a gallant house at the t'other end; ah, many sousing soakings have I had in his cellar! there have I sail'd top and top-gallant, all sails aloft, and bravely boarded the French-man, the high Dutcher, the Spaniard, the Grecian; then, sir, there hath made up to me a fleet of Algerines, Tunis, and Sally* men, (for so I call the drunken dogs). A sail, a sail! quoth I; strike for Algier, quoth they! strike for Dantzick! quoth I; then to't we go, and board one another with small shot, pint glasses, and the like; from them we go to cuddy-guns, and so to demy-cannon, whole cannon, and all our lower tier, romers of an ell; and then there's bloody work; here sinks a galley, there a galleass; there a stout frigate turns up his keel; then high for the main, boys! cry I.

The. What a tedious impertinent fellow is this!

* Sallee.

Lud. And what high wall is that, that faces to the Count's gardens?

Land. That's the monastery wall I told you of.

Paul. Will this fellow never ha' done?

Lud. You don't know who those young gentlemen are that lodge in your house, do you?

Land. Not I. They are pretty youths, strangers, speak but bad Polish; I askt 'um when they came, Rosmepopolsky? said I, no Rosmepopolsky, quoth they: but one may make a shift to understand 'um.

Lud. How came you to have any room in your house, at so great a concourse as this of all the nobility and gentry of Poland with their trains, for the election of a King?

Land. How came my neighbour's wife to have any room in her? she was delivered of a boy, and my big-bellied house of a man; and both were brought to bed yesterday morning. The great Count Palatine of Smolensko, if you know him, lodged here; and he whipt out o' town upon some bickerings betwixt him and the Cardinal: he told the Cardinal his own, he made a most brave mutinous speech in the Diet, which is highly applauded. I have a copy on't in my pocket.

Lud. No matter for the copy, Landlord.

The. This fellow's tongue hath the perpetual
    motion;
Good my lord, rid yourself of him! [*Aside to Lud.*

Lud. Well, Landlord, I have a little business with my servant; you'll excuse me.

Land. I think I ha' lost the copy of this same speech. I must run in to find it. I'll be back presently.   [*Exit.*

Theo. Heaven be prais'd!

Paul. So now I'll venture to him.

Jo.   Do, and we'll stay behind. [*Exit Jo and Alex.*

Theo. Ha! who's this follows the Duke?

My lord, retire ! here's some one follows you.

[To Lad.

Lad. Some of the lodgers for the morning air.
Theo. No, no, my lord, he makes directly to you.
Lad. I think he doth, as if he'd speak with me.
Paul. My lord !   *[Goes up to the Duke.*
Lad. To me, sir ?
Paul. Yes, to you, my lord.
Come make it not so strange, I know you well
    enough.
Lad. Oh ! heavens, betray'd !
Paul. Nay, be not startled, sir !
I've no design but what is honourable.
Lad. Surely you do mistake your person, sir ;
I'm but a stranger here.
Paul. I know you are not, sir,
You lately came out of Muscovy ; you were a
    pris'ner there,
Sir, were you not ? Yes, sir, I'm sure you were,
And your name is Ladislaus, Duke of Curland.
Lad. Ha ! he names my name,
How came I thus discover'd ?
Paul. So, 'tis he ;
Now I have borne him down with confidence.
Lad. I know him not, but since he names my
    name,
Let him be man or devil, friend or enemy,
I'll not disown it. Sir, I am Ladislaus
Duke of Curland ! what's you business with me ?
Paul. That letter, sir, that letter will tell you.

[Gives the Duke a letter.

Lad. Whence is this ?
Paul. Read, and you'll see it.
Lad. Ha ! subscribed Demetrius :   *[Peruses it.*
What ! is this from Muscovy ? where's the Prince !
Paul. The letter, sir, will tell you.
Lad. (*Reads*) I am now at the frontiers of Poland ;

my errand you yourself may conjecture, and I had rather tell you with my sword than my pen ; which I had done, if an unhappy accident had not confin'd me to a small village, and my chamber ; and enforc't me to make use of the kindness of the bearer, my cousin, the Duke of Novogrod, to seek you. The acquaintance you have had of my temper will easily give you to believe, that I had rather fight ten battles than write six lines ; and therefore you must not expect long epistles from me. Then, in short, you have abus'd me with dissembled friendship ; affronted and ruin'd me, by stealing away my Princess ; your crimes are unexpiable by anything but your life, which I expect you tender me on the point of your sword. The circumstance, as of time, place, and weapon, I refer to yourself ; and you may acquaint my cousin, the Duke, whose return from you I expect with impatience.

DEMETRIUS.

Lud. The prince is very severe, and his charge
    is high.

Paul. Sir, I suppose he hath reason.

Lud. That he ought to have been assur'd of, ere
He had condemned his friend.

Paul. Well sir, in short, your answer.

Lud. My answer is, sir, that the Prince hath
    wrong'd me,
I've not abus'd him with dissembled friendship,
Nor stole his Princess ; she remains with him
For ought I know, so may my friendship too,
If't pleases him.

Paul. Oh heavens ! how unfortunate
Am I in my love. See, he disowns my flight,
And he'll disown the marriage too, and I
Shall pass for some base prostrate thing.   [*Aside.*

Lud. You seem disorder'd, sir.

Paul. I am disorder'd sir, at what y'ave said. I

only thought before, the Princess lost to all her
friends and fortunes; but now 'tis worse, I see
she's lost to honour, and fallen into the hands of
one that basely disowns her.

    Lud. You are too quick and fierce in your asser-
      tions, sir.

    Paul. No fiercer, sir,
Then the case merits. Had you own'd her flight,
And own'd a marriage too, it had been honourable;
For upon other terms she would not fly.
But let me tell you, sir, in the same breath
In which you disown her flight, you little less
Than call her strumpet.

    Lud. Do you come here, young Duke, to talk or
      fight?

    Paul. Sir, which you please,—
To fight. O, that I had a fury's whip
To tear thy heart, and scourge thy perjur'd soul!

    Lud. Must it be so?   *[Draws, aside.*

Enter JOANNA *and* ALEXEY.

    Jo. Oh! murder, murder!

    Alex. Hold, hold your hand, sir! save that
      tender life,
Here is an enemy more fit for thee.

    Theo. What villains are these?   *[Draws.*

    Lud. Ha! an ambush.

    Paul. Begone! what mean you to betray me
      thus?   *[Aside to Jo. and Alex.*
I am but humouring my part: retire!
These are my servants, sir; regard 'um not, *[To Lud.*
I'll play you no foul play. Retire! I say.

                        [To Jo. and Alex.
Come, come, my lord! let us put up our anger;
The time and place are not convenient   *[Puts up.*
For this: besides I exceed my commission in't.
I should displease the Prince to take your life,

1   4

And grieve him to lose my own.   Come, let us talk !
By all that's good, I honour you,
And do believe you'll tell me sacred truth.
Then tell me truly, by the faith and honour
Of a brave man, do you know where the Princess
Is fled ?   And are you married to her, or no ?
   Lad. Then by these sacred things, by which
      you so conjure me,
By any thing that's more Divine then they,
I know not of her flight, nor am I
Married to her.
   [*Paul. walks up and down in a passion and disorder.*
   Paul. Oh ! horrid, horrid ! I shall sink and die.
                              [*Aside.*
   Lad. Sir, you look pale : how do you ?
   Paul. I could find in my heart to stab him.
                              [*Aside.*
   Lad. Your countenance changes, sir; I fear you're
      ill,
And but dissemble it in complaisance.
Pray, let me wait upon you to your chamber.
   Paul. No, good my lord ! no ceremony pray.
Sweet-natur'd devil !   [*Aside.*

   Enter SHARNOFSKY *conducting* JULIANA, *followed*
      by HYPOLITA, EMILIA, *and* FRANCISCA ;
        the women all vizarded.

   Lad. Ha ! what is't I see ? It is a vision ! Count
Sharnofsky conducting a lady out of yonder
monastery, she and her train all mask'd, what
should it mean ? my lord, I beg your pardon, I'll
wait on you instantly.
   Paul. Oh ! my sweet lord !   [*Ironice.*
Ho, there !   [*To her, Jo. et Alex.*
   Jo.
        } Madam, the news ?
   Alex.
   Paul. Curland's a monster !

Alex. I'll run and kill him!

Paul. No, let me alone!
I'll kill him, but it shall be with torments!
Steel, poison, fire, racks, scorpions, hell!
Oh, me unfortunate!

Jo. She's grown distracted.

Paul. Lead me! I faint!

Jo. She swoons! help, help! [*They carry her out.*

Al. Who should these be?

Theo. Who're these my lord is gazing on so
earnestly? Ha, it should be his friend, the Count.
But what's that vizard, lady? See, she unmasques.

Jul. Where are we now, my lord?

Shar. I'm sure not far from Count Colimsky's
    gardens.

Theo. It is the Princess!

Lad. Heavens! 'tis my Princess;
'Tis she, 'tis she! my guilty soul retires
At th' apparition of that bright divinity
Which my soul whispers I have now offended.
Just so a suffering saint that long had been
Triumphant over all the arts of sin;
And in all combats made a brave defence,
And still preserv'd entire his innocence:
But yet at last, before he is aware,
Begins to slide into some pleasing snare;
By heaven surpriz'd, his soul is then afraid
Of joys for which he had endur'd and pray'd.

Shar. I see the garden gate. This, this way
madam!   [*Exeunt Shar., Jul., &c.*

Lad. Ha! vanquish't thus! heavens unfold this
    mystery;
It is too dark for me, and I must follow
To see the opening of this cloudy scene.   [*Exit.*

Theo. See, my lord chases 'um, I dread the event!
I wish some mist had screen'd this horrid vision
From his sight.   [*Exit.*

The Scene, a Garden, *at the one end a palace.*

Enter Sharnofsky, Juliana, Hypolito, Emelia,
Francisca.

Jul. Heavens! in what shady paths my fortunes
     lead me.
And must I hide my head in nature's nunnery,
Among these virgin flowers to save myself
From him, who now though he so proud can be,
Hath often for his safety fled to me?
Nor would it grieve me, if I did but know
For what it is he persecutes me so;
Or how I ever did offend this proud
Aspiring man, that he should seek my blood.
     Shar. The tyrant, madam, thinks the Duke and you,
Do all his towering policies undo;
And then his active brain wants no design
The strongest innocence to undermine:
Then for the State, he doth bewitch their sense
With the love-powder of his eloquence:
His sliding tongue doth with its charming strains,
Like a smooth serpent, coil about their brains,
And with its sting not only taints the blood
Of fools and bigots, but the wise and good;
But yet in spite of all such arts as these,
We'll darken his proud stars, and on his knees
Yet make him, ere w' have done this fatal strife,
At these fair hands thus humbly ask his life.
     [*At the instant that Shar. kneels to kiss her hand,*

Ladislaus *and* Theodore *enter.*

Lad. Heaven blast my eyes rather than see this
     sight.
I'm abus'd; villain!   [*Draws.*
     Theo. Oh, my lord, what mean you? [*Holds the*
                                 Duke.

     Lad. Loose me, Theodore! or thou diest.
     Theo. I die! ah, sir, 'twill be a fate too glorious

To die by your hand! thus saving of your friend.
Shar. Hark, I hear a noise!
Hyp. See, see, the guard!
Jul. Fly, I command you, fly! We are betray'd.
[*Jul. pulls Shar., who retreats with his sword in
hand; the women run off shrieking.*
Lad. See, she entices him, and the coward flies!
And hast thou lost thy courage with thy honesty?
This man was valiant once, I've now done more
Than I have seen whole armies do before:
But guilt now so unmans him, that he flies
What once he had the courage to despise:
But I'll pursue thee to thy base retreats.
Ha! the gates fastened! are they barricadoed?
Fetch me a torch, I'll fire my way to 'um,
And kill him in the arms of that false woman:
Yea, rage perhaps may tempt me to destroy
Her, whom I once thought heaven to enjoy.
Theo. Oh! how his passion, like a clap of thunder,
Rends her great soul. But ha! they fire upon us.
My lord! you will be shot, a shower of bullets
Flies from each corner.
See some musqueteers upon the battlements.
The fatal hail falls thick.
Lad. Poor men, how dangerously
They stand against so numerous an army!
How bloodily they wound the drooping flowers!
Theo. A flight of arrows
Covers the garden with a poison'd shade;
And one just glanc't your side: you're shot! you
    bleed!
Lad. I feel it not.
Theo. 'Tis fallen at your foot;
Shot from some Tartar's bow. Curse on the slave,
The horse-fed dog! oh, let me suck the wound,
For fear the dart was venom'd.
Lad. Ha, I bleed!

Indeed these are Juliana's darts of love :
Thank you, kind Princess. Come then, Theodore,
I will retire, I ought not to resign,
T' each common shaft, a life so great as mine ;
No, perjur'd woman ! I will live to have
Such a revenge as shall be great and brave ;
Suiting thy birth, and mine, and be above
My injured honour, and affronted love :
And when I've done I'll make my last retreat
To her, that never hath deceiv'd me yet,
Honour, a mistress worthy of my mind,
Both fair and great, as thou, and far more kind.

[Exit.

The SCENE, a ROOM in COLIMSKY'S palace.

Enter JULIANA, SHARNOFSKY, HYPOLITA.

Jul. Fire on 'um still !
Shar. I can descry but two from the terrace walk.
Jul. They're behind the trees.

Enter FRANCISCA and EMILIA running.

But see, the affrighted maids !
  Em. Oh ! out of breath.
W'ave been pursued by such a crew o' rogues !
  Fra. Ay indeed, madam, there was horse and
     foot.
I was pursued at least by twenty pikemen.
  Em. And sixteen musqueteers ran after me.
  Jul. The Count ! My lord, did you not meet
     the guards ?

Enter COLIMSKY.

Col. Not I.
  Jul. Then sure we are pursued by phantoms.
  Col. Well, madam, I've had fortunate success,
And rais'd a force very considerable
For the small time I had to do it in :
I find the young nobles, and many commons,

And almost all the ladies, highly sensible
Of your great wrongs, and ready to engage with you.
Madam, in short, fear not the Cardinal's threats ;
But, above all things, trust not his promises.
Hell's not so false, madam ; you can but die,
And you had better bravely give your life,
Than be deluded out on 't ; but I hope
You'll be constrain'd to neither, if a wall
Of fifty thousand bucklers can protect you.
   Jul. Blest news ! let's arm ! I will have Poland see
My father's royal soul survives in me.   [*Exit.*

THE THIRD ACT.

Enter PAULINA, JOANNA.

   Paul. Marry a lady o' my quality, and then
Deny the marriage ! oh, perfidious ungrateful man !
And was it then for this [I] trampled on
My self, my honours, fortunes ;
Ran on the pikes of my great father's anger,
Bestow'd thy life, when all thy friends abandon'd
    thee,
And for thy sake am now become a poor
And wand'ring exile ; and thou thus reward me,
Basely abandon me ? oh, horrid, horrid !
Weep, bleed, die, fall at my feet thou tyrant,
Quick, quick ! or see this steel is in thy heart.
   Jo. How wild she looks, and talks ; oh, my poor
    Princess !
How deadly pale she is ! now weeps again.
   Paul. What shall I do ? in a strange country
    here
Exposed to shame, yet strangled if I return,
Death waits me at home, disgrace and ruin here ;

Like a poor ship thus lab'ring in a storm.
I view the angry ocean o'er and o'er,
And see a thousand waves, but not one shore.
   Jo. Oh, that I were a witch to torture him !
   Paul. To-night, he dies ! where is Alexey gone ?
   Jo. Gone out to see what mean these strange
     confusions,
Shouts, clamours, cries, billows and tides of people
Flowing in the streets, calling to arms, to arms !
   Paul. Alexey knows his chamber. Then to-
     night,
When weariness betrays him to his rest,
And he lies coffin'd in the vaults of sleep,
Haunted with mournful dreams, I'll to his bed,
Unwrap his breast, anatomize his heart ;
Here runs a vein of courage, there of falsehood,
This fibre shows him man, but that a devil ;
Then if he groans, or else, with cast up eyes,
Shall sigh a prayer, I'll stab it as it flies,
And beg of heaven both soul and prayer may
To those blest regions never find their way :
But then lest heaven should deny my prayer,
I'll kill myself, even to torment him there.
           Enter ALEXEY.
   Alex. Oh, Madam ! there's the strangest news
     abroad.
The Princess and the Count are up in arms.
Poland's in a blaze, all's in confusion,
The general Diet's equally divided,
And millions of reports fly to and fro :
Some say they design to crown the Duke ;
Others to murder him, and crown themselves.
The Duke lies sick of an invenom'd wound,
But more of jealousy ; I listened at his chamber,
And heard him groan of both ; his soul is bubbling,
A little heat would boil him to a height.
   Paul. I'll go, I'll go, I'll sting his poison'd soul,

Put fire under his heart, I'll boil him, boil him,
Till in his rage he runs and kills his friend,
His mistress, and himself; then we'll be merry,
Be jolly, carouze, drink healths in their blood.

Jo. Our Landlord too's a talking newsmonger,
I'll go and stuff the fool's cranny with all the
rascally news I can invent.

Paul. Do! all tools shall help; there's nothing
        now
So base I would not do to have revenge:
Revenge to me doth even seem above
Celestial joys, or the delights of love.
Ye powers!
Let but revenge give me one minute's ease,
And cast your other joys to whom you please.

The Scene, THE TOWN.
Enter OSSOLINSKY, CASSONOSKY, LUBOMIRSKY,
and their trains, at several doors, running in confusion.
TWO GENTLEMEN.

Om. To arms, to arms!
Osso. Not mounted yet, my lords? the Cardinal
    is ready to march into the field.
Casso. Heaven speed his Eminence, I hope he
is in his coach; for if he was a horseback, and his
horse trotted as high as his designs, he would jolt
the old man's bones.   [*Aside.*
Lub. I thought what would become of these
violent proceedings.
Casso. So, here's Machiavel, policy in the
abstract; the wind of to'ther party blows a little
dust in's teeth, and he wheels about.   [*Aside.*
Osso. You thought! were not you as forward as
any one?
Casso. So, blunderbuss, my lord grand lubber;
be sure if there be any simple knavery, thou wilt
be forward enough in it, but thou want'st wit to

be an ingenious knave. And yet this fool got the marshal's baton from me, thank the good King.

[*Aside.*

Lub. As forward as any one ? no, I was not as forward as any one, sir.

Osso. I hate this.

Lub. Well, and I hate, sir.

Osso. Nay, sir, ben't so passionate ! farewell to you ; I'll stand by the Cardinal my self.

Casso. So, these Lords will go to cuffs about state, you shall see ; come, my lords, no dissensions, we have enemies enow.

Lub. Sir, I am as ready to draw my sword i'th' Cardinal's defence, as he can be.

Casso. No doubt, no doubt, my sweet noble lord ; all the world knows you're loyal, wise, and valiant. My sweet Count Simpleton, all the world knows you to be a coxcomb, and so do I : well, I am so out o' humour, I could hate all mankind.

Osso. Then what need all this quarrelling among ourselves ?

Casso. Enough o' this, my lord. I must reconcile 'um for my own ends, or else they might fight and hang [*aside*]. Well, what shall we do with these impertinent women that are engaged against us ?

Lub. Is your lady amongst 'um, my lord ?

Casso. Ay, I have an impertinent hen amongst 'um, that would crow o'er all the cocks in the Kingdom, if she could.

1. *Gent.* Sh'as reason, for half the cocks in the kingdom have crowed o'er her. [*Aside.*

Osso. They'll have the wit to keep out o' danger. By this time the Cardinal is ready. Bid 'um sound to horse. [*Ex. Osso., Lub.*

Casso. So, thus am I forc't to solder 'um together to keep our rotten building from falling in pieces, till I requite the kindness of the King upon his daughter, for opposing me in all the offices of state I stood candidate for, great seal, gold key, preferring these, and every phlegmatick fellow before me; and now 'tis I have rais'd all this storm, and the overwise Cardinal thinks to make me a tool in his design, and I make him an instrument in mine.   [*Exit.*

2. Gent. This is pretty, the women in arms: ha, ha! is thy mistress amongst 'um, she with the high Roman nose?

1. Gent. Ay, and thine too, she with the low flat French nose.

2. Gent. Ha, ha! how I shall laugh to see the little pretty uptails come to make a home-thrust at a man. Prithee, let's follow our lords, and see this desperate camp.

1. Gent. But first let's arm, back and breast, bodkin proof.

The Scene, A LARGE PAVILION.

Enter JULIANA, HYPOLITA, EMILIA, FRANCISCA, *and ladies in hats, feathers, vests; with gilded pole-axes in their hands, followed by* SHARNOFSKY, COLIMSKY, *and* GUARD *at a distance,* DEMETRIUS *and* BATTISTA *as among the crowd.*

Dem. Not one face here that doth resemble his.

Bat. My lord, you'll be observ'd.

Dem. Stand back, Battista! I'll view 'um all; and if thou dost provoke me, I'll fight 'um all.

Jul. Let all the gazing crowds withdraw, and place strict guards about the tents!

Bat. Come, let's withdraw in time among the crowd.

Dem. I'll not withdraw: Curland is among 'um, And I will make their close cabal deliver him.

Bat. Yes, yes, be cut in pieces by the guards.

Guar. Avoid the tent, all, all!

Dem. Slave, who do you speak to? [*Draws.*
Guar. Ha, sir, who are you?
2. *Guar.* Cleave his head!
Bat. Hold, sir, for heaven's sake! [*Interposes.*
Shar. }
Col. } What mutiny's that?
Guar. A traitor comes to murder the Princess.
Jul. A traitor?
Dem. A traitor, you mercenary slaves?
Bat. Oh! gods, what work is here?
Shar. Deliver, sir! [*Disarms Dem.*
Jul. Who employ'd you, sir, on so wise an
    errand?
Dem. A thing, which I'm afraid Poland ne'er
heard of yet, call'd honour. 'Tis to seek a person
hid in your false cabals, as false as they.
Jul. The youth's distracted.
Bat. This generous person is but a stranger, one
of high quality, and only comes in curiosity to see
th' election.
Dem. Sirrah, you lie! I come to seek the Duke,
and I will have him here, or fire their tents about
their ears.
Jul. He is a little craz'd: he hath his liberty.
Convey him home, and send for one of my
physicians to him.
Bat. I humbly thank your highness.
Dem. Am I your buffoon, then? send your
physicians to me!
Shar. Go, young sir, another time you shall be
welcome hither; at present, sir, indeed you must
excuse us.
Dem. Take notice, sir, I will revenge th' affront
when y'are a King; at present you are all beneath
my anger. [*Ex. Dem., Bat.*
Col. What a mad fiery youth is this!
Jul. And now must I with humble patience wait

Upon this scarlet minister of fate,
Who comes with slow and a majestic pace
To speak a Prince's doom with greater grace,
And with a specious gravity to hide
His traitorous design, and haughty pride.
Yes: To his grandeur I owe more esteem,
I at his own cabals should visit him:
And, if he stays, perhaps I shall prevent
With fifty thousand swords his compliment.
In th' interim I'll divertize my self and these
noble ladies. Command my music to sing a song
of Triumph:
Fierce and heroic tempers cannot stay
To court a victory with long delay,
Like a dull bridegroom for his wedding night,
But conquer and triumph, and then they fight.

THE SONG.

Awake, awake! thou warlike genius of our state,
  Who once didst glorious things;
    But hast of late
  Lain sleeping under drowsy Kings;
Arise! and on triumphant beauty wait:
    See, see, he comes,
  Rous'd with the noise of trumpets and of drums,
The air all flaming wheresoe'er he went,
And now he hovers o'er our Prince's tent.

2.

    Fair Amazon, the day's thine own,
Thine enemies look pale to see thy warriors stand
Impatient for thy great command,
  Whose looks do make the fainting villains groan;
    And by and by
Shall on the altar of the field
    Ten thousand victims lie.

Then church and state
Shall on thy triumphs wait,
  Mitre and crown
Shall at thy feet lie down
To flatter thy victorious charms ;
Away ! to arms ! to arms !

Enter an OFFICER.

Off. Madam, the Cardinal's come into the field,
And all the lords that join with him.
  Jul. The lords ! and doth his piety distrust
Heaven's protection of a cause so just ?
But he, good man, though he is arm'd with prayer,
And hath battalions marshall'd in the air,
Yet will make use of other guards beside,
And rather will in temp'ral arms confide :
My Lord Sharnofsky, draw up the squadrons of
horse into battalia. I'll head 'um myself in person.
  Col. We have a braver appearance than could
b' expected on so little warning.

Enter another OFFICER.

Off. Madam, the Cardinal desires to treat in
person with you, and demands caution, for the
security of himself and those that shall attend him.
  Jul. Let sufficient caution be given.
  Shar. Open to the right and left to make way for
the Cardinal.

Enter CARDINAL, OSSOLINSKY, CASSONOSKY,
  LUBOMIRSKY, *and train. The* CARDINAL
    looks about and smiles.

Card. The women arm'd ! then sure w'are all
    mistaken ;
This preparation's only made
For some great Masquerade.
  Jul. A play ! 'tis only to divert you, sir,

And call'd, The downfall of the Cardinal.
  Card. And was it this, you and your mighty
    poets
Have so long studied on ?   The plot's too mean
For such great wits, and such a mighty scene :
An usurp't crown a better plot would be
For arm'd tragedians, such as here I see ;
And if we make inquiry, we shall find
'Twas such a plot your poetry design'd :
And to deny it, madam, is in vain,
For we have searcht your vaults, and found your
    train ;
And 'twill but set you higher on the score
To justify your ills, by doing more.
But if in this contempt you will proceed,
Then thank your own ambition if you bleed ;
You are an orphan, so is the Kingdom too,
And no less trusted to my care than you.
  Jul. How blest am I, with this great state to share
In such a holy guardian's pious care,
Whose thoughts are busied for me night and day,
That my good angel may have leave to play :
Whose love to that romantic height is flown,
That he to save my soul would lose his own :
For though in compliment he seem'd t' approve
The little youthful vanities of love ;
And did my marriage with the Duke advance,
To show the King and me his complaisance ;
Nay more, did to my dying father swear,
Our mutual loves should be his chiefest care :
He had a far more heavenly intent,
And swore in courtship what he never meant :
For he, who from his youth hath understood
The pleasing mysteries of flesh and blood,
And knows how seldom those that are in love
In their embraces think of joys above :
He therefore charitably breaks his oath,

And becomes perjur'd to preserve us both.
   Card. I am not ignorant what you design
By ironies like these, so sharp, so fine ;
'Tis true, I promis'd I would ever bear,
Even of your loves, a most religious care ;
And that I would endeavour to redeem
The captive you did then so much esteem,
And faithfully engag'd when that was done,
I would complete the vows you had begun;
Things good and just like these I vowed to do,
But not to uphold you in all evil too ;
I did not swear if you should both combine
T' o'erturn the state to share in the design ;
Though with my honour you so pleasant be,
And, think to laugh me into perjury ;
Sport with me, madam, as your scorn thinks fit,
We can distinguish innocence from wit ;
And, if I'm perjur'd, Poland then shall know
Their safety did require it to be so :
For know, my lords, th' ambitious Duke and she
                            [*Turning to the Lords.*
Whom I have injur'd, as she charges me,
Have sought this crown by treason to obtain,
Which by just ways they did despair to gain ;
And to all Princes have addresses made
The commonwealth by fire and sword t'invade,
Seeking that throne which they despair t' enjoy
By mean revenge and envy to destroy ;
And here their partizans do seek by stealth
To gain upon the sleeping commonwealth.
And now to stop so evil a design,
Stepping to take the actors in the mine ;
Enrag'd their enterprise shou'd hinder'd be,
They strive to blow up both themselves and me.
   Shar. No more, proud priest ! how dar'st thou at this rate
      this rate
Sport with a Princess, and a Kingdom's fate ?

And charge us boldly with this black intent,
When as thy conscience knows w'are innocent?
But thou whose valiant conscience never fears
To rifle urns, and sell an orphan's tears,
To break thy oaths made to a dying King,
Must have a soul debauch't for any thing.
Alas, poor man! here are ten thousand eyes
That see thy plots through all their vain disguise:
Poor vulgar spectacles can sit at home,
And read thy darkest policies at Rome;
At Rome, the market for thy royal ware,
Thou chaffer'st Poland for the Papal chair,
And here thou striv'st to beat that interest down,
Which spoils thy trading for the triple crown:
Nay more, for fear thy chapmen there should fail,
Thou to all Princes set'st this crown to sale.
'Tis plac't upon thy private stalls,
And cheap'ned in thy dark cabals:
No pacquets come, nor envy doth resort,
But brings thee pelf from every Christian court:
And not a Princely suitor sends to woo,
But thy good will must first be courted too;
Each royal youth of Europe panting lies,
For fear the Cardinal his consent denies.
And now because some cannot bear to see
A priest make merchandize of royalty;
That money should the throne invade,
And turn the crown into a trade;
He all impending evils to prevent,
Accuses us, to be thought innocent.
   Card. Well, sir, then since you have so good a
      cause,
Repose your life and honour in the laws,
Deliver yourself unto the State, and I
Will lay my maces and my scarlets by,
And from my office, waving all pretence,
Will to the State submit my innocence:

I   5

Then let the Diet freely try
Which is the traitor, you, or I.   [*Card. party shout.*
   Osso. 'Tis bravely spoken.
   Lub. Greatly, like himself!
   Casso. Knavishly, like himself.   [*Aside.*
   Shar. Agreed! Here, bind my hands.
   Jul. My lord, you shall not.
   Shar. His proposition's fair; the Cardinal
Never preach't any thing so much divine,
And let no blood be shed but his or mine !
   Jul. 'Tis all deceit, through you he aims at me,
That he my father's throne might freel' invade,
And proudly triumph o'er his royal shade ;
But that he shall not do whil'st I've a hand
To hold a spear, and armies to command.
   Card. And, Madam, do you think that fate is
      amorous ?
Or to find any courtship from a bullet ?
They, like raw travellers, court all they meet ;
Nor can we send a guide to give advice
Whom to respect, but let 'um take their choice.
   Jul. Their rugged courtship, sir, I shan't deny,
Send them abroad, and give them all supply
That may defray the charges of their flight,
Draw bills of death, they shall be paid on sight ;
I will your faithful correspondent be,
And pay as fast as you can draw on me.
   Card. Madam, I'm sorry you resolve t' expose
Yourself, and such a lovely guard as those,
To all the sad uncertainties of fate,
To try your skill in fencing with the State ;
For justice at a traitor's life doth fly,
And when it makes a pass you put it by ;
But if the sword doth hap' to run astray,
Then thank your self for standing in the way.
         [*Exeunt Card., Osso., Casso., Lub., shouting
               and waving their fauchions.

Jul. Come, valiant friends! the talking pro-
      logue's done;
The curtain's drawn, the mighty play's begun!
The music of the field in martial rage
Calls us to enter on this fatal stage,
Where each brave man shall doubly have applause,
Crown'd by his courage, and his glorious cause;
A cause more glorious there cannot be,
I for the kingdom die, and you for me.
Ex. Jul. and train shouting and waving their pole-axes.

The SCENE *the* DUKE'S *chamber.*

Enter THEODORE, *and a* SURGEON.

Theo. Offer to let my master go out in this
condition?

Sur. I could not hold him, sir, he would go out
whether I would or no. But there's no danger, his
wound's not great, nor was the arrow venom'd, as
first you fear'd.

Theo. Oh! he'll hear all the news,   [*Aside.*
And then I tremble at the consequence.
Now comes this babbling rascal.

Enter LANDLORD.

Land. Nay, I thought 'twould be as I said: the
Count is to be King, and marry the Princess.
How, now, where's your master? I've news for him.

Theo. Get you gone with your news, you prating
bufflehead, or I'll set you down stairs. Come here
with your news?

Land. Prating bufflehead! and you'll set me
downstairs? Do you know who you speak to,
sirrah? Come, come, you lie, you lie! you don't
know who you speak to, and you're drunk, sirrah,
you would not talk to me at this rate else, sirrah:
get me down stairs with my news, sirrah? I'd have
[you] to know, the best men in the kingdom are
glad of my intelligence, you drunken rascal, you.

Theo. Yes, no doubt you have all the intelligence. Pray Mr. Corantoe-Master-General, what may your envoys and spies in foreign courts cost you yearly ?

Land. What may they cost me, sir ? pray what may your envoys and spies which you maintain with the Duke o' Gally-pots, Count Palatine o' Glister-pipes, Marquess o' Mouth-glue, and Baron o' Bathing-tubs, for the support o' your rotten body politic, cost you yearly ? Ha, Sir Ragmanners, my intelligence comes from better men than you or your master either. I met no less now (because you prate) than six lords of my old acquaintance coming out of the field together all of a knot.

Theo. What knot ? a bow-knot ?

Land. A bow-knot, saucy-chops ! when did you see six lords tied of a bow-knot ? Ha ! can you tie your nose of a bow-knot ? You had not best provoke me, sirrah. But so, here comes my man, now it shall be seen whether I am a liar or no.

Enter JOANNA *and* ALEXEY *peeping.*

Jo. How, not here ! where did we lose her ?

Alex. I'll hold a wager the person we met in the cloak was the Duke, and she went after him somewhere, and is lost in the crowd.

Land. Come, come, sir ! you Mr Peagoose that stand peeping there, pray, sir, thrust in your nose a little further : I have some employment for you.
                                   [*Pulls in Jo.*

Jo. The rogue will discover all my design, and render us suspicious to the Duke's servant, I am afraid. Come in, Alexey, and help me to out-face the fool.   [*Aside to Alex.*

Land. Come, sir, did not you hear in the field, as much as to say, as if the Count was to be made King, and to marry the Princess ? Come, answer directly to the point ; why don't you speak, sir ?

Jo. Who, me do ye mean?

Land. Ay, you, sir. Who should I mean else?

Jo. I hear it! how should I hear it? was I in the field to-day?

Land. Why you impudent stinking lying rascal! you won't tell me such a lie, will you?

Alex. You mistake me, Landlord, and ha' met somebody like him.

Land. No, sir, I don't mistake; I can see when I see, surely; I don't carry my eyes in a hand-basket, and more than that, 'cause he goes to't, he's the very man, and no other, from whom I'd all this news now.

The. Is this your six lords of a knot, you ninny? I see you can invent for a need.

Jo. Oh, a most grievous impertinent lying fellow! I'm so plagued with him sometimes.

Alex. Hark you, Landlord, are not you troubled with a dizziness in your noddle, a megrim sometimes? I am afraid you eat too much mustard, and such hot things.

Jo. Some snush* would purge your simple brain.

Land. A little more would make me run distracted. Don't you tell me o' your megrims, your snush, and your mustard; a company of rascals! sirrah, did not I meet you coming out o' th' field, and I ask't you what news, 'cause I was loath to go farther, 'cause I was to go buy a pole o' ling for the women's dinner that lie in my house here; and you told me all this bibble babble, and bid me go no farther, but go to my lodgers with it: deny't if you dare, sirrah! I'll promise you if you do, I'll churn those buttermilk-chops o' yours, and let your master take it off. I care not if you and your master both get out o' my house, I can ha' customers for my rooms.

Alex. Come, enough o' this Landlord.

<hr>

* Query: Snuff? *Scotice,* " Sneishin."

Land. I han't enough, sir. I won't be made a liar on.

The. Why, what a troublesome fellow art thou.

Land. And what a troublesome fellow art thou. I won't be borne down by a company o' saucy valets that are good for nothing but to twirl a whisker, and a shave the crown o' some Sir Nicolas Emptipate, his master; and be kickt thrice a day for a cast suit and bread and cheese.

Alex. Come, Landlord, I perceive you are abusive; this is not to be endured. You must be corrected out o' this humour, it will be for your good another day; and now our masters' backs are turn'd, we'll make bold to give you a taste of our parmesan.*

The. And I'll give him one lick for the sake of his Corantoes. Come, sir, since you're so good at Corantoes, pray, let's see how you can dance a Coranto. Come, up with your news quickly.†

Land. Rogues, you won't murder me, will you?

The. On the fourteenth instant, at the Port of Hucklebone, was drove in by storm a vessel call'd the Royal Cudgel, bound for back, bum, belly, noddle, or any part of the kingdom of coxcomb.

Jo. And near the same port another.

Alex. And another laden with snush, for the cure of the megrim.

Sur. They'll kill their Landlord.

Land. Rogues, rascals, thieves! Will you murder me?

Why, Surgeon, wilt thou stand by and see me
Murder'd? I'll lay my death to thee.

---

* Also "Parmesan," sometimes "Parmasent."

† Coranto, from the French "Courante," means a nimble dance, or anything that runs quickly, such as a paper of news. There have been many newspapers called "Courants" in Great Britain within the last two hundred years. At the present time there exists in Scotland a deservedly popular Conservative newspaper, which originated about the commencement of the last century, called *The Edinburgh Courant.*

Sur. Pray, gentlemen——

Alex. How now, sirrah? do you prate, shaver o' shin-bones, drawer of gum-stakes, grafter o' broken stilts, trapanner o' crackt coxcombs? I'll teach you more manners.

Land. Murder, murder!

The. See, our lords!

They beat Landlord and Surgeon off o' th' stage : and Enter LADISLAUS *and* PAULINA.

Lad. And is it thus? Come, Theodore, my sword!

The. Oh, heavens! what is't I hear?

Paul. Come, sir, I know they're wrong'd by the fond talking world : they're constant, generous, they're angels! angels, not a pound a flesh about 'um, sir; and doth it sting thy soul? [*aside*] Crawl, crawl, about his heart, thou serpent jealousy, until he foams with poison.

Lad. [*aside*] Heavens! I fear something is strangely amiss with the young Duke : he hath talked all day at this distracted rate. What should the reason be? Some secret sorrow sets heavy on him; but I'll take no notice. Come, Theodore!

The. My lord! upon my knees——

Lad. No more, I'm wrong'd, abus'd, by my false friends,
And I will in, and die in their defence,
Since they have lost their guard of innocence :
If in a cause so bad my blood is spilt,
I have revenge by adding to their guilt.
My noble lord, farewell! a thousand blessings
[Lad. turns to Paul.
Crown your sweet youth ; and, when you see th
 Prince,
Do me the right t' inform him of my story,
And recommend me to his noble thoughts ;
Tell him the dying Duke o' Curland begs
A place, a monument to his fair soul ;
And so, heaven bless you both!

Paul. Oh ! oh, I faint.   [*She swoons.*
  Lad. Now, Theodore——
Farewell to thee, if I ne'er see thee more,
Here, take these jewels, they are all I have
At present to reward thy love and faithfulness.
And now, dear Theodore, when the day is done,
And with it me, seek out my lifeless carcass
Among the dead, and give it a private monument :
Let not my Princess's insulting eye
Find out where injured Curland's ashes lie ;
Lest she in scorn should visit him, and there
Profane my tomb with a dissembled tear.   [*Exit.*
  The. My lord ! be sure I shall do this and more,
Ten thousand times, if I'm not dead before. [*Exit.*
  Paul. Ha, is he gone ? and hath he left me
      thus ?
Ne'er was false lady so belov'd as she,
Nor any so unfortunate as me !
But see, he is not gone ; there, there he stands !
Come here, my kindest lord, and kiss me once,
But once before I die, for I am going
Where poor Paulina 'll trouble you no more.
  Jo. Oh, heavens ! her grief mislays her noble
      reason,
What shall we do ?
  Alex. I'll run and kill the villain.
  Paul. Alexey, see what shadow's that ?
Is't not a coffin ? 'tis !   Come, lock me in !
I know not whether I am dead or no,
But if I am not, I would feign be so.
  Alex. Oh, I shall run my sword into myself.
  Jo. And I shall break my heart.
  Paul. Sirs, lead me in !
Well, since th'art gone, brave Ladislaus, adieu !
I'd not have dealt thus cruelly by thee ;
But I forgive thee, and when no one's by,
I'll pray for thee, then fetch a groan and die.

The Fourth Act.

The scene AN OPEN FIELD COVERED WITH TENTS.

Enter OSSOLINSKY, CASSONOFSKY, LUBOMIRSKY :
After, shouts and acclamations without.

Osso.
Casso. } All's our own.   Victory, victory !
Come, for the plunder of the Princess'
tent !

Enter DEMETRIUS *and* BATTISTA.

Lub. But see, Prince Radzeville, Commander of
the Transilvanian horse ! what news from the dead ?
Did not I see thee fall under thy horse feet ?

Casso. Come ! for the plunder of the tent, brave
Prince.

Osso. Move, slow devils.

[*Exeunt Osso., Casso., Lub., shouting.*

Dem. Never did such a gale of fortune blow.
I'll sail in tides of blood up to their tents, and
take the Duke o' Curland's mistress prisoner,
carry her to Moscow, and keep her captive till
Poland ransoms her with Curland's blood. Follow ;
brave men !   [*Exit.*

Bat. Go, 'tis in vain to hinder thee
When honour calls, nor will I stop thee now,
Although he fights, he knows not where, nor how.
[*Exit.*

Enter COLIMSKY.

Col. Must we not only fight with men, but
devils ? Radzeville, Commander of the Transilvanian horse, who fell by my sword, is mounted
afresh, hath broke through all our troops and
stands o' pikes, and flies like lightning to the

Prince's tent, and doth greater things, now dead,
than living.   Pursue the warlike ghost; all, all to
the Prince's tent !   But see, whole troops of flame ;
[*a flame flashes through the tents*] a thousand fiery
spears pierce every way, and a bright cloud of
fire breaks from the town !   What should it mean ?

Enter an OFFICER *running.*

Osso. My lord, to the Princess' tent, or she is
lost.

Col. Teach me my duty, you slave !
[*Strikes him with his sword.*
What means this flame ?

Osso. It is some valiant stranger, but who I
know not, that hath flown about just like a fire-
ship in seas of blood to grapple with whole fleets :
and seeing the enemy flow all in tides up to the
Princess' tent, hath set the tents and all the town
on fire ; and here with five hundred resolute
cavalry he comes to force his passage.

Col. Brave men, I'll lead the way to glory ! all,
all to the Princess' tent !   [*Exeunt.*

Enter LADISLAUS, THEODORE, *and followers with
flambeaux in their hands.*

Lad. Come, valiant men ! let's give 'um brave
    diversion,
Let's set their tents afloat in blood and flames,
And fill the air with clouds of human ashes ;
Set all on fire, the town, the tents, the temple ;
Spare not the very houses of religion.   [*Exit.*
  The. Brave Prince, how generous thy actions
    are !
Unseen he changes all the scenes of war,
And with a noble scorn he fights for them
Who both his courage and his love contemn ;
These glories must at last themselves betray,

And through all gloomy clouds must pierce a way.
                                        [*Exeunt.*

*The scene is chang'd to the Princess's pavilion; a
noise of arms, the women shriek within: And enter
HYPOLITA, EMILIA, FRANCISCA, running.*

Hyp.
Em.   } Murder, murder! the Princess will be
Fran. } murder'd.

*Enter SHARNOFSKY, defending the Princess, pursued
by DEMETRIUS, OSSOLINSKY, CASSONOSKY,
LUBOMIRSKY, BATTISTA, and GUARD; the
women run about shrieking and crying murder.*

Jul. Stand by, Sharnofsky! I'll defend my self.
Shar. Madam, for heaven's sake do not deprive
me in the last moment of my life of that which
I have liv'd and fought for all this while;
For if without defending you I'm slain,
I lose my honour, and I die in vain.
Jul. That honour you shall have, but not alone,
Nor rob my courage, sir, to crown your own.
Shar. Oh! whither doth she rush? For shame, ye
cowards, set not your swords against a lady's
breast, your princess too: she bleeds! You saucy
villains, y'ave wounded a divinity th' Americans
would have kneeled and prayed to. Ye powers!
what, are ye all asleep above the clouds? If ye are,
lend me your thunder. Oh! she's lost.
Osso. You are my prisoner, sir.   [*To Shar.*
Dem. You, Princess, are mine.   [*To Jul.*
Casso. So now shall I have a full draught of
revenge.
Dem. Now know, fond Poles. I have deluded
you; I am not Radzeville, but Demetrius, a Prince o'
the Imperial house o' Muscovy; a mortal, an eternal

enemy to you all. I come to search [out] your General, the Duke of Curland, who like a treacherous Pole, after I had took him prisoner, shew'd him kindness, hath stole my Princess, and I'll enslave his, and, the next time I come, enslave you all. And now stand by me, valiant Transilvanians! I'll give you all a hundred crowns a man.

Bat. Oh ! the good heavens, he betrays himself.

Osso.
Casso. } Ha ! what saith Radzeville ?
Lub.

Shar. This is distraction.

Jul. Must I be carried then a slave to Moscow ?

Hyp.
Em. } Oh, the Princess ! oh, this Russian
Fran. } slave !   [*Dem. drags her along.*

Osso.
Casso. } He's mad ! he raves !
Lub.

Casso. Hold, sir ! Cleave the rebel's head, slaves!

Fran. Heaven ! what stupid lethargy hath seiz'd thee ? Assist, unbind me, or else strike me dead rather than torture me with such a sight.

Osso.
Casso. } Hold rebel, villain !
Lub.

Osso. My lords, command all your men, horse, and foot, to surround the Transilvanian troops, and make 'um fling down their arms, or die.   [*Exit.*

Lub. Let all the cossacques wheel.

Dem. Fire, give fire ! a hundred of you stay, and guard the prisoners.

Bat. Oh ! the unruly fire that governs thee, Where will it lead thee ?   [*Exit.*

Casso. Now, to guard the prisoners shall be my work.

Jul. How am I made the sport and scorn of

fortune! abus'd by Curland, trampled on by slaves; and now led bound to follow the triumphant chariot of scarlet perjury.

Shar. My soul is torn with grief and rage.

Casso. Come then, I'll ease you both? Alas! I pity you; but chiefly you, good Princess. Your kind father, I thank him, eas'd me of many a burthensome employment, and I in gratitude will ease your shoulders of such a weighty head laden with sorrow.   [*Call Osso., Dem., Bat., bound.**

Hyp.
Em.   } Oh, bloody villain!
Fran.

Jul. Insolent slave! dares such a thing as thee threaten a Princess' life?

Shar. Barbarous dog! bring me but to him, I'll kick his dirty soul out of his body.

Casso. I'll snap thy saucy head from off thy shoulders first. Guards, kill the prisoners! I'll not allow the formality of praying; and he that asks what orders I have for it, let 'um know I wear my orders by my side; this is my Cardinal, Senate, and my King. [*shews his naked faulchion,*] Off with their heads, his crooked majesty commands it.

Shar. Thou monster of mankind, hast thou no sense of pity or humanity, nor of thy own, nor of thy country's honour, which such a horrid act will render infamous to all the world? Here quench thy barbarous thirst of blood with mine, open all my veins, take my life, my fortune, honour, all I have, but spare, oh, spare the daughter of thy King!

Jul. No more, my lord, swell not the villain's pride by falling prostrate to it. Quick, Hypolita, give me a poinard!

Casso. Fetch a wrack, an engine, I'll torture him

* *i.e.,* Instructs Osso, to have Demetrius and Battista taken away and bound.

to death. But ha! more sport, de'e come to put
affronts upon the Kingdoms?

Enter OSSOLINSKY *and* GUARD, *with* DEMETRIUS,
and BATTISTA *bound.*

Osso. In the face of the whole army, sir, I'll
cool your fiery insolence.

Dem. Yes, murder me, you slaves!
I do deserve this punishment, and more,
That my revenge should be so low and poor;
I ought t' have set it at no lower rate
Than the whole ruin of your Polish State,
All of you huddled in one common doom,
Curland the cipher to make up the sum.

Casso. Tame the proud rebel; Guards, off with
his head!

Osso. Hold! strike who dares, till I give the
command!

Dem. Come, villains, level me right against the
        clouds,
And then give fire, discharge my flaming soul
Against such saucy destinies as those
As dare thus basely of my life dispose;
Then from the clouds rebounding I will fall,
And like a clap of thunder tear you all.

Osso. Well then, sir, since your spirit is so high,
Your head shall be as lofty by and by;
Yes, your exalted thoughts shall have their due,
Your head shall stand in both the armies' view.

Casso. Guards, are you asleep? Cleave all their
heads at once.

Osso. ⎫
        ⎬ Strike!
Casso. ⎭

*All the women give a shriek, and at that instant
        Enter* LUDOMIRSKY *running.*

Lub. Hold!

Osso. ⎫
        ⎬ Count Lubomirsky, the news?
Casso. ⎭

Lub. All's lost! I am in such a confusion I cannot speak. Some devil in human shape hath quite turn'd all the fortune of the day, hath fir'd the town, the tents, and here he's coming on waves of blood and flame.

Lasso. Hell take thee for thy news! Where is this devil?

Casso. } The Guards retire; stand, villains, or
Osso.   } you die.

Lub. Stand, cowardly slaves!

Dem. Is fortune penitent? Battista, loose me!

Bat. I am bound too, sir.

Dem. Are your teeth bound too, sir?

Shar. Ha! is the scale turning?
A thousand crowns but for one hand loose.

Jul. Deliverance swift like lightning! Heaven,
I thank thee.

Enter LADISLAUS *driving the* GUARDS *before him,
followed by* THEODORE, *and* CAVALIERS.

Lad. Stay, flying cowards! Disparage not my
   sword,
Let it be said at least I fought with men.

Osso. }
Casso. } We are lost! [*They are taken prisoners.*
Lub.   }

Dem. And must I stand to be a thing of pity,
To receive the charity of this man's sword?

Shar. I blush at our own chains, and this man's
   glory.

Lad. Secure the lords! Madam, the scene is
   chang'd,
You're all at liberty.
And now my next great deed shall be
To set my heart at liberty from thee. [*Aside. Exit.*

The. My noble lord
Thus through the field with unseen triumphs flies,

As souls make their entradoes in the skies;
Sure heaven some mighty glory hath design'd,
At last to crown such an illustrious mind.   [*Exit.*
 Jul. What prodigy's this?
 Hyp. 'Tis your angel, madam.
 Jul. A thousand crowns to know him.
 Shar. A warlike phantom,
By heaven created for this exigence.
 Dem. His haughty valour hath affronted me,
I'll out and kill him for his insolence.
And, when he's dead, I'll hug him for his bravery.
         [*Exit.*
 Bat. To arms again; thus doth his active soul
Leap from one danger to another;
Here we destroy, and there we save,
As vessels tost from wave to wave.   [*Exit.*
 Shar. Let's out, and help to reap this glorious
   harvest;
But hark, a loud volley of martial shouts.
 All within. Long live Juliana, our Queen!
 Shar. Blest noise; your name is bandied in the
   clouds;
There's a victorious tempest in the air,
And see a thousand lights approach the tent.
 Casso. Oh, cursed sight! and cursed noise.

Enter COLIMSKY.

 Col. Now, madam, all's our own! Your enemies
have all flung down their arms. Some come to crave
your pardon, others fly in multitudes to the
Cardinal's tent; the Cardinal, in transports of rage
for his misfortune, confest his horrid villanies, and
fled. I sent an officer to conduct him to a private
grotto in a neighbouring grove, pretendingly for
his security; in the interim the crowds rifled his
tent, and found the crown conceal'd, and here

they're coming sailing along with shouts and acclamations, resolving to repose it on your brow.

Jul. The weight's too great for me.

All, within. Secure the distracted State!

Col. The people grow impatient.

Jul. I'll sacrifice myself t'appease the crowds.
Heavens! never was such a turn of fortune known,
From a scaffold to a throne.
In one moment to be seen,
A dying captive and a Queen.   [*Exit.*

Col. So now, my good lords, you may be all at leisure for holy contemplations.

Shar. Guards, see especially
To that malicious Count.   [*Ex. Shar., Col.*

Casso. I know your kindness, I need not go to an astrologer to know my doom: what a long neck shall I have when my head's set upon a pole on one of the city gates.

Osso.   } This is the giddiness of fortune.
Lub.   }

              [*Led away with Guard as prisoners.*

Enter DEMETRIUS *and* BATTISTA.

Dem. This way the spirit went, and as it walk't
I saw a kind of shape resembling Curland.

Bat. My lord, your fancy in the heat of passion forges a thousand images.

Dem. If 'twas his ghost, I'll find out his abode: let it be air, earth, or fire.

Bat. If it walks any where, 'tis there amongst the Queen's triumphant train.

Dem. I hear 'um shout, I'll amongst 'um.

Bat. Hold, sir! pray let 'um not discover you for fear the Poles revenge th' affront you did their Princess.

I.   6

Dem. Then I'll revenge th' affront the Poles did
me.   [*Exit.*

  Bat. Heavens! what a task have I. It is the
    same,
To bridle a tempest, or to steer a flame.   [*Exit.*

   The SCENE, A HOLLOW ROCK IN A GROVE.

Enter the CARDINAL *conducted by an* OFFICER.

  Card. Heaven! have mercy! whither dost thou
    lead me?
Osso. I was commanded to conduct you hither:
The Count will come to you here, and bring the
    news.
Card. He is a worthy friend.
Osso.   'Tis dark and private,
Here you may lie with safety.
  Card. Thus in a moment is my sun gone down.

   Enter a GENTLEMAN *running.*

  Gent. My lord, convey your self away with
speed, all's lost! your men are fled, your tent is
plunder'd; the Princess crown'd, and all your
friends betray you. My Lord Grand Marshall's
coming with a guard from the Queen to secure you.
  Card. Then, there's no trust in man.
  Gent. This way, sir; hasten!
  Osso. Hold, sir, not so fast.
  Card. Art thou set here to betray me too?
  Osso. To guard you, sir.
  Card. To guard me as a victim for sacrifice! I
am at last outwitted in villany.
  Gent. Oh, heavens! sir, you're lost,   [*Shout.*
The Queen approaches; hark, the dreadful shouts.
A thousand streaming lights flow all this way.
  Card. And let 'um come, I have a friend in
private will not betray me.
              [*Pulls out a handkerchief.*

Gent. A poisoned handkerchief, I fear.
Card. The little winding-sheet of all my glories ;
Ah ! had I studied but as much to gain
Heaven, as this world, I had not sweat in vain :
Instead of horrors that pursue me now,
Immortal crowns had waited for my brow ;
But my amazing miseries now are
Beyond the aid of penitence and prayer :
To my own idols I too long did bow,
To put that fawning cheat on heaven now :
For he hath made my religion understood
To be but craft, and my devotion blood.
My heaven was t'ascend the Papal throne,
Where to save other's souls, I've lost my own.
And now, alas ! 'twere folly to deny
Myself the pleasure to despair and die.
May all great men learn by my wretched fate,
Never to stake their souls at games of State ;
For though a while perhaps they seem to win,
They'll find at last there is no cheat like sin. [*Dies.*
   Gent. He's gone ; irrecoverably gone ! his great
     soul's fled,
And see a thousand lights usher the Queen ;
She comes to see her mighty enemy
Lie a cold statue prostrate at her feet.
         [*The scene shuts upon the Card.. &c.*

Enter JULIANA *crown'd,* HYPOLITA, EMILIA, FRAN-
   CISCA, SHARNOFSKY, COLIMSKY, *and* GUARDS,
   at one end of the theatre, PAULINA, *as mixt with
   the crowd.*

   Om. Long live Juliana, Queen of Poland !
   Jul. My lords, I thank you for all this great
     honour.
   Paul. I've stole from Count Alexey and Joanna
                   [*Aside.*
To seek my lord, and I'm afraid to find him,

Or with my rival here, or with the dead :
If here I find him, I'm resolved he dies,
Only to spoil the triumphs of her eyes ;
But see, my servants come ! I'll get away.   [*Exit.*

Enter ALEXEY, JOANNA, *and* LANDLORD.

Jo. Heavens ! where is she wander'd ; and how came we to lose her ?

Al. What do'st thou do crowding in here ? Idle body, come help us to look our master.

Land. I look your master ! Go ! hang yourself with your master.

Jul. What murmuring's that ?

Col. See, guards, what means that noise ?

Land. No, rascals, I remember your megrim, your smush, and your mustard. I'll make you pay dear for that mustard ; it shall be costly mustard.

Guar. Oh ! is it you, sir ? [*Lays hold on Landlord.*

Col. Guards, keep off the rabble ! Take that rude fellow, clap him neck and heels.

Alex.   ⎱ Begone, quick, quick ! and leave the
Jo.   ⎰ rogue i'th' bilboes.   [*Ex. Alex., Jo.*

Land. Oh, good your honour, I beseech your sweet honour.

Col. Sirrah, what's your business here ?

Land. Nothing, an't like your honour, but a couple of idle quarrelsome rascals that lie at my house ha' lost their master, and they'd make me look for their master. Now, if they ha' lost their master, I'm not bound to make good their master by no law in Poland. I refer it to your honour.

Col. Get you about your business, sirrah, and make no references to me.

Land. I thank your honour, I believe your honour knows me. Don't you remember where you lay when your honour kept the fat lady, the Lady

Chmsky!   You could make references to her for all your pride.   [*Aside.*

Col. Begone, sirrah!

Land. I thought I should put you in mind of a reference.   [*Aside.*]   I've done, an't like your honour.

Jul. Now, my lords, what news of the Cardinal?

Col. Nigh to this part of the field is the grotto where I commanded him to be convey'd ; and see ! the officer I sent to guard him.

Enter an OFFICER.

Off. My lord, the Cardinal

Osso. Where is he?

Off. Dead !

Om. Dead ?

Off. He lies so near, torches may show him you.

The scene is drawn, the CARDINAL, *presented dead in a grotto, a* GENTLEMAN *waiting by him.*

Land. Oh, 'bominable ! kill'd ! and is the Council o' Trent, and Pope Paul come to this ? Thou must know, honest guard, I'm a merry man, and I us'd to visit this good man's back cellar o' Rhenish, and then I call'd it the Council o' Trent, and there was a great tun, great grandfather or gossip at least to the great tun o' Heydelburgh, and that I us'd to call Pope Paul the third, and there did the Beef eaters o' the guard and I ——

Guar. Beef-eaters, you rascal !

Land. Sit in council about the good o' Christendom, till at parting we did our reverences to Pope Paul, fall down and kiss his great toe, the spigot, and let the heavenly benediction drop into our mouths.

Guar. You'd have my halbard drop into your mouths, would you Beef-eater, you saucy cur ?

Jul. A mournful spectacle! How died the
 Cardinal?

Off. Proudly, as he liv'd; he would not stoop to
 pray,
Or if he pray'd, 'twas so, as he would seem
He expected heaven should first pray to him;
He gave up's glory, but with such a pride,
He scorn'd to keep it, since he was denied;
And though with death he found some little strife,
Rather than ask, he would resign his life.

Land. What a wicked fellow was this! Oh, fie
upon him! not say his prayers when he died! how
doth he ever think to come to good? My lord, he
was as arrant a——

Col. Guard!

Land. I ha' done, an't like your honour.

Guar. Sirrah, I could find in my heart to beef-
eat you.

Jul. I'm sorry for his soul, but heaven's merciful! Ah! had this great man's piety been equal to's
wisdom, and his many other noble virtues he had
been a man too glorious.

Land. Nay, truly, he had as good a study of
books, I'll say that for him, good old authors, Sack
and Claret, Rhenish and old Hock. Come, said I, to
the library keeper, tap me St. Gregory, or that
good old father a tilt that looks like St. George a
horse-back; take his nag by the spigot, and give
our brains a leap, said I.

Guar. Thou hast a mind to be laid by th' heels
with thy Pope Paul.

Land. I ha' done, honest Guard.

Shar. He was too self admiring and conceited:
The Church and we did to his wisdom owe
All honours Rome or Poland could bestow.

Land. He was something self conceited indeed,
that's the truth on't.

Col. He had a soaring spirit.

Shar. Reaching wisdom.

Col. Unsatiably ambitious, and inexorable.

Land. He was a notable man.

Jul. No more, my lords! What he hath done, he's gone to answer for; then for the reverence we owe religion, let him be interr'd with decency.

> [*They take up the Car.*

Land. And for the reverence I owe burnt Claret, I'll be at's funeral.

Jul. Now all the storms are past, the winds are
    down,
The waves transport me gently to a crown :
Kind heaven smiles, and I am got above
All other tempests but the world and love :
And now I'll seek religion's flowery shore,
And be expos'd to all these storms no more.
My lords attend me, and you all shall know
How I'll my person and the crown bestow. [*Exit.*

Land. Well, I swear this is a delicate woman. I'd give all I am worth in the world I were a young Prince for her sake. I'd so jumble her and tumble her, I'd set her upon her head, and her heels, and kiss this end, and that end, and all in an honest way too.

Col. These words are of dubious and mysterious sense.

Shar. To a cloister, I fear.

Hyp. My lords, prevail with her,
I can assure you she designs a cloister.

Col. Let's attend her to the palace, and then meet in council. [*Ex. Om., Manet Land.*

Land. Well, it's a lovely creature; I love her so well, I could be contented to a little shock for her sake, that I might lie in her lap, lick her lips, and be strok't. But hang't, it would but puff me up, I should be too proud and self-conceited. But here's

a devilish fall in my wishes, now I think on't, from
a Prince to a puppy-dog : but love is humble.   Well
now, there's a harvest a coming, a coronation ; oh,
what a crop of dollars will I reap for my windows,
and balcony : I'll have a rix dollar for every
quarry in my window, and a hundred for my
balcony ; that is to say, fifty for my bell, and fifty
for my coney.
In all, I'll have in current Polish money,
A hundred rix dollars for my bell-coney   [*Exit.*

Enter BATTISTA.

Bat. Heavens ! I've lost him : whither is he
    wander'd ?
What new fury hath transported him ?
But ha ! the glittering of a naked sword ;
A person tall, and of my Prince's stature,
Walking about ! and hark, I hear a voice !

Enter PAULINA.

Paul. Heavens ! I walk about here in the dark,
And hear the labours of departing souls ;
A thousand aiery forms fly round about me,
And fan me into cold and dewy sweats :
Oh ! if my lord be dead, would I were with him.
    Bat. The place is enchanted.

Enter DEMETRIUS *with his naked sword.*

    Dem. There the dying voice fainted away, by
that old wall—— no, liar, that was an echo.
    Bat. My Prince ! some frightful apparition leads
him about.
    Dem. What art thou that usurp'st the sacred
name of my divinity ?
Speak, or I'll turn a ghost as thin as thee,
And torture thee.
    Paul. Hark, the Guards are near ! I will avoid
'um, and go fetch a torch, and seek my lord among

the dead, in those pale groves he is unkindly wander'd t'avoid his poor Paulina.   [*Exit*.

Bat. Hark, the voice cries Paulina.

Dem. Paulina, still! what saucy spirit mocks me with that name? could I but find thee, I'd tear thy aerial body into atoms; and I'll have light, or I'll fire this grove, Ay, and set thee on a rack of flame to make thee confess, who, and what thou art! And a light comes from behind that wall! a youth with a torch, I'll run and fetch it.

Bat. He's grown distracted! I must speak to him, sir.

Dem. And dost appear at last?   [*Runs at Bat.*

Bat. 'Tis I! Battista, Sir.

Dem. I know I might have kill'd thee so; I'm led about with voices, groans, illusions. Fetch me that torch.

Bat. A fair and lovely youth walking among the dead! sure 'tis some spectre.

Dem. Fetch me that torch!

[*Jo. and Alex. run over the stage.*

Jo.   There she is alone walking with a torch.

Alex. Where?

Jo.   Under that tree.

Alex. I see her: let's run, let's run to her!

Dem. Hark, a concert of voices.

Bat. Let's leave this dismal place! there's a cabal of melancholy spirits that haunt it. See two flying shapes come towards this youth.

Dem. I think the dead hold here their rendezvous; hark, there are some come from yonder grove! I'm tortur'd, plagu'd. Fetch me the torch, I say.

[BAT. *Ex., and*

Enter LADISLAUS *and* THEODORE.

Lad. Now, Theodore, press me no more,
I now renounce her and her sex for ever.

And now I've steer'd her safely to a throne,
I'll leave her in her ports, and to my own,
From whence the war she hath on me begun,
Shall now on all the world be carried on;
And captive Monarchs shall of her complain,
And curse my injuries and her disdain,
Whil'st I shall still by blood and slaughter prove
The scorn and hate I bear to her, and love.

Dem. Ho! stand, what are you? Battista, come with a torch!

Lad. Hark, the perdues call to the guard; I'll in my chariot to town; do you ride before, Theodore, and get post-horses ready this night. I'll onward on my way to Curland. [*Ex., Lad., Theo.*

Dem. To Curland! Ye powers, stand, stand! Come with the torch, you slave.

Enter BATTISTA *running and lays hold on* DEM.

Bat. Sir, sir!

Dem. I see a chariot, villain! Stand by, or I'll kill thee.

Bat. Are you distracted, sir? Yonder's your Princess. I've overheard their talk.

Dem. Yonder's Curland's chariot, and the slave holds me.

Bat. Ha! I see a chariot, I'll after it. Do you go to your Princess. Here, here, sir!

Enter PAULINA, JOANNA, ALEXEY *with a torch.*

Paul. Hark, I hear a voice!

Alex. It is the guards.

Bat. Here, sir, by all that's good, this is your Princess.

Dem. After the chariot then, fly! Sir, a word with you.   [*To Paul.*

Paul. The guards call to us. Out with the torch, Alex.

Paul.) Run, run! murder, murder!   [*Jo. Paul.*
Jo.   {   *The torch is put out.*   *run off.*
Alex. Fly, madam, I'll make good your retreat.
                                              [*Draws.*
Dem. Curse on my folly! I've lost 'um in the
dark.

Bat. Ha, lost them and the chariot both? Curse
on this rashness; here, here they flee.
        [*Both run confusedly crossing each other, and
    know not which way to take.*

Dem. Here, here's a path.

Bat. I see the chariot going straight to town.

Dem. I see the shape flying on the wind before
me.   [*Both run off.*

The Last Act.

The scene A Hall.

Enter BATTISTA.

Bat. With much ado I've overtaken the chariot,
and I'm so out of breath I cannot speak. Ha,
stop't her, by that balcony! this is our lodging! it
is, and see the persons coming out of the house
with a light. Where do they go? I'll watch 'um.
                                              [*Exit.*

Enter PAULINA *and* JOANNA.

Paul. Oh! I am faint with running, and the
fright. Where's Alexey?

Jo. He stay'd behind to guard us: but see! he
hath been here before us.

Enter ALEXEY.

Alex. Oh! madam, the Duke is newly alighted

at the door, and on some news, I know not what
it is, he's gone straight to the palace.

Paul. Heavens ! what should it be ?

Alex. They talk, the Queen is gone into a
cloister, some say to marry.

Paul. Oh ! what comes into my head ? Joanna,
slip to my chamber, and get a feather and a
better periwig, and follow the Duke with all the
speed you can.

Jo. I run, I run !   [*Exit.*

Enter DEMETRIUS.

Dem. 'Twas here they came, this was the house
I'm sure.   Ho, ho, the house !

Enter LANDLORD, *beating his servant.*

Dem. Ha ! my Landlord ! what, am I at home ?

Land. You rogue, you dog, I'll kill you, sirrah,
I'll murder you ; would not you tell me this before.

Ser. Murder, murder !

Dem. Hold, come along with me quickly, shew
me all your rooms.   Here's a Princess lodges here.

Land. Don't tell me o' Princess.   The rogue
hath undone me.

Dem. Sirrah, come along ! or I'll send your soul
before me.

Land. Sirrah, hold your prating.   I've lost more
than thee and all thy generation are worth ; I've
lost five thousand crowns, and I'll stop it out of
his wages, I'll not pay one of 'um a farthing.   But
what will that do ? that's some fifty dollars ; what's
that to five thousand crowns ? undone, undone !

Dem. Dog, I'll set fire on's house.

Land. Will you so, sirrah ? a brave amends for
my loss ; but, sirrah, I'll keep you fast enough for
that.   Go quickly, boy, run and fetch a constable.

Dem. A constable, rascal !   [*Draws.*

Land. Murder, murder; ho! there, sirrah, come back again, I shall be kill'd: you bloody rogue, will you murder me?

Ser. Good, sir, don't kill my master. [*Holds Dem.*

Land. Hold him whilst I go run and fetch a constable and secure his cloak-bag, and then I must to the palace, after this base cheating Duke. I've a pack of brave lodgers: here's one young blade, that I'm much mistaken if he or his man be n't a whore; and the Duke's run away and paid me no rent; and this vapouring Jack would kill me, and then set fire to my house; brave doings, is't not? but I'll feage * you all. [*Exit.*

Dem. What Duke's that?

Ser. The Duke o' Curland an't please you, sir.

Dem. Curland! where, where? quickly slave.

Ser. I chanc't to spy him, and came and told my master, and for this he would ha' kill'd me.

Dem. Where, I say, villain?

Ser. Sir, he is just gone to the palace; a young gentleman that lodges here brought a courtier that told him the Queen was to be married to-night, and they are all run to the palace together.

Dem. I'll make one o' the company. His soul shall dance levaltoes in the air at the Queen's wedding. [*Exit.*

Ser. Well, I was a fool he did not let this gentleman kill my master, or fire his house. I would he had!—teach him to belabour me for my good will. [*Exit.*

The scene A PALACE TO THE STREET.

Enter LADISLAUS, PAULINA, JOANNA, *drest like a courtier,* ALEXEY, THEODORE, *at a distance* - BATTISTA.

Bat. So, I have overtaken 'um, [*Aside.*

---

* Censure, chastise.

And here's some great mysterious thing in hand,
The Duke has some design about the crown.

Lud. Knock at the gate, Theodore.

The. Indeed, my lord, this courtier is mistaken;
all say positively the Queen's resolved t' resign the
crown, and go into a cloister, and that she spends
this night among her priests and women in
devotion to prepare for it; and now all the Lords
of the Council are gone in to dissuade her.

Lud. Knock! when I bid you.

Paul. Come, good my lord, do not expose yourself to so much danger; the gentleman's misin-
form'd.

Jo. Perhaps so, sir, I only told you what my
sister, who is a Maid of Honour to the Queen, told
me.

The. Your sister!

Lud. My lord, let it be true or false,
I am resolv'd to be conceal'd no longer:
Thus to the sinful world revenge divine   [*Aside.*
Moves gently on with paces slow as mine:
And heaven stands behind the clouds awhile,
And lets deluded man himself beguile:
And seems as if his law he did not own,
But with brave scorn to let the world alone,
Till man, grown impudent, begins to play
His villanies in open scenes of day;
Then strikes, strikes home, and then his arm doth
    fall
With such a weight, one blow may serve for all:
Thus my revenge I do a while retain,
That when I strike, I may not strike in vain.
Why dost not knock, Theodore?

The. I do, my lord, and none will answer
within. Ho there, open the gate!

Porter [*within*]. What would you have there
Here can none come in.

Land. Give the fellow forty crowns.

The. Here are persons o' great quality, you shall have forty crowns to open the gate.

Porter [*within*]. Bear back there! guard, keep off the crowd.

People [*within*]. Oh, pray, Mr Porter.

Paul. I dread th' event. I wish I had not done this.   [*Exit.*

The. Take notice, sir, if any mischief befalls my lord, you, and your Duke's lives shall answer for it.   [*To Jo. Ex. Theo.*

Jo. Do you threaten, sir? Alexey!

Alex. I hear the slave. Let him have a care I don't cut his throat, and his master's, the worthy Duke.   [*Exit Jo. Al.*

Bal. I'll after you all to see the meaning o' this.   [*Exit.*

Enter LANDLORD. *The scene continued.*

Land. Now I warrant shall I ha' much ado to get into the gate after this cheating knave the Duke, I must speak 'um fair. Porter! honest old crony, friend and fellow soldier in the wars o' Bacchus, open the door, my drunken bulley.

Porter [*within*]. What saucy fellow's that? get you from the gate, sirrah, or the guard shall lay you by the heels.

Land. Oh, the rogue, he pretends not to know me, he knows me well enough; why honest bulley Cerberus, corporal-turnkey, squire o' the house, nointer o' page-bums, engineer general o' double locks, spring-locks, pad-locks, and mouse-traps, open the placket o' the house, call'd the wickets, and let's in, boy. Dost not remember the Council o' Trent, and Pope Paul the third?

Porter [*within*]. Prating rascal! you've a mind to be laid by th' heels?

Land. O th' cunning rascal! he thinks I ha' company with me now, he's as cunning! but here come my slaves; what ha' you set fire on my house yet?

Enter DEMETRIUS.

Dem. How now, the gate barr'd? open the door here.

Land. Nay, if I can't get in, I believe you'll hardly get in, for all your brave cloak-bag.

Dem. Open the door, or I'll set fire on't.

Porter [*within*]. De'e threaten, sirrah! Guard, out quickly, here's a traitor threatens to fire the palace gate.

Guar. Bear back there! let's come out.

People [*within*]. Oh, you crowd me.

Land. So, so, you have done finely, we shall have our brains knock't out; come, come, a spell quickly afore they come. I know the rogues as well as if I were in the bottom of their bellies; come, half a dollar or so——

Dem. Open the door, fellow, thou shalt have fifty dollars.

Porter [*within*]. If I do let you in, you can't get into the presence—the guard-rooms are all crowded. I let in a gentleman just now, and he stands in the crowd still.

Land. The rogue begins to be pliable.

Dem. Open the door, I say! here's thy money.

Porter [*within*]. Bear back there! keep off the crowds.   [*Exit Dem.*

Land. Now, you can bear back with a pox to you, now, you hear o' money; well, I see this money will make every thing bear back, and fly open.   [*Exit.*

One within. Ah, Mr. Porter, we'll give a rixdollar, betwixt four of us.

Porter [*within*]. A rope between four of you.

The scene, A ROOM IN THE PALACE; *a table with the crown, sceptre, and regalia at one end, and beads and books at the other.*

Enter JULIANA, HYPOLITA, EMILIA, FRANCISCA, COLIMSKY, SHARNOFSKY, *and a* PRIEST.

 Col. Well, Madam, since we must despair t'
  obtain,
We'll cease those pray'rs, which we thus make in
  vain ;
For to our sorrow we confess it true,
This Kingdom hath not glory enough for you,
In those celestial crowns you'll only find
Exalted glories equal to your mind :
We only beg you'll help the shrinking throne,
And save ten thousand souls besides your own.
For, madam, whatsoe'er your priests pretend,
You may by crowns to other crowns ascend :
And cells on earth will cells in heaven find,
Large crowns for mighty bounties are design'd.
 Shar. And, madam, one thing I would beg, that
  when
You at the sacred altar stand again
So to address yourself, think on what score
You at those very altars stood before.
When vows with vows, altars with altars jar,
It seems to breed in Heaven a civil war ;
It is not for the Duke I intercede,
I now in the behalf of honour plead :
Though to the sacred church I freely bow,
No doubt, they can absolve you from your vow ;
Yet with the reverence to their power is due,
Methinks, I would have honour do it too :
In other worlds devotion may have bliss,
I'm sure 'tis honour that must save in this ;
And generous honour passes doom on none,

Till first their crimes are clearer than the sun.
  Jul. My lords ! on either side I've heard your
      pleas,
And very much regard your kindnesses :
But now my soul's employ'd on things above,
Concerns of empire, and much more of love.
As for the Duke I cannot censur'd be,
I quit not him, but he renounces me ;
Nor for the throne, I found it in distress,
And mildly leave it in the calms of peace :
And now eternally I bid adieu
To love and empire, to the Duke and you :
And here, my lords, I do your crown restore,
And now retreat to what I was before.
  Confessor. Great victory ! you saints above make
      room,
A mighty spirit doth in triumph come.
  Col. Hold, madam ! ere you fall so great a
      weight,
And break in pieces our disjointed State ;
Rather than we will rush again once more
In the wild chaos we were in before ;
'Tis voted by us all, that you alone
Shall fix some person in our shaking throne.
We swear allegiance to whomsoe'er you choose,
Yea, and the death of him that shall refuse :
'Tis all our votes.
  Om. All, all !
  Jul. The trust is high, and great, and needs
many solemn thoughts, and you must give me some
time to pause.
  Con. Madam, the better to compose your mind,
And fortify your soul in these last conflicts
With earthly glory ; please to rest a while,
We'll use the devout arts of holy church.

*The Queen seats herself in a throne ; the ladies stand
in order on her right hand, and the lords on her
left, whil'st a chorus of voices sing.*

THE SONG.

How nobly heaven doth receive
    Whate'er a pious mind
Is in devotion pleas'd to give,
    As if he crowns resign'd ;
        The sacred vaults with joy resound,
        The altars all with roses crown'd,
        And the poor saint in triumph brought
        To offer up one holy thought.
And if to that such honour's due,
What glories wait, great Queen, for you !
    Chorus,—And if to, &c.

If heaven thinks an humble bow
    To him devoutly meant,
Then we whole hecatombes bestow
    In one devout intent ;
        When Queens lay youth and glory by,
        To seek our crowns of chastity,
        Some brighter stars must sure compound
        The wreath wherewith her head is crown'd
For more than common honour's due
To royal saints, great Queen, like you :
    Chorus,—For more, &c.

Then blest be all my storms of love,
    Though they discourteous were,
That on our peaceful shore hath drove
    A saint so great, so fair :
        Now let the boy, with all his train
        Of griefs, go weeping back again :
        Whil'st you set sail before the wind,
        And leave this floating world behind.

Till spooning * gently on, and fair,
You turn an angel unaware.
          Chorus,—Till spooning, &c.

Con. Now, that your royal soul is flown aloft
Upon the wings of divine harmony ;
We'll keep it there by holy representation,
First of the vanishing glories of the world,
Its splendid entrances, its shady exits.

Enter two QUEENS *followed by two* GHOSTS. *They pass
          slowly over the stage.   Soft music.*

Con. Saw you those royal shadows pass the
          round
With all the charms of power and beauty crown'd ?
Would not the glory which they did display,
Make the world think none are so blest as they ?
Alas, had they but look'd on either side,
They might have seen what would have damp't
          their pride :
Two pining spirits that were once as fair,
Showing with sighs where they must all repair :
Such are th' unseen shadows that attend
All earthly glory, and in those they end.
Now the next thing that we shall represent,
Is chaste devotion, recluse piety.
It's humble entrances, its glorious exits.

Enter two NUNS *clad in white, followed by two*
          ANGELS *crown'd.   They pass as the former.*

Con. Saw you those virgins pass in holy state
Observe how angels on their triumphs wait :

------

* "To spoom," says Johnson, quoting Bailey, " in sea language
is when a ship, being under sail in a storm cannot bear it, but
is obliged to put right before the wind." "To spoom" bears
nearly the same signification.
          " When virtue spooms before a prosperous gale
          My heaving wishes help to fill the sail."—*Dryden.*

Their souls are as their beauties fair and bright ;
Their thoughts are as their garments pure and
       white :
Their dreams are visions, and their breath is pray'r :
They're fasted into spirits thin as air ;
Nor can you them from holy angels know,
Since these are nuns above, and they below.
And now, you in a solemn dance shall see,
How all these move to divine harmony :
Confus'dly mixt each in their several states,
Walking around the changes of their fates ;
The world is a great dance in which we find
The good and bad have various turns assign'd ;
But when th' have ended the great masquerade,
One goes to glory, t'other to a shade.

[They all dance.

Col. What tumult's that ?

Enter a GENTLEMAN.

2d. Gent. My lords, here is a person of unknown
quality desires admission ; by's habit we conjecture
'tis the same that fought to-day i'th' head of all
our troops, and sav'd the Count and Princess in
the field.

Osso. He's highly welcome ; let him have
admission.

Enter LADISLAUS *disguis'd, followed by* PAULINA,
   JOANNA, ALEXEY, THEODORE, *at a distance,*
       BATTISTA.   *All the* LORDS *bow to* LAD.

Lad. It seems the bridal masque is done. [*Aside.*
Bat. So, I ha' crowded in among the rest, [*Aside.*
To see the event of this mysterious business.
Jul. I have considered on't, my Lord Shar-
nofsky ! heaven and your own merits design you for
the crown.

She takes the crown off the table, and presents it to
    SHARNOFSKY, *who seems to refuse it, and the*
            Lords to constrain him.

Lud. Ye powers !   [*Aside.*
The. What tragedies will here be straight ? [*Aside.*
Paul. She's false, indeed !   [*Aside.*
Shar. Great madam !   [*Seems to refuse.*
Lords. Kneel, and receive the crown. [*Sh. kneels.*
Lud. Ha ! is it so ?
Then now I see, I have not been deceiv'd,
Sharnofsky, as thy glory so thy fate
Is very near, and thus successful villany ;
Heaven let's it to the top of glory come,
Then strikes it dead with unexpected doom.
Sharnofsky, draw ! there's one obstruction more
Lies in your way to all your glories ;
The Duke o' Curland's sword.
    Om. The Duke of Curland.
                        [*Lud. draws and discovers.*
Jul. Ye powers ! the Duke ! I faint, Hypolita,
Emilia, hold me !   [*Swoons in her woman's arms.*
    Theo. Help the Princess !
Shar. The Duke of Curland's sword ! and can
    that sword
Be set against my breast ? for what is this ?
    Lud. That shall afford us talk in th'other world.
Shar. I fall !   [*Shar. falls : the Guards call "trea-*
    son," and run at the Duke : Colimsky interposes.
Col. Hold, villains ! 'tis the Duke, your General ;
what cursed devil poison'd the Duke's soul with
jealousy of his brave friend ?
    Tde. What fatal work is here ?
Paul. Oh, heavens ! Joanna, what have we
    done ?
Bat. What should this tragical confusion mean ?
Jul. What vision have I seen ? where am I ?

Am I awake ? or is't a martial dream ?
See, the Count bleeding ! who hath done this deed ?
  Lad. And dost thou then lament him to my
    face ?
Oh, thou apostate ! shame of royal blood ;
Is this thy gratitude for all the martyrdoms
I've suffered for thy love ? 'Tis I have done it, and
    done it
To revenge my injur'd love. And I but just
    should be,
Now I have punished him to punish thee ;
But that, alas ! 'twould be so poor a deed,
My very sword would scorn to make thee bleed ;
And if my passion should the thing request,
'Twould turn in rage against his master's breast.
No, I shall leave thee to a higher doom,
And now, go wait thy lover to his tomb.
  Jul. Ha ! doth he go ? and leave me thus in
    scorn,   [*Proffers to go.*
Guards, stop the traitors ! I'll revenge my honour,
And the Count's blood. In the interim,
Carry him out, and use your utmost skill
And care about him.
  Col. Madam, he breathes, and whilst there's life
There's hope. Guards, stop the Duke !
                        [*They carry out Shar.*
  Theo. She'll kill the Duke ; but I'll not long
    survive him.
  Jul. Curland, thou diest ; but first thou must
    explain
The mysteries of this thy proud disdain ;
Say then, what fury did thee hither send,
To wound my honour, and destroy thy friend ;
For none in Poland hath this treason wrought,
Nor dare they wound my honour with a thought.
  Lad. None dare ! 'twere sacriledge to make it
    bleed.

None but your valiant self dare do the deed,
And you are grown to that insulting height,
You scorn the modest whispers of the night.
Trumpets must speak, and banners must display,
And to your lover's arms you fight your way.
   Jul. This is distraction!
   Col.   His Russian bondage hath mislaid his
      reason.
   Jul. He's mad!
I once to punish him had an intent,
And now I pity him, and those thoughts repent:
And yet it may be those distractions are
Only th' effect of pride, and wild despair:
The sinner finds he's damn'd, and prays in vain,
And now by blasphemy would ease his pain.
   Lad. Yes, as a man damn'd by a false religion,
When he finds all his piety in vain,
Doth curse his gods, and wish he had liv'd profane,
So all my merits lost, I now repent,
That I have been so fondly innocent,
That I in Muscovy so vain should prove,
In seeking crowns and armies for thy love;
And cruelly my heart refused to give
To one who wanted it that she might live.
   Jul. What, then! it seems thy killing eyes have
      there
Done many murders too, as well as here;
And what if I thy triumphs should disgrace,
And in a grave should hide thy conquering face,
Where ladies' hearts it might no more surprise,
Nor women be in danger of thine eyes?
Sharnofsky's blood forbids to let thee live:
Yes, Curland, thou shalt die! it shall be seen,
In this one glorious act, I am a Queen;
And let thy sovereign title plead thy cause,
Let Poland talk of privilege, or laws,
In this great doom I uncontroul'd will be,

And trample on the State, their laws, and thee :
And let the glory of thy fate contain,
And sum up all the glory of my reign.
Guards, kill the Duke ! hold, but kill him so,
That he may live within an hour or two.   [*Aside.*
Methinks I now a little weakness find,
And my heart tells me, I would fain be kind :
Fool that I am ! I weeping melt away
Even all the crowns, and triumphs of the day :
The conqueror doth quit the field and fly,
Whil'st the proud captive stands insulting by ;
That ever I should play so weak a part,
To be entic't thus to resign my heart !
A heart, design'd for things so far above
The petty troubles and concerns of love :
Yet now led captive, can so prostrate be
To worship him, who ought to worship me :
But for these follies I'll myself dethrone,
Forgive his sins, but will chastise my own.
Lead to the chapel ! I'll to-night——

Con. Hold, madam, your soul's disorder'd, it
must be calm'd with penitence and prayer, before
you can be fit.

Jul. I cannot help it, I am but woman. [*Weeps.*

Lad. Ha ! and have I wrong'd her ?
What cursed charm hath led me in this maze ?
Surely I have been abus'd ! Young Duke of Novogrod,
[*To Paul.*

Have you not told me lies ? I fear you have,
And done it to revenge your friend, the Prince.

Bat. Hark, he calls my Princess, Duke of
Novogrod.   [*Aside.*

Jo. Discover to him——

Alex. Madam, undisguise ! and let the Duke
Affront you if he dares.

Paul. Yes, sir, I've led you in this maze of
   jealousy ;

And done it to revenge my injur'd honour.
                                        [*Discovers.*
    Om. A woman !
    Jul. A woman !
    Paul, Yes, and a Princess, madam,
Great as yourself by birth, greater in misfortunes ;
The daughter of the mighty Czar of Muscovy,
Become a wandering pilgrim, hidden lies
In the poor hermitage of this disguise ;
By Curland's treachery, now brought so low,
I even am asham'd myself to know.   [*Weeps.*
    Bat. Now, I perceive the mystery.   [*Aside.*
    Lud. The Princess, Paulina !
    Paul. And dar'st thou mention then Paulina's
      name,
And proudly stand without remorse or shame ?
Because in war thou hast a captive been,
Wilt thou, in spite thy victories, begin
On virtue, on religion, love, and me,
And hate my name because I pitied thee ?
When all the world forsook thee, I alone
Bestow'd thy life, and made thy chains my own,
Yea, more, so fondly I betray'd my flame,
At thy petition, I thy wife became.
When crowns lay at my feet, I married thee,
Who hadst no armies, crowns, nor liberty ;
Yet promis'd one, but meant in that above,
A crown of martyrdom, for injur'd love.
Yea, after all, perfidious man ! to fly
And leave me in thy chains condemn'd to die ?
And when I found thee basely to disclaim
Thou hadst relation to Paulina's name.
Know, Duke, I do abhor thee, and to-day,
This hand, this steel, had ta'ne thy life away,
But that some power did the blow withstand,
And, when I proffer'd, did withhold my hand ;
But my revenge now alters its design.

The death it aim'd at thee now shall be mine;
Not that I die because I grieve to part,
But thus to punish my rebellious heart.
[*Offers to kill herself, but Jo., Alex. snatch the dagger.*
    Jo.   } Oh, she hath hurt herself; oh, madam;
    Alex.   }   madam!
    Paul. What means this cruelty? oh, let me
        die!
    Bat. I now perceive the maze in which they
        wander;
Oh, I have been too slow in my discovery.
    Jul. And have I wept and bled for this?
    Lud. What cursed phantom did abuse my shape?
As ever, heaven, thou'st regard to truth
Or innocence, now by thy thunder show
If it was I that wrong'd this lady so.
    Jo. Oh, horrid, horrid!
    Alex. Oh, immortal powers! and can you suffer
        this?
    Jul. Prodigy!
    Con. Oh! Madam, rule your haughty passions,
There is a ring of angels made about you,
To see how you'll come off in this great combat.
    Jul. And let 'um make a ring--they to them-
        selves
The pleasure of revenge would not deny,
Were they but flesh and blood as well as I.
    Bat. I must reveal in time, before more mischief
ensues.   Royal madam——
    Jul. Ha? what art thou?
    Bat. I'm one, whom if you please
Can in one word rectify all mistakes.
'Tis a deceitful marriage then breeds this
Confusion: the Princess was not married
To the Duke, but to my Prince Demetrius,
He who to-day was, Madam, in your tent [*To Jul.*
Condemn'd to die

Lod. My innocence is cleared by miracle.

Paul. Is Prince Demetrius here? and did he
  abuse me so?

Bat. Madam, he ventur'd on so grand an enter-
  prize,
Partly t' allay the torment of his love,
And partly for revenge upon your father,
Who, having promis'd you, as a reward to him
For taking the Duke prisoner, slighted his royal
  word,
Upon the news of the King o' Poland's death,
And proffers you to the Duke, with a great
  army,
Only in hopes to make you Queen o' Poland.
The Duke, indeed, did nobly slight the proffers.

  Jul. So Count Sharnofsky said.
What have I done to wound that gallant man?

  Bat. My fiery Prince resenting the affront,
As proudly as the Emperor did his,
'Twixt rage and love did by a wile entice you
Unto the castle, where the Duke was pris'ner,
Pretending danger, penitence, and love,
And, if you remember, married you in the dark,
Because he would not trust, as he pretended,
The priest himself with such a dangerous secret.

  Om. Amazement!

  Bat. And ere you could discover the mistake,
You fled away in fright, and ere you went
Brib'd the Cipier* for the Duke's liberty;
Then he, in innocence forsaking you,
And you, as innocent in pursuing him,
Occasion'd this unhappiness.

  Col. Heavens! 'twas this the Cardinal took
advantage on to breed all this disorder.

---

* Halliwell, in his Archaic Dictionary, has " Cippus, the
stocks or pillory." " Cipier" probably means " jailor" or
keeper of the stocks.

Om. Now all's come to light.

Paul. How have I been abus'd? unhappy I,
Born to misfortunes.

Bat. See, my Prince is here!

Enter DEMETRIUS *and* LANDLORD, *struggling with
the* GUARD.

Lad. I think, my Landlord, the Prince perhaps
was the other stranger lodg'd in the same house:
petty humour of fortune!

Land. Come, honest Cardinal Bembo, dost thou
not remember   [*To the Guard.*
I made thee a Cardinal at the Council o' Trent!
Hast thou forgot Pope Paul's great toe, boy?

Dem. Slave, shall I stay here all night?

Guar. Well, what would you see? all's done!

Land. Nay, I told you I'd get you in, if any
body could; the rogues all know me as well as a
beggar knows his clap-dish.*

Dem. Curland, have I found thee? 'tis not thy
    friends,   [*Draws.*
Nor the Queen's guards that shall protect thee.

Bat. Hold, sir! all's well.   [*Holds Dem.*

Dem. Not till Curland or I fall.

Land. Why, what a mad fellow's this; draw in
the presence! why, sirrah, do you know where
you are, you malapert lad you? I shall be hang'd
for bringing in a quarrelsome jackanapes. If I had
known I would ha' kept him at home, I warrant
him.

Bat. Oh! hold, and turn your eyes on that sad

---

* "Clap-dish," or "clack-dish," a box with a lid to rattle and
make a noise when shaken, carried by beggars to attract notice
and bring people to their doors. Forby mentions that there
is a phrase still current, "His tongue moves like a beggar's
clap-dish." In Kenneth's time the term was applicable to
"a wooden dish wherein they gather the toll of wheat and
other corn in markets."

object that there lies weeping, bleeding for your
crimes.

Dem. My Princess! I'm in a trance; oh, bloody
    vision!
What cursed hand hath done this wretched deed?

Paul. 'Tis you have done it.   Oh, Demetrius,
How have you injur'd me? what horrid dangers
And miseries have you expos'd me to?

Land. This young man hath been in a scuffle, I
see.

Paul. I'd lost my life under my father's anger,
Had it not been for this good Count Alexey,
Who had the charge of me, and help't me away;
And now in passion I have chas'd the Duke,
Thinking him guilty of forsaking me
His lawful wife, and made him kill his friend,
Injure his Princess; and had fallen himself
By my revenge, this steel had pierc't his breast,
But Heaven to whom his innocence was known,
Thus made me turn the blow against my own.

Land. What's the meaning of all this blind
story?

Dem. And have I injur'd thus the Duke, and you?
What miseries, what torments are my due?
First by some slave, or villain, let me die,
And, when I'm dead, then stab my memory.
By my own hand, or your's, to die, would be
A death too brave for such a fiend as me:
And, when I'm buried, to my grave repair,
And throw in scorn my ashes in the air:
But lest you prove unjust, and pardon all
My horrid crimes, thus at your feet I fall.
           [Proffers to fall on his sword, and
              is prevented by Land., Paul., Bat.

Land. What! art mad? wilt thou kill thy self,
sweetheart? bless me, he makes my heart ake;
take the sword from him, fie upon't! who let's such

young fools ha' swords, that don't know how to use 'um?

Paul. Hold, Prince Demetrius, live! your wife, Paulina, doth beg it of you.

Land. Your wife, Paulina! what, I warrant this young man is that young man's wife; why, sure my house was enchanted to-day, lodg'd Princes, and Dukes, like mummers and masqueraders; and women and wenches in men's cloathes, and cloak-bags, and scufflings, and they kill one another, and they're alive again, and this, and that, and I know not what. Here's work indeed!

Dem. And, can you pardon me, my kindest Princess?

Paul. Yes, my dear Demetrius, I have charity enough to pardon you, and virtue enough to love you.

Dem. Blessed minute; I shall die with happiness.

Alex. And I with joy.   [*All weeps.*

Dem. Now, generous Ladislaus, can you forgive me?

Lad. My princely friend.

Land. Ay,—— hug,——— but you're but a couple o' knaves both on you.

Paul. Great madam, may not we embrace, as well as our dear lords?

Jul. Yes, madam, and perhaps with an affection as generous as theirs.

Om. Celestial sight!

Col. The charm that rais'd this tempest o' confusion
Is now undone, the horrid spectre's vanisht;
All ends in friendship, let it end in glory;
Love now is crown'd, let honour be so too;
Let's place the crown upon the head of him
Who in a thousand fields hath purchas'd it.

Land. With all my heart, truly, though I must

tell you, you're none of th' honestest to run away
and pay me no rent.   [*Aside.*

Col. Great Duke, it is decreed you are our king,
And you our queen.   [*To Jul.*

Om. Long live Ladislaus, King of Poland, and
Duke o' Curland!

Om. Long live Juliana, Queen of Poland, and
Duchess of Curland!

       | My Lords, we thank you for all this
Lad. | great honour,
Jul. | And shall endeavour still to make this
       | crown
Rather the kingdom's glory than our own.

Land. Your humble servant; nobody questions
it.   Well now, an't please your majesty——

Lad. Go, I forgive thee.

Land. Forgive me; thank you heartily: I come
to dun him for money, and he cries, he forgives
me; right courtier, i'faith; but if you forgive me,
I won't forgive you: in the first place, for cheating
me of five thousand crowns, but that I'll take no
notice of. [*aside*] Why, sir, for my rent, and
several other courtesies, as procuring, conniving,
angling for trouts; no courtesy in this age; come,
come, sir, a feeling, a feeling, and I'll take no
notice, otherwise my tongue doth naturally hang
so loose,——but nothing is better for it than a
little Aurum Potabile.*

Lad. This fellow is strangely impertinent.

Land. Besides, do I deserve nothing for my
honesty for concealing you? I knew you well
enough.

Lad. I doubt, Landlord, if you had, my head
had not stuck fast upon my shoulders.

Land. It may be, sir, if I had been put to a

----

* See Davenant's Works, vol. i., p. 72.

great strait indeed, I might have borrowed a little money upon your nose, or so——

Lad. Rid me, Theodore, of this fellow, and give him a hundred dollars.

Land. Thank your majesty!

Enter one of the GUARD, *who whispers* COLIMSKY.

Col. Sir, the Grand Marshal and the other Lords desire to have admission to your majesty, t'implore your grace and pardon.   [*To the King.*

Enter GUARD *with* OSSOLINSKY, CASSONOSKY, *and* LUBOMIRSKY, *as prisoners.*

Osso. } Heaven crown your majesty with a
Casso. }   long and happy reign!
Jul. Oh, my good Lords; what ha' you chang'd
    your tunes?
But you, poor men, sung but the Cardinal's notes:
My lord, forgive 'um.   Thou malicious Count
                                [*To Casso.*
That wouldst have murder'd me in my tent to-day
And mixt my blood with my great father's ashes,
Know, slave, some of my guards shou'd strike thee
    dead,
But that thy very baseness saves thy head.
Who merits my revenge and hate, must prove
As brave and great, as he who gains my love.
I pardon thee: retire out of my sight——
And now go home, repent thy crimes and see
If heaven will be generous like me.

Lad. My lords, you have your pardons; your lives and fortunes we shall not touch, your offices and governments we must bestow on men of better maxims.   Count Colimsky, the baton of Grand Marshal we confer on you. Their Governments and Palatinates we shall consider of.

I   8

Paul. I'll beg a command of the King for you, good Count Alexey.

Alex. No, madam, I'll serve none but your Highness. Let me but live in your favour, 'tis all the glory I am ambitious of.

Casso. Now will I go home and hang one-half of my slaves, starve the other, kick my wife out o' doors, be drunk nine and fifty hours together, breed a mutiny at home, and a rebellion in the Kingdom; and at last lose my head for my pains, and there's an end of good Count Cassonosky.

Lad. Now, let us all go visit my brave friend.

Enter a GENTLEMAN.

Gent. Great sir, I now came from him. His wound is search't, and is found not so dangerous as first was fear'd. At his return to sense, he seem'd amaz'd, as having lost all memory how he came wounded so; nor was he concern'd, but only enquir'd about the Queen's health.

Lad. Brave friend!

Jul. The Count was ever generous.

Om. Lights for the King and Queen!

Lad. Thus do our fortunes lead us blindly on,
And to be happy we are first undone;
And thus the mighty storms have all combin'd
To cast thee on the shore which I design'd.
Now I am blest with happiness above,
My own ambition with a crown and love.

THE EPILOGUE.

SPOKEN BY PAULINA AND LANDLORD.

Land. Now, gentlemen, a word.
Paul. How now, you lout,
What are you speaking?
Land. Ha, th'ast put me out,
I know not what it was.
Paul. Oh, I can tell!
The Epilogue; yes, it becomes you well,
You gentlemen! and why, I pray, to them?
What, do the ladies merit no esteem?
Good sirs! I know not whether 'tis your due,
But poets still direct themselves to you:
      [*Turning to the audience.*
Don't the fops know in this and every age,
'Tis beauty rules the world, much more the stage.
When you ha' done your best, the scribbling clowns
Lie at the mercy of the ladies' frowns:
And not a critic of you all but knows,
No repartees are half so sharp as those.
Land. Why, prithee, 'twas the women wits I
  meant,
'Tis not the men I'm sure that pay my rent;
For they are grown so hect'ring now-a-days,
They kick my customers, and damn their plays,
That I am ruin'd by your critic blades;
What, d'ee think I keep fiddlers, men, and maids
For nothing? and, besides that dreadful charge,
I'm building a new house, that's brave and large;
If you're so curious as y'ave been before,
I must e'en lay the key under the door.
Paul. Prithee, ha' done!
Land. No, sir, I've more to say;
Then if the liquor I ha' broacht to-day

Be good, commend it, but if it be dull,
I'faith e'en damn, and ram your belly full.
    Paul. Away, rude fool ! fair English Diet then,
Senate of ladies, lower house of men,
I humbly pray, decree before you go
If marriages like mine be right or no,
At least resolve in pity of my pain,
To sit to-morrow on the same again.

THE HISTORY OF CHARLES THE EIGHTH OF FRANCE.

The History of Charles the Eighth of France, or the Invasion of Naples by the French, as it is acted at his Highnesses the Duke of York's Theater. Written by Mr. Crowne. Honestum est secundis tertiisve consistere. Qu. London. Printed by T. R. and N. T. for Ambrose Isted, at the sign of the Golden Anchor, over against St. Dunstan's Church in Fleet Street. 1672. 4to.

Ib. 4to. 1680. With the difference of a fresh title page.

THE first new play brought out in Dorset Garden was the History of Charles VIII., or the Invasion of Naples by the French. It was performed, according to Geneste, "six days together and now and then afterwards."* Adopting the fashion of the writers of tragedies in France, and aware of the prejudice of Charles II. in its favour, Crowne, following the example of Dryden in his siege of Grenada and other tragedies, and of Lord Orrery, in his successful dramas of Mustapha and Henry the Fifth, has ventured to woo Melpomene in rhyme.

As Betterton performed the character of Charles VIII., Harris that of Ferdinand, son and successor of Alphonso the King of Naples, Smith the Prince of Salerne, and Mrs Betterton Isabella, widow of John Galeazzo, Duke of Milan, it is not surprising that the piece so well cast was successful ; indeed, more so than some of Dryden's tragedies in verse, the absurdities of which were at the time admirably satirized by the Duke of Buckingham in his comedy of the Rehearsal, of which Sheridan's Critic, a century later, was a clever but inferior imitation.

Alphonso, king of Naples, was represented by Mathew Medbourne, who was author of Tartuffe, a translation of Moliere's comedy of the same name, of which there are two editions, one 1670 and the other 1707, 4to. This drama, of which a favourable opinion is expressed in the Biographica Dramatica, was represented at the King's Theatre with very great applause. In 1718, Cibber's Nonjuror appeared, taken from the same source, "and the principal character in it, Dr. Wolf, is a close copy from the same original." In 1768, Bickerstaffe's Hypocrite was performed at Drury Lane with great success. It is an alteration of Cibber with the addition of the character

* History of the Stage, vol. i., p. 124.

of Mawworm. It still holds its place among the acting plays; and fortunate indeed are they who have had the gratification of witnessing the inimitable impersonation of Dr. Cantwell and Mawworm by Dowton and Liston.

Medbourne is believed to have written another drama, a tragedy entitled Saint Cicily. He was a zealous Roman Catholic, and was caught in the meshes of Dr. Titus Oates. He was committed to Newgate, November 26, 1678, where he died the 19th March following. He was an actor of great eminence, and deserved a different fate.

Although the conquest of Naples by Charles VIII., the abdication of Alphonso in favour of his son Ferdinand, and some other circumstances, are true, still the greater portion of the incidents in the present play have little historical foundation, and appear to be either the fruits of the author's own imagination, or taken from some old Italian novelist.

Charles was the son and successor of Louis XI, whose character has been given in Quentin Durward with such perfect accuracy by the author of that admirable romance, that it may be accepted as the most complete and truthful portrait of that monarch extant. Charles came to the throne in the year 1483, at the age of thirteen years and two months.* "The king his father," says Commines, "had brought him up at Amboise in such solitariness, that none beside him besides his ordinary servants could have access unto him: neither permitted he him to learn any more Latin than this one sentence, *He that cannot dissemble cannot reign*, which he did not that he hated learning, but because he feared that study would hurt the tender and delicate complexion of the child. Notwithstanding, king Charles, after he came to the crown, grew very studious of learning, and gave himself to the reading of stories and books of humanity, written in the French tongue, and attempted to understand Latin."† Unlike his father, Charles was a man of high and honourable principles, and of great personal

* Henault's History of France, by Nugent, vol. i., p. 326 — 5th edition, London, 1782, 8vo.

† History of Philip de Commines, Knight, Lord of Argenton—4th edition, London, 1674, folio, page 225. Translated by Thomas Danett. Originally printed in 1596, and dedicated to Lord Burghley.

courage. His reign, although short, was a beneficial one to his country, and his demise on the 27th April 1498, before he attained the age of twenty-seven, was deeply regretted, although his successor, the Duke of Orleans, his cousin, obtained as Louis XII., the title of " The father of his people."

The right of Charles to the kingdom of Naples was by no means clear, being founded on a testament or will of Joanna, queen of Naples, the existence of which was questioned. His Holiness the Pope, who assumed a right to all monarchies that could not find owners, especially claimed Naples as coming under the papal power, and, as he wished to propitiate the pious Louis XI., obligingly proposed to make it over to him, but the cautious monarch would have nothing to do with the tempting offer, which was renewed to and accepted by his son. Accordingly, so soon as Charles had arranged with infinite success many matters of great importance to France, and settled his quarrel with Britany, by his nuptials with the Lady Anne, in 1491, thus permanently uniting that valuable principality to France, he proceeded to enforce his claim to the Neapolitan diadem in direct opposition to the advice of his councillors, who desired that he would content himself with his own dominions. He invaded Italy, and within a period of time not exceeding six months, came, saw, and conquered. Upon the 21st of February 1495-6, Charles VIII., clad in imperial robes, made his triumphant entry into Naples, where he was received with enthusiasm by the citizens.

Alphonso, the Neapolitan ruler, becoming unpopular, had, previous to the French occupation, prudently abdicated in favour of his son Ferdinand, a young prince of great courage. and beloved by the people, whose detestation of his father, coupled with a terror of the French arms, had so completely paralysed them that no opposition was offered to the invaders.

Time usually works wonders, and it did so in this instance. An union of potentates, including Pope Alexander VI., who succeeded, Pope Innocent VIII., in 1492, the Venetian Republic, Henry VII. of England, and the Emperor Maximilian, who had designed to marry Anne of Britany himself, the youthful and gallant ruler of

France compelled Charles to retire from his conquests. He had great difficulty in retracing his steps; but defeating the allied army, commanded by the Marquis of Mantua, at the battle of Fornova, on the 6th of July 1496, where Charles displayed the most signal proofs of valour, his return home was comparatively easy.

Charles, having recruited himself, was anxious once more to try his fortune in Italy, but was dissuaded by his cousin of Orleans, who dreaded the consequence of his demise in a foreign country,—an event which, from his indifferent health, was far from improbable. The apprehensions of his subjects were soon realized, as he died in July 1498. "Charles VIII.," says Commines, "was but a little man, so good natured that it was impossible to meet with a better creature." Upon his decease, his wife, Anne of Britany, put a black knotted lace round her coat of arms, a custom which prevailed until the first Revolution. She became the wife of his successor, Louis XII. in 1499, and died 8th of January 1513.*

The departure of Charles from Naples having removed all difficulties, Ferdinand recovered his kingdom, but he did not long enjoy this return of his prosperous fortune, for dying soon after without issue, he was succeeded by his uncle Frederick. Thus, says Guiciardini, in the space of three years, the kingdom of Naples had five kings—Ferdinand I., Alphonso, Ferdinand II., Charles VIII., and Frederick.

Lewis, Duke of Orleans, is a prominent character in the play. According to Brantome, Anne, the sister of Charles, was fond of him but he did not return her love. He was thrice married. His first marriage with Joan, the daughter of Louis XI., was not consummated; his second, with Anne of Britany, was a happy one, and his third, with the Princess Mary of England, is said to have caused his death, as he had, for her sake, en-

* This lady's matrimonial adventures were singular enough. She had married the Emperor Maximilian by proxy; but she broke the contract, and espoused Charles VIII. On his death Louis XII. became her husband; but to bring this about he had to divorce his wife Joan, the daughter of Louis XI., who had forced him to marry her. By the obliging aid of the Pope he obtained a declaration of nullity of the marriage, and by means of it was enabled to marry his cousin's widow.

tirely altered his manner of living, " for before he used
to dine at eight o'clock, and now he was obliged to dine
at noon; it had been likewise his hour of going to bed
at night, and now he frequently sat up till midnight." *

He died on the 1st of January 1515, aged fifty-three,
having reigned seventeen years, and was interred at
St. Denis. His death was the cause of general lamen-
tation—the bellmen went about ringing their bells, and
crying along the streets, "the good king Louis, the father
of his people, is no more." †

The French Commander Montpensier, a nobleman of
high position, was appointed Viceroy of the Kingdom of
Naples by Charles VIII. In 1496, at Pozzuolo, he fell
a victim to the plague.

Isabella was the widow of John Galeas, or Galeazzo,
Duke of Milan, who was poisoned in 1494 by his uncle
Ludovico, or Lewis Sforza, usurper of the duchy, in the
possession of which he was confirmed by the Emperor.
Sforza, after exercising great influence in the affairs of
Italy, changed sides in a manner worthy a man of
liberal views. Ultimately he was taken prisoner by the
French, and confined to the castle of Loches, where
he died in 1510. He was surnamed the Moor, not
from his complexion, for he was rather fair than swarthy,
but from an allusion to the Italian word Mora, which
signifies a mulberry tree, and which he had taken for his
device, considering this tree as a symbol of prudence. ‡

The love passages alluded to by the Duchess Isabella,
in the play, as passing between her and Charles are
pure fictions, besides, she was not a widow when
Charles invaded Italy. Commines says, that when
the French monarch was at Milan, before he entered
Naples, John Galeas, the Duke of Milan, was alive,
but confined in the castle of Pavia, with his "wife,
daughter of King Alphonso, in a very piteous estate,
her husband being sick," and that husband and wife
were held in this castle, "as under guard, and her
son who is yet living with a daughter or two. The child
was then about five years old, and him every man might
see but no man might see the Duke; for myself passed
three days before the King, and by no means could be

* Henault, p. 352.   † Ib. 339.   ‡ Ib. 342.

suffered to come within." The King, however, saw him, but would not speak on his behalf, for fear to offend Lord Ludovic. " At the same time the duchess fell upon her knees before the said Ludovic, desiring him to have pity upon her father and brother. He answered that it could not be. But to say the truth, she might better have entreated him for her husband and herself, being at that time a goodly young woman." * This statement of Commines nearly fixes the time when Duke John was " done to death " by his strong-minded uncle, and it could not have been very long after the conversation with Charles, who proceeded to Naples, never imagining that the murder of the Duke would follow. Probably, the *prudent* Ludovic was apprehensive that the success of Charles at Naples would be followed by the liberation of his victim. As it was, this versatile Prince very soon afterwards, with his associate, Pope Alexander Borgia, a potentate alike distinguished for vice and villany, assisted by the Venetians and the Emperor Maximilian, futilely attempted to cut off Charles on his return to France.

Although a real personage, the Prince of Salerne, except to the effect of spurring up the French monarch to invade Naples,† had little concern with what was doing in the city, as represented in the drama. He was a Neapolitan, chief of the noble family of St. Severin, and had been banished from his native country for rebellion. Trivultio the turncoat, despised equally by Charles and Ferdinand, Ascanio, Cornelia, the widowed Queen of Cyprus, and Julia, are, we suspect, indebted for their existence to the author himself.

Of the merits of this tragedy in rhyme it may be fairly said that it is just as good as any other of the time. Where Dryden failed it is not very likely Crowne would succeed. No one would suppose that the author of All for Love and Don Sebastian, tragedies of the first rank, would have wasted his powers upon such exaggerated extravagances as Almanzor and Almahide, or Tyrannic Love. But such was fashion—the King admired rhyming plays, and his courtiers were bound to do so also. It is a remarkable instance of the low ebb to which the public taste had descended, when the vigorous

* Commines, page 257.   † Commines, page 276.

language of Shakespeare, Jonson, and their contemporaries was in a manner banished from the English stage, to make way for the insipidity of French feeble rhythmical declamation. It was to Buckingham's Rehearsal, that we owe the cure of this Gallic malady.

The patron to whom Crowne dedicated his tragedy was a nobleman of good descent, the grandson of Charles Wilmot, created an Irish viscount and English baron by Charles I. He defeated Sir William Waller, at Roundway Down in Wiltshire, in July 1643. His son Henry received the higher dignity of an Earl from Charles II., and was the first Earl of Rochester of the name of Wilmot. Dying in 1659, he was succeeded by his son John, the last Earl, who married Elizabeth Mallet, daughter of John Mallet, Esquire, of Enmore, by whom he had one son, Charles, who predeceased his father, upon whose death in July 1680, before he had completed his thirty-second year, the Earldom and inferior dignities came to an end in the name of Wilmot.

Of the life and conduct of this well-known ornament of the dissolute court of the merry monarch it is unnecessary to give an account. The Earl has been placed by Dr. Johnson amongst the poets of England, and to that account of Rochester the reader is referred. Suffice it to say, he lived a profligate, and died a penitent.

In the 'Biographica Dramatica,' Rochester has been accused of ridiculing some lines by Crowne in the present drama. It is asserted that in an imitation of the third satire of Boileau, called Timon, Rochester wrote as follows:

> Kickum for Crown declar'd, that in Romance
> He had outdone the very wits of France.
> Witness Pandion * and his Charles the Eight,
> Where a young monarch, careless of his fate,
> Tho' foreign troops and rebels shook his state,
> Complains another sight afflicts him more,
> Viz., the Queen's Galleys rowing from the shore
> Filling their oars and tacking to be gone,
> Whilst sporting waves smil'd on the rising sun.
> *Waves smiling on the Sun!* I am sure that's new
> And 'twas well thought on, give the devil his due. †

* Pandion and Amphigenia, or the History of the Coy Lady of Thessalia, adorned with Sculptures, London, 1665, 8vo. of which there is a copy in the British Museum.

† p. 148.

Referring to the Works of his Grace, George Villiers, Duke of Buckingham, third edition, London, 1713, vol. first, page 164, it appears that the satire called Timon is said to be by the Duke of Buckingham *and the Earl of Rochester*. It thus is by no means certain that the extract just quoted is from the pen of the last mentioned nobleman, who is also asserted to have assisted in the composition of the 'Rehearsal,'—to what extent, it would be desirable to ascertain. It is not safe always to hazard an opinion, but we are much inclined to suspect that Buckingham not Rochester penned the lines in question, which, whoever was the author, are not beyond the bounds of fair criticism.

Flatman, notwithstanding his unpoetical name, has some verses on the death of Rochester, with whom he was cotemporary, from which we quote the following, which certainly possess great elegance:

> As on his death-bed gasping Strephon lay,
>   Strephon ! the wonder of the plains,
>   The noblest of the Arcadian swains.
> Strephon, the bold, the witty, and the gay,
>   With many a sigh and many a tear he said,
>   Remember me, ye shepherds, when I'm dead,
>
> Ye trifling glories of the world Adieu,
>   And vain applauses of the Age ;
>   For when we quit this earthly stage,
> Believe me, shepherds, for I tell you true,
>   The pleasures which from virtuous deed we have,
>   Produce the sweetest slumbers in the grave.

These stanzas are quoted by Park, in his edition of 'Walpole's Royal and Noble Authors,' from the third edition of Flatman, to whom Pope owes obligations which he repaid by censure. It is to Flatman he is indebted for the most striking lines in his celebrated short poem of 'the Dying Christian to his Soul.'

TO

THE RIGHT HONOURABLE

JOHN, EARL OF ROCHESTER,

One of the Gentlemen of His Majesty's Bed-Chamber, &c.

My Lord,—Perhaps your lordship may admire to see your name fixed before this trifle; but it is the fate of persons of your obliging temper to receive persecutions of this nature, in return of candour and indulgence; which I must confess is so ill a requital, as it may make your lordship cautious henceforwards of bestowing your favours, since this must be the troublesome consequence. But greatness like beauty attracts all on whom it smiles, and we frail writing sinners cannot content ourselves with the secret enjoyment, but think half the pleasure lost if we do not boast of it to the world. This vanity occasions your lordship the present trouble; and, next to this, a design to overawe with your name any the briskest enemies this poem may meet with; for when I tell 'em your lordship thinks it not much unworthy your favour, they will judge moderately of it,—at least not be too forward in censuring anything which you are pleased to defend. The enemies it has already met with have been fewer than a play in verse (and an ill one too) could expect; considering how many there are, that exclaim against rhyme, though never so well writ. Some of them I am afraid do it from the same unjust pique that Women of cruel hearts, but peaceable Beauties ever have against a Mode, wherewith they despair to kill. But I shall not much concern my self with their little quarrel: I am fortunate enough in your Lordship's approbation, and can dispense with the rest of mankind. And this I am bold to affirm though I have not the Honour of much acquaintance with your Lordship; for it is sufficient that I have seen in some little sketches of your Pen, excellent Masteries and a Spirit inimitable; and that I have been entertained by others with the wit, which your Lordship with a gentile and careless freedom, sprinkles in your ordinary converse, and often supplies vulgar and necessitous wits where-with to enrich themselves, and sometimes to treat their friends; and when your Lordship is pleased to ascend above us, you do it with a strange readiness and agility of mind, and by swift and easy motions attain to heights, which others by much climbing, dull industry, and con-straint cannot reach. Nor is this vast wit crowded together in a little Soul, where it wants freedom, and is uneasy, but fills up the spaces of a large and generous mind, infinitely delighting to oblige all, but especially to encourage any blossoming merits; and ready to for-give large and voluminous faults for the sake of any one thing tolerably said or done. And now the world sure will not blame me that I esteem my self extremely happy in Your Favour, and secure in Your Patronage; and this being to me, like some great and sudden Fortune to the poor, I know not how to manage my own transports, but must make my brags to my friends. This, my Lord, is a great infirmity, but it is incident to human nature, and very common with all of our tribe; and I do not doubt but your Lordship will pardon it among other defects to,

    My Lord,

        Your Lordship's most humble

          and most obliged Servant,

            JOHN CROWNE.

PROLOGUE

TO KING CHARLES THE EIGHTH.

Now the rough sounds of war our ears invade,
Some think the Muses should retire to shade,
And there, like mournful birds with hanging wing,
Alone and sad some doleful ditty sing:
For now our gallants all to sea are gone,
Muses as well as Misses are undone,
And both of 'um must to their grief allow,
They can expect but sorry trading now;
But though kind Miss may sit at home and whine
For some brisk airy Sir, that kept her fine;
Wit has not so much reason to complain,
And wit no more than beauty can abstain.
Hot English mettle must to working fall,
And do for love ere they'll not do at all.
Let dull Dutch jilt over a smokey stove,
Sit sighing for the loss of some fat love;
Let frighted burgers——
Shut up their shops, and to their fate submit,
Whilst we keep ope' both shops of trade and wit.
Whilst our brisk critics are become their fate,
And damn the farce of their mechanic state,
You, gentle sirs, that here behind remain,
We with a martial play will entertain;
You shall see wars and death as well as they,
But it shall be in a much safer way:
Nay, now their backs are turn'd, we'll watch our time,
And be so bold to fight and die in rhyme;

I   9

For our dull author swears he but aspires
To please the city wives and country squires;
And all the sober audience of the town,
Those of the long robe and the talking gown,
With serious men of trade, who well or ill,
Seldom good men protest a poet's bill;
'Mongst whom all stuff does find such present vent,
We durst ensure our plays at three per cent.
With these our author's dull insipid rhyme,
He durst not have produced another time,
He hopes is safe, and if his sense is low,
He can compound for't with a dance or show.
And to conclude, he swears—
He does not doubt but he shall feast to day
Your sober palates with a serious play.

THE NAMES OF THE PERSONS.

ALPHONSO, *King of Naples* . MR. METBOURN.

FERDINAND, *Son to Alphonso* . MR. HARRIS.

PRINCE OF SALERNE, *a fierce and valiant young Rebel* . } MR. SMITH.

ASCANIO, *Friend to Ferdinand* . MR. YOUNG.

TRIVULTIO, *an old General, and Commander of the Neapolitan Army* . . . } MR. SANDFORD.

GONSALVO, *Admiral of Queen Cornelia's Galleys* . . } MR. BURFORD.

GHOST, *of Galeazzo, Duke of Millane* . . . . } MR. CADEMAN.

CHARLES THE EIGHTH, *King of France* . . . } MR. BETTERTON.

LEWIS, *Duke of Orleans* . . MR. CROSBY.

MOMPENSIER, *a French Commander* . . . . } MR. NORRIS.

———

ISABELLA, *Daughter to Alphonso, and Widow to Galeazzo, the young Duke of Millane, who was poisoned by his Uncle Sforza* . . } MRS. BETTERTON.

CORNELIA, *Widow Queen of Cyprus* . . . . } MRS. SLAUGHTER.

IRENE, *her Friend and Confidant* . . . . } MRS. SHADWELL.

JULIA, *Sister to Isabella* . . MRS. DIXON.

PORTIA }
EUPHEMIA } *Maids of Honour to* { ISABELLA.
SYLVIA } { JULIA. CORNELIA.

OFFICERS, GUARDS, ATTENDANTS.

The Scene : NAPLES.

THE HISTORY

OF

CHARLES THE VIII. OF FRANCE:

OR,

THE INVASION OF NAPLES BY THE FRENCH.

THE FIRST ACT.

After several shouts and noises without,

Enter ISABELLA, JULIA, PORTIA, *as from their beds.*

Isa. Oh heavens! what mean these sad dis-
    tracted cries,
This confus'd noise, which through the palace flies,
And puts a horror on the face of night,
Dreadful to th' ears, as visions to the sight?
  Jul. The city hath receiv'd some strange alarms;
For in the streets they call, to arms! to arms!
The palace echoes with a dreadful sound,
And martial noises from the streets rebound.
  Isab. Portia, enquire the news!—
  Por.   Madam, I go;
And yet I dread to ask.—   [*Exit Por.*
  Jul.   And I to know.
  Isab. What can w' expect? The enemy is come!
Although last night some said he was at Rome.
 see the slave, who the false news did bring,
Came with those tidings to betray the King.
When once a shaking monarchy declines,
Each thing grows bold, and to its fall combines.

Jul. Oh heav'ns ! how strange a dream I had to
    night !   [*Aside.*
Visions of glory walk'd before my sight ;
Crowns, Cupids, bowers, and, in my pleasing trance,
I thought my self no less than Queen of France.
What the presage should mean I fain would know,
And yet I dare not let the secret go.
    Isab. Does haughty Charles his anger still retain,
                              [*Aside.*
To come from France with armies in his train ;
To ruin Naples, and usurp the crown ;
'Cause his feign'd passion I did once disown ? *
I'll make him know, by sad experience too,
What a wrong'd Princess in despair dare do !
Perhaps he thinks I am grown humbler since,—
Th' afflicted widow of a murder'd Prince :
But the proud King shall find, when 'tis too late,
My mind hath grandeur, much above my state.
Since darts of beauty could not wound his pride,
Those darts shall now with daggers be supplied.
    Jul. These sad confusions will disturb, I fear,
Our Royal stranger drove by tempests here,
The distress'd Cyprian Queen, who will conclude
By her hard fortunes she is still pursued ;
That she in vain took refuge from the winds,
Whilst in the port she a new tempest finds ;
Which though for Naples 'tis alone design'd,
Will have impression on her generous mind.
    Isab. The distress'd fortunes of that beauteous
      Queen,
Have by my soul deeply resented been ;
And I the more for our confusions grieve,
In that no aid we can her fortunes give.
But see, she comes !

  * This is fiction. Charles was to have married Margaret the
daughter of the Emperor Maximilian,—but broke the contract
and married Anne of Brittany, thereby securing to France her
Duchy.

Enter CORNELIA, IRENE, SYLVIA.

Cor. Ah madam, what should mean,
The sad distractions which I now have seen ?
Wak'd from a gentle slumber soft as those
Of lovers charm'd with music to repose ;
I rose, and in confusion went to see,
What 'twas that had divided sleep and me ;
And to my window straight I did repair,
And setting wide those sluices of the air,
I in the streets saw waves of people flow,
Like the sea billows when fierce tempests blow.
Among the surges of th' unruly throng,
Came fleets of armed troops sailing along,
Like ships pursued by angry winds, and straight,
They all were landed at the palace gate.
    Jul. Heavens ! we shall be murder'd !
    Isab. —W' are betray'd !
The enemy is got into the town,
Villains have sold my father's life and crown.
    Cor. Madam, you judge too soon, and judge the
        worst,
Forbear till you have heard the story first.
Then, Madam know, the Guards opposed awhile ;
But 'twas like reeds upon the banks of Nile,
Weakly resisting an impetuous flood,
Of armed troops, and of a floating crowd.
The King your father then in person came,
Compass'd with lights, that he seem'd arm'd with
        flame.
When from the terrace first he did appear,
Their awful silence shew'd a general fear ;
Till some more insolent than all the rest,
Presum'd to set their pikes against his breast :
But when the Prince appear'd, the martial ring
Proclaim'd aloud, that he should be their King.
By the respect they did your brother shew,
Judge if they were your enemies, or no.

Jul. Oh heavens ! How durst you stand in dead
  of night,
So unconcern'd, to see that dreadful sight ?
  Iren. I saw all this the Queen doth now relate,
From my own room which views the palace gate.
And the fierce tumults fill'd me with such dread,
That in a fright I here for safety fled.
  Isab. And could the traitors find no fitter time,
But this the more to aggravate their crime ?
When heaven abandons a declining King,
Rebellion then grows a religious thing.
Though on heaven's party they devoutly fight,
To whom all Kings must bow their sovereign right!
And this with vulgar heads succeeds so well,
Success seems heaven's commission to rebel.
  Jul. Hark, hark, the shouts increase ;—They're
  louder yet.
  Iren. And now they nearer to the palace get.—
                                        [*Shouts.*
  Isab. The rebels still are insolent and loud,
The King will fall in the rebellious crowd.
Madam, you're cast upon a fatal shore,
                          [*Turning to Cornelia.*
Where you meet tempests greater than before.
The noises and unruly crowds appear
Less civil then the storms that forc'd you here.
But heaven, that judges these misfortunes due
To us, designs no share of them to you.
  Cor. Heaven to us all doth equal share design,
Since friendship makes all your misfortunes mine.
  Jul. But Portia comes! And see she comes in haste.

Enter PORTIA.

Ah ! Portia speak.   Is all the danger past,
Or doth it still increase ?
  Por. Madam, this noise
Is but the people's loud tumultuous cries.

Jul. The Queen already hath the story said!
Tell us th' event, is my great father dead?
What have the traitors done? and can we fly,
Or must we tarry and prepare to die?
    Por. It is in vain the fatal truth to hide!
Madam, we are beset on every side,
Your enemies are come, the French are here,
All round the walls their warlike troops appear,
And their approach such terror doth display,
As almost frightens back the infant day.

    Cor.   ⎤
    Isab. ⎬ Ye powers!
    Jul.   ⎟
    Iren. ⎦

    Por. And every minute comes a post,
With news of towns surrendered, cities lost:
With this the people are distracted grown,
Some would have straight deliver'd up the town!
Others that had with wrongs been much opprest,
Now seek revenges whilst the King's distress'd.
The public dangers they do all contemn,
Crying, all tyrants are alike to them.
And thus the city did with clamours ring,
The French besiege the town; the town the
    King.
    Isab. What would the villains have?
    Jul.   My father's life
I fear will be th' event of all this strife!
    Por. The King retir'd in a profound despair,
And left the people to the Prince's care.
Then did the armed crowds the Prince surround,
And in the noise and tumult he was crown'd!
    Cor. [*Aside.*] I feel within my heart a sudden
    flame
Rise at the mention of the Prince's name: ⎞
Not all the noise that doth his reign begin, ⎬
Exceeds the tumult which I feel within.   ⎠

Iren. Of brave Ascanio still I nothing hear,
           [Aside.
Heaven grant he meets with no misfortune there !
For in his King's concern his passion's high,
And his ungovern'd zeal too far will fly.

Isab. Then I perceive the Kingdom is undone,
The crown of Naples from our line is gone :
For these convulsions in a dying State
Some high and dangerous ills prognosticate.
Come, madam, let us go !   *[To Cor.*
And since the worst that fate designs, we know,
If it be day, let's on the western tower
View this dark cloud which threats so fierce a
  shower.   *[Exeunt omnes.*

Enter ALPHONSO, FERDINAND, ASCANIO,
   TRIVULTIO.—GUARD.

Alph. Depose their King, and fly from his defence
When they've the highest need of innocence !
T'engage all Kings and fortune of their side,
To guard their wealth, and prop their falling pride :
But since my son they've seated on my throne,
They in some measure do their sins atone.
Dear Ferdinand, thou hast thy people's voice,
And art thy father's and the kingdom's choice.
Like blind idolaters they worship thee,
With dark devotion by blaspheming me.
They finding my dim glories to decline,
With torches of rebellion light up thine :
But like a God, their ignorance disdain,
And shine upon 'em with a glorious reign.

Ferd. Ah ! sir, I humbly crave—
You'd not such orders on my duty lay,
Which I must be disloyal to obey ;
Nor by resigning up to me your throne,
Force me to make the people's guilt my own.

I'll not such favour to rebellion shew,
To wear a crown the people do bestow,
Who, when their giddy violence is past,
Shall from the King th' ador'd revolt at last ;
And then the throne they gave, they shall invade,
And scorn that idol which themselves have made.
No,—live and govern, to revenge on them
Those crimes which only now you can contemn.
    Alph. No, Ferd'nand, I the choice of heaven
      allow,
And to my fate, not to my vassals bow,
In all the changes that to crowns befall,
There is a power unseen that governs all,
Orders the moves, and plays the mighty game,
Whilst only Kings and Kingdoms have the name.
'Twas heaven for Naples safety did decree,
By all those tumults to make choice of thee.
I freely then the Royal power resign.
Proclaim your King.   [*Ferdinand seems to oppose.*
No more! the Crown is thine !
I will for ever quit that glorious weight,
And now retire from all the toils of State.
Long live Ferdinand King of Naples!   [*All shout.*
    Ferd. What guilty acclamations do I hear ?
'Tis known to heaven how small a part I share
In that disloyal joy the people shew.
    Asc. Accept the crown, sir, since it must be so.
Our ruin'd kingdom flies to your defence
As to a Prince fram'd for this exigence,
With sublime courage to support the weight,
Disperse these clouds, rebuild the falling State.
    Alph. Now, son, the glories of my life are done !
But ah ! thy troubles are but now begun ;
For know this crown to that distress is come,
Abroad 'tis pitied, and betray'd at home.
Thy subjects mutining, and thy allies
Fly from their own approaching destinies.

The less Italian States that us'd to ride,
In calms of peace close by each others' side,
Have with this tempest broken every chain,
And now are tost like gallies on the main,
That to unite again, they seek no more,
Each flies for safety to a several shore.
Venice and Rome, on whom I did rely,
Buy their own peace, and from the tempest fly;
Which swells this Monarch with no less design,
Than the world's ruin to begin with thine.

    Ferd. He on the world hath past a haughty
      doom ;
But we may make his thoughts contain less room.
    Alph. 'Tis true, my son, but thou art left alone,
And hast no sword to trust to but thy own.
And that with high rebellion's broke in two,
That none, my son, dare manage it but you.
Those that should serve thee in this high contest,
Turn all their swords against the Monarch's breast,
That in this exigence 'tis hard to say,
Which are more dangerous, the French or they.
    Asc. The Prince of Salerne heads the rebel
      crew.
    Ferd. He does,—and I the villain will pursue
In his fierce chase of power with so much flame,
He shall let fall his prey, and change his game,
And curse his pride which his ambition led
To play with thunder till it strook him dead.
    Alph. Yes, Ferdinand, thou must the slave
      destroy,
On that young traitor first thy arms employ.
He thinks his bold pretence is just and good,
Thus to revenge his rebel father's blood;
Nay, his successful pride so high doth swell,
He dare demand thy sister Isabel :
But make him know it is a safer thing
To blaspheme Heav'n, than to depose a King.

Between the French and him thy arms divide,
The war is just and brave on either side ;
Rather than by a slave in triumph led,
Throw down thy falling kingdom on his head,
Blow up the French, the villain, and the town ;
And if thou canst not save, thus lose the crown.
Thou wilt be brave and glorious in thy fall ;
But thou hast courage to subdue them all.
    Triv. The King revengeful grows when 'tis too
       late,
Thus mighty spirits struggle with their fate.
    Asc. Had this great counsel been pursu'd in time,
T'had sav'd our ruin, and that rebel's crime.
    Ferd. In these expressions of your Royal mind,
I both my duty and my glory find.
And, sir, I'll pay them such sublime respect,
To your revenge I altars will erect ;
Where I will consecrate my sword, and he
With all his train shall the chief victims be.
Then for my other foes I will prepare,
And with devotion thus begin the war ;
And if I conquer, prostrate all my fame
And glory at your feet, from whence they came.
    Asc. Brave Prince !
    Triv. But this devotion, I'm afraid,   [*Aside.*
Will sacrifice the crown upon your head.
    Alph. Ah son ! thou fill'st my heart with secret
       joy,
My high prophetic thoughts my fears destroy.
Some mighty glories treasur'd up by fate,
For virtues that attain so great a height,
When thou hast through a thousand glorious toils,
Trode on rebellion, and hast reapt the spoils
From the ambitious French ; the news to me
Will even a second coronation be :
Then, freed from all these cares, enjoy thy throne,
And raise the glorious name of Arragon.

And now, my son, farewell ! this painful hour
Presses me more than e'er did weights of power.
But I shall conquer it.   The powers divine
Take to their guard, a virtue great as thine !
Now let thy galleys to the Asian shore
Conduct thy father hence—thy King no more.
   Ferd. This flood of sorrow let me first unlade,
Then, sir, your sad commands shall be obey'd.
[Ex. Alph., Ferd.
   Asc. Tragical sight ! the brave Alphonso's gone!
Despoil'd by rebels of that glorious throne,
In which his soul whilst living was enclos'd :
For kings are truly murder'd when depos'd.
When they the souls of power from Empire fly,
They turn a wand'ring regal shade, and die.   [*Ex.*
   Tri. And art thou gone, brave Prince ?   Thy
     short-liv'd reign
Hath been of troubles one continued scene.
The giddy multitude, who never fear
A threat'ning danger, till they see it near,
Do fondly from their own protection fly,
And just assistance to their King deny.
Oppos'd by some, forsaken by the rest :
All will be conquer'd, rather than opprest.
But when destruction on themselves they bring,
They then revenge their follies on their King.
This scene once past, the next thing I must
     know,
Is how my fortunes I had best bestow.
Ere since the armies of this crown I've led,
Laurels have never wither'd on my head.
The State is wholly at my devotion grown,
And as I please, I can dispose this crown.
And I therein shall fortune's smiles pursue ;
All my allegiance to my self is due.
As fortune favours, so shall I advance
The interest of Naples, or of France.

Enter PRINCE OF SALERNE.

But ha ! the fierce young Prince of Salerne here,
How dares he thus among the guards appear ?
    Sal. Trivultio, seek not to retrieve the guard,
I will from no accesses be debar'd.
                              [*Shew several men armed.*
Nay, my unbounded power to let you see,
The King shall have no other guards but me.
'Tis to my interest ye high honours do,
Those who make idols must preserve 'um too.
    Tri. I know your interest, sir, and wish your
        power
Were something less, or loyalty were more.
    Sal. My loyalty !
Go talk of that to dull obedient fools,
Whom laws and tame pedantic virtue rules.
My honour's safe in that my cause is good,
And I am loyal to my father's blood :
And shall be bold, in such a glorious cause,
To tread on Kings, and loyalty, and laws.
By nature's high commands my sword I draw,
And nature's dictates are the highest law.
    Tri. No doubt, to nature's universal sway
                              [*Ironice.*
All laws must bow, and Kingdoms must obey.
But, sir, imperious nature might have chose
A fitter time for her commands than those,
When King and Kingdom are embroil'd in war,
That for the crime of one all punisht are ;
If 'tis a crime for Monarchs to defend
Their crowns from every sacrilegious hand.
But power it seems can change the names of
        things,
Call treason, virtue ; and make rebels, Kings.
But grant your father's blood unjustly spilt,
Must Naples suffer for their Monarch's guilt ?

Sal. Sir, I'll revenge my father's blood on all
That saw, and dares survive his funeral :
On all that to his execution came,
And did not set all Naples in a flame.
Blaspheme the Heavens, and, in transports of rage,
'Gainst Kings and Gods in some high act engage.

   Tri. No doubt 'twas pity when he lost his head,
But all mankind had suffer'd in his stead.
                                [*Ironice.*
But I must wait a more important care.

   Sal. Stay, sir, and to the King this message
      bear.
Tell him, that now his father I've chastis'd,
My high revenges are in part suffic'd :
That when h'ath wip't his eyes, which for a while
Must drop some tears for the old King's exile,
I am content my passion to subdue,
And if he please our friendship to renew.
And that th' alliance may eternal prove,
I've thought his sister worthy of my love,
And shall descend t' accept her as my bride,
If I'm petition'd for 't on every side.
But if my alliance he dares disesteem,
Tell him, I both his sister scorn, and him.
To wear his crown were to descend too low ;
Him and that trifle I'll on Charles bestow.   [*Exit.*

   Tri. To what prodigious heights his spirit flies,
The fates and crowns of Monarchs to despise.
These are portentous signs, and I'm afraid
The crown will fall from our young Monarch's head.
And with its heavy fall 'twill ruin those,
Who fondly in its support their lives expose.
Too long I've borne the weight for no reward,
Now time calls loud my fortunes to regard,
And leave this barren place,——
Which for this twenty years with blood I've sown,
And nothing reapt but beggarly renown.——[*Exit.*

The Scene, a fair Country before the Walls of Naples.

Enter CHARLES, LEWIS OF ORLEANS,
MOMPENSIER, GUARDS.

Ch. The day draws on, the sun appears in view,
And we to-day have much brave work to do.
Send, in my name, a herald to the town,
Tell King Alphonso I demand the crown !
That crown his ancestors usurpt from mine.
And he, the third usurper of his line,
Detains——if he refuse——bid him prepare
For all the worst calamities of war.
    Lew. They dare not, sir, oppose your mighty
        claim,
The world's subdu'd already with your fame.
The Italian States like herds to covert fly,
Whilst you are like a whirlwind passing by.
Yes, Rome her self declines her sacred head,
And by obsequious fawning shews her dread.
But this lost Kingdom, upon whom the ball,
Folded in clouds of fire, designs to fall,
Shakes with the fears of its approaching doom,
Whilst smoking a far off they see it come.
    Mon. Yes sir, your power, like an impetuous tide,
Breaks down their yielding banks on every side ;
That raving with despair, they wildly run
I'th midst of all those dangers they would shun.
Our spies within have all disorders found,
The King is banisht, and his son is crown'd.
Hurried into the throne by crowds of those,
Whom now instead of guarding, they oppose,
Within their city's of a blazing fire ;
Without their army ready to retire.
Nor town nor army will their King obey,
That you will meet no enemy to day.
    Ch. Yes, sir, the rebels are my enemies,
And every King's concern as well as his.

Rebellion is a monster would devour
The Kingly dignity, and Sovereign power.
A sort of atheism, that doth crowns blaspheme,
And styles the sacred power of Kings a dream.
And as blasphemers call the heavenly powers
To arm their thunder; this awakens ours.
Go to the King then e'er it proves too late,
[To Momp.

And if you find the rebels desperate,
The party strong, and the young King afraid
He cannot conquer 'um, I'll lend him aid.
When that is done, tell him the crown's my right,
And I expect that he resign or fight.
  Mon. Great sir, I shall obey.
  Cha.   Next to the town
Proclaim, that I all rebels shall disown,
For though 'tis true I am their lawful Prince,
To whom they all allegiance owe ; yet since
Titles of Kings are mysteries too high
Above the reach of ev'ry vulgar eye,
They must the present shrines of power adore,
And pry into their duty, and no more ;
For those with new religions will be bold,
Who dare with high contempt profane the old ;
And he who doth his own false God despise,
And with atheistic pride and scorn denies
That worship, which he thinks is but his due,
Would do the same if he ador'd the true.
Bid 'um be loyal then, whilst we dispute,
And their false worship I with arms confute. [Exit.

Act II.

The Scene a Room in the Palace.

FERDINAND, MOMPENSIER, ASCANIO, TRIVULTIO.

Ferd. Your master's haughty message I despise,
Who knows not how to conquer, but surprise.
He owes his victories to my distress,
As he derives his title from success;
And has my vassals into fears betray'd
With th' empty noises which his fame hath made :
But they are ready, by a brave defence,
To cloud his fame, and blast his false pretence.
Then let him know his proffer'd aid I slight,
And dare retain my crown, if he dare fight.
Perhaps his army is in some distress
With tedious marches, want, and weariness :
To pay the debt he on my fame hath laid,
I'll send the rebels forces to his aid.
   Mon. I shall acquaint him, sir.
   Ferd. Trivultio—go !
To the proud enemy my standards show,
And, in the form that I my army drew,
Advance my troops, and fix 'um in their view.
   Triv. The armies, sir, already are so near,
That now they in each other's view appear;
And only want their King's commands to join.
   Ferd. Let all my squadrons stand prepar'd for
     mine !   [*Exit Tri.*
Ah ! my Ascanio ! Heaven doth still provide
New ways and arts to have my courage tried.
I do not mean by all those angry stars,
Which thus begins my reign with various wars;
By all the clouds that o'er my crown impend,
And in black tempests ev'ry hour descend
Threatening my life, my father, and my throne
Beset with foes and rebels, left alone

T' encounter all, whilst fearful spirits fly
In panic terror from their loyalty.
These meaner griefs my courage can remove ;
But I am tortur'd with despairing love !
  Asc. Why, sir, should you afflict your royal mind
With griefs, for which you soon redress may find ?
Time and some little patience will destroy
Those griefs which lie but in your way to joy :
Your own despairs, the blushes of the Queen,
And all the other guards which stand between,
Will soon remove their stations, and be gone ;
When all the empty forms of love are done.
  Ferd. Alas ! thou speak'st as if the piercing dart,
That wounded me, had toucht her gen'rous heart.
No, her unconquer'd heart is too severe ;
For all the happy time she hath been here,
Too much, I fear, against her will confin'd
By the kind force of an obliging wind,
With all my services I ne'er could gain,
The least allay to my insulting pain.
  Asc. Love in her sex must some resistance make
To a brave enemy for honour's sake.
But, sir, to better news I can pretend,
From the fair mouth of her own beauteous friend ;
For I, who in my confident address
To her fair friend, have met with more success,
Do find by her, that, sir, your noble flame
Is not contemn'd, nor doth she hate your name !
  Ferd. What is't thou say'st ?
  Asc. Yes, sir, I say the Queen,
With eyes betraying love, hath oft been seen
To glance on yours, but with such caution move,
As poets make the gods in stealths of love :
Watching with care the motions of your eyes,
To guard her timorous honour from surprize ;
And then retreating ere she was betray'd,
Falls into the ambush which her blushes made.

Nay, once——
Pursu'd to her retreats by her fair friend,
She was o'er heard to sigh——Prince Ferdinand!
And to the private echoes of the grove,
Intrust the dang'rous secrets of her love.
    Ferd. Prithee no more such pleasant tales as
       these,
As hard to faith as heavenly mysteries.
Thou think'st, with golden dreams and pleasing art,
To fan this burning fever in my heart ;
And blindly lead'st me to the wars of love,
With tales of Paradise, and joys above
My hope or faith, as Turkish priests delude
To war and death their cheated multitude.
Yet if 'twere true, and I in vain have mourn'd,
The inconstant wind is with my fortune turn'd,
At the same view in which I saw to-day
The French their standards on the hills display,
Another sight appear'd which griev'd me more,
All the Queen's galleys rowing from the shore,
Fitting their oars and tackling to be gone,
Whilst sporting waves smil'd on the rising sun.*
    Asc. Your Royal orders may remove that fear,
And for a while confine her galleys here ;
And though in honour she displeas'd may seem,
All her lost favour you may soon redeem,
And clear the guilt contracted on that score ;
For, sir, perhaps you can't oblige her more.
    Ferd. No more, my friend ! these flatteries are
       vain !
Thou like an artist doth delude my pain
With gentle promises, and hopes of cure,
When the anguish grows too violent to endure.
But since
All ways are fled to in a desp'rate case,
Thy dang'rous counsels I'll for once embrace,

---

* Ridiculed in "Timon"—the satirical poem mentioned in the
Introduction.

And will resume my courage. Prithee, go
And let the Adm'ral of her galleys know,
I must confine him in the port to-day ;
But then from me assure him that his stay
Not the least damage to the fleet shall bring,
And his compliance will oblige a King.
 Asc. Sir, I shall hasten on the bless'd design,
Since the concern is both my King's and mine.
[*Exit.*

 Ferd. I'll to the Queen and by confession own
The devout crime my trembling love hath done ;
Like those who still in hopes of pardon sin,
And all their crimes with penitence begin.
[*Exit.*

 Enter ISABELLA, *followed by* SALERNE.

 Isab Rebel, begone! Thy passion I disdain.
 Sal. And I those frowns which you employ in
  vain.
The debt which to my fathers' blood I owe,
I yet have paid with a revenge too low.
The abject blood of vassals I have spilt,
And blush that fame on such mean crimes I've
  built.
To kill your brother were revenge sublime,
And the great cause would consecrate the crime ;
But yet that debt I shall in part forgive,
And for your sake shall let your brother live.
The regal style I'll suffer him to bear ;
But I shall ease him from the regal care.
I have another enemy beside,
The hopes of Charles which nourishes your pride :
But from those flames I shall your heart redeem :
For I'll at once both kill your hopes and him,
And pull your pride and all his glories down.
And fetch that Monarch's head, or lose my own.
[*Exit Sal.*

Isab. Who ever heard an insolence like this ?
But this is rather fortune's crime than his ;
He finds successes smile on his offence,
And now he swells to all this insolence;
And does so proud of his rebellion grow,
He thinks all virtues must to treason bow.

Enter PORTIA.

Por. Madam, the Cyprian Queen is coming here !
Isab. To take her last adieus of us I fear.

Enter CORNELIA, JULIA, IRENE, SYLVIA.

COR. Madam, I come with sorrows to complain
Of my hard fate, with which I strive in vain.
My friends, the winds and seas have all combin'd
To make me both ungen'rous and unkind ;
And force me from you in your great distress,
The only time my friendship to express.
    Isab. Madam, in this your friends do faithful
        prove,
And act like Heav'n, who always doth remove
The souls he loves from evils he fore-knows,
And kindly takes them to their blest repose.
    Cor. Madam, this sacred truth I can't deny,
It is the same to part with friends, or die.——
                                    [*Weeps.*
    Iren. I find it so ; yet, must my joys resign,
                                    [*Aside.*
Ere by possession I can call 'em mine,
That I the brave Ascanio ne'er had seen,
Or could command my friendship to the Queen.
My love and loyalty my soul divide,
I flatter both and dare take neither side.
    Isab. Madam, this death you safely may embrace,
Since you will only leave a mournful place,
Which seems like some wild melancholy shade,
For the dark walks of guilty spirits made.

Nothing but terror haunts us every where ;
Pale sighing cowards turn'd to ghosts with fear.
Shouts of the valiant, fainting women's cries ;
All intermixt with the loud martial noise
Of guns and swords, and, which is yet more loud,
The saucy clamours of the rebel crowd :
Which like the groans of spirits in the night,
Women and cowards with the noise affright.
   Jul. This is our dismal state, and yet I find [*Aside.*
The last night's dreams of love so haunt my mind
With bright and glorious shapes, that I'm afraid
My heart will be insensibly betray'd.
I feel an inward flame I dare not own,
And love a Prince which seeks my father's crown.
If nature doth his passion disapprove,
Oh! nature pardon my ambitious love!
   Cor. I by this death to strange Eliziums go,
Not joys and crowns to gain, but to bestow.
That I the better world forsake I fear,
And leaving you, leave joy and angels here :
But I must yield to my imperious fate,
For my kind fathers, the Venetian State,
Do at their wills dispose my crown and me ;
But I've reserv'd my self this liberty ;
Nor winds nor seas shall intercept the share,
I'll in your sorrows, and misfortunes bear.
   Isab. Ah! Madam, you such generous kindness
    shew,
You seem like a bright angel sent below,
To comfort us in our dejected state ;
Or like a vision to foretell our fate.
Such lightnings some have had when near the
    grave.
Why may not dying Kingdoms visions have !
   Iren. My Queen great friendship has to her
    exprest,——   [*Aside.*
Whilst still her thoughts are to the King addrest.

Like one that praying would his saint conceal,
To a wrong image does devoutly kneel.
  Jul. Do visions death foretell ? What do I
   hear ?——   [*Aside.*
Then I'm afraid my death for love is near.
Oh heaven ! If I from life so soon must fly,
Grant me one vision more before I die.
  Cor. Could I your fate foretell, I would not own
Any ill news to you, nor to this throne :
But Madam, if what fame has said is true,
Crowns and not sorrows are design'd for you.
'Tis said, if Charles shall this fair Kingdom gain.
'Tis he shall triumph, but 'tis you shall reign.
  Isab. Of Princes' honours fame makes small
   esteem,
And speaks low things of me, and false of him.
He scorns his ancient passion to retain,
And I as much a crown from him disdain.
  Jul. Ye heavens ! what power doth my heart
   surprize ?
For I as much adore what you despise. [*Aside.*
My inward grief I can no longer bear,
To my fair friend I must impart a share.

    [*She whispers Irene, and they both go out.*

  Cor. But love oft hovers long within the breast,
Which is by beauty upon youth imprest.
I've heard the King receiv'd his first alarms
Of youthful love from your victorious charms.
  Isab. Madam, 'tis true, fame made a large report,
Whilst I i'th' glories of the Gallic Court
Sometimes consum'd, of that young Monarch's
   flame ;
He shewing me all the gallantry became
A youthful Monarch, but ere that pretence
Was well discover'd, I retir'd from thence.
  Cor. Against your will I fear.——

Isab. By a command
I durst not disobey, of Ferdinand
My grandfather,
Who then design'd me a less glorious throne ;
And the young Duke of Millane being grown
To man's estate, he sought alliance there——
Confining me within that narrow sphere.
   Cor. And this great King, finding his passion vain,
Comes to revenge himself on your disdain.
   Isab. Some would that compliment on me bestow,
But his ambitions do not aim so low.
I can derive it from a truer cause :
For, Madam know, when to obey the laws
Of Heaven and nature I subdued my mind,
To fix my self where the old King design'd,
I found the Duke of Milane, when I came
T''enjoy of Sovereign nothing but the name.
His youth was not so tender as his soul,
He and his sceptre under the control
Of wicked Sforsa, who, with the pretence
Of being guardian to his innocence,
Betray'd th' unguarded Prince, and hourly sought,
Which way his death might be with safety
      wrought.
When I the treason came to understand,
I speedy aid from Naples did demand,
The villain lest we should his plots surprise,
And his unfinish'd villanies chastise,
Raises these storms of war on Naples' throne,
To sink the power he fear'd and save his own.
   Cor. Would France, that does so much at glory aim,
At such a traitor's call pursue his claim ?
   Isab. Princes in eager chase of crowns ne'er mind
The way they take ; but ride o'er all they find.
   Cor. Since France this war had to the world
      declar'd,
How came th' old King thus strangely unprepar'd ?

Isab. The good old Monarch of a peaceful mind,
More to devotion then to arms inclin'd,
Grown credulous and dull with age and sloth,
Lov'd all those false reports that flatter'd both.
And so by Sforza was with lies betray'd,
That France some other crown design'd t'invade.
And till the French in Italy were come,
Was unprepar'd for all things but his tomb.
Then when his life and crown he could not save,
He quitted both and crept into his grave.
And left my father in a ruin'd state ;
Opprest with wars, and with the people's hate,
Whose most unhappy reign was scarce begun
Ere he resign'd the Kingdom to his son.
    Cor. But what becomes of wicked Sforza still,
Durst he proceed in his intended ill ?
    Isab. The rest, like a dark secret from the dead,
Told by some walking discontented shade,
Too full of direful guilt and horror grows,
Safely to hide or freely to disclose.
The villain, having rais'd by magic skill,
These throngs of martial spirits at his will,
To fill with noise of war th' Italian air,
Whilst near his circle no one durst repair,
Now takes th' occasion of this cursed time,
When he with safety might pursue his crime,
When none might hear his dying Sovereign groan,
Or could revenge the murder when 'twas done,
To bring the poor young Duke to his command,
And wring the sceptre from his tender hand ;
And to acquaint you with a fatal truth,
Poisons at last the sweet and princely youth.
    Cor. Oh monster !——
What will not some men do high power to gain,
And wear a while a guilty crown with pain ?
    Isab. I must retire, my grief imperious grows,
And on my reason doth too much impose. [*Ex. Isab.*

Isabella goes out weeping: As Cornelia is following,
SYLVIA *enters.*

Syl. Gonsalvo, madam, does your pleasure wait.
Cor. I know the haste of the Venetian State
To have my crown.   But, since I must away,
My master's haughty pleasures I'll obey.
Admit him in !

Enter GONSALVO.

      Your galleys, sir, prepare.
Gon. Madam, they're ready, and the wind is fair.
The storms, that lately rag'd upon the coast,
Are out o' breath, and all their fury lost.
But whilst the sea is smooth, and air is clear,
Madam, we meet another tempest here.
A storm not from the sea, but from the Court,
The King has stopt your galleys in the port.

Enter FERDINAND.

Ferd. Yes, madam, seeing my just accuser
      come,
I came to own my crime, and know my doom ;
For on my honour I have wars begun,
And own the great offence my love hath done.
Cor. Am I your subject, sir ?   Doth Naples own
Dues from my Kingdom, yet to me unknown ?
Ferd. Naples, its crown, and Monarch claims no
      due ;
But as they're conquer'd to be ruled by you.
Cor. Am I by laws of nations captive made,
'Cause without leave I did your shores invade ?
For so 'tis said——
When unarm'd Princes to strange lands betake
Themselves they voluntary captives make.
Ferd. Madam, 'tis true !   But you come arm'd
      with power,
Which makes me captive and you conqueror.

A power so charming all things must obey,
And where 'tis seen will have Imperial sway.
　　Cor. Nor subject, nor a captive! then from whence
Arises, sir, this high and great pretence
Of power, t'imprison here a sovereign Queen?
　　Ferd. From that ——
Whence all rebellions in the world have been,
From flaming zeal,——
Which to all order we destructive find,
And loves a zealous rapture of the mind.
　　Cor. You act those things of which you are
　　　　asham'd,
Then zeal and love must for your crimes be blam'd;
So to those virtues you injurious prove,
And bring an ill repute on zeal and love.
But, sir, you better reasons can relate,
Some secret cause or interest of State,
Or pride to let your Kingly power appear,
You exercise it first on strangers here.
And you make wars, as you have well exprest
On those, who, sir, are like yourself distrest;
But you had enemies enough before,
First conquer those ere you make wars on more.
　　Ferd. Madam, perhaps 'twas interest of State,
Since on your aid depends my Kingdom's fate!
For what can a despairing Monarch do,
To save his crown, who is condemn'd by you?
　　Cor. I know not what despair 'tis you pretend,
Nor yet what aid a depos'd Queen can lend.
Did I enjoy my crown, perhaps I might
Support another injur'd Prince's right:
But then I never would afford my aid
To those by whom I was a prisoner made.
　　Fer. You with the same devotion are detain'd,
As Heav'n with prayers and incense oft is chain'd,
Who seldom frowns on a devout offence,
And ne'er chastises sacred violence.

Cor. What is 't I hear? His love too generous
    grows,
And like rash valour doth itself expose
To mighty dangers which it can defeat.
And from which honour suffers no retreat. [*Aside.*
These trifling follies, sir, you may forbear,——
                        [*To Ferd.*
Your kingdom rather does require your care,
And if your cause and title, sir, are just,
You may your life and crown to Heaven entrust;
Whom in your aid I often shall implore,
And in my state you can expect no more.
                   [*Exit Cor., Syl., Gon.*

   Fer. Are they too trifling? Yes, fair Queen, with
    you,
Who those tormenting follies never knew;
How shall I bear this pang? It is above
My strength t'endure, or courage to remove.

      Enter a MESSENGER *in haste.*

  1. *Mes.* Your army, sir, with high impatience
    waits
Your presence, whilst the French approach the
    gates.

      Enter a SECOND.

  2. *Mes.* The crowds once more, sir, are rebellious
    grown,
Threat'ning to let the French into the town.
   Fer. Let city, army, Kingdom, perish all,
And share in their unhappy Monarch's fall;
Insulting love will no compassion learn,
And nothing else is worthy my concern.
But since the fair Cornelia will be gone,
I'll guard her hence, and haste to be undone.

And see ! her Admiral.

Enter GONSALVO.

Your fleet convey
From hence no longer for my orders stay.
  Gon. Y'oblige us, royal sir, with your consent,
But we are still confin'd ; for, since I went,
A fleet of galleys row'd in with the tide,
And fill the harbour's mouth on every side.
And the Admiral, that doth his flag advance,
In his main top displays the arms of France.
  Fer. Ha ! from my enemies shall I receive

[Aside.

That kindness which the Queen disdains to give.
The pow'rs of all mankind shall ne'er detain
Those glories here my service cannot gain.
Remain a while I will your passage clear,
I'll send to sea, and first I'll fight 'em there.

[Exit Gons.

Ferdinand is going out, and is met by Ascanio,
who enters in haste.

  Asc. Ah ! Sir, with speed this trait'rous town
    forsake,
And to some place of strength yourself betake !
The false Trivultio to the French is fled,
And hath some thousands of your army led.
The citizens within once more rebel,
And your guards side with those whom they should
    quell ;
And whilst we wait your orders to engage,
City and army both are in a rage ;
Nay, seek your life, and are resolv'd to buy
With their King's blood the Kingdom's liberty.
  Ferd. How ! With my blood the rebels safety
    bought ?
The slaves dare die, ere entertain that thought.

No, my brave friend ! Let not thy loyalty
Betray thy soul into kind fears for me.
Army and rebels both shall at the sight
Of me
Fear their own thoughts, and shall not dare but
    fight.
As for Trivultio, if Charles is brave,
From him he'll the rewards of treason have :
If not, let Charles and all the traitors join,
'Twill from his glory take and add to mine.

[Exit.

The Scene a fair Country before Naples.

Enter Charles, Trivultio, and Guard.

Ch. And is my fame so little in this place,
Thou dar'st adventure on an act so base ?
I thought my deeds my temper might have shewn,
And that my character was better known,
But thou in malice would'st be entertain'd,
To stain the many laurels I have gain'd ;
Thy King, despairing to preserve his crown,
Would thus by arts make war on my renown.
Tri. Sir, I came here on no such false design,
Nor is that Monarch any King of mine :
Though I have serv'd that Kingdom twenty years,
But of that long apprenticeship appears
No fruit, but loss of blood and many scars,
And some small fame got by success in wars,
And now grown old and poor, if I desire
To serve some other Monarch, or retire,
May n't I my service as I please bestow ?
Hard fate of soldiers if it must be so.
Ch. And had'st thou such a low esteem of me,
That I would entertain thy villany ?
And doth thy mercenary treason dare
Thy fortunes with the falls of Kings repair ?

If from that service did no profit spring,
It was reward enough to serve a King;
And for a King 't had been a soldier's pride
For no reward but glory to have died.
But since for gain, th'ast to my banners fled,
Thy treason I'll reward, and send thy head
To Ferdinand——unless thou dost from hence
Withdraw thy troops, and fight in his defence.

*Trivultio goes out, and enters in haste the Duke of
Orleans.*

Lew. Sir, they have made a sally from the town,
And all the force they have is pouring down.
The fierce young King doth in the head appear,
Dispensing death, and slaughter ev'rywhere.
And what success he finds he doth pursue,
Through all your squadrons, sir, to seek out you.

Enter MOMPENSIER.

Mom. The enemy, sir, doth your guards assault,
And all those men that lately did revolt
Repent their crimes, and do your guards betray..
Whilst through your troops King Ferdinand cuts
    his way.
Ch. Go, sacrifice the villains at my feet !
Let 'em my anger feel : whilst I go meet
The brave young King, and, since he's hither flown,
Afford him yet one trial for his crown.
                                        [*Ex. Om.*

ACT III.

The Scene of the field continues.

Enter TRIVULTIO *and an* OFFICER.

Tri. No hopes my ruin'd honour to regain !
Off. No hopes ! your men are either fled or slain !
Tri. This was the ambush of some cursed star,
That envied all the fame I got in war.
Both Kings disdain me, and I've lost the day,
And all my hopes,—my fame's damn'd every way.
One scorns my sword, the other my defence,
Charles slights my aid, Ferdinand my penitence.
But ah ! there's yet some hopes, on yonder hill
I see King Ferdinand's banners waving still.
Off. And I descry on yonder rising ground,
A Prince with armed throngs encompast round ;
And lion like he strives to get away,
Or make the hunters to become the prey.
By all that at this distance I can see,
By habits, plumes, and courage, it is he !
Here's one that can inform us.

Enter a SECOND OFFICER.

Tri. Where's the King ?
2. *Off.* Lost without aid,—encompast with a
    ring
Of hot French cavalry, in yonder grove,
Where for defence he did his troops remove,
Finding his passage to the town oppos'd,
And now with all their troops he is enclos'd.
Tri. The King is safe, for to his aid I come,
With those few troops I'll yet reverse his doom.
And now the bloody fate of Charles is near,
And see, the valiant Prince of Salerne here !

Enter PRINCE OF SALERNE.

Tri. Welcome, thou fate of Kings! What power
   divine
Sent thee to raise thy own renown and mine?
Our stars are penitent! In yonder shade
They've laurels for us hid in ambuscade,
To crown us if we bravely fetch 'em thence.
Both Kings have there refer'd their great pretence
To our decision, as we please we may
Give crowns, and rule the fortune of the day,
And Kings destroy or save.   Let's, ere we go,
Resolve on which we Naples will bestow.
  Sal. On neither: on myself.
  Tri.   I do agree.——
  Sal. They are both equally contemn'd by me;
Nor do I fight to give 'em crowns, but tombs.
  Tri. They both shall die; we will decree their
   dooms!
We'll fall on Charles to raise our sinking fame,
And save young Ferdinand for an after-game.
  Sal. Pursue thy fortune.   I'll destroy or save,
As I, and not as men or gods would have.
In the high chace of fame I'll not be shewn
What way to take, but will pursue my own.
I hate both Kings and firmly have decreed,
Both by my sword successively shall bleed.
But in the field, I'll a brave death afford
To Charles, who seems most worthy of my sword:
The other is by fortune brought too low,
His life on Isabel in pity I'll bestow.   [*Exit.*

*The Scene is drawn, and there is presented a thick
  Grove filled with armed men, Batallions surrounding
  it at a distance, out of which comes Ferdinand and
  Ascanio with a party.*

  Ferd. All the remainder of my army gone!
And left me in this high exigent alone?

Asc. Sir, they are all revolted, slain or fled,
Mixt with the French, the rebels or the dead.
    Ferd. Then I perceive
I've tempted my high destiny too far,
Wading too boldly in the depths of war ;
And 'tis but valour's heresy to fly
At mysteries of fame that are too high,
And Monarchs, though high priests of fame they be,
Have not, in arms, infallibility.
But if I have err'd in courage, 'tis to you,
My brave Ascanio, all the blame is due.
    Asc. To me, sir !
    Ferd. Yes, thou fought'st with so much flame,
Thou mad'st thy Monarch jealous of his fame ;
Rushing where e'er I could most danger see,
Only in honour to out-rival thee.
    Asc. I only fought in duty, sir, to bear
Of all those wounds you sought some little share.
    Ferd. In this thy King thy courage disapproves ;
Thou ought'st to save the man thy Monarch loves,
And not so easily expose to fate,
What Monarchs value at the highest rate.
    Asc. Subjects or Kingdoms are but trifling things,
When laid together in the scale with Kings.
    Ferd. In this despair what shall's resolve upon,
To stay or cut our passage to the town ?
    Asc. Sir, their whole army doth the grove
        surround ;
All we can do is to maintain our ground.
    Ferd. Why are they at a stand, and make us stay
Guarded like hunted lions at a bay ?
    Off. 'Tis said, their King commands 'um to
        forbear,
He saith your person is too great a share
For common swords, a purchase so divine
As a King's due, to's own he doth design,
And see, he comes !

Enter CHARLES, LEWIS, MOMP., *and* GUARD.

Ferd. 'Tis he! stand by me all!
In this great hour shall France or Naples fall.

Charles stops and views Ferdinand.

Ch. Ha! my fierce enemy thus left alone, [*Aside.*
And by wild fortune at my mercy thrown!
Me thinks a braver man I have not seen,
He views his fate with an undaunted mien,
And with such pride maintains his fatal ground.
As if my army came to see him crown'd.
Heav'n! That I could recall that fatal breath,
Which rashly swore so brave a Prince's death.

 Ferd. Ha! is this he that must enjoy my throne!
           [*Aside.*
Ye powers! your favours have been well bestown:
Could I have chose the Prince that must invade
My throne, no other choice I would have made;
Scorning that any Prince less brave than he
Should e'er aspire to be my enemy.

 Ch. King Ferdinand, your fate hath been severe.
Through all my squadrons to conduct you here
With feign'd successes to deride your sword,
And then no safety to your life afford;
For now you must with speed your sword resign,
Else as I've won your crown your life is mine.

 Ferd. My fate in this what I desir'd hath done,
Here I enjoy the conquest I have won,
And here triumph. and, whilst I this retain,
         [*Shews his Sword.*
Our lives and crowns on equal terms remain;
But by the care you of my life have shewn,
You seem to doubt the safety of your own.
Glad if I would this dang'rous sword resign,
Which threats your life, whil'st you are begging
  mine.

Ch. King Ferdinand, 'twere more generous to spare
These haughty words to him, who shall forbear
To use his sword on one he can chastise,
And tread on him who at his mercy lyes.
Were y' in the head of armies you should see,
In half this time I'd try your gallantry ;
But for that high contest you're brought too low,
And now, say what you will, I'll pity show.
   Ferd. How, pity me ! whence does this baseness
      spring,
To talk of childish pity to a King ?
Kings' falls are glorious like the setting sun,
And crowns are splendid when they 're trampled
      on ;
And since this secret is to thee unknown,
Thou merit'st not the glory of thy own.
And for the blasphemy thy tongue has said,
To revenge Kings I'll snatch it from thy head.
   Ch. Are you some god that you can wonders do ?
   Ferd. Can none but gods the mighty Charles
      subdue ?
   Ch. That human valour must be strangely great,
Whose single sword whole armies can defeat.
   Ferd. You'll to the refuge of your army fly !
   Ch. A King may shun an angry deity ;
But, valiant Ferdinand, do not tempt your fate !
Let's find some way to end this high debate :
Princes like you unfortunately brave,
It is my glory to oblige and save.
   Ferd. If you're inclined to end this fatal strife,
And return home in safety, beg your life.
   Ch. I must not this high insolence forgive,
Heav'ns ! He'll not suffer me to let him live. [*Aside.*
A generous pity long has held my hand ;
But my wronged fame does now your life demand.
Though 'gainst my glory you have nought to stake,
Yet of these odds I'll no advantage make,

But end the warlike game I have begun,
And for this crown, which I have fairly won,
Here in the face of the whole Kingdom fight,
And, till the combat's done, disclaim my right.

Asc. Rather than tribute pay to his renown,
Sir, let us force your passage to the town.

Ch. Yes, you shall die, for I have sworn——
Who e'er I find possest of Naples crown
Shall die, if of the house of Arragon.
This vow I in my father's life-time made,
When I decreed this Kingdom to invade.
Nay, and this sword,——
Was then made sacred to the high design
Of rooting out the Arragonian line:
And now you die, and die by none but me,
Out of respect to Kingly dignity.

Ferd. If you have made that vow
To your dead father, and the pow'rs above,
Employ your army lest you perjur'd prove.

Ch. Let fall your braving vein, lest all that hear
Suspect y' endeavour to disguise your fear.

Ferd. My fear! Wer't thou a god I would not bear
So rude a word, and none that mortal are
Shall dare to think it.——

Ch. Now, I find you're brave;
But after all, mayn't I your friendship have?

Ferd. Yes, Charles, I give it thee, and as to him,
Whom only upon earth I can esteem:
And if thy valour dooms me not to live,
I freely shall thy generous sword forgive,
And die thy friend, and thank the Heav'ns and thee
For my brave fate, and braver enemy.

Ch. Let's with embraces then, my valiant friend,
Begin that friendship which too soon must end.

Lew. The King too grand excess of honour shews.
                    [*Charles* and *Ferdinand embrace.*
Mom. He doth, but yet I dare not interpose.

Asc. Can there no way be thought on to unite
These two great rival Monarchs, ere they fight?
Whose sacred blood, that must profusely flow,
Out-values all the crowns the earth can shew.

   Ch. Command my troops some distance to
     remove: *[To Momp.*
And let my guards of horse surround the grove!
On pain of death let not a man presume
To interpose, what e'er may be my doom:
And if my fortune does my fall decree,
Pay him the loyalty you owe to me.
               [Lewis and Momp. go out.

   Ferd. With what large wings his glory takes her
     flight,
And leaves my fainting honour out of sight.

*The two Kings are preparing to fight, and are
interrupted by a noise of arms without, and
Mompensier re-enters.*

   Mom. Great sir, a noise of arms from yonder hill
Doth all your squadrons with disorder fill.

   Ch. Haste! meet 'um with my troops, whilst we
     conclude,
Ere these new fighters on our ground intrude.

         Enter LEWIS *in haste.*

   Lew. Sir, from the vaults of yonder spreading
     wood,
O' th' sudden opes new scenes of war and blood,
Their rallied troops new courages display,
And demand back the triumphs of the day.
Some th' old revolted General does head;
But the most daring are by Salerne led;
He and the General unite their force,
And break through all your pikes and guards of
     horse.

   Ferd. Shall I my crown to slaves and rebels
     owe?

Villains ! [*Proffers to go out and is stayed by Charles.*
   Ch. Hold, valiant friend ! I beg you stay !
   Ferd. Your life's in danger, sir, with this delay.
   Ch. And so is your's : those horrid slaves design,
No doubt, to take your life as well as mine ;
For all their rage from desperation springs,
And they hate all that bear the name of Kings.
   Ferd. My sword shall teach 'um what to Kings
      they owe.
   Ch. Rather that duty to my troops allow.
   Ferd. Perhaps 'tis more than all your troops
      can do.
Rather I'll out, and save your troops and you.
   Ch. Fear not ! my army can their force withstand.
   Ferd. And I'm their King, and can the slaves
      command.
   Ch. You may command 'um then. Leave me to
      fight !
   Ferd. You've had your turn t' oblige, now 'tis
      my right.
Which you in justice ought not to invade.
   Ch. We shall contend till we are both betray'd.
   Ferd. My sword shall from that danger set you
      free,
The glory of your death's design'd for me ;
But now your life in honour I'll defend,
Till we with equal fame our high debate shall end.
                       [*Exit.*
   Ch. End it you shall, for I'll perform my vow ;
But I'll not take your life till glories shall allow :
Till then this little friendship I'll receive ;
But I'll protect your life, without your leave.
Go, aid the King, and cut the rebels down !
                   [*To an officer.*
Then with my army guard him safe to town.
   Lew. He may get safe to town, but, sir, I fear
He will but small security find there :

For trembling Naples, of your arms afraid,
On their high walls your banners have display'd,
Willing to pay you the allegiance due
To th' Crown of France, and own no King but
      you.
Ch. Sir, you mistake, 'tis to my sword that they
All their submission and allegiance pay.
Those, who are rais'd to glorious heights of power
The vulgar with implicit faith adore,
Whilst noble spirits oft dispute too late,
And so become the Martyrs of the State.
I'll go receive the town in my command,
Punish the traitors, and save Ferdinand,
Lest he mistaken to their refuge fly,
And by some base mechanic villain die.

The Scene changes to a Room in the Palace.

Enter JULIA and IRENE.

Jul. You see how all my follies I declare!
Oh, do not trust 'um to the moving air :
For here I kneel, and vow if e'er they're known,
I'le kill my self, and will the truth disown.
Iren. Why so? Is't such a vile and abject thing
To love a youthful conqu'ror, and a King?
'Tis generous love, and shews your courage high,
That you disdain for less than Kings to die.
Jul. I but to love a shape, a flying thought,
A dream, an image in the fancy wrought!
Iren. 'Twas strange indeed! But oh! I long to
      hear
In what bright shape this vision did appear.
Jul. 'Twas late last night,——
When various noises flew in ev'ry room
Throughout the palace, crying, Charles is come ;
And with the mournful sound of news so bad,
All eyes were weeping, and all hearts were sad :
I to my apartment went.

Iren.   And so did I.
To such misfortunes who could tears deny ?
    Jul. Where, for a while contending with my fears,
My soul o'er flow'd with grief, my eyes with tears,
My heart with love, my courage with disdain,
My tongue with pray'rs and vows, my head with pain,
My mind with Charles' glory and renown ;
Opprest with all these weights, I laid me down.
And listened to a gentle slumber's call,
Which husht the noise, and reconcil'd 'um all.
    Iren. And whither then did gentle sleep entice
Your wand'ring thoughts ?
    Jul.   To a fair Paradise,
Planted with bright abodes for heavenly powers,
Shaded with pleasant groves, perfum'd with
        flowers,
Cool'd with soft winds, which gently walk'd the
        round,
Still dancing to their own harmonious sound,
And to each grove and palace did repair,
And as they danc'd fan'd odours through the air.
    Iren. From these abodes the shadow did appear?
    Jul. Yes, in a shape too bright for mortal eyes
        to bear.
From his fair brows the glories of a crown,
Like dazzling streams of day, came flowing down
To pay their shining tribute to his eyes,
And then rebounding with more glory rise.
In his stern looks, beauty and courage strove,
Both threatening war, and yet inviting love ;
In all his stature, beauty, garb and mein,
Something so charming and divine was seen ;
Revelling gods might in those beauties play,
Or dress themselves on some triumphal day.
    Iren. Oh ! I am charm'd ! Heav'ns, I can hear
        no more,
And did you not the God-like shape adore ?

Jul. In a soft qualm, I fell upon my knees,
Fainting with love and dying by degrees,
My sinking spirit ready to withdraw ;
Which when, me thought, the royal shadow saw.
With a soft voice he cried, see, see, she dies,
And gently came, and kist my closing eyes.
   Iren. Oh heav'ns ! that I could such a vision see,
Or dreaming so, dream to eternity.
   Jul. Then rais'd with words and kisses so
     divine,
Me thought he clasped his royal hand in mine,
And in my rapture led me all along,
O'er flowry greens, and through a martial throng,
To a fair temple in a shady grove,
Where pilgrims visited the shrines of love,
Without, 'twas all beset with shades of night,
Within, bespangled with celestial light,
Me thoughts I sigh'd !
   Iren. But sure you would not wake,
You would not such a pleasant dream forsake ?
   Jul. Not till a sacred Priest, by his commands,
Had at a chrystal altar join'd our hands.
   Iren. Love courted you, disguised in masquerade;
But yet
How came this mask within your fancy played,
Where no machines of love before were brought,
To move and raise the pleasant scenes of thought ?
   Jul. I had been frail before.   I oft had sate
And heard my sister Isabel relate
The glories of that King:—Had seen his picture too,
And my heart snatcht new flames at every view.
But see ! Euphemia comes, and in her eyes
Discovers grief, and in her mein surprize.

Enter EUPHEMIA.

Ah ! thy unhappy message quickly say.
   Euph. Madam, undone, the King has lost the day !

And now distrest, and by his foes subdu'd,
Is by his own rebellious slaves pursu'd.
   Jul. Oh Heavens! where will my royal brother
    fly?
   Euph. Heaven knows! This cursed city does deny
To save their King, nay, rather are at strife
Which way they shall dispose his sacred life.
   Jul. Oh, cursed traitors! oh, I faint with fear.
                           [*Exit.*
   Iren. Be not disturb'd so much at what you
    hear;
Angels will be his guard:——But see, the Queen!

    Enter ISABELLA, CORNELIA, PORTIA, SYLVIA.

I fear she is preparing to be gone.
   Euph. All her retinue, madam, left the town
Some hours ago.   [*Exit.*
   Iren. That I had left it too, when first I came,
Or going now could leave behind this flame, [*Aside.*
   Isab. How, not a letter, not a message yet.——
                         [*Aside.*
From the proud King? Doth he my name forget?
Unconstant Charles! th'ast made my honour bleed,
To take thy life were an heroic deed.
   Cor. The Duchess highly doth her state resent,
Her soul is fill'd with haughty discontent.
   Isab. Madam, my grief is troublesome, I fear,
I beg your pardon if I leave you here,
My sorrow doth a share on you impose,
And sorrow flatter'd more imperious grows.
   Por. My Princess is disturb'd, and I perceive
For what it is her swelling heart doth grieve.
   Isab. Portia, the jewels which from France I
    brought.
And those were sent from thence, let 'um be
    sought.
   Por. Madam, they shall!   [*Exit Isab.*

I thought from whence this mighty grief did spring,
She does resent the unkindness of the King.
                         [*Aside.   Exit Por.*
  Cor. Now, to allay her sorrows she is gone,
I have got freedom to discourse my own.
Ah! Ferdinand, how much I pity thee;
And though my kindness thou shalt never see,
To my own bleeding heart is sadly known
Those pains which honour now forbids to own.
Unhappy storm that did me here convey,
And sav'd my fleet, but cast my heart away.

Enter FERDINAND, ASCANIO, *and* GENTLEMEN *with
  drawn swords, vizarded, and muffled in their cloaks.
  At their entrance the King and Ascanio fling off
  their cloaks and vizards.*

  Cor. But see! the King is here! and in disguise,
At his own gates afraid of a surprize!
                         [*Ascanio discourses with Irene.*
And now my last and fatal hour is nigh,
Which will my love and all my courage try.
  Ferd. Madam, my fate hath my hard sentence
       past,
And now I come to offer up my last
Devotion to the shrine which I adore,
And where perhaps I ne'er shall offer more;
For all those glories I am doom'd to lose,
Which might my high aspiring flame excuse:
But, now uncrown'd, I must no more pursue
The envied glory of adoring you.
  Cor. Sir, since you first was pleas'd to talk of
       love,
You know I all occasions did remove
From treating wi' you, on a design so vain,
Which I in honour ne'er could entertain;
For though as Sovereigns we equals are,
And so you had no reason for despair:

Yet as a widow Queen, that lately paid
Her solemn sorrow to the royal shade
Of her dead lord, I surely must reprove
All new addresses of a second love.
    Fer. These forms of sorrow may a while remain:
But shall the dead over the living reign ?
They in the other world their joys receive,
Must we not share in this without their leave ?
    Cor. The dead but absent are, and out o' sight,
Shall they for a short absence lose their right ?
If to your memory my tears were due,
You would not have me be unjust to you.
But ——
'Tis not my temper, sir, this may convince !
T'insult at all o'er a dejected Prince.
                    [*Puts her Handkerchief before her face.*
No, sir, I've found a shelter in your port,
Respect from you, and honour in your Court.
For which I would in gratitude restore
Your ruin'd fortunes, were it in my power:
But how can she support another's throne,
Who is depos'd and banisht from her own ?
A distrest Queen, who since the old King died,
Have been too much opprest on every side.
The Egyptian Sultans threating every hour
T'invade my kingdom with their mighty power,
And none to guard me from this threat'ned fate,
But my good fathers, the Venetian State.
                            [*Ironice.*

Who wisely did adopt me in design,
My falling crown t'entice me to resign.
Thither I go, forc'd by a fate so rude,
To spend my days in pious solitude.
Then, sir, since I shall never see you more,
May Heav'n your royal family restore !
And that I may a little grateful seem,
You shall not want my prayers, nor my esteem.

Ferd. Ah, madam! now you shew your generous
    mind,
You pity most where most distress you find.
Your timely bounties succour the forlorn,
When all his dying patience was out-worn.
I feel a pleasing extasy of joy,
Which does all present sense of grief destroy.
But, ah! how soon will all my pain return
When I shall think I must for ever mourn?
To air its wings love takes a soaring flight,
And then must fall in endless shades of night.

Enter a GENTLEMAN *in haste.*

Gen. The King! The King! You're lost, sir, if
    you stay,
The traitrous rabble will your life betray;
Or else in chains your royal person bring
A present to the new triumphant King.

    Ferd. Alas, poor men! It is no news to find
Fear, driving all the herds of lower mankind;
The timorous hare will o'er the hunters leap,
When sh'as no other way for her escape.
Could there no other means for safety be?
These would betray their God as well as me.

    Iren. And will you have poor wanderers in mind?
No, my Ascanio, when the fleeting wind
Has snatcht us hence, my soul may bid adieu
To this fair shore, to hopeless love and you.

    Asc. D'ye think I will commit a crime so great?
Can humble votaries their saints forget,
To whose fair images they hourly pray,
Whose ador'd shrines they visit every day?
My dear, my fairest saint, to think of thee
Shall all my pleasure and devotion be:
But why should we despair to meet again?

    Iren. Yes, we may meet, but Heav'n knows
    where or when!

Asc. Then you may stay behind.
Iren.   And you may go!— -
Asc. What, to forsake my King ? That were
    below
The faithful subject I have ever been.
    Iren. And 'twere as bad for me to leave my
      Queen ;
But when I'm gone I shall lament in vain,
Your heart some happier love will entertain.
I die to think !——
    Asc.   By all that's good I swear !
    Iren. O, my imperious grief I cannot bear !
New pangs of sorrow do besiege my heart,
Like those of death,—when soul and body part.
    Asc. She swoons !   [*She swoons in his arms.*
    Ferd. I now like tortur'd souls look up with pain
On joys of angels which I can't obtain.
They from those visions fly to deep despair,
And I from joys of love to blood and war ;——
                        [*Aside.*
For if from friends I any aid can find,
In some brave death I'll ease my wounded mind.
Come, madam, since my heavy doom is past,——
                        [*To Cor.*
As men condemn'd to execution haste,
To ease their souls of weight they cannot bear
Of griefs unknown, which more than death they
    fear ;
So give me leave to haste those joys away,
Which are but torment whilst they vainly stay.
And thus that wealth I to the winds restore
They lent awhile, and ne'er will lend me more.
                        [*Ex. Om.*

ACT IV.

The Scene the Town of Naples.

Enter PRINCE OF SALERNE *and* TRIVULTIO, *muffled
in their cloaks and disguised.*

Sal. How! March in pomp and triumph through
   the town,
Whilst I that name, which threatened Kings
   disown!
Must I be buried thus alive, whilst he,
Advanc'd by fortune's servile flattery,
Marches in State to meet the haughty charms
Of her I love, and revel in her arms!
Damn'd be this tame disguise, —— I will appear,
And Charles from th' arms of love and fortune tear.
   Tri. Hold! let not valour, sir, your life betray;
                     [*Sal. offers to go.*
Nor demand debts which fortune cannot pay.
I know his triumphs to your sword are due:
But, ——
   Sal. But what? do'st thou adore his fortune too?
   Tri. How, I adore it? —— No sir, curs'd be he,
That shall deny by any treachery
To take that life he to our swords does owe,
When fortune shall a fair occasion show:
But I'd not dun my stars when they are poor,
And so gain nothing but enrage 'um more.
   Sal. If bankrupt fortune's poor, I'll fall on
   those,
On whom profusely she my wealth bestows.
Charles has my mistress, does my triumphs wear,
My wealth's in's hands, and I'll arrest it there.
I'll kill him,
Only to let th' imperious woman see
The arrogant folly of disdaining me.
                     [*Offers again to go.*

Tri. Hold! since you'll go, let us our fortunes join,
I'll share i'th glory of this great design ;
Besides th' revenge to my lost fame is due,
I've some concerns of love as well as you.
For Julia I a long hid flame have borne,
Though I've supprest it ;——
Knowing too well the Arragonian scorn,
Who to my sword have paid so small regard,
They thought their service was its own reward.
But now I'll clear the scores another way ;
Her beauty all my old arrears shall pay.
  Sal She's thine! there's nothing shall be left
    undone,
That may bring down the pride of Arragon.
  Tri. Let's go, then, whilst our raging blood does
    boil, ——
Whilst the French guards, wearied with this day's
    toil,
Disperst in quarters to their rest betake
All but whom lust and wine may keep awake ;
Whilst they in pleasure, or repose engag'd,
Our friends alarm'd and the town enraged,
We'll go to th' palace in secure disguise.
  Sal. No more! I scorn to kill him by surprise!
What I'll attempt, I'll do in open day,
And let his guards and genius stop my way :——
Then if I live or die, destroy or save,
Success or death I equally will brave.   [*Exit.*
  Tri. This high ungovern'd flame I must allay.
I seek revenge!——
But then I'd seek it the securest way.
But heav'ns! Which way shall this great deed be
    wrought,
My soul is lost in a wild maze of thought!
But yet I'll boldly on.——
He who through dang'rous ways does fate pursue,
Must not the depths of precipices view :

But with high courage, and a bold address,
Spur on, and leave to fortune the success.

[Exit.

The SCENE changes to a Room of State.

Enter CHARLES, LEWIS, MOMPENSIER, GUARD.

Ch. Gone to attend the Queen ?——
Lew. To guard her hence!
Ch. What need of guards, where there's no violence
Design'd ?——
   Mom. He fear'd lest the Venetian fleet
Might from your galleys some obstruction meet.
   Ch. Going to serve a Queen, regain his crown,
To raise my honour, and repair his own,
Could he suspect my fleet would stop his way ?
No, ——rather all my galleys shall convey
The King to any port, where he intends
To try his fortune, or has hopes of friends.
   Lew. Going with those, whose masters have declar'd
Themselves your enemies, he justly fear'd
Your anger, sir!——
   Ch. He did ?—— That treacherous State
Has disoblig'd me at the highest rate,
Have broke their faith with me, and out of fear,
And envy to my rising glories here,
Creep into leagues, and private friendships court,
That I might fire their galleys in the port :——
But since they attend the Queen——
I'll spare their galleys, and reprieve the doom
Of that false State, till my returning home ;
But to the Queen——
Command my Admiral that he honours pay,
And whilst she stays her orders to obey.——

[To an Officer who goes out.

Mon. But dares, great sir, the false Venetian
    State
Abuse your friendship?——
    Ch.   That we'll now debate!

CHARLES *seats himself, and enter a* SECRETARY *with
    Papers and Despatches.*

    Ch. Not only they,—— but all
Th' Italian Princes are in Council sate,
Each fears to lose his little coronet.
Nay, by th' intelligence I've now receiv'd,
All Kings and States with my success are griev'd,
Doubting themselves, and knowing not how high
Ambition raised, with victory may fly.
Rome, Millane, Venice, Germany, and Spain,
With all the little Princes they can gain,
Are all in bonds of strict alliance tied,
To check, as they pretend, my growing pride,
That I must now make war on half mankind,
And gain that Empire which I ne'er design'd.
    Mon. Rome perjur'd too?
    Ch. Yes, Venice, Millane, Rome,
Agree to intercept my passage home,
Are arming frontiers, raising troops with speed;
Which the fam'd Duke of Mantua must lead,
The great Gonzaga, one whose fame is high,
And on his conduct they do all rely.
    Lew. Sir, that an envious and mechanic State,
Whose nature is crown'd heads to fear and hate,
A Prince's glory thus should undermine,
I not admire;——but such a low design.
That Rome should aid?——
    Mon. And join with Sforza too!
A barb'rous Prince, who did his hands embrue
In his young master's blood,——and basely made
Our wars his opportunity, to invade
His life and crown, and act his villanies!

Ch. That bloody traitor Sforza I'll chastise!
But now that Rome should join in league with
    these,
When for his fame had given me hostages,
Enrages me! ——
   Lew. You must betimes disperse
These gathering clouds that threaten storms so
    fierce.
   Mom. First shake your rods o'er th' Ecclesiastic
    chair!
That busy-headed priest, you must not spare.
He is Heaven's usher in the world's great school,
Only to teach, for Kings have highest rule.
   Ch. Whate'er his office or commission be,
I'll make Rome know his duty now to me.
He shall not baffle Kings, under pretence,
With all Heaven's laws his office can dispense;
He swore me faith! and, if the powers divine
Slight their own honour, none shall sport with mine.
Cousin of Orleans march to-night away,
With all my choicest men! ——
   Lew.   Sir, one night's stay
Your wearied men for rest would humbly crave.
   Ch. Then let 'um short and gentle marches have:
But move this evening, though you march not far;
For expedition is the life of war!
   Mom. Send not too many for your safety sake,
Lest this rebellious town advantage take.
And what's so desp'rate as an angry slave,
When by adventuring he revenge may have?
   Ch. Leave fifteen thousand foot.   Your march
    direct
To Rome —— I'll follow and no time neglect.
                      [*Exit Lew.*

What, did you visit yet as I desir'd,
The Duchess Isabel?
   Mom.   Sir, she retir'd

To her apartment, and with haughty pride
Retains her State, and visitants denied.
 Ch. Alas! she well might have that pride
  forborne,
To one that values not her love or scorn.
She, that had such a Monarch in her chain,
Would a young petty rival entertain,——
Makes me contemn the name of royal slave,
And slight the little wounds her beauty gave:
But now we've settled all our grand affair,
And the declining day begins to wear
His milder beams, let's out, and taste a while
The fresher air; for I with this day's toil
Am weary grown!
 Mom. The gardens, sir, are nigh,
From hence they open to your prospect lye.

*CHARLES and MOMPENSIER go out, and the Scene is
drawn and a fair garden is presented. JULIA sitting
as asleep in an Arbour: EUPHEMIA waiting by.*

A Song within.

Whilst the Song is sung, CHARLES and MOMPENSIER

Enter. CHARLES gazes on JULIA.

The Song sung to JULIA in the Garden.

Oh love! if e'er thou'lt ease a heart,
  That owns thy power divine,
That bleeds with thy too cruel dart,
And pants with never ceasing smart;
  Take pity now on mine.
Under the shade, I fainting lye!
A thousand times I wish to die;
But when I find cold death too nigh,
   I grieve to lose my pleasing pain,
   And call my wishes back again.

But thus as I sat all alone,
    I'th shady myrtle grove,
And to each gentle sigh and moan,
Some neighbouring echo gave a groan,
    Came by the man I love.
Oh ! how I strove my griefs to hide !
I panted, blush'd, and almost died,
And did each tattling echo chide,
    For fear some breath of moving air,
    Should to his ears my sorrows bear.

Yet oh, ye powers ! I'd die to gain
    But one poor parting kiss !
And yet I'd be on racks of pain,
Ere I'd one thought or wish retain,
    Which honour thinks amiss.
Thus are poor maids unkindly us'd,
By love and nature both abus'd,
Our tender hearts all ease refus'd ;
    And, when we burn with secret flame,
    Must bear our griefs, or die with shame.

  Ch. I'm startled, see ! What divine shape is
    there ?
Some angel sure, —— no mortal is so fair !
  Mom. Some airy vision does deceive our eyes.
  Ch. Heavens ! like a bright unbodied soul she
    lyes
Wrapt in a shape of pure ætherial air,
To some fair body ready to repair.
Know'st thou whom this bright shape resembles
    most ?
  Mom. None but the Princess Julia, sir, dare
    boast
These angel beauties ——
She to the Duchess's apartment came,
Whilst I was there : these beauties are the same.

Ch. The Princess Julia!
Mom. How his eyes are fixt! ——   [*Aside.*
Sir!
If any knowledge of your heart I learn,
You view this lovely shape with some concern.
    Ch. I do! and must acknowledge
I feel within my heart a passion move,
Like the soft pantings of approaching love.
And if from war I could the leisure gain,
Th' insinuating guest to entertain,
My heart might be seduc'd by one so fair
To love, and fix my roving passion there! ——
But to
Remoter parts o'th' gardens let's repair,
To take [our] breathings of the evening air.

*They go out betwixt the Scenes, as into the garden, and
    enter* SALERNE, *and* TRIVULTIO, *follow'd by several,
    all habited like the French Guards.*

    Tri. So, we 've securely past in this disguise, ——
Let's watch a fair occasion for surprize.
    Sal. Surprize?—make an alarm,—for he shall
        die,
Were all his guards, and his whole Kingdom by.
    Tri. But let us wait for the approach of night—
    Sal. Let night be damn'd,——
I'll kill him new in Isabella's sight,
That every wound I give him she may feel!
And, when he's fallen by my revengeful steel,
She wild and raving may his death bemoan,
Tear out his bleeding heart and stab her own.
See there!—He walks——
                    [*Looks within the scenes.*
    Tri. Silence!—for Heaven's sake.——
    Sal. Nor Heaven——
Nor hell shall hinder the revenge I'll take,

Were death 'twixt him and me I would not stay.
                    [*Goes out 'twixt the Scenes.*
  Tri. Ye powers, he'll our designs and lives betray!
Haste! let the garden avenues be barr'd,
                    [*To one of his followers.*
Before we give suspicion to the guard.——
Thou to the postern run, where our men wait,
                    [*To a second.*
On a sign giv'n t' aid, as in our retreat,
Unlock it with this key, and then remove
Part of our men, to th' private myrtle grove.
Place'um i' the grotto, by the dark descent,
Where we may fly, if the French guards prevent
Our other passage! Heavens! what is't I see?
The Princess here!—blest opportunity!
Now!—now's the time! you run and aid the Prince,
You stay and help me to convey her hence!——

They go out several ways, TRIVULTIO *and a party
towards* JULIA, *who shrieks and runs off the Stage,
crying, murder! At the same time clashing of
swords within is heard, and immediately enter*
CHARLES *defending Julia, and pursued by* SALERNE,
TRIVULTIO *and his party;* SALERNE *beating down
the sword of* TRIVULTIO, *and the rest.*

  Sal. Villains retire! I don't your succours need,
The tyrant by my hand alone shall bleed! ·
  Ch. Thou'rt brave! who e'er thou art!

*As Salerne and the rest are going about to assault
Charles; Enter* MOMPENSIER *and a* GUARD,
*rushing on all sides of the Stage, crying treason!
and assist Charles, all assaulting Salerne, who with
Trivultio are forced off the Stage by Charles and the
Guard, after which Julia recovers herself from her
surprize.*

  Jul. Oh heavens! in what confusions have I been.
With what my heart has felt, my eyes have seen!

Sav'd by the King? my ruin'd heart's betray'd
Into an ambush which my stars have made.
Punisht for doting on an airy shape,
My enslav'd heart must never hope to 'scape!
    Euph. Fate seems not,
By this surprize, your flame to disapprove,
Rather exalts it to a generous love.
    Jul. But all in vain.
    Euph. A Princess young and fair!——
Such youth and beauty's yours should ne'er despair.
    Jul. But when I love a Prince I ought to hate,
What passion can be more unfortunate?

Enter CHARLES *as from the Chase of Salerne, &c.*

    Jul. But see, he comes! My yielding spirits fly!
Help me Euphemia!——or I faint,—— and die!
    Ch. Madam! How much am I asham'd, you find
Such barbarous treatment here, where I design'd
You with all honour should be entertain'd?
Giving commands, that whilst you here remain'd
My slaves the same respect to you should bear,
As if the King, your father, govern'd here.
But since my guards——
Did not this horrid villany prevent,
Your own fair mouth shall name their punishment.
    Jul. Sir, rather let
Those slaves of ours, if they are fled, be sought,
Who 'gainst your life have this bold treason
        wrought;
For, sir, the horrid villany th'ave done,
I know my royal brother will disown;
And punish too if he had so much power.——
And though from the obliging conqueror,
By all brave ways he will his crown redeem,
For this great act——
He will his gen'rous enemy esteem.

Ch. Ah, madam! though by my unhappy fate
I've been too much expos'd to your just hate,
And in pursuit of fame have been betray'd
To all those wars, ——
I with the house of Arragon have made.
I now acknowledge I so vanquisht am,
That I for ever do renounce the name
Of enemy, ——
And do repent the crimes my sword has done, ——
And at your feet will lay the crown I've won.

Jul. Sir, you know best your guilt or innocence,
I shall not judge you for your wrong pretence.
Let heaven do that to whom our right is known:
But if my brother e'er regain his crown,
The obligation, now on us you have laid,
Shall be, some gen'rous way, by him repaid.

As JULIA *is going,* CHARLES *proffers to lead her by the hand, which she seems to refuse, and withdraws her hand: At the same time enter* ISABELLA.

Isab. As from my close retirement I withdrew,
Methoughts wild noises from the gardens flew,
And horrid cries loud echos did repeat. ——
Has the proud tyrant some disaster met?

Discovers CHARLES *leading* JULIA *within the Scenes.*

Isab. But, ha! the tyrant, and my sister
    there!
Oh! cursed vision quickly disappear! ——
I'll charm you, be you spirits bad or good, ——
I'll rend your shapes, I'll circle you in blood.

JULIA *goes,—and* CHARLES *turns and sees* ISABELLA.

Ch. Ha!
The Duchess Isabel!
Isab. Yes, sir, 'tis I!
I fear I have disturb'd your privacy;

If so, great sir! I do your pardon crave.
  Ch. Madam, for that you need no pardon have,
Since all the palace is at your command!
  Isab. I'm glad my liberty I understand;——
But pray, sir,——
On your fair Princess to'r apartment wait,
This kindness then we farther will debate.
  Ch. Madam,—your counsel I do well approve;
But none need teach me——
What duty I should pay to those I love!
  Isab. Thou lov'st!—Immortal powers! with un-
      mov'd brows
Dar'st thou relate how thou contemn'st thy vows?
  Ch. The vows
To Isabel of Arragon I made,
To Millane's Duchess ought not to be paid.
  Isab. But Millane's injur'd Duchess shall chastise
Th' inconstant Prince, that dares her love despise.
Heavens! thou inflamest me to so great a rage,
That nothing but thy blood shall it assuage.
  Ch. Good madam, what should this great passion
      mean?
Is it because you have inconstant been,
And now into a fit of rage are flown,
To hide those faults which you disdain to own?
  Isab. Tyrant, I never did a crime commit,
But when my heart did to thy love submit.
Thy love! thy hate! thy scorn! for which I now
Would stab that heart which would so poorly bow,
And with false meteors so deluded be,
But that I live to have revenge on thee.
  Ch. Madam, first seek revenge on your own
      scorn,
Which vainly slighted crowns you might have
      worn,
And your preposterous pride, did in my stead,
Advance a puny lover to your bed.——

Whose little coronet——
   Isab. Preposterous pride!
   Ch. Yes, when for Millane, France should be
     denied.
   Isab. Thou fir'st my blood! I'm rackt with
     grief and shame,
Wouldst thou have had me stay, and court thy
     flame?
Thy feign'd addresses did not I receive,
And for thy loit'ring flame in silence grieve,
Waiting the motion of thy painted fire,
Till modesty compell'd me to retire?
Then by a thousand differing passions led,
Was I not forc'd into that Prince's bed,
By such commands I durst not disobey,
And by distractions of more power then they?
And now of him and all my friends bereft,
The kingdom lost, and no assistance left,
Opprest both by thy falsehood, and thy sword,
Dost thou such recompence as this afford?
   Ch. Madam!
   Isab. No more,—no more, insulting Prince!
Treat not a lady with this insolence!
Is this your valour, mighty King! t'oppress
A poor afflicted Princess in distress?
Go hide thy head with shame, and with some fear!
For know thy fall!—thy fall,—proud King, is near;
Th'ast robb'd me of all my friends, ——
Thou shalt not rob me of my courage too;
I will do more than all our troops could do.
The glory of our house I'll yet regain,
And all thy laurels in thy blood I'll stain.   [*Exit.*
   Ch. Alas poor lady! I her pain perceive,
She sees 'tis vain for her old scorn to grieve;
And now, to soften her remorseless fate,
Flatters herself with pride, revenge and hate. ——
But see Mompensier here,

Enter MOMPENSIER.

And by his looks do some ill tidings bear.
   Mom. Ah, sir! ——
The bearer of ill news I'm forc'd to be. ——
Not only the actors of this villany
Have scap'd our hands, and made a safe retreat,
But in the harbour the Venetian fleet——
   Ch. How! does my Admiral my orders slight,
Or without leave dares he presume to fight,
Or stop the fleet?—his boldness I'll chastise,—
Fire on my Admiral from the batteries!
On him, and all my galleys till they cease,
And of King Ferdinand humbly beg for peace.
Fire on 'um! —— Haste!——
   Mom. Alas! sir, all's too late,
Both Princes have already met their fate.
The Queen—is lost. ——
   Ch. What wast thou saidst, the Queen?——
   Mom. Yes, sir, her galley in distress was seen
Rowing to land, but, ere it gain'd the shore,
Sunk in the billows, and was seen no more.
   Ch. Oh! fatal accident! which way shall I
Make satisfaction for this villany ——
To Heaven, and all that will her blood demand,
And which is more to injur'd Ferdinand?
   Mom. Sir, 'twas the King himself did first
     engage,
Fir'd with a haughty and ungovern'd rage,
To see his fleet confin'd, and yours controul
The shore along the channel, and the Mole,
And he must at your Admiral's pleasure stay,
He fought through blood and flame to make his
     way,
And had destroy'd your fleet,
Had not the news of the Queen's loss done more
Than bullets could to save it from his power;

For with the news he fell,——and with him——
Victory fell, his galleys sunk with fear,
And all his scenes of triumph disappear!
And fortune, whom his valour had constrain'd,
Stole from his sword, and liberty regain'd,——
And now——
After the wonders which his sword had wrought,
He is among guards ashore a prisoner brought.
   Ch. A prisoner! My Admiral dies for this!
With a strict guard ashore the villain bring!
                         [*To one that waits.*
Thou with a train go meet the injur'd King,
                              [*To Momp.*
Wait his commands, pay all submissions due
To his high quality and valour too.
Declare my innocence, his pardon crave,
And, whilst he stays, let him all honours have. [*Exit.*
   Mom. With how much glory these two Kings
      contend,
Each other's generous enemy, and friend.
My King
To Ferdinand's crown and friendship does lay
     siege,
And strives at once to conquer and oblige:
But Ferdinand judges it a greater thing,
To subdue Heaven and fortune than a King.
But see! he comes,—and ha!——

Enter FERDINAND *and* ASCANIO *brought as prisoners
by the guard.*

A weighty grief hangs on his royal brow,
His mighty soul does to his sorrows bow!
   Ferd. Cornelia dead! what is't I have done?
My fair Cornelia, whither art thou gone?
Celestial shade! If yet there may not be
Too many clouds 'twixt my dark soul and thee,

Look down, and see my grief, and oh ! forgive
That fatal pride, which would not let thee live ;
But rather would to fate thy life expose,
Than take one kindness from my conquering foes :
I am thy murderer, and at my hand,
Fair Queen ! thou must thy guiltless blood
    demand ;
Nor shalt thou ask in vain, and be denied
His wretched life by whom Cornelia died ;
Rather new torments for myself I'll find,
And, dying, beg the curse of all mankind.
   Mon. His sorrow does his royal soul oppress,
            [*Momp. beckons away the Guard.*
That 'tis no time I find for my address.
   Asc. Now he begins his passions to disclose,
And now, alas ! I dare not interpose !—— [*Aside.*
   Ferd. For the Queen's body let all search be
    made,
And, when she's found, and I've appeas'd her shade,
Inter us in such decent state,———
As may our royal qualities become,
And lay us both together in one tomb.
This kindness to thy care I recommend ——
               [*To Asc.*
The last thou e'er shalt pay thy King and friend.
To stoop to Charles my spirit is too high,
Though, if I ask'd it, he would not deny
That friendly act ; for I have found him brave,
And this is all the recompense I crave
Of him, or of the angry pow'rs above,
For my lost crown, and unsuccessful love.
             [*Exeunt Omnes.*

Act V.

Enter EUPHEMIA, *with a light, conducting* JULIA.

Euph. Oh, madam! Fly from hence, I've over-
    heard
Your sister's dark designs, and now a guard
Of her own slaves are coming here with speed,
To bring you to her hands, alive or dead.
    Jul. Oh heavens! What shall I do?
    Euph. This,—This way fly!——
I'll shew you where you may in safety lye,
And over-hear her talk aloud, and rave,
And vow to Heaven what deep revenge she'll have.
                          [Exit.

Several pass over the Stage, as in search of Julia:
    The Scene changes to Isabella's apartment. Enter
    ISABELLA *followed by the same that past over the Stage.*

    Isab. How, fled? Then, I'm betray'd!——
Which on you, villains, have this treason wrought?
I'll have your bloods if she's not quickly brought.
                       [They go out.
But Heavens, I see!——
All vermin from a falling palace run,
And love to sport in the warm rising sun.
Though I to flatter fate have stoopt so low,
To seek Trivultio's aid and Salerne's too,
They now despise me,——
And I, who was obey'd, ador'd by all,
Must helpless stand and see my temples fall.

    Enter TRIVULTIO *in disguise.*

    Isab. Ha!—What creeping thing art thou?——
                     [He discovers.
Trivultio!——Dull leaden fellow!——

Why hast thou tortur'd me with thy long stay ?
I've been on tedious wracks with thy delay ;
And wracks with less impatience I could bear,
Were thy troops mine, bright day should now
          appear
From the fir'd town, which should in ashes lye,
Ere the least beam of day salutes the sky,
Ere time's least atom Charles should be un-
          crown'd !
His murder'd guards in their own gore lye drown'd !
He at my feet prostrate and bleeding lye,
Begging vain pity from my scornful eye,
His trembling spirit ready to depart,
Tears in his eyes, my dagger in his heart.
    Tri. I stay'd to prepare all things ere I came,
And to entice Salerne here with hopes of fame,
And with much talk prevail'd with him to come,
And gave him keys to the dark passage room,
And vaults through which I came.——
    Isab.   What did you say
Prevail'd with him my orders to obey ?
    Tri. Yes, madam, for he now does proudly own,
He values nought but glory and renown.
    Isab. What, does he value glory more than me !
Or can there any higher glory be
Than dying at my command ?
Go, kill the slave !—Let him the glory lose,
Since he the ways of fame no better knows !
    Tri. Yes,—when he's serv'd your interests let
          him die !
But with his pride we must a while comply,
Or rather with his fortune, since the town
Rebels, and bandits do his interest own.
For on the news,——
That the French troops were on their march from
          hence,
Only some few, left for their King's defence,

A bandit came t'acquaint him,
That fifty troops under Vesuvius lay,
Who might be here some hours ere break of day,
And if he pleas'd would all their fellows bring
To murder the French guards, and crown him King.
   Isab. To a slave's fortune must I humbly bow,
What does the pride of fate subject me too!
   Tri. Madam, he comes!—Command your self
     awhile,

Enter SALERNE.

And soothe his passion with a seeming smile.
   Isab. Salerne! Though thou hast long a rebel
     been,
And all that's infamous,—Yet I have seen,
In thy attempts, a mind so bold and brave,
That for thy courage some esteem I have!
Not that I'll flatter or delude thy fate;
For know thy birth I scorn, thy person hate:
But yet thy flaming spirit I esteem,
And would thy name from infamy redeem:
And therefore out of pity do design
To honour thee with some commands of mine,
Provided still thou do submissive prove,
And first repent thy bold ambitious love.
   Sal. Was it for this you did entice me here,
Only to let your insolence appear?
I thought your soaring spirit was brought down
T'express some sorrow for the pride you'd shown:
But now since this is all,——
Know I already do deserve your love,——
And for esteem I not one step will move,
And your commands I least of all regard:
I serve my self, and will my self reward.
   Isab. How! am I scorn'd!—Ho! kill the traitor
     there!
Shall I contempt from a proud rebel bear?

SAL. *is offering to go out, and is stopped and disarmed
    by several that rush upon him from between the Scenes.
    They proffer to kill him, and* TRIVULTIO *interposes.*

   Tri. Hold, hold I say!—Ah, madam! what d'ye
    intend?
All our designs do on his sword depend.
                                    [*Aside to Isab.*

   Isab. Did the whole Kingdom perish in his fall,
To my revenge I'd sacrifice it all.
Kill him!—Hold! does he not shake
At sight of death, and the revenge I take.
There's something in his soul for greatness form'd
Which will not by ignoble fear be storm'd.
Go, live!—but dare not so presumptious be,
To think of dying for thy King or me.
   Sal. Yes, thy unjust revenge shall be pursu'd,
In spite of thee and thy ingratitude;
For I my noble passion still retain,
And still my firm unshaken self remain.   [*Exit.*
   Isab. This fellow's brave ——
Could fate th' impediments of birth remove,
A crown might make his passage to my love.
   Tri. So madam, now, we've this great spirit won,
Our high designs are ended ere begun.
   Isab. Pursue him straight, and manage him with
    care,
And in the glory of my service share.   [*Tri. Exit.*
Now my impatient soul is all on fire
To know if fate will flatter my desire.——

                Enter PORTIA.

Is the magician whom I sent for come?
   Por. Yes, madam,——all alone,——in a dark
    room,
Hung round with horrors, and the shades of night;
Which seems more horrid with the glimmering
    light

Of the pale moon, which through a crevice shines,
H'as sate this hour scoring o' mystic lines.
Winds, lightnings, whispers, sad and mournful
    groans,
Soft voices melting into pleasant tones,
Fill'd his dark cavern, whilst as magic spell
Fetter'd my feet, and thrice into a swoon I fell.
And see he comes!——

Enter MAGICIAN.

Isab. Speak, speak thy news! 'tis I thou
    tell'st it to,
I, who defy the utmost fate can do ;
For I am fixt as heaven, whose high decree
May change my fortune, but not conquer me.
  Mag. Madam, your doom I dare not yet relate,
Thick swarms of spirits in cabals are met
To read your stars, whose counsels you shall know,
When whispering winds do in my cavern blow.
Now all is still and silent.——
  Isab. Quickly call
Thy drowzy spirits from their dark cabal,
Whilst I their lazy constitutions wait,
I might kill Kings, and overturn the State.
Charles in his shadow to my view present,
And what shall be this direful day's event.
  Mag. I wish that shade you'd not desire to see,
I fear 'twill an unpleasing vision be :
But since it is your pleasure I'll obey,
Then madam in this magic circle stay.
Leave not the bounds in which you are confin'd,
And with firm courage fortify your mind.

PORTIA *goes out, and the* MAGICIAN *begins his charm.*

  Mag. Thou black familiar, who, by firm compact,
Art at all seasons bound my will to act ;
Whom I with fat of strangled infants feed,
And for thy thirst let my veins freely bleed :

Whom I for thrice seven years by name have
    known,
And when as many more are past and gone,
Must lead my soul to that infernal cell,
Where thou, and all thy fellow spirits dwell.
Arise!——and in an airy vision shew
What must befall this prince, to whom
Our conquer'd State does bow.

*There arises a Spirit, and immediately the Scene is
    drawn, and the supposed shapes of* CHARLES
    and JULIA *are presented; royally habited, and
    seated on Chairs of State, at their feet several
    Masquers; and near the Chairs the Music in
    White Robes, and Laurels on their heads. A
    Chorus of Voices and loud Music heard. The
    Duchess seems much disturb'd at the Vision, and
    with a naked poynard moves towards the shapes,
    but is stopt by the Magician, whilst at the same
    time one of the Masquers touches her with a White
    Wand, at which she seems to fall into a slumber,
    and is plac'd on a Chair by the Magician. Then
    the Masquers rise and dance; after a dance the
    Spirit descends, and the Scene closes.*

*The Song of Spirits sung to Isabella as she sits
    asleep.*

They call! They call! what voice is that?
        A lady in despair,
Whose tears and sorrows come too late,
        Her losses to repair.
By too much pride I've lost a heart
        I languish to regain :
And yet I'd kill the man I love,
        Ere own my fond disdain.
        Some gentle spirit shew the fate
        Of him I love, but feign would hate.

In vain! in vain! thou seek'st our aid,
    Thy passion to remove:
For see, alas! The sad events
    Of thy too tragic love.
See! See! The crown thou didst disdain,
    Another brow must wear,
Then sigh and weep no more in vain,
    But die in deep despair.
  May this be all proud beauties' fate,
  Still to repent their pride too late.

When Kings like Gods descend to woo,
    They must not be denied:
Nor may fond beauties damn themselves
    To please a moment's pride.
Beauty was made by th' Pow'rs above,
    Monarchs to entertain;
No greater duty is than love,
    Nor sin than proud disdain.
  Thou then who durst a King deny,
  Haste from its sight, despair and die.

Mag. Her soul's retir'd,——I'll steal away,
And leave her wrapt in sleep's soft arms,
And ere the first approach of day,
  End my unfinish'd charms.   [*Exit.*

The Mag. goes out, and immediately enters the Ghost of young GALEAZZO, *Duke of Millane, with a cup of poison in his hand. The Ghost passes over the Stage, at which* ISABELLA *starts and wakes, as in a fright.*

Isab. Ha! What pale thing art thou? and
    whither fly?
Me thought I saw young murder'd Millane's shade
Walk by in mournful state, and, as it went,
With a sad look exprest its discontent.

In what dark shade has my lost spirits been,
Where in wild shapes I've death and horror seen.
But they are liars all, nor shall defeat
My injur'd soul of a revenge so great.

The Ghost re-enters.

Isab. But ha! the ghastly shape appears again,
My frighted blood retires from every vein;
I am congeal'd at this pale scene of death,
And all my words are stifled in my breath.
Speak! what would'st have? why dost appear
      to me?
Who never wrong'd thy bed or memory,
In one the least unkind, ungrateful thought;
But to revenge thy blood all ways have sought;
And now have on this tyrant past a doom,
To be a royal offering to thy tomb.

Ghost. Cease thy fond thoughts!——for higher
      things prepare,
Employ thy soul in a more solemn care;
For thou, who bidst my memory adieu,
And dost thy vain revenge and love pursue,
Shalt shortly sleep with me in that cold bed,
Where I too early was by treason led,
And all my guiltless blood reveng'd shall be;
But not by traitors, rebels, nor by thee.
Mean while, fond woman, thou dost vainly wait
On hell's black arts, to know thy lover's fate,
What joys he'll have, what troubles undergo,
Does not belong to Isabel to know.
Mind not his fate, thy own is drawing nigh,
Death hovers o'er thy head, prepare to die.
Farewell awhile,——when thy last hour is come,
I'll give thee one more summons to thy tomb.

*The Ghost goes out, and after some pause she seems
   to recollect her Spirits from their disorder.*

Isab. Ha! what curs'd fiend art thou.

That dost the shape of my dead lord assume,
T' accuse me wrongfully, and speak my doom ?
I'd not have shak't at any other form,—— ——
And now I find I must expect a storm,
A dark and heavy storm. Heaven will deny
Success to my designs, and I must die. —— ——
[Weeps.

But since my doom I now have understood,
Naples shall weep my fate in tears of blood ;
Fire, blood, and slaughter, more than I can tell,
Shall be the dying pangs of Isabel.
My stormy life shall yet in glory end,
And Charles, and Julia shall my fate attend.
No pining ghost shall leave his gloomy bed.
To charge me with injustice to the dead ;
No Millane,——
Grutch not* the love thy widow to him bears :
For it shall cost him all the crowns he wears.
[Exit.

Enter PORTIA.

Por. Oh, heavens ! to what a height her rage is
        flown,
The world for her revenge must be undone. [*Exit.*

Enter JULIA, EUPHEMIA.

Jul. Horrid ! Art sure !
Euph. Why, did you nothing hear ?
Jul. Alas ! thou saw'st I often swoon'd with fear.
Euph. I heard it all,—and horrid noises too
That fill'd my ears, and round like whirlwinds
        flew :
Then softly pin'd away,——That I'm afraid
They call'd up troops of devils to their aid.
Jul. Oh, Heavens ! which way shall I this Monarch
        save ;
For oh ! I never shall the courage have

<hr>

Envy not.—Used by Tusser and Ben Jonson.

To tell it him, and yet one hour's delay
Would ruin him, and all our lives betray :
But, hark ! I hear a noise i'th' gallery,

[*A noise of trampling within.*

I think the King's abroad.   [*Euph. runs and peeps.*
  Euph. Madam, 'tis he !——
  Jul. Oh, heavens ! What shall I do ? I faint !—
    I die !
Which way shall I from my own blushes fly ?
Which if I see him will disloyal prove.
And by a thousand signs betray my love ;
But 'tis too late,—his danger I'll impart,
And leave to th' mercy'f Heav'n my fainting heart.

She walks to one side of the Stage, whilst CHARLES,
    MOMP. *and train enter.*

  Ch. In her apartment various noises heard ?
  Mom. Yes, and two seen suspected by the guard,
To be the rebel chiefs,——
  Ch.   And not detain'd ?
  Mom. The guards, sir, from all violence
    refrain'd,
Whilst they in th' Duchess's apartment staid ;
And sir, in that your own commands obey'd,
But waiting for 'um till approach of day,
By private avenues they scapt away.
  Ch. The danger is not worthy my regard,
Nor shall th' afflicted lady be debar'd
From any pleasure, her unquiet mind
In little plots for her revenge can find.
  Mom.——The Princess——Julia——sir——
  Ch. Ha ! th'ast awakened my late kindled flame,
I owe devotion to that sacred name ;——
And see this way all her approaches are,
As if I should for an address prepare.
What fair and blest occasion should it be,
That drives her hither, and obliges me ?

Jul. Great sir, the sister of King Ferdinand,
Lately preserv'd by your victorious hand,
Having this morning heard a fatal doom
Past on your life does now with blushes come,
Thus early sir, the treason to prevent,
And pay your sword her just acknowledgement.
    Ch. Madam !——
    Jul. Nay, haste. sir, hence ;——
For traitors have against your life combin'd,
Which for my brother's valour is design'd,
And do presume t'abuse his sacred name,
To countenance the treason we disclaim ;
And though, as right permits, we'll not refuse,
In our own safety and just cause, to use
All generous ways our low estate affords,
We would not have you die by common swords.
    Ch. What is't I hear, do my kind stars take
        care
To save my life and crown by one so fair ?
Nay, and by her, whose beauty I have seen,
With so much rapture, that my soul has been
In high displeasures with my treach'rous fate,
That by success betray'd me to her hate :
But now my fortune in her own defence,
T'appease my soul, and make me recompense,
That all her guilty smiles I might forgive,
Finds ways by your commands to make me live.
    Jul. Oh, heavens ! I find my honour I've
        betray'd,
I fear'd such ill requitals would be made :
And therefore long did with myself contend,
To let you die ; but honour was your friend
And now your friend, which would so formal be,
To repay favours to an enemy ;
And 'gainst a thousand blushes forc'd me on,
Must suffer for the folly it has done.
            [*And puts her handkerchief before her eyes.*

Ch. Ah, madam! these resentments are severe,
Must I in all a criminal appear?
I but in humble words express the sense
Of a soul, wrapt in love and penitence,
Griev'd for past guilt, which it would fain remove,
Opprest by favours, and inflam'd by love.
    Jul. Oh, heavens! I feel within delightful
        pains   [*Aside.*
Of joy and love, that shoot through all my veins:
But I new sorrow's for my heart prepare,
And lead my self into a pleasing snare.
Sir, I perceive you ill constructions make
Of what I've done, only for honour's sake;
But there's a pride peculiar to our blood,
Who ne'er till now misfortunes understood,
That when we wrongs or kindnesses receive,
We revenge both, and never can forgive.
And now in that revenge
My injur'd honour was content to bleed:
But now we are from all obligements freed.

                                    [*Exit.*

    Ch. She's gone displeas'd,——but has such
        honour shewn,
And something so like love,
That now my vanquisht heart's entirely won.

            An alarm within.

Hark! the storm's begun,
Haste! Haste! and guard her to some safe retreat.
                                [*To Momp.*
Lest unexpected danger she should meet;
For all th' esteem and value I did bear
To crowns or fame, is wholly plac'd on her.   [*Ex.*

        Enter FERDINAND *alone.*

    Ferd. Oh, my Cornelia! how does thy fair shade,
Each corner of my restless thoughts invade?

Methinks I see her from her floating grave,
Sighing with grief, and pointing to the wave,
That does the treasure of her body hide :
And in whose cold and watery arms she died,
Then with kind looks she beckons me away.
Chiding my soul for its too tedious stay.
And, Heavens !——
Why do I stay, when fortune does remove
All I esteem, my glory, crown, and love :
And which increases my impatience more,
By Charles's gallantry I'm triumph'd o'er ;
Who gives me freedom, but to make me wear
Those hated chains no royal mind can bear.

Soft music within.

Ferd. Ha ! would they flatter my imperious grief,
These fond diversions give but small relief.
Asc. Ah, sir ! for Heaven's sake.——

Enter ASCANIO *in haste.*

Ferd. What hast thou seen ?
Asc. An airy phantom or the Cyprian Queen.
Listening to find whence these soft airs should come,
I chanc'd to look in an adjoining room,
And saw two shapes lean on a silken bed,
They seem'd too fair, and lively for the dead,
And if in some transport I have not been,
They are Irene and the Cyprian Queen.
Ferd. Thou dream'st,——
Or else their disturb'd spirits wander here,
To pursue me their guilty murderer.
[*Ferd. and Asc. go out.*

The Scene is drawn, and CORNELIA *and* IRENE *are
presented asleep upon a Couch, and at their
feet* SYLVIA. *The* KING *and* ASCANIO *enter.*

Ferd. What is't I see ? I die with high surprize,
Some fair enchantment does delude my eyes,

And in a vision does my Queen restore,
In all the beams her living beauty wore!
  Asc. Surely they live, or else the waves and
    wind
Has all their beauties faithfully resign'd.
  Ferd. The lovely vision strikes a sacred awe
Into my soul,—Let's near the altar draw,
Where the fair shape enshrin'd in beauty lyes,
Lest it too quickly vanish from our eyes.

FERD. *and* ASC. *go to the Conch, and kneeling kiss the
hands of* COR. *and* IRENE.

  Ferd. She gently breathes! her hand is soft and
    warm!
This cannot be some fair deceitful charm.
With all the devout rev'rence which we pry
Into some great and sacred mystery.
I'll draw the scene, which, from my longing sight,
Vainly conceals a mystery so bright.
Wake! my ador'd Cornelia, wake and see
Impatient Ferdinand upon his knee,
Watching to see thy eyes their light display,
Like devout Persians for the dawning day.
               [Cor. and Iren. awake.
  Cor. Where am I now!——bless me the powers
    divine!
What voice is that that calls?
  Ferd. Fair Queen, 'tis mine,
  Cor. The King!
  Ferd. Your poor adorer,—one that dies
With the high rapture of excessive joys:
What kind power sent you here on angels' wings,
To bless the world, and save the lives of Kings?
  Cor. That gentle power of pity which we find,
Sways in the empire of each gen'rous mind.
I was inform'd, you did my death bemoan,
And now you've lost both freedom, and a throne.

I thought 'twas cruelty
To let a mere delusion ask a share
Of tears, when real grief had none to spare.
   Ferd. Oh ! What a melting joy o'erflows my
     breast,
Like drooping flowers with morning dew opprest !
But, Heavens ! How did you scape the fatal day ?
   Cor. We in another galley got away
To the next shore,—where in a grove we stay'd
Till fields and plains were gloomy as the shade ;
Then, all is darkness, solitude, and fear,
We wander'd on the shore we knew not where :
Still trembling at each little noise we heard.
Till near the morn we met some of the guard,
Of whom I beg'd safe conduct to the town !
And though they knew me not, yet I must own
They shew'd me all the due respect became
My sex's honour, and their nation's fame,
And brought me here,——where I decreed to stay
For some few hours, and sail by break of day,
When by a message from me you had known
That all was well, and I in safety gone.
   Ferd. Ah ! will you shew me Heaven in all its
     light,
And then for ever close it from my sight ?
   Cor. Alas ! Sir, you attempt a vain design,
Only to wed your miseries to mine.
Suppose I should so kind and yielding prove,
Only t'oblige your importuning love ?
W'are of our crowns bereft, where should we fly,
In what dark cave should we obscurely die ?
   Ferd. Madam, forgive me that, without a throne,
My bold pretences I still dare to own :
But if th'ador'd Cornelia lov'd like me,
A cell or grotto would a Kingdom be.
   Asc. Now my Irene we are blest again,
The joys through so much danger we obtain

Let us preserve,
As one would the rich treasure, which he saves
By unexpected aid from rocks and waves.
   Iren. You know my heart is yours, but we must
     wait
Our Prince's fortunes, and th' events of fate.
                              [*An alarm.*

   Ferd. Whence is this?
   Asc. There's some contention grown
I fear, 'twixt the French army and the town.
But see, the Princess!

       Enter JULIA *with a Guard.*

   Jul. Ah, royal brother as e'er——-
For being great and good, you'd honour'd be
Go save the life of your brave enemy!
Who midst slain guards, does now forsaken
     stand.
Whilst barb'rous traitors do his life demand;
And using your great name for their pretence,
Do act their treasons with high insolence:
This from the palace eastern tower I've seen,
Where by his guards I have protected been.
   Ferd. This is bold Salerne, and my sister too,
Her fond revenge and malice to pursue.
   Jul. My sister is too faulty in't, I fear:
But be not, sir, too much displeas'd with her,
You know whence her high passion does arise,
Spare her, and her bold followers chastise.
   Ferd. I go!   With passion, madam, I
     implore   [*To Cor.*
You will not leave us in this fatal hour;
Nor take away the aid your presence brings,
As sent from Heaven in the support of Kings.
   Cor. Sir, 'tis so generous——
To save your royal foe in his distress,
That in that cause I wish you all success.

Ferd. Sir 1 commit the ladies to your Guard,
                              [*To one of the guard.*
Your loyal service should not want reward.
                              [*Ex. Ferd. and Asc.*

*As the Guard is conducting out the Ladies, they are
    met by* MOMPENSIER, *who enters in haste.*

  Mom. Hold! Hold! The ladies must not move
    from hence,
This place alone is left for their defence ;
The enrag'd Duchess strives to seize the tower,
And we're too few to guard it from her power!
What more is done I could not understand :
But to an officer I gave command,

                Enter an OFFICER.

To bring the news, and see, he's here !——
                              [*The news.*
  Off. All's well !—King Ferdinand's leap'd into
    the throng,
And like a God drives all the crowd along.
The Duchess has receiv'd a wound in fight,
And to the Domo ta'ne a speedy flight.
  Mom. Blest news! I'll on the battlements and
    see,
The valiant Kings pursue their victory.
But see, another comes in haste.

              Enter another MESSENGER.

  2. *Off.* Undone, undone !
With all your Guards to th' King's assistance run !
The town is all with troops of bandits fill'd,
Lead by a traitor, to whom all parties yield,
And the mock title of a King does bear,
And with success pursues us everywhere.

I   I I

Cor. Oh heavens !　　[*Cor., Jul. seem to faint and are supported by their women.*

Mom. runs out as to the King's assistance. Enter FERDINAND *with a Guard, chasing Salerne.*

Sal. O curse ! and is my glory thus betray'd ?
Ferd. Help, help the King ! I do not need your
  aid,　　　　　　　　[*The Guard goes off.*
Salerne I've chas'd thee from thy trait'rous herd,
Not t'have thee cut in pieces by the Guard,
But to appease my own revenge and hate,
And give thy valour a more glorious fate.
 Sal. Thou'rt brave ! I wish thou hadst not sent
  'um back ;
For now I shall be forc'd thy life to take.

They fight, the Ladies shriek, and run to the side of the Stage. SALERNE *is disarmed and wounded.*

 Ferd. Now Salerne, ask thy life ! and on thy knees
Humbly beg pardon for thy villanies.
 Sal. And dost thou this insulting temper shew,
My life's not in thy power to bestow.
My enrag'd soul is leaving its abode ;
But if it were not, and thou wert a God,
And for submissions wouldst whole Kingdoms give
To gain thy Godhead, I'd not ask to live.
Go back ! and scramble for thy fallen crown,
Which from the trembling tree my arm shook down,
And which I sought now to bestow on thee,
That crown'd, thou might'st a glorious victim be :
For yet my father's tomb no trophy wears,
His blood has only had thy father's tears :
But fate would to my cause no aid afford,
But rather basely thrust me on thy sword ;
Which high dishonour ere I'll tamely bear,
    [*Tears his wounds, and dies.*
Thus, thus a passage for my soul I'll tear.

Ferd. H'as torn his wounds, and now the gushing
 blood
Breaks from its sluices like a swelling flood :
I pity his misfortunes, since I see
He was misled by too much bravery :
But see ! they still press on ! the guards retire !
Command 'um from the battlements to fire.
         [*To the Guards within.*

   Enter CHARLES, ASCANIO, MOMPENSIER.

 Ch. Convey to the fleet the ladies, and their
 train !
For fear the rebels should the palace gain.
 Asc. The traitors, sir, have seiz'd the postern
 gate,
And all the barges there ! 'tis now too late.
 Ch. Ha ! am I then decreed a fate so low,
My glories must at last to rebels bow.
 Ferd. Ye powers ! what proud ambitious
 traitor's this,
That chases Monarchs with so high success ?
 Asc. They come !

An alarm within, and they all stand upon their guard.
  Enter ALPHONSO *followed by several with drawn*
  swords.

 Alph. Enough, retreat without delay !
         [*The Guards retreat.*
He dies that once refuses to obey.
 Ferd. Ha ! 'tis my father or a thing that bears
That royal shape.—— [*Ferd. and Jul. kneel to Alph.*
 Alph. 'Tis I remove your fears,
I find amazement sits on every brow
To see me here :——
But that will cease when I acquaint you how
A sudden tempest cast me on the shore,
Where I, scarce sav'd, fell in these bandits' power !

Who struck with grief their banisht King to see,
Seem'd to repent their past disloyalty,
Told me the state of the distracted town,
And proffer'd me their swords to gain my crown ;
I, fearing ill events, if I deny'd
Their proffer'd kindness, with the slaves comply'd.
But here——revenge and rapine was so sweet,
The villains ran confus'd in every street,
Where they could ravish, kill, or booty gain,
Nor could my power their savage rage restrain.
For th' ills they've done, sir, I your pardon crave ;
                                        [*Turns to Charles.*
For I declare, I no intentions have
To seize the kingdom, or your glory cloud ;
But for that friendship which fame speaks so loud,
You to my son in his distress have shewn,
I come my high acknowledgments to own.
Proud, if this way I can so happy be,
T'oblige, and serve so brave an enemy ;
And now resign the crown, which is your due,
And do become a prisoner, sir, to you.
  Ch. Heavens ! I'm amaz'd at his high gallantry,
                                        [*Aside.*
I've sought his crown, and he obliges me ;
I see there does the same high courage run
In all the haughty blood of Arragon.
Sir, I confess the Kingdom is my right ;
But you've subdued me with so great a height
Of honour, as my courage scarce endures ;
And now I find— —
I came not here to raise my fame, but yours.
But sir, I'll be so just to your renown,
That as your gift, I will accept this crown :
But since for honour, not for crowns I came,
I also must be just to my own fame,
And must return to you, sir, that Kingdom back,
Which only to oblige I stoop to take ;

And that your honour may have safe retreat,
I'll beg a gift more generous and great
Than that of Kingdoms, this fair Princess' love,
                              [*To Julia.*
Whose beauty will reward me far above
The highest flights of honour I have shewn,
And I have sought no interest but my own.
  Alph. By this high honour you oblige us more.
But sir, since you who are our conqueror,
What's our advantage, make your own request ;
Thus gladly, sir, I end the high contest.
                              [*Gives him Julia.*
    Ch. Without your love the gift's imperfect still.
    Jul. Sir, I obey my royal father's will. [*To Jul.*
    Ch. Madam, I do not doubt your duteous mind,
But shall I only cold submission find ?
    Jul. He'll force my heart a secret to infold,
I fear my blushes have already told.   [*Aside.*
At present, sir, you must no more obtain
Than this that duty shall my heart explain.
    Alph. Madam, I beg you will complete our joy.
                              [*To Cornelia.*
That want of crowns may not our hopes destroy ;
Once more to exile I will gladly go,
And on my son my Kingdom will bestow,
And shall be happy, in some safe retreat,
To sit and view felicity so great.
    Ferd. Madam, some pity to a heart allow,
                              [*Kneels to Cor.*
Which never came in view of hope till now ;
And now it sees some little glimpse of day,
Grows much impatient with the least delay.
    Cor. The memory, sir, which to the dead I owe.
                              [*Raises Ferd.*
And my own honour too must make me slow
In granting these requests, but yet I find
A secret fate o'erpowers my yielding mind,

And I but struggle with a high decree,
Which is as wilful as my heart can be.
    Asc. And now, my fair Irene, shall not we
Add to this joyful day's felicity?
Shall we not land, whilst this fair gale does blow?
    Iren. Why should you ask, what you already
        know?
But my suspicions now I find too true,
You love to triumph where you can subdue.
    Ferd. Now, sir, to shew I've your commands
        obey'd.   [*To Alph.*
See the revenge to your wrong'd fame I've paid.
                            [*Shews Sal. dead.*
    Alph. Ha! Salerne dead! I pity the bold slave;
For had his soul been loyal as 'twas brave,
He had deserv'd my favour;——
But where's the treacherous Trivultio?
    Asc.   Slain!——
His head does on the eastern tower remain,
Where to rebellion he incites no more,
But frights the traitors he seduced before.
    Alph. Treason's just fate,—but you forget to tell
How fares my unhappy daughter Isabel.

                Enter a GENTLEMAN.

    Gent. The Duchess, sir!
Bleeding and faint is from the Domo led,
Where she to th' altar was for refuge fled.
    Alph. Bleeding!
    Gent. Some base unmanly sword has plac'd
Too deep and dangerous wounds in her fair breast.
From whence her life flows unregarded by,
Not gaining the least pity from her eye;
And now, of your arrival, sir, she hears,
Life with impatience for a while she bears.
And she is brought along with bleeding wounds,
By gentle steps, and at each step she swoons.

The DUCHESS *enters led between two ladies,———*
bleeding.

Isab. Sir, I come here to take my last adieu
Of all my glory in this world, and you.   [*To Alph.*
For any ills I in my life have done
I beg your pardon,——though I know of none ;
For to my glory you so just must be,
To own I've honour'd our great family,
And liv'd in fame, though the small crown I wore
My brows with blushes and impatience bore ;
And now I walk in grandeur to my tomb,
By such a death as does my blood become ;
Though dying, sir, I generously own
I sought not to restore your vanquisht crown
So much, as for revenge on that false Prince,
                                        [*To Charles.*

Whose base inconstancy and insolence
To punish deeply I to arms did fly ;
Yet, oh my fate ! now unreveng'd I die.   [*Faints.*
   Ch. Ah Madam !——why ?——
   Isab. Take hence thy hated sight,
Thou stop'st my soul in its eternal flight.
Oh, I am going !——Ha, what is't I see !

Enter GALEAZZO'S GHOST.

My murder'd lord again to visit me !
   Alph. What is't she sees ?
   Isab. I come ! I come ! poor shade !
   Alph. Alas ! She raves, her reason is mislaid.
What wouldst thou have ? oh, speak thy last
      commands !
   Isab. See you not Millane's Ghost ! there ! there
      he stands !
Father revenge his blood, and let not slaves
Their glories build on murder'd Princes graves.
                [*She dies and the Ghost goes off.*

Ch. Madam, for honour's sake, and for your own,
Your lord's revenge shall be my work alone;
But ha! she hears me not, and seems to die,
Displeas'd and pain'd, whilst one she hates
    stands by.
  Alph. She aim'd at glory which her fate
    denies,
And, now enrag'd at fortune's hate, she dies.
  Ch. Now royal friend, let us embrace at last,
                                          [*To Ferd.*
And bury thus all wrongs and quarrels past!
That vow which me into this war betray'd,
Shall vanish in the fleeting breath 'twas made:
If to the dead this an offence will be,
I rather will offend the dead than thee.
But, sure, revenge and blood can never prove
Things more divine than valour, friendship, love!
  Ferd. Brave Charles, thy sentiments are so
    sublime,
That nothing thou canst do can be a crime;
If such high virtue an offence can be,
I'll my religion change and worship thee.
  Alph. Heavens! to my soul 'tis a transporting
    sight,
To see our hearts and families unite.
Now let us all to some repose betake,
And joy in decency a while forsake:
Till solemn rites we for the dead prepare,
The dead must now be our succeeding care:
And when those sad solemnities are done,
You may complete the joys you have begun.
Thus human life does various forms display,
And grief and joy succeed like night and day.

EPILOGUE.

With how much patience have you heard to day
The whining noise of a dull rhyming play ?
This obstinate incorrigible rhyme,
Though lasht by all the critics of the time ;
Our dullest writers can no more forbear,
Than your ill faces vizard masks to wear.
Yet you appear'd so grave and so devout,
You neither hist nor stamp to put us out,
A thing our critics would no more ha' done,
Then to a dull phanatic meeting gone ;
And there, amongst a serious whining throng,
Stay'd out a holding forth of nine hours long.
As for the play our author will not dare,
Like you, good men of trade, to praise his ware :
But unskill'd customers he may advise ;
Then, Sirs, since on your verdict it relies,
Resolve to save the play before you go,
For fear it should be good for aught you know.
Howe'er it makes heroic virtue shine
In royal breasts, where it shews most divine.
And so does Kings and Monarchy advance,
Nay, guarded with the names of Charles and France,
Names that now shake the world, sure, you'd not dare
To damn a play, where these united are ;
Let it be ne'er so bad, who dares arrest
The meanest slave that wears the royal crest?
Join not with small cabals of wit, that pry,
How they may damn the play, and no one spy ;
Being much ashamed in these tame wars t' appear,
When their high mettle may be shewn elsewhere.
Now, they're divided, let's have aid from you,
Them and their factions party to subdue ;

I　　　　　　15

Then, ere the parliament of wits that sate,
And govern'd here like a proud petty State,
Return from sea in a triumphant rage,
We'll get a full possession of the Stage;
Meanwhile our poet, with your forces join'd,
May damn the Rump of wits that stay behind.

CALISTO.

Calisto : or, The Chaste Nimph. The late Masque at Court, as it was frequently Presented there, by several Persons of Great Quality. With the Prologue, and the Songs betwixt the Acts. All Written by J. Crowne. Printed by Tho. Newcomb, for James Magnes and Richard Bentley, at the Post-Office in Russell-street in Covent-Garden. 1675. 4to.

Owing to the influence of John Wilmot, Earl of Rochester, to whom Crowne had dedicated his History of Charles the Eighth of France, he was employed to compose the Court Masque of Calisto, in which the principal characters were represented by the daughters of James II., then Duke of York, and the chief nobility of England. The right of preparing this performance belonged properly to Dryden, as poet laureat, but he made no remonstance, and kindly composed an Epilogue, which, through the interference of Rochester, was not accepted.*

In his address to the reader, Crowne, after speaking of the merits of the piece with great humility, and pointing out the many difficulties that presented themselves to him in its composition, assures him "that the dancing, singing, musick, which were all in the highest perfection, the most graceful action, incomparable beauty, and rich and splendid habit of the Princesses, whose lustre received no moderate increase from the beauties, and rich habits of the ladies who had the honour to accompany them and share in the performance, must needs have afforded you a delight so extraordinary that this, (meaning the Masque) in its printed form, will appear very insipid."

According to the Biographia Dramatica, it was the Duchess of York by whose command the Masque was prepared, but there is nothing to be gathered from the work itself to warrant this assertion. From the dedication to the Princess, subsequently Queen Mary, it would rather appear to have been at her request that this cherished pastime of her grandfather's times was attempted to be revived. In this instance the experiment succeeded, as the author informs the public that the entertainment, so much "honoured and adorned, was

* Scott's Dryden, vol. x., p. 337, 2d Edition, Edin. 1821, 8vo.

followed at innumerable rehearsals, and all the representations, by throngs of persons of the greatest quality, and designed for the pleasures and divertisements of their Majesties, and Royal Highnesses, and accordingly very often graced with their presences."

The Princess Mary was born at St James' 30th day of April, past one o'clock in the morning, 1662. Sandford says she "is a lady of great beauty and eminent virtue, and is now happily become the wife of William Henry of Nassau, Prince of Orange, their nuptials being privately celebrated in her bed-chamber at St James' aforesaid upon the 4th of November, about eight of the clock in the evening, 1677."* She consequently could not have been more than thirteen years old when Calisto was produced, and fifteen when she was married. The Princess Anne, according to the same authority, was born on the tenth of February 1664, "thirty-nine minutes past eleven at night." "She was for her health sent to France in 1669," and since "her return not only acquired a healthful constitution of body, but those accomplishments of mind which are very seldom found in a person of her years." At the date of the Masque she would be about eleven years of age.

As Anne Hyde, mother of the two Princesses, died upon the 31st of March 1671, the Duchess of York of 1675 could only have been Mary D' Este, daughter of the Duke of Modena, who became the second wife of the Duke of York upon the 21st November 1673, when hardly fifteen years of age. Crowne in the dedication to the Princess Mary never in the slightest manner refers to her stepmother, or even her father, although it is certain that his Royal Highness took a deep interest in the representation.

Evelyn, in his life of Mrs Godolphin, mentions that she, when "Margaret Blagge," and Maid of Honour to the Queen, performed the character of Diana, the Goddess of Chastity, and "had on her that day near twenty thousand pounds value of jewells, which were more set off with her native beauty and luster then any they contributed of their owne to hers." After the

* Sandford's Genealogical History of the Kings of England, 1677. p. 567, folio.

performance "a dissaster happened which extreamly concern'd her, and that was the loss of a Diamond of considerable vallue which had been lent her by the Countess of Suffolk; the stage was immediately swept and diligent search made to find it, but without success, soe as probably it had been taken from her, as she was oft environ'd with that infinite Crowd which 'tis impossible to avoid upon such occasion. But the loss in question was soon repaired, for his Royal Highness, understanding the trouble she was in, generousely sent her wherewith all to make my Lady Suffolke a present of soe (as?) good a jewell."* It may not unnaturally be assumed that, as the two princesses were performers, their Royal Parent would deem it a duty on his part to repair the loss which had occurred, the more especially if the entertainment had been by his order.

James II. had inherited from his mother, Henrietta Maria, a taste for exhibitions of this kind, and both he and his sister Henrietta Maria took part during their banishment from England in a Masque of which the following is the title: "The Nuptials of Peleus and Thetis, Consisting of a Mask and a Comedy, or the Great Royal Ball, acted lately in Paris six times, by

> The King in Person.
> The Duke of Anjou.
> The Duke of Yorke,
>   with divers other Noble-men.
>   ALSO BY
> The Princess Royall Henrette Marie.
> The Princess of Conty.
> The Dutchess of Roquelaure.
> The Dutches of Crequy.
> With many other Ladies of Honour.

London. Printed for Henry Herringman, and are to be sold at his Shop at the Ancor in the lower walke of the new Exchange 1654."

This is a translation or adaptation from the French by James Howel, the author of the once popular

* The Life of Mrs Godolphin, by John Evelyn, Esq., p. 99, London, 1848. Edited by Samuel Wilberforce, Lord Bishop of Oxford, Chancellor of the most noble Order of the Garter.

and still interesting volume called Epistolae-Hoelianae, and is dedicated by him to the Lady Katherine Marchiones of Dorchester, the wife of Henry second Earl of Kingston, who obtained the Marquisate of Dorchester in the county of Dorset 25th March 1645. The Marchioness had the honour of being godmother of Henrietta Stuart, third daughter of the Duke of York, and Anne Hyde his first wife. The Princess was born upon the 13th day of January 1668, but did not live more than ten months, dying upon the 15th day of November 1669.

It is remarkable that the Masque of the Nuptials of Peleus and Thetis should during the Commonwealth have been openly sold with the publisher's name and address, as both the Duke and his sister are not only given as performers on the title, but the verses spoken by the Duke could not be very agreeable to the ears of the dominant faction in the metropolis of England. His Royal Highness was born upon the 14th of October 1633, and must therefore have been just of age when with the Fishers of Coral, and " representing a Fisherman," he spoke as follows :—

> 'Tis not for me to fish for Corrall here,
> I to another coast my course must steer,
>   A fatal ground
>   Which Seas surround ;
> There I must fish upon an angry main
> More than two Crowns and Scepters to regain.

This is not all, for " Madam Henriette, the Princess of England, representing the Muse Erato, which fell to her by lott," says—

> My Stemm is more then of a mortal race ;
> For to *great* Henries' *grandchild* all give place.
>   My innocent and young aspect
>   Inspires both pitty and respect,
>   And he who loudly would complain
>   Of *Princes'* falls and *People's* raign,
>   Of angry stars and destiny,
>   Let him but cast his eyes on me.

At this time the Princess, who was born on the 11th June 1644, was only ten years of age; her verses were prophetic of her future fortunes. She married the Duke of Anjou, better known afterwards as Duke of Orleans, the brother of Louis the Fourteenth and died suddenly in the month of June 1670 at the early age of twenty-six. The general belief was that she was poisoned.

Bishop Burnet, whose authority cannot always be relied on, asserts that upon the return of the Princess to France from England, her husband had heard such things of his wife's behaviour that he ordered a great dose of sublimate to be given her in a glass of succory water, of which she died a few hours after in great torments: and when she was opened her stomach was all ulcerated."* He also asserts that she was attached to the Count de Guiche. The same accusation occurs in the Memoirs of Sir John Reresby. It is probable that the acquaintance of the Princess and De Guiche commenced with the Masque of 1654. He was one of the performers first as a Fisherman, when he says :—

> Upon the side of a still fearful pond
> I use to fish, and dare not go beyond.
> The time will come that I may also seek
> The River's Banks, and haply a Sea-creek.

Subsequently there enters a " Quire of Lovers "— " Mounsieur," the King's brother—the future husband of Henrietta, " representing the first love," has these lines :—

> Ladies from this tender spray
> There may some danger come one day ;
> Ye with caresses flatter him, he you,
> Ye kiss and hugg him, but you'll find it true
>   It is a Lion's cubb which you do stroke,
>   Who with his paw in time may make you smoke.
> He sports with you, he smiles and mocks,
> Plays with your jewells, fancies, locks,
> But take yee heed, for he at length
> Will gather more encrease of strength ;
> Yet I foresee he will wean quite
> Himself from all such soft delight,
> And marching in the steps of his great sires,
> Make *Glory* the sole *Queen* of his desires.

Next came De Guiche, " representing another love," who says :—

* Burnet, vol. i., p. 552. 2d Edition, Oxford, 1833, 8vo.

> All those Loves I do behold
> Brighter than the burnished gold
> Are nothing if compared with me,
> Whether Fire or Light they be,
> I do discover in effect
> I am all love when I reflect
>   upon myself.

The Princess was very beautiful and accomplished. She brought the Duke one son—the Duke de Valois, who died in infancy—and two daughters, Louisa, the elder, who became Queen of Spain but died without issue, and Anne Maria the younger, Duchess of Savoy, whose descendants became heirs of line of the race of Stewart, and would have excluded the House of Hanover from the British throne, had it not been for their professing the Roman Catholic faith.

The first entry of the Masque was " The Grand Monarch," who as Apollo was attended by the nine muses, represented by ladies of the highest rank, at the head of whom was the English Princess, as the Muse " who singeth of love and marriage."* Thus Erato reversed the adage, for marriage came first and love afterwards.

The Masque of Calisto is taken from the second book of the Metamorphoses of Ovid, where Jupiter, accidentally meeting the daughter of Lycaon, King of Arcadia, whilst perambulating that country with the intention of repairing the injuries it had sustained through the folly of Phaeton in his ambitious attempt to guide the chariot of his father, became captivated by her beauty. Calisto was one of the favoured attendants of Diana, whose form Jupiter assumed, and was thus able to accomplish his wishes. The result was a child called Arcos, which she hid in the woods. Juno, having discovered what had occurred, changed the unfortunate victim of her husband's imposture into a bear, whereupon Jove made her a constellation with her son under the name of the Bear. She was called " Virgo Tegeava," from the city Tegea in Arcadia.†

* Ovidius de Arte Amandi, Lib. ii., 16.   F. 568.
    " Nunc Erato : nam tu nomen amoris habes."
† Sed tibi nec Virgo Tegeava, comesque Bootæ
        Ensiger Orion aspiciendus erit.
Ovidius de Arte Amandi. Lib. II.   F. 555, Tom. I.   Lug. Bat. 1670, 8vo.

The fable is one not exactly adapted, it might be supposed, for a Royal Masque. Nevertheless, as the virtuous Evelyn assures his readers, "however defective in other particulars, it was exactly modest and suitable to the persons, who were all of the first rank and most illustrious of the Court."* This opinion is somewhat remarkable, coming as it does from a man generally supposed to be an exception to the class of individuals who fluttered about Charles and his brother, for little can be said of the modesty of the masque, which might nevertheless be quite adapted to the taste of most of the distinguished audience that witnessed its representation. One fact is elicited from the testimony of Mrs Godolphin's biographer, that even with individuals free from the taint of the period, a freedom in diction and tolerance of expression was permitted, which in the present day would be considered highly objectionable.

Crowne, in executing the task imposed upon him, has added an underplot, for which he was not indebted to Ovid. He introduces Mercury as one of the Dramatis Personæ, who falls in love with one of Diana's attendants called Pseeas, "an envious nymph," and an enemy of Calisto, who assists Juno in wreaking her vengeance on the heroine. Instead of a son Calisto, is given a sister called Nyphe, and after a vindication of the reputation of the former, Jove winds up with soliciting her to

> Accept the small dominion of a Star.
> There you and beauteous Nyphe may dispense
> With cooler beams your light and influence
> On the great ceremony, Hermes wait,
> Let all the Gods give their appearance strait,
> Their virgin consecration nought debars,
> I will in full assembly crown 'em stars.

Pseeas, for her mischief-making, is rewarded by the gentle Juno, and received into her friendship, whereupon Jupiter sarcastically remarks :

> A most harmonious friendship this must prove,
> The fates designed 'em for each other's love,
> For none love them, and they have love for none,
> Their kindness centres on themselves alone,
> And they are so exactly of a make
> Each may the other for herself mistake.

* Life of Mrs Godolphin. p. 99.

Mrs Godolphin, then Miss Blagge, during the progres of the Masque, was one of the maids of honour to Catherine of Braganza, the Queen of Charles II., and was anxious to have resigned the situation prior to the performance, but retained it from the difficulty of getting any satisfaction as to the allowance usually made when any of these ladies gave up her appointment. In a letter to Evelyn, written on the 22d September, she informs him, " my buissiness makes no advance, and that where I least expected difficulty I find the greatest. The King sayes nothing to my Lord Treasurer, nor my Lord to him ; soe that for ought I perceive 'tis likely to depend thus a long tyme : well, God's will be done as in Heaven, soe on earth ; in the meantyme, I am extreamly heavy for I would be free from that place and have nothing to do in itt att all : butt it will not be for the play goes on mightyly, which I hoped would never have proceeded farther. Dear friend, I begg your prayers this cloudy Weather, that God would endow me with patience and resignation. Would you believe itt, there are some that envy me the honour (as they esteeme it) of acting in this play, and pass malitious Jests upon me. Now you know I am to turne the other cheeke, nor take I notice of it."

For a young lady of a mind so serious it would undoubtedly have been peculiarly unpleasant to have enacted the part of a goddess who had patronised Endymion, and had not repulsed Hypolitus,—as the naughty P'secas chose to assure Juno was the fact. However, the Royal order settled all scruples. " She had her part assigned her, which as it was the most illustrious, soe never was there any perform'd with more grace and becoming the solemnity." Evelyn continues, that during the time the performance was proceeding and her presence was not required, she returned to the " tireing roome, where severall Ladyes her companions were railing with the gallants trifleingly enough till they were called to re-enter, she, under pretence of conning her next part, was retired into a corner, reading a booke of Devotion without at all concerning herselfe or mingling with the young company,—as if she had no further part to act who was the principal person of the comedy." The writer who witnessed her performance particularly remarked the " surprizing and admirable aire she trode the stage and performed her part, because she could doe nothing of this sort, or anything else she undertook indifferently, butt in the highest perfection. · Butt whilst the whole theatre were extolling her, she was then in her own eyes, not only the humblest, butt the most diffident of herself, and least affecting praise." " For the rest of that dayss triumph I have a particular account still by me of the rich apparel she had on her, amounting besides the Pearles and Pretious Stones, to above three hundred pounds, but of all which she immediately disposed her selfe soe soone as ever she could get clear of the Stage. Without complimenting any creature or trifling with the rest who staid the collation and refreshment that was prepar'd, away she slips like a spiritt to Berkley House, and to her little oratorye; whither I waited on her, and left her on her knees thanking God that she was delivered from this vanity, and with her Saviour againe. never, says she, will I come within this temptation more whilst I breath."

Evelyn is not very precise here as to the exact time his heroine abandoned the stage, for Crowne assuredly could hardly have been mistaken in stating, as he does in the title of the Masque, that it was *frequently* presented at Court " by several persons of Great Quality." It is obvious that she must have performed the character during the entire period of the representation, which does not appear to have continued after the publication of the play in 1675.

Margaret Blagge, born upon the second of August 1652, was the youngest daughter of Colonel Thomas Blagge of Horningsherth, in the county of Suffolk, a Groom of the Bed-chamber to Charles I., and Governor of Wallingford. Upon the restoration, he was made Governor of Yarmouth and Languard fort. He did not long enjoy his appointments, as he departed this life 14th November 1660, leaving by his wife Mary North, daughter of Sir Roger North of Mildenhall, four daughters, the eldest of whom, Henrietta Maria, figures in Grammont, and married Sir Thomas Yarburgh of Snaith; Dorothy, the second, died unmarried; Mary, the third daughter, was Maid of Honour to the Duchess of York; and Margaret, the friend of Evelyn, the youngest, became the spouse of Sidney Godolphin upon the 16th May 1675. and died 9th September 1678, shortly after giving birth to their only son Francis.

Her widowed husband never remarried, and devoted himself to politics. In September 1684 he was created Lord Godolphin of Rialton when First Lord of the Treasury. He became Lord High Treasurer and Knight of the Garter in 1704, and was elevated to the Earldom of Godolphin 29th December 1706. He died in 1712, when his only son Francis succeeded him. He married the Lady Henrietta Churchill, Duchess of Marlborough in her own right. · Of this marriage there was issue one son, William, Viscount Rialton, subsequently Marquis of Blandford, who dying without issue 24th August 1731, the Dukedom of Marlborough and Marquisate of Blandford passed to the Earl of Sunderland, whilst the Godolphin representation, by reason of Henrietta her elder sister, Duchess of Newcastle, dying without issue, was inherited by Mary her only sister, who married Thomas Osborne, fourth Duke of Leeds, whose son Francis Godolphin Osborne succeeded his father 23d March 1789, and died 31st January 1799.

The fifth Duke of Leeds was twice married. his first wife was Amelia D'Arcy, only daughter and heiress of Robert fourth Earl of Holderness, and in her own right Baroness Conyers, whom he divorced May 1779 for adultery with John Byron, Esq. By her he had George William Frederick, the sixth Duke, who succeeded upon the demise of his father 31st January 1799, and died in July 1838, having married Charlotte, daughter of the first Marquis Townshend, on 17th August 1797. By her his Grace had two sons. the elder of whom became seventh Duke, but although married, died leaving no issue. His younger son was accidentally killed at Oxford 19th February 1831. The eldest daughter, Lady Charlotte Mary Anne Georgiana, born 16 July 1801, married 22d June 1826 Sackville Lane Fox, Esq., M.P.; and upon the death of her brother, the representation as heir of line of Margaret Blagge and Sydney, first Earl of Godolphin, came, after the demise of his mother, to be vested in their son, the present Lord Conyers.

Some very interesting particulars, contributed by John Holmes, Esq., of the British Museum, relative to Colonel Blagge, the father of Mrs Godolphin, who preserved " his

Majesty's George" after the battle of Worcester, will be found in the appendix by the Bishop of Oxford to Evelyn's memoir of the lady. His Lordship has prefixed to the volume an engraving of Mrs Godolphin from the original painting at Wootton. "A portrait of Colonel Blagge is at Gog-magog Hills, near Cambridge, the seat of his descendant the present Lord Godolphin," 1842.

In his account of the English stage, Geneste, in a brief notice of Calisto, observes that, on the whole, it "does Crowne credit rather than otherwise—the principal fault of it is its length, for it extends to five acts." In adapting the legend for representation, the author has shown considerable skill in deviating from Ovid, and avoiding, as the author says, "writing what would have been unfit for Princesses and Ladies to speak." Even purified as the masque has been by the judicious alterations of Crowne, enough of the original leaven still remains to create some surprise how any parent could permit the selection of not the most reputable adventure of the King of the Gods, as the subject of a Drama in which his two daughters were to be principal performers.

In his address to the Reader, the author gives an amusing detail of the difficulties under which he laboured in preparing the Masque of Calisto for representation— the chief one arising from the selection of the plot and his assuredly hazardous attempt to represent the deceived daughter of the King of Arcadia and attendant of Diana as an impersonation of Chastity. It is not probable that Crowne would have made the experiment without permission, and Charles himself may possibly have suggested the idea, as it is understood his Majesty was by no means indisposed to offer his advice in dramatic matters, and that he did so is established by his recommending Crowne to take two Spanish plays and form them into one, an advice the Poet followed, and produced Sir Courtly Nice, a Comedy which became deservedly popular, and of which the critic Dennis says, "the greatest comic poet that ever lived in any age might have been proud to have been the author."

THE LADY MARY.

Eldest Daughter of His Royal Highness
THE DUKE.

MADAM,—Being unexpectedly called out of my Obscurity, to the glory of serving your Highness, (and indeed the whole Court) in an entertainment so considerable as this; my fears and amazements were such as (I believe) shepherds and herdsmen had of old, when from their flocks and herds they were call'd to prophesie to Kings. I know not how to interpret the meaning of that command, which laid on such feeble shoulders, a burden too heavy for the strongest to bear. Fain would I have shrunk back again into my former shades, and hid my self in my native obscurity; but fearing to dispute with oracles, and resist Heavenly Powers, I adventured on dangerous obedience, knowing that if I must perish, it was better to perish a Martyr than a Criminal. But recollecting my self, I remembered that Divine commands were Presages rather of Favour than Ruin; that when Heaven pressed any to his wars, he gave them courage, as well as pay. This made me hope, that in the glorious work to which I was called, I should be inspired.

And this I thought it my duty to believe, when I remembered in whose service I was employed, in the service of a Princess, over whose great and victorious Father a glorious Genius always hovered, assisting the meanest of his followers, when engaged in services of his, of what kind soever; and sure, thought I, he will not neglect me, now I serve so fair, so excellent, and so considerable a part of him; now I am under the shadow of his wings, I shall partake of his influence. This made me think it a sin to despair, and thrust me on with all the boldness and giddiness, but, to my sorrow, not with the exalted raptures, of one inspired : for, after all, it was not with me according to my Faith. This Poem savours too little of inspiration, and too much of my own weak unassisted self : nay, as it was first written, it came even short of my self, and sure that must be a wretched thing which wants the perfection I can give it. And though no man is to blame for having no more wit than he has, yet he is an ill-mannered Churle who will not spend his whole stock to entertain such a Guest. For my defects and inabilities, Nature alone must answer, and I am heartily sorry for them, but I must, with all submission, charge your Highness with being the occasion of my latter offence. If you will invite yourself to the greatest table in England, and not give them time to prepare, you will not find an entertainment fit for you. A poem is a thing consists of many and different images ; and though a man's estate be but small, yet if it lies in many hands, it will require time to get it in. Nature herself proceeds always slowly, and gradually to perfection : nay, we find Heaven pondering and consulting when he was to make a creature on which he meant to bestow excellence. I will not pretend that I have materials in me to have formed a poem of such perfection as so great an occasion required ; but I am certain I could have written something more worthy of your Highness' favour, and the great honour to which this was preferred, had I had time enough allowed me to ripen my conceptions. But, Madam, if your Highness did expect, I should have indited thoughts fine as your own, and made you speak as excellently as you think, you then laid a task on me too great for anything but an Angel. For none can have Angelical thoughts but they who have Angelical virtues : and none do, or ever did, in so much youth, come so near the perfection of Angels as yourself, and your young Princely Sister, in whom all those excellencies shine, which the best of us can but rudely paint. But, Madam, what need was there of that perfection of wit, the charms of your person, youth, and mein, the lustre of your high quality, and the extraordinary grace that attended everything you said and did, spoke to the eyes and souls of all that saw you, in a Language more divine than wit can invent, in a Language wherein Nature entertained them with her own Ingenuity, and by a thousand charming expressions so took up all their attention, that the best of writers could not have made you speak anything, your audience would have been at leisure to regard, or for which they would have descended from one moment's pleasure of admiring you. The foresight of this made Fortune, who always loves to favour the least deserving, throw the honour of this service on me: she knew there was no need of excellence in a Writer, when there was so much in you; and since the best of Writers would not have appeared considerable, indulged her humour in selecting the worst: a favour which in many respects exalts me above all my Contemporaries, and will make the world judge me, though not the best, the happiest Writer of the age.

But, Madam, as it is the Fate of all things to be subject to inconstancy, and neither happiness nor misery last long, especially when in extremes: this Poem, made like the first man, by the command and for the service of a Divinity, almost out of nothing too, and placed, at the instant of its formation, in a paradise of happiness and honour, now driven from its blest estate and its ever-flourishing gardens, is going to wander round the world, in a condition of poverty, misery, and exile; where, instead of its past felicities, the many visions of Heaven, when the Sovereign glories of this isle descended frequently to visit, and seemed to recreate themselves in, its bowers; instead of the extreme lustre it received from the most graceful action of your Highness, of the Princess Anne your sister, and of the other young Ladies, which like so many beautiful Angels attended you, it is now condemned to want and nakedness, to starve under the cold wind of censure, to all the sufferings that the native of a rich and happy soil must expect when banished to cold and barbarous Regions. In this condition, forced by its misery, and bound by the duty of a Creature, it makes this humble sacrifice of itself to your Highness, to beg such a share of your Protection and Favour as may enable it to live in a condition becoming a creature which had once the Honor to be

so near to you, and to receive such particular Graces
from you. Your Highnesses favour will yet make it spend
its days in Honor, revive with pleasure the remembrance
of the past glories, and give an immortality, not only to
this poor Poem, but to the otherwise most obscure
name of,

MADAM,

Your Highness' most humble

· and most devoted Servant,

JOHN CROWNE.

READER,—If you were ever a spectator of this following entertainment, when it was represented in its glory, you will come, if you come at all, with very dull appetite, to this cold, lean carkass of it. The dancing, singing, music, which were all in the highest perfection, the most graceful action, incomparable beauty, and rich and splendid habit of the Princesses, whose lustre received no moderate encrease from the beauties and rich habits of the ladies who had the honor to accompany 'em, and share in the performance, must needs have afforded you a delight so extraordinary, that this will appear very insipid. If you have never seen it, then perhaps you may receive some pleasure; but yet, I fear, not so much as you expect. You, no doubt, will imagine, and you have reason, that an entertainment so much honoured and adorned, followed at innumerable rehearsals, and all the representations by throngs of persons of the greatest quality, and designed for the pleasures and divertisements of their Majesties, and Royal Highnesses, and accordingly very often graced with their presences, should be some superlative piece. But you will be disappointed, you will find nothing here answer those swelling expectations. How it happens to be so, it is enough to tell you, that it was written by me; and it would be very strange, if a bad writer should write well; but, which was as great an unhappiness, I had not time enough allowed me, to muster together, on so great an occasion, those few abilities I have; I was invaded on the sudden, by a powerful command, to prepare an entertainment for the court, which was to be written, learnt, practised, and performed in less time than was necessary for the writing alone. True, it was not performed till some months after the time first decreed, but that hapened from the discretion of those on whom the dancing and musical parts depended, who found it required time to do any thing in perfection; but I not knowing it would be so deferred, finished my part within the time first allotted me, which was scarce a month : not only for the *play*, but the *prologue*, and *songs*, the nature of which I was wholly a stranger to, having never seen any thing of the kind ; and by these means, I was forced upon a brisk dullness, writing quick, but flat. I was also confined in the number of the persons ; I had but seven allowed me, neither more nor less : those seven to be all ladies, and of those ladies two only were to appear in men's habits. Next, for my subject, it was not, I confess, imposed upon me by command, but it was for want of time to find a better : for I had but some few hours allowed me to choose one. And as men who do things in haste, have commonly ill fortune, as well as ill conduct, I resolving to choose the first tolerable story I could meet with, unhappily encountered this, where, by my own rashness, and the malice of fortune, I involved myself, before I was aware, in a difficulty greater than the invention of the Philosopher's Stone, that only endeavours to extract gold out of the coursest metals, but I employed myself to draw one contrary out of another ; to write a clean, decent, and inoffensive play on the story of a rape, so that I was engaged in this dilemma, either wholly to deviate from my story, and so my story would be no story, or by keeping to it, write what would be unfit for Princesses and Ladies to speak, and a Court to hear. That which tempted me into so great a labyrinth, was the fair and beautiful image that stood at the portal, I mean the exact and perfect character of Chastity in the person of *Calisto*, which I thought a very proper character for the princess to represent ; nor was I mistaken in my judgment, the difficulty lay in the other part of the story, to defend chastity was easy, the danger was in assaulting it ; I was to storm it, but not to wound it ; to shoot at it, but not offend it ; my arrows were to be invisible, and without Piles ; my guns were to be charged with white powder ; the bullets were to fly, but give no report. These were niceties required skill to perform, and would have puzled a finer invention than mine ; and, indeed, I did a little fail in my first attempt : my arrows, though as fine as I could then in haste turn them, yet were too course for a

Court.   I often pared 'em, and much difficulty I found
to make 'em thin enough to pass through nice and
delicate ears, without wounding 'em, an art which
with much pains in this emendation I attained. The
last, and not the least, difficulty imposed on me in the
entertainment, was in the Chorusses.   I was obliged to
invent proper occasions, to introduce all the entries, and
particularly for the closing of all with an entry of
Africans. How I have succeeded in it I leave the
reader to judge.   Under all these difficulties did this
poor poem labour even before it was an *embrio*, and when
sleeping in its causes; and when in the womb it was
squeezed, and hindered of its due growth by intolerable
strait lacings; and lastly, forced on an immature and
hasty birth. By all which inconveniences it was impossible
it should prove otherwise than a weak, lean, ricketty,
deformed piece, and as such, notwithstanding the kindness it received from others, it was looked on by me,
and accordingly I was impatient till I had strangled it,
and in the room produced something less imperfect,
something of a constitution strong enough to endure the
blows of its enemies, and of a complexion beautiful
enough to delight its parents and friends, and such a
thing, in some low degree at least, this is which you see.
Far be it from me to say it is as well as it ought to be,
or as others of greater abilities would have written it.
Nor, give me leave to say, so well as I myself would
have done on a better subject, and in less haste; for this
was written in a hurry as well as the former, being
finished and learnt between the second and third representation; but having the advantage of features and
dead colours laid, it was easy to work something on
that foundation better than the former; and I undertook
the trouble, not only to repair my own reputation, but
to give some refreshment to the audiences, who would
have been weary of a better play at the second or third
representation, and therefore must needs be weary of
that at the 20th or 30th, for near so often it had been
rehearsed and acted.

   Some, perhaps, will expect I should not only apologise
for not writing better, but daring on such an occasion
to write at all; but having said it was done by Command,

none can have so little manners as to expect I should make excuse for obedience. I must confess it was great pity, that in an entertainment where the sense* was so deliciously feasted, the understanding should be so slenderly treated; and had it been written by him, to whom, by the double right of place and merit, the honour of the employment belonged, the pleasure had been in all kinds complete. However this appeared not so contemptible but it attained the felicity for which it was made, to afford some delight to his Royal mind, to whose pleasure all our endeavours ought to be, and this more particularly was devoted. And of this I have full assurance, by the best, and to me most pleasing testimony of it, that of his most princely bounty. Having said this, the devouring critic must cease his pursuit, for the poor sinner is out of the reach of his fangs, and safe in glory. And now it is at my courtesy to make any farther apologies, yet because I know the critics will be nibbling at anything they think they can catch, I must now answer for some errors, which I suppose they hope I have ignorantly, but I confess to have wilfully committed. I have in the *Prologue* represented the river *Thames* by a woman, and *Europe* by a man, contrary to all authority and antiquity. To that I answer, I know of no sexes in lands and rivers, nor of any laws in poetry, but the fundamental one to please; they who do that, follow the highest authority, and agree with the best antiquity. The principal part of the *Prologue* being the river, my business was not to consider how the *Latin* poets painted it, but how to represent it best and most beautiful on our stage: not to trouble my head with *hic, hæc, hoc,* to please the *Grammarians,* but how to have the part sung best to delight the Court; and the graceful motions and admirable singing of Mrs *Davis* did sufficiently prove the discretion of my choice. And *Thames, Peace,* and *Plenty* being represented by women, I was necessitated in spite of the lady that bestrid the bull to make *Europe* a man and to call it not *Her* but—*His fair Continent*—otherwise I must either have spoiled the figure, and made three parts of the world men, and one a woman: or worse, by representing them all by women

* Sight !

have spoiled the music by making it consist all of trebles.
But these are criticisms for none but those of school-boys'
learning, and school-boys' understandings. Some other
faults there are in the style and expression, which,
Reader, if you can discover, you may insult over as you
think fit, the whole having obtained the happiness to
please, I shall not concern my self for every trifling
error which slipt from me unawares, and which I had
not leisure to mend; perhaps you may find fault with
my different numbers, that I have not kept to one kind
of verse. but written part in Pindaric, and part Heroic.
To that I answer, the Pindaric is what I left of the old
play uncorrected, as not needing emendation; and I
chose that kind of measure at first, not as the best and
most pleasing to the ear, but as the readiest and quickest
for one that was in haste; it being in comparison of the
grave Heroic, a kind of mixed pace betwixt ambling and
galloping, where the poet is not bound to wait the
leisure of a stubborn syllable to rhyme, but to take the
rhyme where he can catch it, without any more trouble.
But upon the correction, I chose the Heroic as more
majestic, lofty and musical, and as I hope made
emendation, both in sense and sound.

Having made this little vindication of my self, I were
now bound in gratitude, before I conclude, to record
the due praises of those whose admirable performances
in their several kinds lent this entertainment much of
the praise it had: namely, the singers, and the composer
of all the musick, both vocal and instrumental, Mr
Staggins; but their excellencies lying far out of that
road my understanding travels in, I should praise them
so ignorantly, if I should attempt it, that I should discover my own folly more than their merit. But if the
judgments of others, and those the most skilful too, be
not mistaken, Mr Staggins has not only delighted us
with his excellent composition, but with the hopes of
seeing in a very short time a master of music in *England*
equal to any *France* or *Italy* have produced. No less
praise may be said of the best and choicest of the singers.
But, Reader, I shall detain you no longer, now take
what pleasure you can find in the perusal of the following pages.

PROLOGUE.

*The Curtain is drawn up, and there appears a Nymph
leaning on an Urne, representing the river* THAMES,
attended by two Nymphs, representing PEACE *and*
PLENTY : *near her are the four parts of the world,
seeming to make offerings to her.   On the opening of
the scene, lamenting Voices are heard on both sides of
the Theatre, at which the Nymph of the River seems
affrighted.*

Voices within. Fly, fly, help, oh ! help, or we die.

Tha. What mournful cries are these on ev'ry
   side ?
The winds waft nothing to this island o'er,
But the complainings of some neighb'ring shore,
And all the echoes are in groans employ'd.
The fair Augusta* too, I weeping see,
Though none so fair, so rich, so great as she ;
       Alas ! my fears encrease :
You gentle Nymphs of Plenty and of Peace,
       Shall now go seek some other shore.
And you that with your presents wait,
       Shall bring your gifts no more.
  Plen. I to no other dwelling will betake.
  Pea. Thy beauteous streams I never will forsake.
  Euro. And we our presents still will make.
  Om.   We our presents still will make.
  Plen. Thy stores with all my plenty shall be fill'd.

* London anciently so called.

Pea. My halcyon on thy banks her nest shall
  build.
Euro. Thou shalt in all my noblest arts be skill'd.
Asi. My jewels shall adorn no brow but thine.
Amer.   Thy lovers in my Gold shall shine.
Afri. Thou for thy slaves, shalt have these
      Scorched sons of mine.
Pea. } Thy beauteous streams we never will
Ple. }   forsake.
Euro.
Asi.
Afr.   } And we our presents still will make.
Amer.
Om.   We our presents still will make.
Pea. What should so much beauty fear ?
      Round this isle the heavens appear
Like your own streams all undisturb'd and clear.
Tha. These beauteous Nymphs unfrightened too,
Not minding what on other shores they do,
      Their innocent delights pursue.
Pea. See! they, void of grief or fear,
      Come to entertain you here.

*An Entry of Shepherds and Nymphs, dancing round
the Thames, &c., as they stood in their figure.*

  *[Here the Princesses and the other Ladies danced
    several sarabands with castanets. A minuet
    was also danced by his Grace the Duke of
    Monmouth : which ended, Thames proceeds.*

Tha. Oh ! now my spirits I recover,
I've wak'd the Genius of this isle, my warlike lover.

      Enter the Genius of England.

Gen. What cries are these disturb my pleasing
  rest ?
Tha. 'Tis I, my love, 'tis I, thy aid request.

Gen. Is it my Nymph, what dost thou fear ?
Tha. Does not my love sad cries around him
    hear ?
Gen. Wilt thou thy fear at every shriek proclaim ?
Tha.   Am I alone to blame ?
Do you not see Augusta, rich and fair,
Though to her lap I all my treasure bear
    Will for no comfort stay her tears ?

    [*The following stanza is properly part of the
    Genius's speech, being a pertinent reply to
    Thames; but being set extreme pleasantly, and
    for a treble voice, it was sung by Thames.*

    Augusta is inclin'd to fears.
    Be she full or be she waining,
    Still Augusta is complaining :
    Give her all you can to ease her,
    You shall never, never, please her.
Chor. Augusta is inclin'd to fears, &c.
Gen. These fears do not belong to her nor you ;
    Europe only should lament
    The Nymphs of his fair continent.
    Some giants now pursue.
But this sweet isle no monster can invade.
Tha. Oh send those poor distressed Nymphs
    some aid.
Eur. From the mild power of this happy place,
    Who is inclin'd,
To make the world as peaceful as his mind,
    They have already gain'd the grace :
Two heroes of his own celestial race
Are sent ; the one to triumph o'er the seas.
And all the watery divinities.
The other, monsters of the land to quell,
And make the Nymphs in safety dwell.
Gen. The first, in war has all perfections gain'd,

That can by human nature be attain'd :
    The second promises to be
    All that in the first we see.
Eur. Mars to the first does all his glory lend :
The second beauty, youth, and love attend.
    Gen.   Both in high perfections shine :
    Valour, glory, race divine :
    Wait awhile, and you shall see
    Both return with victory.
Pea. Hark, hark ! the triumph's near,
And see ! they both already crown'd appear.

Enter one crown'd with a Naval Crown, attended by
    Sea-Gods and Tritons.

    Rejoice you wat'ry deities !
    The mighty monsters of the seas,
      This valiant Prince has slain.
    The god of this fair isle shall now
    Command, as all his right allow,
      The empire of the main.

Enter one crown'd with a Mural Crown attended
    by Warriors.

Ye gods and nymphs of plains and groves,
Of springs and streams, enjoy your loves ;
This youthful hero has subdu'd
The satyrs now of ev'ry wood :
Has kill'd or ta'n 'em all for slaves,
And chac'd the giants from their caves.

      Chorus of all.

    Let us both their praises sing,
    Whilst we both in triumph bring ;
      Let us all contend to grace 'em
    With our loud and joyfull'st thanks,
    Whilst upon the flow'ry banks
      Of this beauteous Nymph we place 'em.

Two Entries are danced: One of Sea-Gods and the other of Warriors.

Gen. Now welcome heroes to my blest abode,
And to my Nymph belov'd by ev'ry god.
  Tha.   Welcome to my love and me,
       Now we all shall happy be.
  Cho.   Now we all shall happy be.

A Temple of Fame appears.

Plen. Now you whose valour gives the world
  repose,
      See what Fame on you bestows.
Her shining temple shall preserve your names,
And thence her trumpet your renown proclaims.
  Gen. To our Divinity, now let us go,
And at his feet your crowns and trophies throw.
  Eur. I will my thanks in offerings proclaim.
  Asi. I'll lend you spice.
  Amer. I gold.
  Afr. And I the same.
  Tha. I'll be your guide,
My streams beneath his palace hourly slide.
    There it is, not far before you,
    Pleasure, arts, religion, glory,
    Warm'd by his propitious smile,
    Flourish there, and bless this isle!
  Gen. But stay! what wonder does my spirit
  seize?   [*Turning to the King and Queen.*
See! here are both the great divinities.
  Tha. The god and goddess too of this bless'd
    isle!
    Chaste beauty in her aspect shines,
      And love in his does smile.
  Gen.   Quickly, Heroes, as 'tis meet,
      Throw your trophies at their feet,
        Fall down, and adore 'em!

  Whilst with speed we hither call
  The gods of neighb'ring groves, and all
   Their Nymphs to dance before 'em.

An Entry of Rural Gods and Nymphs.

*When the Prologue is done, and all gone off the stage,
Enter two, who sing this following song :—*

  Now for the play, the prologue is done,
  The dancing is o'er, and the singers are gone.
  The ladies so fine, and so fair, it surpasses,
  Are dress'd, and have all tak'n leave of their
   glasses.
Where are the slaves should make ready the stage ?
Here, here are the slaves should make ready the
  stage.

An Entry of Carpenters.

It having been the manner of all those who have had the honour before me, to serve the Court, in employments of this nature, to adorn their works with the names of those great persons who had parts in the representation, I hope I shall not be condemned, if I, following their examples, consecrate this of mine to posterity, by the same policy.

DRAMATIS PERSONÆ.

The Persons of the Play.	The Personators.
CALISTO, *a chaste and favourite Nymph of Diana, beloved by Jupiter,* . .	Her Highness the LADY MARY.
NYPHE, *a chaste young Nymph, Friend to Calisto,* . .	Her Highness the LADY ANNE.
JUPITER, *in love with Calisto,*	The LADY HENRI- ETTA WENTWORTH.
JUNO,	The COUNTESS OF SUSSEX.
PSECAS, *an envious Nymph, Enemy to Calisto, beloved by Mercury,* . . .	The LADY MARY MORDANT.
DIANA, *Goddess of Chastity,*	MRS BLAGGE, *late Maid of Honour to the* Queen.*
MERCURY, *in love with Psecas,*	MRS JENNINGS, *Maid of Honour to the Duchess.*

NYMPHS *attending on* DIANA, *who also danced in the Prologue, and in several entries in the Play.*

THE COUNTESS OF DARBY.
THE COUNTESS OF PEMBROKE.
THE LADY KATHARINE HERBERT.
MRS FITZ-GERALD.
MRS FRAZIER, *Maid of Honour to the Queen.*

* She resigned previous to the publication of the Masque.

The PERSONS *of* QUALITY *of the men that danced, were*

HIS GRACE THE DUKE OF MONMOUTH.
THE VISCOUNT DUNBLAINE.
THE LORD DAINCOURT.
MR TREVOR.
MR HARPE.
MR LANE.

In the PROLOGUE *were represented*

The RIVER THAMES,	by	MRS DAVIS.*
PEACE,	,,	MRS KNIGHT.†
PLENTY, . . .	,,	MRS BUTLER.
The GENIUS of ENGLAND,	,,	MR TURNER.
EUROPE,	.,	MR HART.
ASIA,	,,	MR RICHARDSON.
AFRICA,	,,	MR MARSH, Jun.
AMERICA, . .	,,	MR FORD.

* Both Mrs Davis and Mrs Knight were mistresses of the King.

† Evelyn mentions in his Diary, 2d December 1675, that he met at Mr Slingsby's the master of the Mint, "Mrs Knight, who sung incomparably, and doubtless has the greatest reach of any English woman. She has been lately roaming in Italy, and was much improved in that quality," vol. ii., p. 94. Pepys, in a letter to Viscount Brouncker, March 13, 1681-2, says, "I have not yet been at Mrs Nelly's.* I hear Mrs Knight is better, and the King takes his repose there once or twice daily."

* Nell Gwin.

I   17

In the Chorusses betwixt the Acts.

STREPHON,	The parts sung by	MR HART.*
CORIDON,	,,	MR TURNER.
SYLVIA,	,,	MRS DAVIS.
DAPHNE, .	,,	MRS KNIGHT.
TWO AFRICAN WOMEN or BLACKS, }	,,	{ MRS BUTLER. MRS HUNT.

The SCENE *of the* PLAY

is ARCADIA.

The duration of it,

AN ARTIFICIAL DAY.

* Hart, who had served Charles I. during the civil wars as a captain, upon the Restoration became a performer in the King's theatre, and attained to great eminence in his profession. He was celebrated for his admirable performance of Othello. That very susceptible female, Lady Castlemaine, better known afterwards as Duchess of Cleveland, " was mighty in love with him, and he is much with her in private, and she goes to him, and do give him many presents : and that the thing is most certain, and Berk Marshall only privy to it and the means of bringing them together, which is a very odd thing : and by this means she is even with the King's love to Mrs Davis."*

Nell Gwin is said to have been a favourite both of Hart and Lacy before she attracted the notice of the Earl of Dorset and the King.†

* Pepys, April 7, 1668, vol. iv., p. 415. 1848, crown 8vo.
† Grammont's Memoirs, Notes, vol. iii., p. 265. London, 1809, crown 8vo.

CALISTO.

ACT I.

Jup. How am I tired thus vainly to pursue
A Nymph, I cannot keep in view ?
 I daily through Arcadia rove
 O'er every hill, through every grove,
 But in her ears to sigh my love ;
And may as well the shades and echoes chace ;
 The shades I easier can embrace,
Which grieves me too, whilst I this maze have trod,
There's none to pity a dispairing god.
 Mer. In these Arcadian woods I've lost my
  heart ;   [*Aside.*
 Whilst I the Nymph by whom I smart,
 Pursue, some little ease to get ;
 This Jove I've oft a wandring met :
 He makes my jealousy grow strong ;
What does he do out of his heav'n so long ?
 I'm sure on some fair Nymph he has design,
 And all my fear is lest it should be mine.
 Can no soft beauty be embrac'd,
 But he must still desire a taste ?
That the old Titans from his throne had hurl'd
 This general grievance of the world !
 But I too soon to rage am won,
 Perhaps there is no injury done ;
 Another Nymph has snatcht his eye,
 I'll go discourse with him, and try.

JUPITER *discovers him.*

Jup. Ah! Mercury! What fortune brought thee
    here?
Thou faithful envoy of the gods, come near!
Plung'd deep in sorrow, with despair opprest,
    I now was wishing for some breast,
    Where I my secrets might repose,
And fate has sent the best I could have chose.
  Mer.   What wondrous pain
Is it can make the king of gods complain?
  Jup. My old affliction, love!
  Mer. What do I hear!   [*Aside.*
    This news I did not vainly fear.
Now dare not I what Nymph he loves enquire,
Lest we should both of us the same admire.
  Jup. Thou seem'st disturb'd, what does thy
    passion move?
  Mer.   Only my loyalty for Jove:
    And rage at the tyrannic boy,
    That dares great Jove's repose destroy:
    His boldness Jove too mildly bears,
    Though us poor vassal gods he dares
    Into his chains and fetters bring,
    He is too saucy with our King.
You ought to make his very godhead cease,
For yours and heav'ns universal peace.
  Jup.   Oh let thy vain discourses die!
    Love's is delightful tyranny:
    There is more pleasure in his pains,
    Than all the joys our heav'n contains:
    If love I out of heav'n should chace,
    It would appear so dull a place,
    My self and all the gods would be,
    Even tir'd with immortality.
  Mer. I own these joys, sometimes I try,
    To pass away eternity:

But are they not for Jove too low?
Jup. The world must not the secret know.
We boast great things to be adored and sought;
There is some pleasure to be happy thought
    But for all joys of our abode,
      From earth I would not move:
    Nor be content to be a god,
      To be deprived of love.
Without that joy two vast extremes would join;
Things without sense would equal things divine:
'Twixt us and plants there would be little odds,
And saucy mortals be more blessed than gods.
  Mer. Oh! let not Jove submit to such a fate.
Poorly to envy things he does create.
  Jup. No, if to mortals I present delight,
I to the feast will still my self invite.
  Mer. Yes, yes, we know Jove's appetite; [*Aside.*
    Ere quite abstain from love's sweet feasts,
    He'l humbly dine with birds and beasts.
  Jup.   —— I still provide with care,
    We gods in all delights should share;
    Besides, the loves by us embrac'd
Would kill a poor weak mortal, but to taste.
    We know what pleasure love affords,
    To heavy beasts and mettled birds;
    Here and there at will we fly,
    Each step of nature's perch we try;
    Down to the beast, and up again
    To the more fine delights of man:
    We every sort of pleasure try;
So much advantage has a deity.
  Mer. Nay, if Jove rents the world to man and
    beast,
He may preserve the Royalty at least,
And freedom take to hunt in any grounds;
The pleasures of great Jove should have no bounds.
This distant talk still keeps me sweating here,

In agonies of jealousy and fear;
   And if I do not put an end,   *[Aside.*
   The day he thus will gladly spend.
  I'll not torment my self in vain,
  I'll boldly ask and end my pain.
All joys the world must own their sovereign's due;
   But yet the story does untold remain,
   What beauty did the glory gain
Once more the world's great ruler to subdue.
  Jup. Oh! Mercury! the fairest Nymph of
   human race!
All former loves of mine she does so far surpass,
   I them for beauties scarce allow,
   And never truly lov'd till now.
  Mer. Astonishment!
  Jup. Did they all live again,
   I would not take the pain
   To vex my self into a shape,
   For all the pleasure of a rape;
Except it were to sharpen my desire,
And to return to her with greater fire.
  Mer. What should she be? and where does she
   remain?
  Jup. Oh! that's my grief, she's one of cold
   Diana's train.
  Mer. Oh! I am stabb'd! my fear prophetic
   proves,
I am assured, it is my Nymph he loves.   *[Aside.*
  Jup. Thou know'st what ills of late were done
In heav'n and earth, by Phœbus' frantic son:
I from high heav'n descending to survey
   The half-burnt world, and with a god-like care
   All ruin'd places to repair,
Came here to view my lov'd Arcadia.
   As I in every place did pass,
   To cloath the wither'd fields with grass,
To all the woods new leaves and shades to bring,

Set rivers running, fill each empty spring,
        I chanc'd to spy
This young and beauteous Nymph trip often by.
  Mer. And has great Jove her name yet ever
      heard;
  Jup. No opportunity I yet have got,
She swiftly by like some bright meteor shot
Dazzled my eye, and straight she disappeared.
  Mer. And whither ran the vanishing vision still?
  Jup. ——Or to the woods, or o'er some hill,
    To hunt some dear, or swifter roe,
    Still in her hand a dart or bow:
    Her garb did negligence express;
    For oh! she had no need of dress:
Conceal'd, I oft pursued her, but in vain;
For still at last she mixt with chaste Diana's train.
  Mer. Can she be gain'd?
  Jup. By no enchantment can,
She flies the very shadow of a man:
    She thinks it does her virtue stain,
    If she but sleep where one has lain,
That she is of some purity beguiled,
If she but taste the air, the breath of one defiled:
    If any wand'ring loves by chance
      T'approach her be so bold,
    Away the naked Cupids dance,
      She makes them shake with cold.
  Mer. This in my soul does some small comfort
      breed,
    What then to gain her will ye do?
  Jup.   ——I do not know,
It does the skill of one poor god exceed.
But ha! I see 'em come from yonder grove,
Diana and her train, this way they move.
  Mer. They are preparing for this morning's chace.
  Jup. Let's hide our selves in clouds apace,
Lest we our being here betray,

And quickly chace 'em all away.   [*Exit.*

  Mer. But as they pass I'll watch your eye,

And your lov'd Nymph that way descry.   [*Exit.*

SCENE II.

DIANA, CALISTO, NYPHE, PSECAS, ATTENDANTS.

  Dia. Come! Come away my Nymphs, too long

    we have repos'd,

The morning has her golden doors unclos'd,

And there stands blushing on us!—Come away!

Let us not lose the gentlest part of day;

Princess Calisto, most admir'd, belov'd,

The fairest, chastest, most approv'd

Of all that ever grac'd my virgin throng,

You, who of great and royal race are sprung,

    Born under golden roofs, and bred to ease,

   To every kind of soft delight,

   To glory, power, and all that might

    A royal virgin please.

What could your tender years to pain so soon

    enure ?

And how can you this hard and toilsome life

    endure ?

  Cal. Divinest power ! Can any pleasures be

Compar'd to innocence and chastity ?

From toils of greatness I discharge my mind,

And only in these shades true ease I find.

  Pse. Oh ! with what pride ! and feign'd neglect

    of art   [*Aside.*

This royal favourite storms our goddess' heart,

Conquers it too, and rules her power divine,

Whilst all our merits unregarded shine.

  Dia. I never such a victim had before,

Crown, beauty, youth what all the world adore,

You bring at once in sacrifice to me,

The offering exceeds the Deity.

Pse. Our poor deluded goddess is undone;
                                        [*Aside.*
This favourite has her heart and empire won.

   Ny. How am I pleas'd my sister's praise to hear,
Though like a little star I near appear,   [*Aside.*
Nature and friendship do enough prefer
My name to honour, whilst I shine in her.

   Cal. The crown and glory at your feet I throw
Are for your favour off'ring too low ;
And giving only what I scorn and hate,
I gain your service at too cheap a rate.

   Pse. Oh ! how for praise she spreads a spacious
     net ?
Not one regard to us can passage get :   [*Aside.*
Our virtues will not go for virtues long ;
I neither will, nor ought to bear this wrong.

   Dia. You, Princess ! do adorn, enrich my shade.
Ne'er was so great, so early triumphs made
At once o'er beauty, glory, youth and ease,
All of 'em fair delightful provinces.
None e'er so young such courage did express ;
The Macedonian victories were less.
And better to adorn and guard my groves,
This fair young warrior, 'gainst ease and loves,
You bring to train up here,—before whose eye
I see already vanquish'd Cupids fly,
With wounds a bleeding, and with broken bows,
A fair comparison in arms you chose.

   Ny. She to much honour me, in this prefers ;
And though my courage cannot equal hers,
None to your service shall more zealous be,
Nor still to love a greater enemy.

   Pse. Hark how they bandy praise, and flattery
     round !   [*Aside.*
Each takes her turn to catch it and rebound :
Whilst we desertless fools must patience feign.
And praise our selves, if any praise we'll gain.

Our youth I find we wisely waste,
And are to mighty purpose chaste ;
Since these our kind rewards must prove.
I will in pure revenge go love.
A god-like youth, and vassal to my eyes,
Has long with patience borne my tyrannies.
The humble slave each moment I torment,
And rage which others slight, on him I vent :
But now his sufferings I'll requite,
I'll go and love him out of spite.
Dia. Now, Nymphs, before the rosy morning
fades,
And the day's fury chase us to the shades :
Let's hunt the nimble deer without delay,
We have decreed the martyrs of the day,
And what you all shall kill together bring,
And meet when sun declines at yonder spring.

[Exeunt all but Pse.

Pse. —— No, I'll about another care,
I'll seek my love, discover me who dare ;
On the whole train the shame shall fall ;
I'll swear we are dissemblers all.
From men we only seem to fly,
To meet 'em with more privacy :
That I sincerity approve,
And boldly own to all the world I love.   [*Exit.*

SCENE III.

JUPITER, MERCURY.

Mer. Thanks to the fates ! my heart is now at
ease !
Two different Nymphs our inclinations please.

[*Aside.*

Jup. Ah ! Mercury ! what beauty have I seen ?
Mer. I have with Jove in equal raptures been.
Jup. I in so hot an agony did stay

The cloud, in which I hidden lay,
    Dropt, and melted half away :
That she such beauty should on shades bestow,
And careless love should let her scape his bow.
    Mer. And is it she ?
    Jup. Why dost thou so enquire ?
    Mer. Because I one of the same train admire.
    Jup. Art thou by these cold beauties wounded
        then ?
    Mer. ——Yes, by the scornful'st of the train,
Your Nymph is yielding, if compar'd to mine ;
Yours hates she knows not why, mine with design ;
Yours only flies you, mine returns and fights ;
Yours lets you die, but mine to kill delights :
You have but one aversion to subdue,
I thousands have, which every hour renew.
    Jup. Poor Hermes ! how are we by love opprest ?
    'Two wounded gods here desolate appear,
    Each with an arrow sticking in his breast,
        Goes wand'ring round the woods he knows
            not where ;
Chacing his Nymph, some little ease to find,
And may as well pursue the fleeting wind.
    Mer. Pursue the wind ? rather a storm I chace,
Which turns to dash her fury in my face,
Not in wild shapes, but in all beauty drest,
    That ever did a human shape adorn.
I've met my Nymph, and have my love exprest,
    And never any thing obtain'd, but scorn.
She meets me, true ! but 'tis to mock me still,
And if she ever smiles, it is to kill.
    Jup. Oh ! Hermes ! you your self may happy
        call ;
            When maids shew scorn, they oft are
                near to yield,
    And they who venture once to fight may fall ;
            But mine will not be drawn into the field.

Could I entice her thither any way,
I only for a little scorn would pray.
I'll not to heaven till I obtain some ease,
Let jealous Juno watch me as she please.
   Mer. What will ye do? you no attempt must
     dare.
   Jup. Prithee, what god or mortal can forbear?
T'enjoy such beauty I'd no shape refuse:
     Nay, if I knew what form most pleas'd her eye,
     I'd not deny
To be that thing, and my whole godhead lose.
   Mer. O wondrous power of love!
     Too hard for Jove!
I wonder not he baffles my defence;
He is too mighty for omnipotence!
   Jup. Hermes I've thought! I can my self relieve.
                        [*Starts.*
   Mer. What new Minerva does Jove's brain con-
     ceive?
   Jup. A sure and pleasant ambush I will lay;
I'll in Diana's shape the Nymph betray:
My wanton kisses then she'll ne'er suspect,
     Nor my design detect.
No vice but for a virtue may escape,
If it be acted in a holy shape.
Disguis'd like her, I'll kiss, embrace, be free.
   Mer. Yes, and persuade her too, 'tis chastity.
All actions finely gilded o'er succeed;
Men still the doers mind, and not the deed:
The Nymph will all Diana does allow;
Nay think she liv'd in some mistake till now.
   Jup. 'Tis sacred truth! then firmly I decree,
I will serve her as all mankind serves me.
When on the world they would impose some cheat,
Most strict devotion they will counterfeit:
Look grave on all men, and then whine to me,
With such absurd and apish mimicry,

I scarce from laughter, spite of rage forbear,
And take diversion in the villain's prayer:
This trick of mortals shall be learnt by me;
I to serve love will mimic chastity.
What form wilt thou assume for thy design?
   Mer. What better form than one that is divine!
In human shape no more to her I'll go;
My own true form I thus attired will shew,
When she perceives it is a god does love,
Perhaps ambition the proud Nymph may move.
This satisfaction too I shall enjoy:
'Tis not a shape embraces her, but I,
Whilst our delights we in disguises chuse,
We half the pleasure of enjoyment lose.
   Jup. I like thy plot, thy thoughts agree with
      mine,
Come let us each with speed to his design.
Now vanish from my thoughts all vexing cares,
And rule of human, or divine affairs.
Let gods and mortals what they will pursue,
And fate and fortune their own business do.
Let wrangling elements contend their fill,
And all the wheels of the world's frame stand still:
Let toiling nature if she please go sleep,
Or for her sport a general revel keep.
Let trembling mortals now go curse or pray,
Be good or wicked, which they will, to-day,
I care not what disorders there shall be;
Let heaven and earth slide into anarchy.
   All politic cares of every kind
      I'll from my breast remove;
   And will to-day perplex my mind
      With never a thought but love.   [*Exeunt.*

Enter STREPHON, CORYDON, DAPHNE, SYLVIA.
         Chorus of SHEPHERDS.

   Str. Hark, hark, I hear the merry hunter's horn.

Cor. The sound from yonder hill by winds is
　　borne.
Daph. Diana, and her Nymphs are all that way
A hunting gone.
Syl. So soon ere break of day?
　　　Chorus,　　Let 'em, let 'em go,
　　　　　　Lovers better pleasures know.
Str. Let the cold Nymphs run dabbling in the
　　dew,
　　　Kind love to warmer pleasures us invites.
Daph.　　I do not envy their delights,
Whilst my dear Strephon does continue true.
Cor. Whilst thus severe my Sylvia does remain,
I envy not the hunters, but the slain.
Syl. Poor Corydon, thy flame remove,
　　　I pity thee, but cannot love.
Yet I own, I have something in every vein,
Which moves me to love, could I meet with a
　　swain,
Who were to my mind, and would love me again.
Str.　　See Shepherds, the day is begun :
　　　Come, with our sports let's welcome
　　　the sun.

　　　　An entry of BASQUES.

Sylv.　　Kind lovers, love on,
　　　Lest the world be undone,
　　　　And mankind be lost by degrees :
　　　For if all from their loves
　　　Should go wander in groves,
　　　　There soon would be nothing but
　　　　trees.
　　　Chorus,　　Kind lovers, love on, &c.
　　　　　　　　　　　[*Exeunt omnes.*

　　　FINIS ACTUS I.

ACT II.

JUPITER, MERCURY.

Jup. When shall I get this vision in my sight?
She flies from love, as shadows from the light:
Whilst I pursue her, flaming with desire,
And o'er these hills roll like an orb of fire;
Making the sun the rule of day resign,
To these more bright and piercing beams of mine.
  Mer. 'Tis folly longer o'er these hills to stray:
'Tis noon, and now the golden dust of day
Dissolved, does from the heavenly mountains flow
In fiery streams, and drowns the world below.
In the cool groves our Nymphs we now shall find,
Wading in shades, and bathing in the wind:
        Whilst Phœbus shoots his arrows round,
        And vainly seeks the Nymphs to wound,
        The groves he vainly does invade;
        His fiery darts are quenched in shade.
Fit your disguise, and thither let's repair.
  Jup. At small expense I from the wealthy air
My self with any figure can supply:
Or I can fix an image in the eye.
Come here you wand'ring atoms of the air,
You that are fittest for a form so fair,
And now my beauteous ambuscade prepare.
Into Diana's shape your selves congeal,
Under that ice the burning Jove conceal;
There let me all lie cover'd, like the brow
Of some high flaming mountain hid in snow.
  Mer. See! the assembling atoms do obey,
Or rather the great Jove is fled away:
And the fair goddess of these woods is here.
Hail beauteous!——
    Jup. Oh! Thou rallyest now I fear;
        But canst thou any where
        Descry one beam of Jupiter?

Mer. Not one by your own self I swear ;
There's nothing but Diana can be seen :
Her habit, feature, shape, proportion, mein ;
Nay, and your voice exactly tuned I hear,
And past discovery deludes the ear.
  Jup. Now, you cool atoms, from your ranks dis-
    band,
Flow to loose air again at my command :
Thither return like rivers to the main,
And let me now be Jupiter again.
  Mer. Again the atoms loyally obey,
The snowy shape is all dissolv'd away.
  Jup. Poor god ! No shape at all thou didst
    descry :
I only graved a figure on thy eye :
And the soft voice which you believe you hear,
Was form'd but in the concave of your ear.
  Mer. Ah ! Jove ! How useful, and of what
    delight
Is sovereign power ? 'tis that determines right.
Nothing is truly good, but what is great :
A mortal you would punish for this cheat.
  Jup. I would, and justly ; shall the thing I make
Presume the freedom of a god to take ?
I cannot err, what e'er my actions be ;
There's no such thing as good or ill to me.
No action is by nature good or ill ;
All things derive their natures from my will.
If virtue from my will distinct could be,
Virtue would be a power supreme to me.
What no dependency on me will own,
Makes me a Vassal, and usurps my throne.
If so I can revenge me in a trice,
Turn all the balance, and make Virtue Vice.
  Mer. Jove like himself, with reasons firm and
    strong,
Upholds the Port, does to a God belong :

For I have ever of opinion been,
Gods only should be privileg'd to sin ;
We gild sour Virtue with fine Titles still,
To make men swallow the unpleasant pill ;
But from the sweets of sin they'll ne'er be chac'd,
Ere since the liquorish slaves have got a taste ;
But let us hasten now to seek our loves,
And first examine all the neighbouring groves.

 Jup. See ! something swiftly darted by my
  sight ;   [*Cal. goes over the stage.*
Was it a Nymph, or sudden glance of light ?
 Mer. A Nymph, I swear !
 Jup. Oh ! whither is she run ?
 Mer. See ! See ! to yonder grove she's gone !
There like a glittering star in night,
She tempers all the shades with light.
Fair streams of light seem after her to stray,
Like the bright dawning of some beauteous day.

 Jup. It is my Nymph, none else is half so fair.
  Fly thou ! whilst thither I repair :
  Fly ! or thou ruin'st my design.
 Mer. Nay stay ! perhaps the Nymph is mine :
  If mine, she will to mock me stay.
 Jup. If mine, thou chacest her away.
 Mer. I in a cloud my self will hide.
 Jup. I'm ruin'd, if thou art descried.
 Mer. And I, if mine discover Jove.
 Jup. But mine will fly.
 Mer. But mine may love.
 Jup. I'll be so hid she shall not Jove surprise.
 Mer. But Jove may peep through his disguise.
 Jup. It shall no damage to thee bring.
 Mer. Oh ! no one can resist a King.
 Jup. I will not tempt thy Nymph, I swear.
 Mer. Your glory will, if you forbear.
 Jup. Oh ! thy impertinence ! the Nymph is
  gone !

I   18

Thy saucy wrangling has my hopes undone.
   Mer. For what should all this anger be?
      Perhaps 'tis you have ruin'd me.
   Jup. Surely you ought at my commands to move.
   Mer. Love understands not either King or Jove.
   Jup. What monarch will endure this from a
     slave?
   Mer. What constant lover but is bold and brave?
   Jup. Begone, thou wilt provoke my rage!
     In foolish strife no more engage.
   Mer. Thrice happy Jove! your Nymph I now
     espy?
   Jup. Where, where?
   Mer. In yonder neighbouring wood!
   Jup. So nigh?
Happy contention which my flight delayed!
For I had lost her if I had not stayed.
   Mer. To me the obligations then confess,
And chide no more a lover's haughtiness.
   Jup. Be gone, be gone! and thy own Nymph
     pursue,
Or once again thou wilt thy King undo. [*Exit Mer.*
Now all you troops of winged loves, come see
Your selves reveng'd on your fair enemy.   [*Exit.*

CALISTO.

   Cal. Under the day's oppression tired I grow;
The sun to-day does no compassion shew.
In these cool shades I am compelled to stray,
To shun the merciless fury of the day.
My goddess up the mountain's farther gone,
The Nymphs dispers'd, and I left all alone:
My hopes to find 'em I will now forsake,
And, tired with hunting too, will gladly take
The invitation of this bed of flowers,
In soft repose to pass away some hours:

There lye, my bow, and take thy ease unbent,
Thy weary arms I'll not this hour torment.
And you, my arrows, in your lodging keep,
And there from mischief lull your selves to sleep.
Mine and your travel for an hour shall cease,
And now poor herds go browse a while in peace.

[She lies down to sleep.

Enter JUPITER.

Jup. Oh ! Love ! what pleasure dost thou here
    prepare ?
Dull heaven, I shall return to thee no more ;
    Here is a pleasure I prefer before
All the delights I am possess'd of there.
Now Juno thy disgrace with patience bear,
And to disturb my pleasures do not dare :
My former loves I yielded to thy rage :
    I was contented they should be remov'd ;
    Alas ! I find I only thought I lov'd.
No Nymph but this did e'er my heart engage :
Thou might'st contend for beauty with the rest ;
But this shakes all thy interest in my breast.
Keep in thy heaven, and do not cast an eye ;
There gnaw thy self with rage and jealousy.
    Thou art already half undone,
    Be glad thou dost enjoy my throne :
For plague me now, I'll chace thee from my bed,
And place thy crown upon thy rival's head.

[Cal. wakes.

But I have wak'd my Nymph from her repose,
Her opening eyes a sparkling heaven disclose ;
Wherein a thousand captive Cupids lye,
Opprest and fetter'd all with chastity.
In those two temples full of heavenly light,
At the bright crystal portal of her sight,
Let me in fair Diana's form appear :
And let my voice dissolve into her ear ;

And thither in those pleasing accents flow,
The goddess speaks, when she does kindness shew.
My huntress here at her repose ? which way
                    Did you pursue the chace to-day ?
    Cal.   My goddess here so nigh ?
Hail power! more great than Jove, though Jove
        stood by,
In my esteem !
    Jup. Till now what lover heard   [*Aside.*
Himself with pleasure to himself preferred ?
    Oh ! now my fire does rage within !
        I for the pain,
        No longer can my self contain ;
    Without more forms I must begin.
Princess Calisto, pleasure of my sight !
Grace of my train, my pride, and my delight ;
What courteous god will lend me words and art
To speak the amazing passion in my heart ;
Thy dazzling excellence each moment breeds.
    Cal. My goddess now in praise of me exceeds.
That I from fate or nature did obtain
Any deserts, that might your favour gain,
Must in my soul a noble pleasure raise ;
But now you quite oppress me with your praise.
    Jup. Not half my sense of your desert I speak ;
My heart can never shew it, till it break,
Which swell'd with kindness it will do ere long,
If love can find no passage but the tongue.
    Cal. Chaste power ! I beg you let these praises
        die,
Take some compassion of my modesty.
    Jup. Oh ! Princess ! it is I that pity need.
Shall I the secret tell ? your merits breed
In my lost heart a strange uncommon flame :
A kindness I both fear and blush to name ;
Nay, one for which no name I ever knew,
The passion is to me so strange, so new !

Cal. My wond'ring thoughts you into mazes
		guide!
And your dark meaning close in riddles hide.
	Jup. You are not half so much amazed as I !
My self am frighted at the prodigy.
I daily stand, and wonder at my pain,
And do not know of what I would complain ;
I always sigh, when I your beauties view,
And wish, but wonder why, I wish for you.
Something I fain would crave, but do not know
What I should ask, or what you can bestow.
Some charms about you for my ease you bear,
But know not how they cure, nor what they are ;
But I am certain they could give me ease.
	Cal. Oh ! Gods ! how came you by this strange
		disease ?
Weary with hunting, you to-day in haste,
Of some accursed plant did rashly taste ;
On which some viper left his deadly sting,
Or else you drank at some infectious spring.
	Jup. Some spring where Cupid wash'd his bloody
		darts,
When the young tyrant had been murd'ring hearts ;
That, that the author of my grief does prove,
The pois'nous gore has tainted me with love.
	Cal. Who to that fatal spring your steps
		betrayed ?
Call, call to Æsculapius for some aid.
	Jup. Oh ! none can give me any ease but you.
Sick ! Sick I grow ! ——
	Cal. What would you ha' me do ?
	Jup. Look kindly on me with a pleasing eye !
Smile, smile upon me sweetly, or I die.
Suppose me now, some beauteous god, or Jove
The King of gods, and think your self in love.
	Cal. You do not speak your own desires, I'm sure,
You'd rather die, than ask me such a cure.

Jup. Yes, once I would, but I am alter'd now :
Some kindness now, you may, you must allow.
　Cal. What kindness can I shew? what can I do?
Stand off, or I shall be infected too.
　Jup. That is the reason why I press so nigh ;
To cure me you must be as sick as I.
　Cal. Yes, were your sickness but the plague, I
　　would ;
This for a world shall never taint my blood.
　Jup. In this necessity you must submit ;
It will be only one tempestuous fit,
And we shall both be well, —— you must, you
　　shall.——
　Cal. She raves, I to the Nymphs for aid must call,
Or she will do some horrid act, I fear ;
Help, help ! my goddess is distracted here ;
Come both to mine, and to my goddess' aid !
　Jup. I will not wrong you, be not thus afraid.
　Cal. You cannot help it, you distracted grow.
Loose me, or this into my heart shall go.
[Shews a dart.
　Jup. I find my stratagem is fond and vain,
By other arts I my design must gain,
Or in despair and shame must vanish hence :
Glory has most victorious influence
On women's hearts, that seldom is denied ;
For that subdues their only guard, their pride.
I'll try how that will work upon her mind,
And rush with troops of glories from behind
The ambush, where I lye in vain conceal'd,
And fight her virtue fairly in open field.
The wondrous virtue, royal Nymph, you shew,
Deserves your glorious fortune you should know :
From fair Diana's vanish'd form, see here,
Low at your feet thus prostrate does appear,
Paying his homage to your conquering eyes,
No less than Jove the King of deities !

Who so fortunate, 'tis true, did prove,
At two celestial springs to drink in love ;
But they were these two bright ones of your eyes.
From which he bears such torturing miseries.
Unless you quickly some compassion shew,
You will the world into confusion throw.
    Cal. Oh ! Gods ! have I been cheated all this
        while ?
Talked with a god, and of a thing so vile
As love ? I might have guess'd by all his words,
As men by horrid shrieks of ominous birds ;
Their deaths foretell some fate in secret lay,
To make my fame and innocence a prey :
What sin have I committed, mighty Jove !
You should contrive to punish me with love ?
    Jup. Your killing beauty is one great offence ;
But your chief sin is too much innocence.
    Cal. If beauty does offend you, ruin, blast,
Take what revenge on it you please, —— the last
My virtue, you, nor shall, nor can destroy ;
I all my life will in that sin employ.
    Jup. Then all my life I must be wretched
        made.
Condemn me then to the infernal shade,
    Cal. Let me with speed to any pains remove,
To hell, or any torment, but your love.
    Jup. That way my self I into hell shall doom,
And turn their hell into Elizium ;
For that is heaven where sovereign pleasures are,
And oh ! what pleasure can with you compare ?
Then do not by severity so fierce
Damn the great soul of the whole universe.
    Cal. These fond discourses I'll no longer bear ;
Farewell, you only combat with the air,
And all your high contention vain shall find.
Ha ! He my feet does with enchantments bind !
Release me tyrant ! ——

Jup. Do not yet begone !
I beg, I kneel, I offer you my throne.   [*Kneels.*
   Cal. I scorn the throne, the deity of Jove !
   Jup. Oh ! do but counterfeit a little love.
   Cal. Be gone, the sight of you I cannot brook.
   Jup. I'll give my empire for a smile, a look :
For nothing, —— let me but so happy prove,
To oblige one I so entirely love.
   Cal. If gifts you will bestow, I'll name you one,
Give me my self, and let me straight be gone.
   Jup. Proud and ungrateful Nymph, did I bestow
                         [*Rises angrily.*
Those treasures on you, which enrich you so,
And now, I come a begging to your door,
Can I not gain an alms when I emplore ?
I'll quickly if I please retake my due,
And punish those your saucy virtues too :
For virtues in a soul my Vice-roys be,
And may my empire guard, but not from me.
Their power vanishes when I appear,
Nor shall they dare o'er me to domineer.
I will depose 'em from their high commands,
And take the rule of you into my hands.
Ho ! There the winds ! to yonder valley bear
This Nymph, and for my love prepare her there.
   Cal. Kill me, you tyrant !
          [*Enter* WINDS *and carry off Calisto.*
   Jup. Stop her needless cries !
Now Nymph, it is my turn to tyrannize ;
She is led hence my captive, but I find
My self in stronger chains left bound behind.
Glory and pleasure in my breast contend,
Pleasure would seize what glory would defend :
Her virtues charm my glory on their side ;
But pleasure longs to have his pleasure tried :
For glory like a bragging coward, does here
Only in beauty's absence domineer :

But in her sight 'twill make a poor defence,
And never stand before victorious sense.   [*Exit.*

The Scene *near the* Vale, *whither the* Winds *carried*
Calisto.

Enter Strephon, Corydon, Daphne, Sylvia,
Chorus of Shepherds.

Cho. Come Shepherds quickly hasten to the
     shades,
The sun with all his force the air invades.
Sylv. The open plains let us forsake!
Here is a grove will pity of us take:
The trees in gentle whisperings delight us;
     Here are all things to invite us.
Stre. These pleasures none can well improve,
But we, my shepherdess, who love.
Daph. These pleasures none can well improve,
But we, my dearest swain, who love.
Cor. Oh happy shepherd, and kind shepherdess,
Whom all the gods, above expression bless.
     Here Sylvia cruel, I forlorn,
          Torment our selves each day;
     Whilst I with grief, and she with scorn,
          Waste all our youth away.
Sylv. Alas poor shepherd! the fault is not mine
That to thy passion I do not incline;
I wish thy love and desert were more moving;
For I confess I fain would be loving.
                         [*She pauses and starts.*
     What, on the sudden, do I ail?
     Gentle winds, from yonder vale,
     On the sudden warm my heart.
Sylv. Oh! I'm wounded: Oh! I smart.

Enter Cupids, *and* Winds.

Stre. Sure some god is here descended.
     With a train of loves attended,

Sylv. Oh! I'm wounded: Oh! I love,
　　This is some inchanted grove.
Chorus. This is some inchanted grove.

　　　An ENTRY *of* CUPIDS *and* WINDS.

Stre. Oh! my soul is in a flame.
Daph. I must fly, or lose my fame.
Cor. O what raging passions fill me!
　　Love me Sylvia now, or kill me.
Sylv. Oh! I love, and long to shew it;
　　But my shepherd shall not know it.
Stre. Oh! my Daphne! now or never.
Daph. Strephon, fly my sight for ever!
Cor. I can no longer Sylvia wait thee.
Sylv. Corydon be gone! I hate thee.
Chorus. Curse on this enchanted grove,
　　　We are all undone with love.
　　We are all undone with love
　　　Fly from this enchanted grove.
　　　　　　　　　　　[*Exeunt omnes.*

FINIS ACTUS II.

— —

ACT III.

JUNO.

Juno. Down from the heavenly rooms, and airy
　　　throne,
Where I have long been left alone:
As fast as jealousy my steps could bear,
I come to seek my wand'ring Jupiter:
I am assur'd he does not wait
On any politic affairs of State:
He stays not to employ his public mind,

And fix the general business of mankind.
No, I have too much cause to fear,
Affairs less good and virtuous keep him here.
My blood grows hot!——and must I then be us'd
For ever thus?—— for ever thus abus'd?
Must every trifling Nymph, that looks but fair,
Entice from my embrace my Jupiter?
Must all my charms be every strumpet's scorn,
Only because they by a wife are borne?
Oh! servile state of conjugal embrace!
Where seeming honour covers true disgrace.
We with reproaches mistresses defame,
But we poor wives endure the greatest shame.
We to their slaves are humble slaves, whilst they
Command our lords, and rule what we obey.
Their loves each day new kindnesses uphold,
We get but little, and that little cold!
That a poor wife is with her state reproached,
And to be married is to be debauched.
Now some new rival must my soul perplex;
I'll find her out, or I'll destroy the sex:
And I will Jove too in his thefts detect,
Or I'll each bird and beast I meet dissect.   [*Exit.*

Enter PSECAS.

Psc. Where is this love of mine a wand'ring now!
When I would scarce a look to him allow,
The restless slave would follow me all day,
I could not frown or chide him then away:
And now that I would kind to him appear,
The handsome fool is gone I know not where.
If any of the winged train of love
    Now hover in this grove,
Go fetch the moaning boy to me with haste,
Tell him the happy minute's come at last:
    For by love's bow I swear,
I with my goddess open war declare.

And for the battle all my charms prepare.
Ha! what fair vision's this assaults my sight,
My beauty's love I swear arrayed in light:

Enter MERCURY.

Sparkling in glory brighter than the day;
His splendid train sweeps all the shades away.
    Mer. My Nymph!
    Pse. My love appear to me again,
Welcome as sudden ease to one in pain:
Where hast thou hid thy lovely self to-day?
A whole long morn together from me stay!
I have been seeking thee in every grove,
To give some ease to thy despairing love:
But I'm afraid my trouble I may spare,
The cure's already wrought by one more fair:
Some of the charming goddesses above
From me have spirited away my love.
Venus has chose thee for her page, and she
Has drest thee in this shining livery.
    Mer. Oh! what amazing change is this!
I am a dreaming now in Paradise;
Or this is some kind image of my fair,
My charming Nymph that pities my despair;
Act on this sweet delusion, pretty shade,
What pleasure does my throbbing heart invade?
My panting heart is on the sudden eas'd,
I, since I was a god, was ne'er so pleased.
    Pse. If in my love be any bliss,
Thou shalt have more delight than this.
A kindness equal to my former hate,
Thou shalt not wish thy self a happy fate.
    Mer. Can Psecas then do anything but kill?
Psecas be kind, and yet be Psecas still?
    Pse. The very Psecas who did hate thee once,
But now does all her cruelty renounce:
And with it both my goddess and her train.

Whom now I shun, I hate, disdain,
Throw off the yoke of her unnatural law,
And all my beauties from her camp withdraw ;
And now in love's and nature's cause will fight,
And do my sex, and injur'd beauty right ?
  Mer. Oh ! with what noble courage art thou
    fir'd !
What courteous god these thoughts in thee in-
    spir'd ?
Lead on, we will begin the war to-day ;
I'll fight the cause, and thou shalt be my pay.
These pois'nous fumes we'll from the earth remove,
And cleanse the air with the hot fire of love.
All beings are concern'd in our just cause,
To kill these rebels against nature's laws ;
Who, if they be not to confusion hurl'd,
Will beggar nature, and lay waste the world.
And to encourage us my love the more,
Great Jove himself in person now adore,
Does execution for her proud disdain,
Upon the fairest criminal of the train :
On her who only sways your goddess' breast,
And thou, my Nymph, hat'st more than all the rest.
Look in that vale, and thy revenge delight.
  Pse. Oh ! how I am transported with the sight !
Oh ! that some god now my revenge to please
Would summon hither all the deities ;
All beings mortal and immortal too,
And shew her shame to universal view.
  Mer. My Nymph nor yet her empire under-
    stands ;
See here a god attending her commands.
  Pse. Ha ! what great brightness does around thee
    shine ?
Something beams through thee like a pow'r
    divine.
  Mer. Such glorious vassals are your beauty's due,

And less than gods should not pretend to you.
  Pse. This is a fate more great than I would
    crave;
Have I a god then for my beauty's slave?
  Mer. One of the highest rank, and next the
    throne.
  Pse. This is a love I may with honour own:
For petty gods, like mortals I despise;
But yet I understand not deities.
I fear your passion, I must disapprove;
Gods always make dishonourable love.
  Mer. By love, by Styx, I true to thee will be;
And lose my godhead ere be false to thee.
  Pse. Suppose you constant to your love remain,
I know not how a god to entertain;
Or if I did, perhaps divine delight
May not agree with human appetite.
  Mer. The joys of gods exceed the thoughts of
    men.
  Pse. Oh gods! and shall I be a goddess then?
  Mer. As great as Juno, more belov'd and prais'd.
And have more altars to thy beauty rais'd.
  Pse. What? and have power to torture all I hate,
That will not die with envy at my state.
  Mer. All! All!
  Pse. Oh! then the Nymphs I will torment!
But for Calisto I will plagues invent.
By my great self, this does so pleasing prove,
                        [*Aside.*
My ravish'd heart begins almost to love.
Come to my coronation straight proceed,
Call all the gods and goddesses with speed!
Let the whole air with the bright throng abound.
To shame Calisto, and to see me crown'd.
  Mer. I fly my Queen, and will your will obey;
    But oh! some present kindness you must give,
    To bear my charges in this way

To heaven, and back again, in this one kiss I'll
    live.

Enter NYPHE.

Ny. I heard a doleful cry, not far from hence,
    Of one who in some great distress must be;
The voice seem'd like Calisto's to my sense:
    Oh! all the gods forbid it should be she.
Ha! Psecas, here a lover entertain?
Oh! the vile Nymph, she will disgrace our train.
    Pse. Oh! now I long till I my reign begin,
To plague the Nymphs I hate, and act the Queen.
And see!
Already here a subject for my power,
Thrown in my way by fortune, to devour.
What brings you here my secrets to discover?
    Ny. Not your design to entertain a lover.
    Pse. How dare you so presumptuous be, to spy
My royal, nay, my divine privacy.
    Ny. Royal! divine! and how dare I presume?
Good heavens! what mighty thing are you become?
    Pse. A thing too sacred for your tongue to name
The mighty glories of my swelling fame;
You shall not once into your mouth receive,
Nor dare to look on me without my leave.
    Ny. Since when were you so great, so sacred
      grown?
Surely if any honour must be shewn
The right is mine, who am a Princess born.
    Pse. That's nature's gift, whose charity I scorn.
On my own treasure of desert I live,
And all my glory from my self receive.
    Ny. No, from your lover you some glory gain!
I'll do you right, and spread it through the train.
    Pse. How! do you threaten me? stop, stop her
      flight;
Although my fame is spotless as the light,

My goddess from dishonour less secure,
I'll not th' affront of a dispute endure.
   Ny. Oh! blasphemy! Oh! prodigy of pride!
Crimes black as these do you once hope to hide?
   Pse. Continue still in a contempt so great!
Confine her till my pardon she entreat,
For daring thus my anger to despise,
And 'gainst my honour to believe her eyes.
   Ny. Thy pardon?
   Mer. Will you all you saw deny?
   Ny. I'll tell it all, though I that moment die.
   Pse. Then kill her!
   Ny. Do! thy infamy and shame
My walking ghost shall to the world proclaim.
   Pse. To what a height will this young courage
     grow?
The shame to me design'd, on thee I'll throw.
From hence I charge you let her not remove:
I'll call the Nymph, and swear you are her love.
The lie is sacred, and prevents a crime
Her boiling blood will sure commit in time.
I'll quench the love is springing in the blood,
And blast her vicious nature in her bud.   [*Exit.*
   Mer. Run, run, with speed! I'll charm her in
     this grove,
Shew her with me, Calisto there with Jove.
   Ny. Oh! Traitress!
   Mer. Go, obey my charming rod,
Know 'tis but vain contending with a god!
                  [*Ny. Exit.*
Whilst in this grove, this Nymph with charms I tie,
Straight on my love's commands to heaven I'll fly,
To call my Queen! But oh! what do I see
Juno already here? Oh jealousy!
This jealousy's the ghost of murdered love,
Which turn'd all spirit does outrageous prove:
Groans o'er its grave the poor despairing breast;

But never let's the murderer have rest.
Juno I fear will all our plots prevent,
But I will stand behind, and see th' event.

JUPITER, JUNO, CALISTO.

Jup.   What saucy watchful spies,
    Does Juno place on me where e'er I go ;
  I think the trees of every grove have eyes,
    And winds breathe stories as they blow.
Jun. Is this your business mighty Jove below
Are these the secrets none must dare to know !
For this does Jove in clouds his glory hide ?
Is thus his great omnipotence employ'd ?
How will th' Arcadian Nymphs his praises sing,
And crown with garlands the almighty King !
But what need shapes conceal the wandring Jove :
He is transform'd too much with shameful love ?
Jup. The love I to this royal virgin own,
I take a greater pride in, than my throne ;
And all my shapes do but adorn me more,
As shining armour does a warrior,
To fight this field under the power of love
Is greater glory than to reign above.
Jun. Oh ! blasphemy above an atheist's tongue !
Should men in thought you glory so much wrong ;
The impious slaves you quickly would destroy,
Your thunder now against your self employ :
Or rather there against those trait'rous eyes,
That have depos'd the King of deities.
Jup. She has exalted me above my throne ;
In the short time I have her virtues known :
The joy I felt in loving her, was more
Than endless eyes blest me with before.
Jun. Then all my beauties are forgot it seems,
And Jove for her his goddess disesteems.
A long fruition has a loathing bred,
Of me for ages you have surfeited.

1   19

Jup. I own I have of your imperious mind,
Which to your so much boasted charms, I find,
No small indifference in my breast creates.
    Jun. My haughty mind not half so much abates :
The passion in you for my beauty's due,
As your low mind does my esteem for you.
I scorn my beauties should descend to please
One, who degrades himself to such as these :
With whom if strife were for my grandeur meet,
I now would trample her beneath my feet ;
But that resentment I disdain to shew,
And think the Nymph for my contempt too low.
    Cal. Great Queen ! all honour to your rank is
      due :
But please to know, I am a Princess too,
And do in that respect your image wear ;
Nor does that State from me dishonour bear :
You scorn not more your Monarch should forsake
Your bed for me, than I his love to take ;
And if for love the high contention be,
You scorn strife less, than I the victory :
Not that my hate on Jove alone does fall :
But I disdain, and hate to love at all.
    Jun. When first begun in you this hate to love,
This mighty pride, in the embrace of Jove ?
    Cal. That raise my pride ! True honour you
      blaspheme.
An insect, or a plant, in my esteem
Are nobler beings, and of higher price,
Than Nymph or goddess that descends to vice.
    Jun. Oh ! how in favour boldly you presume !
When had it then beginning ?
    Cal. From the womb.
Rather from fate, which did my choice foresee,
And durst not other natures frame for me,
For fear I should, 'twixt horror and disdain,
Have started to my nothing back again.

Jun. Was e'er such insolence by mortals shewn?
What then, it may be, you disdain my crown?
  Cal. I do; nor by your glory would be bought,
To sin against my honour, but in thought.
All kinds of love to me are so impure,
I hate the marriage bed, which you endure;
Nor would exchange my virtue for my power;
A virgin is a Queen's superior.
  Jun. Amazing haughtiness! This saucy scorn,
If thou wert virtuous, were not to be borne.
  Jup. As Queen she is! more virtues in her shine,
Than you, and all the female powers divine.
  Jun. What virtues yielding easier to your will,
And pleasing you perhaps with greater skill.
  Jup. She gives me greater pleasure in her pride,
Than ever Juno did in being enjoy'd.
  Jun. Oh! how he tortures me! what secret
      pain
I feel, to counterfeit a brave disdain?
Your pleasure with the artful Nymph pursue;
If pride so pleas'd, what did fruition do?
  Jup. Her virtue's more untainted than your own,
And less of yours advanc'd me to my throne.
  Jun. What stay'd you then together in the grove?
Virtue is but of little use to Jove.
  Jup. Rapt with her beauties, but her virtues
      more!
I tarry here her virtues to adore.
They us'd that force upon my vanquish'd mind,
Which once on her bright beauties I design'd.
The fire these kindled th' other did put out.
  Jun. To virtue you are seldom so devout.
And scarce for such insipid joys would stay.
  Jup. Cease your contention without more delay!
Lest you provoke me in this Nymph's defence,
To prove too fatally her innocence.
  Jun. Give her my crown, the trifle I despise;

By being depos'd from thee I higher rise.
To thee no more I will myself debase,
But here condemn thee to this Nymph's embrace.
  Jup. Do, we shall both be gainers by the strife ;
You get more glory, I a fairer wife.
  Jun. A fairer wife ! though I with scorn look
    down
On thy lost heart, and on my falling crown,
Above thy throne, my beauty I surprise ;
I will revenge on thee these blasphemies.
I will ascend, and leave thy hated bed ;
But mounting thus, I'll on thy goddess tread.
  Jup. Hold! lest indeed I raise her to my throne,
And to thy rival make thee vassalage own.
  Jun. Thy throne and heart on whom thou wilt
    bestow !
Without revenge from hence I will not go.
Revenge to my enraged soul shall be,
My throne, my Jove, my heavenly dignity.
  Jup. Nay, then I'll govern your imperious hate.
You airy spirits that on tempests wait,
That all the forces of the air command,
Rain, thunder, lightning, muster or disband,
Employ 'em when, and against whom I please,
Viceroys of all the spreading provinces.
'Twixt earth and moon, quick with your guards
    appear,
And take the loudest of all tempests here,
Your Queen from hence, and keep her close con-
    fin'd,
In the cold rooms, where hail and snow you grind,
Where with more fit companions she may be,
With storms that can reply as loud as she.

Enter AIRY SPIRITS.

Where she her fill of noise may take,
Rail as she will, and no disturbance make :

And do not dare to let her scape from thence,
Till of her duty she has learnt a sense.

[*Spirits seize* JUNO.

Jun. So then, thy Queen must be confin'd above,
That thou below may'st revel with thy love :
Loose me, you slaves, I will not bear this wrong,
I will not stir till I have him along.

Jup. Oh! the eternal plague! my will obey!
This tempest from my ears with speed convey.

Jun. I will not go, you rebel slaves forbear!
Jove, to confinement send me, if you dare.
All the celestial powers shall quickly know,
On what affairs you are employ'd below :
I'll make 'em chuse another in thy throne,
To save both heav'n and earth from be'ng undone.

Jup. Guard, wait awhile !

Jun. Nay, now I will not stay.

Jup. Will you your Queen's, or my commands
    obey ?

Once more I do instate you in my throne ;
Once more this royal virgin's virtues own.
Though had she lov'd, it is sufficient plea
For innocence, that she's belov'd by me ;
For I will be control'd in no amour ;
My love is arbitrary as my power :
I bound all minds and beings but my own,
Am place to all things but my self have none.
On you my largest share of love shall fall,
But no one heart has room enough for all.
I, like my sun, my beams will not confine,
Nor starve all beings by my self to shine.
And like him too, where e'er I shed my light,
I nature do not alter, but excite.
When on a loose and wanton Nymph I smile,
Her blood breeds monsters like the mud of Nile :
But when to flowers and gardens I repair,
With fragrant odours I perfume the air.

Such were the sweets I from her virtues drew,
And you shall own it, yes and thank her too:
Do it I say, and her deserts proclaim;
She of a goddess only wants the name.
    Jun. I will embrace her, since I must obey,
But she by heaven shall dearly for it pay.   [*Aside.*
    Jup. Farewell, fair Nymph!   [*To Cal.*
To that I call my heav'n I now must go;
But leaving you, I leave true heav'n below.
                        [*Jup., Juno, Guards, Ex.*
    Cal. From what a horrid dream do I awake?
I am afraid my sense does yet mistake.
From these celestial tyrants I am freed;
But still the thought does horror in me breed.
I cannot yet compose my restless soul,
The storm is ended, but the billows roll.
But oh! which tears my soul, a shame remains;
My rising blood does almost break my veins:
A fiery blushing flame's around my face;
I'm all on fire with rage at my disgrace:
For I'm enough dishonour'd, and asham'd
To breathe, but in the air, where love is nam'd.
But be disgrac'd with an attempt so foul,
I hate this place, the world, the gods, my soul.

Enter MERCURY.

    Mer. The tempest ended, and no mischief done?
        Calisto's innocence unshaken stand?
    This horrid storm must be again begun,
        I'll fly to heaven, as Psecas gave command:
And to my Queen with lies my self address,
And bring again that raging lioness.
Meanwhile I'll charm the Nymphs within this
        grove:
        Around, around here let 'm rove:
        And visions guard the sacred ground.
        To fright 'em still within their bound.   [*Exit.*

Enter NYPHE.

Ny. How am I kept a prisoner, in the power
  Of this base god! Oh! that revenge to have
I were some mighty goddess for an hour:
  Oh! how I would torment the heavenly slave.
But see! my sister here? and oh! my fears
Her lovely face all delug'd o'er with tears.
Ah! what means this?
Cal. My sister here? be gone,
Leave me to my disorder'd self alone:
And fly these groves, they are the curst abodes
Of satyrs, fiends, or worse, of impious gods.
  Ny. Oh! how you fright me! I grow pale with
    fear;
What fatal accident has happ'ned here?
  Cal. I'm too disorder'd now replies to make:
  Ny. No matter, I will no denial take.
What has befallen you since I parted hence?
  Cal. What you to hear have too much innocence.
  Ny. Not let me know it? this unkind appears;
I will both hear it, and have all the tears.
To yonder mournful shades let us repair,
Which to our sorrows some resemblance bear:
And there to tell your griefs your task shall be,
And I will sit and weep for you, and me.

Enter DAPHNE *and* SYLVIA.

Sylv. Corydon is a noble swain,
  And too long has felt disdain:
  But since scorn I once did show.
  My love I'm too proud to let him know.
Daph. Ah Sylvia! Sylvia! my heart. like yours,
  Pain from foolish pride endures.

I angry with Strephon to-day did appear,
    And now long to reconcile;
Yet in pride for a time will seem severe,
    Though it breaks my heart the while.

Enter STREPHON, CORYDON, *Chorus of*
SHEPHERDS.

DAPHNE *and* SYLVIA *offer to go as they enter.*

Stre. Oh whither does my lovely Daphne fly?
Cor. How long will Sylvia Corydon deny?
Daph. It is my will my kindness to remove.
Sylv. And I shall never, never love.
                    [*Daphne and Sylvia exeunt.*
Stre. Oh! what has chang'd my Daphne's mind?
Chorus. Oh false and cruel woman-kind!
1. *Shep.* Come shepherds, do not complain.
    See, see yonder a merry train
    Of gypsies dancing over the plain.
Call 'em straight, call 'em straight to comfort these
    poor swains.

An ENTRY *of* GYPSIES.

No longer complain,
If your loves shew disdain,
    Be proud and disdain 'em again.
The fools you will find
Will be glad to be kind,
    When they once are despised by the men.
                    [*Gypsies go off.*
1 *Shep.* Hark, hark! in yonder woods the satyrs
    play,
    The echoes bring their laughs this way.
    They with some pleasant sport are pleas'd.
The wanton demi-beasts some Nymphs have seiz'd.

Enter two SHEPHERDS.

Laugh, shepherds, laugh and sing!
Joyful tidings now we bring.

The fair Calisto is disgrac'd ;
Gods and mortals hate the chaste.

An ENTRY *of* SATYRS.

Stre. All this to me but little ease does give.
Cor. All joys are dead to me, why do I live ?
Stre.   In death alone we ease shall find.
Cor.   In death alone we ease shall find.

Chorus of all.

Oh false and cruel woman-kind !

[*Exeunt omnes.*

ACT IV.

Enter PSECAS.

Psc. How long will these malicious woods in
        spite
Conspire to hide my goddess from my sight ?
Were the truth known, she is in private gone
To some blind cave with her Endymion :
For busy tongues are with her honour bold,
Or she with love does correspondence hold.
Some beauteous youths that do her fancy please,
Have reconcil'd those bloody enemies ;
I scorn and hate her, though these falsehoods be,
That she delights in any thing but me.
At her my generous revenge does aim,
I in Calisto would my goddess shame.

Enter MERCURY.

But ha ! my vassal Mercury so nigh ?
Put me in humour with some pleasing lie,
For my lost goddess I can no where find.

Mer. I bring you news, my Nymph! will tune
　　your mind,
Much better news than did I only aim
To please and flatter you my wit could frame.
　　Pse. Oh! Speak! the expectation does delight.
　　Mer. The minute that I parted from your sight,
Our jealous Queen descended from above,
And found Calisto, as you wish'd, with Jove.
　　Pse. Oh! Joy! and kill'd her straight?---
　　Mer. She was debar'd,
The Nymph was then under her lover's guard.
　　Pse. What strange event must that encounter
　　have!
　　Mer. All his Queen's rage my monarch did
　　outbrave.
With her fair rival forc'd her to comply,
Nay, ask her pardon for her jealousy.
Not daring then to trust her with his love,
Compell'd her to return, and fled above.
　　Pse. Tyrant! That I had been his Queen an hour,
I would have plagu'd and exercis'd his power!
Will Juno then put up affronts so rude?
　　Mer. No, no, the angry Queen I straight pursued,
Fired all the mines of sulphur in her soul,
The active flame through ev'ry vein did roll,
That she wept fire, and her whole soul did blaze.
The frightened gods did at the wonder gaze,
Believ'd the world once more with fire undone,
And Jove look't round for a new Phaëton.
　　Pse. The world for ruin surely must prepare!
Let her destroy it, ere Calisto spare.
Oh! I'm impatient till she does appear,
Why tarries Juno? when will she be here?
　　Mer. Ere you can think again.　I left her now
This instant standing on the shining brow
Of a celestial arch, of wondrous height,
With her robes girt, and ready for her flight.

Calisto's dead by this time, or at least
Roaring beneath the figure of a beast.

Pse. Oh! Shall she be a beast?

Mer. If any ease it will give you,
She shall,—what beast you please.

Pse. Oh! Let me think! Some very ugly one,
Uglier than yet by nature e'er was shewn
With all her skill and power, let Juno try
To outwit nature in deformity.

Mer. She shall observe your pleasure to the full,
She shall discover nature's fancy dull.

Pse. My most obedient deity! But stay,
May not Calisto have escap't away,
And found our goddess, whilst you fled above?

Mer. I charm'd both her, and Nyphe in that
    grove.
There round they wander, chaced by panic fear,
Take for a sighing ghost each wind they hear;
At their own voices start, and shadows stare,
And think the lofty trees tall phantoms are.

Pse. Observ'd to every tittle my command,
Nay, guessed my very wishes, take my hand,
Here pay thy self, for thou hast pleas'd me so,
My favours unpetition'd I'll bestow.
Now Nyphe's ruin I must next contrive;
For no one my displeasure shall survive.

Mer. For her disgrace do not disturb your
    thought;
Go, let your goddess to the grove be brought.
To shew her fav'rite's virtues there pretend,
My jealous Queen will soon your cause defend.
Calisto's fall will soon dishonour throw
On her young friend, and, to pursue the blow,
Charge her with confidence of love to me.
Then I, as if I fear'd discovery,
And of my mistress' honour cautions were,
Will gently call, but so as all may hear,

Nyphe, my love. —— My Nyphe, why so slow ?
Come to me here, for I impatient grow.
   Pse. How active an invention dost thou prove !
Thou half deserv'st the glory of my love.
I could descend to smile now, if I durst ;
But that's too great a favour at the first :
And to rash youth 'tis an unhappy fate,
To come too early to a great estate.
Much wealth, much honour, I design my slave,
But I the management of all will have.
   Mer. My glorious mistress does her kindness
      shew,
With the vast wealth I should distracted grow.
But yet some mark of favour let me wear,
This little arrow from your quiver spare.
   Pse. 'Tis thine !—But stay, not that ; the dart
      you have
My goddess in reward of service gave.—
No matter, take it, I her favours slight ;
Nay, to affront her, wear it in her sight.
   Mer. How will I strut among the powers divine
With this, and make 'em at my fortune pine ?
Psecas's Knight, my self I now declare,
And this the badge of my Queen's order wear,
But see, the Nymphs walking their fairy round !
This of their circle is their utmost bound.

Enter CALISTO, NYPHE.

   Pse. Oh ! Let me run and wound 'em with my
      eye !
But now I think on't —— by my frowns to die
Will be a fate too glorious and sublime,
And I shall look 'em dead before their time.
They are of use that huntress to disgrace,
Which, 'cause she is of a celestial race,
Usurps the title of a power divine,
Though her deserts inferior are to mine.

Howe'er by birth she's not below my hate,
I'll shew her folly, and dismiss her straight.
Then these may live. ——
    Mer. See! See! I have descried
Your goddess.
    Pse. Where?
    Mer. There by that river side ——
Run, run, my Queen!
    Pse. In yonder thicket stay
Till my return ——
    Mer. My Queen, I shall obey.
                              [*Exeunt several ways.*
    Cal. How long shall we this black, this cursed
        place,
The hated horrid scene of my disgrace,
In wild and frightful mazes wander round?
    Ny. Sure we are here by black enchantments
        bound.
    Cal. Where e'er we go, wild shapes around us
        move!
And every tree appears to me like Jove.
    Ny. These frightful shadows are his guard, I fear,
And for some black design, imprison us here.
    Cal. They are! What shall we for our safety do?
Run, and the phantoms swiftlier pursue!
Shoot, and our arrows fly we know not where,
Are lost in mists, or only wound the air.
They come!—Stand off, ye fiends!—
    Ny. How pale they shew!
    Cal. And every thing is blasted where they go.
That some brave man of the old Tytans' race,
Would help me to revenge my great disgrace.
If any god will tempt my soul to love,
Let him depose that hated tyrant Jove.
    Ny. Oh! That the gods should be such wicked
        things!
Now this into my soul the reason brings

Why heav'n is hated by the young and fair ;
It seems, the deities abuse 'em there :
For which, the old and slighted do not care.
Is it for this priests bid us worship Jove,
And these the joys they promise us above ?
But we are safe, my goddess does appear.

                                      [*Looks within.*

  Cal. Disguis'd again the tyrant Jupiter.

  Ny. Do you not see the Nymphs around her
    there ?

  Cal. Cheats, phantoms, all !—Delusions of the air.
My heart fears for you, sweetest Nyphe, cease !
Leave me to suffer my own miseries.

  Ny. Why with unkindness do you love repay !
I hope you do not think I will obey.
Besides, I'm fetter'd in enchantments too ;
Though I need none to fasten me to you.
The foolish gods may their enchantments spare,
Stronger than theirs about your self you bare.

  Cal. Fortune, who sends me suff''rings, does in you
Send me the sweetest of all comforts too.

  Ny. Discourse no more, I cannot bravelier die
Than in your aid, and by a deity.

  Cal. Then let us bravely perish in defence
Of injur'd chastity and innocence ;
And when we both are dead, oh ! if there be
In heav'n, but any friend to chastity,
Some goddess of our purity have care,
And to some private tomb our bodies bear. [*Exeunt.*

DIANA, PSECAS, NYMPHS.

  Dia. The chaste Calisto sin ? if thou would'st try
To scare us with some frightful prodigy,
Thy stories within bounds of reason feign ;
Those who out-talk their mark derision gain.
Who use invention must with art proceed,
They, of all merchants. the most cunning need.

Psc. I scorn the traffic, and your friend, nay
    you
May love, ere I speak anything untrue.
   Dia. Of one most useful virtue you have store,
Of confidence, to charge you with no more.
But know, no ill can her fair soul invade,
Her whole composure is for virtue made,
Her body in so pure a mould is wrought,
Her very body may a soul be thought;
A soul to highest purity refin'd,
Visible virtue, a celestial mind
Condens't to beauty, in that fair disguise
Descending to the view of human eyes.
Gross passions can no more find dwellings there,
Than men can breathe in the ætherial air.
There is no fuel there for earthy fire,
The starving flame must instantly expire.
   Psc. Oh! How much curious art you make
    appear!
How finely you would paint us nothing here;
Your colours are so fine, your strokes so small,
That they no strokes nor colour have at all.
I know not how invisible, and pure
Her body may be, 'tis not so obscure,
But you may see her now in yonder grove;
There but this instant in the arms of Jove,
She humbly condescended to my view.
   Dia. I say, 'tis false! Nay, it is nonsense too.
   Psc. Nonsense to see! That does indeed sur-
    prise!
Nymphs in your service must have witty eyes.
   Dia. That it is nonsense I again proclaim,
The gods for her must a new nature frame,
Ere sin in her the least possession gains!
No longer then Calisto she remains,
Who says Calisto then does spot her fame,
Says she's at once another, and the same.

Pse. How for Calisto you employ your wit,
How virtuous 'tis to be a favourite!
Her crimes with glosses as you please disguise,
You shall not argue me out of my eyes.
    Dia. Proceed in insolent contention still;
Cease your disputes! And know it is my will,
You never more presume to touch her fame,
Nor mention, but with high respect, her name.
    Pse. Gods! Gods! to rev'rence her I much
        incline!
What pity 'tis she is no power divine.
Yes! I will spread her virtues and your own,
What virtues too they are shall well be known,
    Dia. Call in dispute my virtues?—Seize her
        there!   [*Nymphs seize Pseus.*
    Pse. Is this the love to chastity you bear?
    Dia. Who boast of it so much, oft-times have
        none!
    Pse. My chastity is equal with your own.
    Dia. Amazing pride!—— Confine her!
    Pse. If you dare!
I'll work on flowers the story with my hair;
Which round the world some courteous wind shall
        blow,
Till it with zeal into a tempest grow.
    Dia. With pride and malice she begins to rave;
Convey her to some beasts forsaken cave.
I doom her by her restless self to dwell,
And that at once both fury is, and hell.

    As they are guarding her out, enter JUNO, *who*
        stops them.

    Jun. Hold! Goddess, do you thus your Nymphs
        reward,
That with such loyalty your honour guard?
Is this the place where chastity's profest?
Has love so strong a party in your breast?

Dia. Has love in any breast a greater foe?
Jun. Do you your hatred to that passion shew,
By guarding those who wrong my bed and throne?
Am I excepted from your rules alone?
Dia. On any such did e'er my favour fall
Who will not bear my Nymphs should love at all?
Jun. Does not this Nymph in seizure here
    remain,
For charging the most vicious of your train?
Whom you from infamy defend with might,
For no desert, but being your favourite?
Dia. The merits of Calisto well I know,
My favour rashly I on none bestow.
Jun. And shall my eyes then be affronted too?
Dia. It was some shape abused both her and you.
Jun. That cursed shape still somewhere haunts
    this wood,
And it shall bleed if it be flesh and blood.
Pse. See! with dart fixt, and how completely
    bent,
She comes from yonder grove.
Jun. As if she meant
To give us an assault.
Dia. And Nyphe there?——
Pse. Of virtue she has much her sister's share.
I thought to tell you, if I durst proceed,
How Mercury her forward youth does breed,
And make already most expert in love,
But I perceiv'd I should your anger move.
Dia. Ignorant nature, if these Nymphs be ill,
To temper spotless chastity wants skill,
Or flesh and blood is of too coarse allay,
And she may waste the fire of souls away,
And in her vain experiments grow old,
Ere that base metal will be turn'd to gold.
In them I'm sure she did at virtue aim,
And never yet so near projection came.

Enter CALISTO *and* NYPHE, *in a posture of defence.*

Cal. Now, now the satyr comes, let us prepare!
Ny. Guarded around with spirits of the air
In shape of Nymphs.
Cal. Let's make a brave defence,
Who knows what charms may be in innocence?
'Twas virtue to the gods their godheads gave,
Dare they, what made 'em impiously outbrave?
Ny. If that gave godheads, we, who virtue have,
Are above gods, and Jove is but our slave.
Cal. Fear not, but valiantly our selves defend.
Jun. See! See! I think for battle they intend.
Dia. Amazement! let us their intention know.
Princess, what mean you by that bended bow?
Cal. Tyrant! I mean to guard my self from you.
Dia. Do you not know me?
Cal. Yes, and hate you too.
And will my honour to the death defend.
Jun. This is your royal virgin!
Pse. This your friend!
Jun. She knows her guilt too public to be hid,
So does to honour bold defiance bid.
· *Dia.* Why sacred honour do you dare to name?
Is honour, since we parted, turn'd to shame,
And vice grown virtue? Riddles you express.
Cal. That virtue is a vice which you profess.
Ny. Practise no more on us that stale deceit!
You wear that shape of chastity to cheat.
Dia. The wonder almost stupifies my sense;
Run Nymphs, and bring 'em here by violence.
Cal. Stand off, you shapes, and do not venture
near.
Ny. Go play your masquerading tricks elsewhere.
Cal. Stand off, I say, if further you proceed,
If shapes have any blood I'll make you bleed.
Dia. See! to the height they insolence pursue.

Now to all honour and esteem for you,
And everlasting farewell; now I'll know
If against me you dare to bend your bow.
　Ny. We dare, and will. ——
　Cal. And could we make you fly
From your strong guard of immortality,
Let heaven and nature of themselves take care,
Or stand, or fall, to kill you we would dare.
[Both strike Diana with their darts.
　Dia. I'm wounded!
　Jun. They to violence proceed,
And have presum'd to make a goddess bleed.
Immortal blood runs trickling from her veins.
　Pse. Oh! the infernal deed! fetch engines,
　　chains!——
　Jun. They shall this instant at my altars die,
I will revenge my injur'd dignity.
Not Jove himself shall his lov'd mistress save.
　Pse. And I the honour of the priesthood crave.
　Jun. 'Tis thine, the glory to thy zeal is due.
　Pse. Now all my malice is devotion too.
　Cal. Like one from strong infernal chains un-
　　bound,
Whose soul is after long distractions found,
To sense and reason, I begin to wake,
And doubt and tremble at my sad mistake.
Is it our goddess? are you Nymphs indeed?
For heaven, for goodness' sake, reply with speed.
Yet if you do, delusions still I fear,
Who will secure me, it is you, I hear?
I dare not trust my cheated ears or sight.
　Dia. Ah! Princess! do you thus my love re-
　　quite?
Do I displease you then in being too kind?
And is this wound a punishment design'd?
　Cal. Am I betray'd into so black a guilt?
Is it your sacred blood which I have spilt?

Oh ! Look not on me with that wounding eye,
Speak not, unless to sentence me to die.
No other word but death I can endure,
My impious hands from further ill secure.
Kill me, if you design revenge to gain,
Ere I grow mad, and have no sense of pain.

Ny. My goddess cannot save me if she would,
For I am fainting in her loss of blood ;
If to herself she does revenge deny,
I of her bleeding wound alone shall die.

Pse. Now they begin again their Syrens' song,
The tunes which charm'd my goddess' soul so long.

Jun. Hope they to be forgiven crimes like these ?
Abuse at once two mighty goddesses ?
The spotless blood of chaste Diana shed,
And yet more horrid, durst invade my bed ?

Cal. Believe it, I will scorn to make defence,
Nor to beg life, pretend to innocence.

Pse. The reason for it is but too well known !
In spite of you, you are ingenious grown.
This injur'd Queen, my goddess here and I
May thank your guilt for so much modesty.

Cal. Your office, Nymph, I do not understand,
Who to implead us, gave you the command ?
From whom do you derive a place so high ?

Ny. I shall inform you, 'tis from Mercury.
Her charms that god her humble vassal make ;
He would not be a god but for her sake.
And she, that she may kind and grateful prove,
Revolts from chastity, and sides with love.
Nature has to th' amphibious creature lent
An art to live in either element.

Pse. Malicious ! Will you wipe your stains on
        me,
And soil my honour with your Mercury ?
Though could I bow to love my noble sense.
Love then would be a thing of excellence.

My nature is so godlike and sublime,
That nothing I can do can be a crime.
  Ny. My Mercury?
  Pse. Yes, yours, who should he be?
He durst not have presum'd to think on me.
  Ny. Did I not find him with you making love?
  Pse. Did I not leave you with him in the grove?
  Ny. You did, but do you not the reason know?
  Pse. Must I a reason for your vices shew?
  Ny. Oh! Gods! Are there such things as wrong,
    or right?
As truth, and falsehood? And is seeing, sight?
If truth be true, and seeing be to see,
You love and are belov'd of Mercury.
  Pse. Which way can I such confidence confute?
But yonder's one will finish our dispute.
  Dia. See, Mercury indeed in yonder grove.
  Jun. Listen, he gently calls.
  Mer. [*within.*] Nyphe, my love!
Steal to me, I will help thee safe away.
  Ny. Steal to thee? who art thou?
  Mer. [*within.*] Haste, haste away.
  Ny. Villain, impostor, had I but a dart,
I'd steal to thee, and fix it in thy heart.
  Pse. Now truth is true, I hope, and seeing sight,
Now pray inform us who is in the right?
  Ny. I am, and this some wicked plot must be
Invented by thy lying god, and thee.
  Jun. Astonishment! So soon to vice begin?
Your youth an early riser is in sin.
Love is in so much haste he cannot stay,
But must set with you ere break of day.
  Pse. Now where's your chymistry –your beaten
    gold?   [*To Dia.*
Your spiritual flesh and blood? A finer mould
Than souls are made of? All's a cobweb cell,
Where her black soul does like a spider dwell.

Dia. Embitter not thy words with gall like this!
Treacherous love has rob'd my paradise,
And pluckt the fairest fruit that there did grow;
The gods in vain plant virtue here below,
It ripens not by any sun or time,
This world for virtue is too cold a clime.
   Jun. Her thoughts, still for her favourites,
     partial stay;
Virtue can sooner faulty be than they.
You may forgive the blood of yours they shed,
But she shall die for injuring my bed.
   Cal. Yes, let me die! I many deaths would bear,
Rather than once these foul reproaches hear.
   Ny. Death on a rack would be a greater bliss
Than life in such a lying world as this.
   Cal. Chaste goddess, my petition is to die,
Hearken no longer to your clemency;
Death for your sacred blood alone is due,
Let me not live to wound your honour too.
I can a plea produce yet, if I please,
Not only all my clamorous enemies
Could vanish, quite, but silence, if I would,
The loudest cries of your immortal blood.
Not only quell my foes' injurious hate,
But make your blood become my advocate.
That very dart, would I the truth reveal,
Which wounded you, my bleeding fame would
    heal.
But that would too much love for life display;
And I so hate the evils of this day,
My self I out of fortune's way would hide!
My innocence will for it self provide.
If that shines by me in my shady tomb,
I shall sleep sweetly in that mournful room,
And dream not of the world's censorious doom.
   Dia. Unhappy Princesses, your fate's severe!
Your prayers I most unwillingly must hear,

Your cause I cannot with my honour own :
A torrent of misfortunes bears you down.
In spite of all my kindness you must die ;
Nay, I must banish too your memory.
What plea you have your innocence to clear
I cannot guess ; but I have cause to fear
None, that can all these witnesses oppose :
At least, subdue the malice of your foes.
If you shall suffer an injurious doom,
Oh ! may your honour blossom from your tomb !
I'll build my arbour there, and every hour
Come and bedew with tears the sacred flower.
If you be faulty, and disgrace your due
Eternal shades conceal your names and you.
    [*Diana goes off weeping, Nymphs guard off*
      Calisto and Nyphe.
  Jun. See ! in deep sorrow she is parted hence !
Her love to virtue is but a pretence ——
She is unchaste her self.
  Pse. Is that unknown ?
Have you not heard of her Endymion ?
Nor of her young Hippolitus that fled
From every Nymph, in private to her bed ?
She to the world has been a long mistake !
Pretends to chastity for pleasure's sake.
For secret love does in the forests dwell !
They understand each other's meaning well.
  Jun. She shall disgrace our dignity no more,
I will depose her from her heavenly power.
And crown thee in her stead a power divine !
I will !——the empire of these woods is thine.
Meanwhile I to my first revenge will fly,
Thy foes and mine shall at my altars die. [*Ex.*
  Pse. Oh ! how I am transported with success !
Courted and sought my fame and happiness !

Enter MERCURY.

But how malicious does my fortune prove?
Now he comes here to pester me with love.
  Mer. My fairest Queen!
  Psc. Thou troublest me, begone!
  Mer. What change is this?
  Psc. I'm busied in fruition
Of a new love.
  Mer. Do you say this, to try
If with despair I at your feet will die?
Name him!
  Psc. My self.
  Mer. Oh! Now farewell despair,
I hope in that fruition I shall share.
  Psc. I must feign love, that I may freedom gain.
                                        [*Aside.*

Another time you shall.
  Mer. Oh! where, and when?
  Psc. Perhaps this evening.
  Mer. Where?
  Psc. In yonder grove.
  Mer. Will you not fail me?
  Psc. Ask a maid in love,
If she will fail to meet with her delight?
  Mer. With expectations of this pleasant night,
Till it arrives my thoughts I will employ.
                                        [*Exit.*

  Psc. Do! Expectation's all you shall enjoy.
If in the grove he tarries till he sees
Me there, he shall stay longer than the trees.
                                        [*Exit.*

Enter DAPHNE *and* SYLVIA.

[Concerted piece.]

  Daph. Oh! whither are our poor despairing
    shepherds gone!

I fear I have my Strephon slain.
Sylv.   And I my Corydon.
Daph. Oh my sorrow! Oh my pain!
          Could I my Strephon find:
          Could I my dearest Strephon find,
               I'd never be unkind.
I'd never be unkind to him again.
Sylv. And I, my love would passionately own,
               Could I find my Corydon.
Daph.   Do I dream? Do I rave?
          Look towards yonder cave.
Sylv. Our shepherds come from yonder cave.
Sylv. ⎫
Daph. ⎭ Our shepherds come from yonder cave.
Sylv.   From empty pride I'll be free,
          It shall bring no more mischief upon me,
          Since I love as well as he,
               I'll not hazard my joy,
               In being foolishly coy,
          It had like to have undone me.

DAPHNE *and* SYLVIA *go and meet* STREPHON *and*
     CORYDON : *each brings in her* SHEPHERD.

Daph.   Dear Strephon, give despairing o'er,
               Unkindnesses are gone,
I never will be cruel to thee more.
Sylv.   Nor I to Corydon.
Cory. Oh, what kind god does Sylvia's hate re-
     move?
Str. And made at length my Daphne grateful
     prove?
Sylv.   The god of love.
Daph.   The god of love.
Sylv. ⎫
Daph. ⎭   The gentle god of love.
Cory.   Oh happy tidings!

Str.   Blessed hour !
               Ever kind and gentle pow'r.
Cory.   Ever kind and gentle pow'r.

Enter Chorus of SHEPHERDS, *followed by*
                BACCHUSSES.

Chorus.

Joy, Shepherds joy ! Diana's disgrac'd,
Love has had to-day revenge on the chaste.
The Bacchusses here our mirth to improve,
Come hither to follow the triumphs of love.
No mirth without Bacchus, nor joy without love.

An ENTRY *of* BACCHUSSES.

After the dance.

Cor. Since all our grief thus joyfully ends,
Let each shepherdess make her shepherd amends.
        To the temple let's go,
        And then we will show,
What every lover, by loving intends.
                              [*Exeunt omnes.*

ACT V.

Enter MERCURY.

Mer. The time is past, whilst vainly round I
      pace,
As yet encount'ring nothing in this place
But the long evening shadows of the grove ;
And shadows are but slender food to love.
No, it is substance ! substance ! must delight
Love's wholesome frame and eager appetite.

Malicious fortune must this stay contrive,
Some sudden ill to Psecas must arrive.
Nothing that's common could my Nymph retain,
For when Nymphs love, they fonder grow than
    men.
Their melting hearts in kindness does excel ;
And I am sure my Psecas loves so well,
That were she dead, her spirit would appear,
And leave th' Elyzian joys to meet me here.
Well, patience ! patience ! time rides proudly by,
And looks upon me with a scornful eye ;
But I, in spite of all his swift career,
Will overtake him when my joys appear.

Enter PSECAS.

Pse. The mighty victim's ready to be slain !
    Heaven's Queen a vassal to my merits grown.
Diana now no more my sovereign ;
    The shady empire of these woods my own.
Th' impoverisht stars have nothing to bestow,
But what for my acceptance is too low.
My next affair is quickly to cashier
My loving patient slave that waits me here.
    Mer. My Nymph, appear ? oh ! now my planets
        smile !
What has detain'd thee from me all this while ?
I have been wand'ring here in grief and fear.
    Pse. Who bid you do't ? Could you expect me
        here ?
    Mer. Can the kind vows my Queen was pleas'd
        to make
Her just and noble thoughts so soon forsake ?
    Pse. Do I such trifling contemplations use ?
Will I my memory with you abuse ?
    Mer. Though I deserve not such a glorious place,
My goddess will not from her mem'ry chace
The noble creatures which she being gave,

I mean, the promises she made her slave.
  Pse. Well, if I did, I'll break 'em if I please!——
Am I oblig'd to keep my promises?
  Mer. Nothing can sov'reign power oblige, 'tis
    true,
But its own will, that sov'reign power have you;
But yet there is one mighty thing above
Even your own pow'rful self, and that is love.
  Pse. Can any one such insolence endure?
Love above me? You would affront me, sure.
Who should, or can I love? Where is there ought,
Except my self—that's worthy of my thought?
  Mer. True! But since love to me you did
    express,
Your love confers on me some worthiness.
  Pse. My love! Why can you think 'twas love I
    meant?
Dare you to hope it be so insolent?
  Mer. Why?—should I rudely think you speak
    untrue?
  Pse. Am I oblig'd to speak my thoughts to you?
  Mer. Do you not love then?
  Pse. Dare you hope I do?
  Mer. Are you in earnest?
  Pse. What should I intend?
Should I with my own slaves to mirth descend?
  Mer. And am I fool'd then?
  Pse. Well! What if you be?
Is't a dishonour to be fool'd by me?
  Mer. And will you all my service thus requite?
  Pse. Challenge reward as if it was your right?
  Mer. Your service then is with it self re-paid.
  Pse. Supposing not? What service did you do?
Invent a falsehood? Shame a harmless maid?
    Well! when you please, I'll lie as much for you.
  Mer. Exceeding well! Did I then toil and
    sweat,

At last, this mockery to get?
None serve you for your fools but heav'nly powers!
   Pse. Mortals are yours, you may sometimes be
     ours.
   Mer. What! I must then to your contempt
     submit?
   Pse. I cannot help another's want of wit.
   Mer. You do continue in your boldness still?
   Pse. 'Tis you are bold, who dare dispute my
     will.
   Mer. Thou empty foolish female, who to please
Thy sickly longings, with the fond delight
Of thy vain sex, or rather their disease
Of pride, resists thy nobler appetite.
Though now when thou so coy pretend'st to be,
Thou'dst give an empire I would ravish thee.
But I'll not stoop to gratify thee so;
That joy some bestial satyr shall bestow!——
Ho! there!——
   Pse. A rape! here!
   Mer. Call out, if you dare,
I'll all your lies and villanies declare.
   Pse. Rape! Rape! here!

Enter JUNO, DIANA, NYMPHS.

So! 'tis well you do appear!
Virtue has excellent protection here.
Much safety your good government affords,
The spreading trees are not so full of birds,
The caves of beasts, as all the woods around
Of wanton gods who ev'rywhere abound,
Waiting to make our chastities a prey,
And gins and toils do for our honours lay.
On our occasions we can no where move,
But straight we fall into some trap of love.
   Dia. Dare you affirm it is a fault of mine?
Can I the gods to their abodes confine?

If they be weary of their heavenly bliss,
Must I be guilty?——
   Pse. You are too remiss,
And both our honours and your own neglect.
   Dia. You are too bold and full of disrespect.
   Pse. Wherein do I that confidence express?
Is hate to love and vice grown sauciness?
Your pardon for my dullness I implore,
I never knew they were your friends before.
It seems your meaning we must backward read,
And we a key to all your cyphers need.
By chastity, you zealous love intend;
By hate and coyness, kindness to a friend.
Your nimble wits have found it out;—but I,
Dull fool, am hardened in my chastity.
You should have plainly told me what you meant,
Before your wanton gods to me you sent.
For I affront 'em all, and spoil the sport,
And quite disorder your mysterious court.
   Dia. Immortal gods! was e'er celestial power
In her own presence so blasphem'd before?
What! I am turn'd a Venus, and my groves,
Private retreats and nurseries of loves.
Hence from my sight, and in the forest howl
In some beast's shape, deformed as thy soul.
   Jun. Stay, Nymph, and fly to me, I'll have it
     known
Here is a power superior to her own.
   Dia. What in my forests here have you to do?
I in my empire am supreme to you.
Go exercise your goddess-ship above,
There you may share authority with Jove.
   Jun. Your Nymphs diminish there my royal due,
And I will have reprisals here on you.
   Pse. Her love to virtue now I hope is shewn,
And how much wrong I have her honour done.
She has but one chaste Nymph in all her train.

And she enjoys no rest till that is slain.
   Mer. Boldness above belief! I've watcht an
     hour
    From all these cloudy mists to set you free,
    And disentangle the whole mystery,
And never yet could get it in my power.
I will no longer bear the pangs and throws,
I now will speak, and none shall interpose.
She then who dares your anger so outbrave
Is my sworn female, my devoted slave!
Bought to my pleasure at no dearer rates,
Than ruining the Nymphs she so much hates.
I help to gain her her malicious ends,
And for that hire my pleasure she attends.
   Pse. Oh! hellish falsehood!——
   Dia. I believe it true!——
   Jun. I think it false.
   Pse. Th' opinion is my due!——
I scorn to fear he can my fame remove.
   Mer. That let th' event of my relation prove.
I shall bring proofs will make your courage fall.
   Pse. I'll hear no more.
   Dia. But I will hear it all.
Can you the honour of my Nymphs restore?
And are they innocent?
   Mer. They are; and more,
Calisto's virtue is above divine,
And Nyphe at the least a heroine.
   Pse. How he exalts the praises of his love!
   Jun. And flatters servilely the vice of Jove.
   Pse. In your own presence dares your rival
     praise.
   Jun. To affront me, he does her honour raise.
   Pse. He is no doubt the cause of your disgrace,
And first allur'd your Jove to her embrace.
   Mer. What horrid monster art thou? of what
    kind?

How fortified in body or in mind?
Under what species does thy nature fall?
Or human, hellish, or divine, or all,
So many gods thou dar'st deride, defy?
To conquer thee, will be a victory
Great as the sun's o'er Python, nay, above
That over all the Titans gain'd by Jove.
But with the force of truth I'll make thee bow,
And yet will batter down that brazen brow.
    Dia. Melt it with shame!—For though she virtuous be,
Malice so great dishonours chastity;
They should not dwell together in one breast,
It is a serpent in a Phœnix' nest.
Say then, why call'd you Nyphe in the grove?
    Mer. Vile Psecas her dishonour to remove,
And fasten it on Nyphe's spotless youth.
    Dia. That was not wise, it would not look like truth,
To clear your stains with innocence so pure.
    Mer. Neatness alone some maladies does cure.
Contagious soonest taint the finest blood,
Unwholesome rooms they love to change for good.
But us on all these pikes her virtue drove,
She chanc't to make discovery of our love,
And rather chose a thousand deaths to die,
Than hide a crime of the least infamy.
    Pse. Where lodges truth, if gods such liars be?
He knows all this is only true of me.
Cause by my zeal his Nymph is doom'd to die,
He sought revenge here on my chastity,
And now with falsehoods does my fame pursue.
    Mer. Against such confidence what can I do?
    Pse. What? but your self a foul defamer own.
    Dia. Despise her boldness and the truth make known.
    Jan. I am confirm'd that Psecas suffers wrong.

Pse. If e'er did Nymph from a defaming tongue.
Dia. With sacred truth he does her honour
  blast,
Why should I judge a mind so vicious, chaste?
Jun. Nor chastity, nor any thing that's good,
Can lodge in one that shares Calisto's blood.
  Pse. My vice, I fear, to your disgrace will
  prove
Too much severity to vice, and love.
  Dia. Hermes! Release me from this viper
  here!
Who in my sacred honour, does not fear
To fix her teeth, and venom to distill
On that, which is an antidote to ill.
Make but Calisto's fame, as Nyphe's clear,
And this bold Nymph a punishment severe
For all her blasphemies shall quickly bear.
  Pse. When he clears her, then do you what you
  dare.
  Mer. Her divine virtues and unspotted fame,
Incense and victims only should proclaim,
All wordish praise she is so much above,
That eloquence would profanation prove.
  Pse. Oh! how the woods must with her praises
  ring!
Such were the words entic't her to his King.
  Dia. Praise on, and Psecas's reproaches slight,
Torment her envious nature to the height.
And did Calisto triumph over Jove?
  Mer. O'er him, o'er pleasure, empire, glory, love.
Despairing to subdue by open storm,
He first stole to her in your beauteous form,
Hoping by ambush his design to gain;
And finding that fair stratagem in vain.
Himself and all his glory he display'd;
Himself his heaven at her feet he laid.
He sued, commanded, threatened, and implor'd,

I   21

Nay, wept, bow'd, kneel'd, and at her feet
    ador'd;
But could not or by promise, force, or guile,
Entice, compel, or cheat her to a smile.
Her fort of chastity to buy, to break,
Heaven was too poor, omnipotence too weak.
   Pse. This to torment you sure is some design.
   Jun. It tears my ears.
   Dia. 'Tis harmony to mine.
The brave Calisto's praise still boldly tell!
My pleasure is their rack, my heav'n their hell.
   Jun. Fond goddess, who triumph'st in thy
    shame,
Preferring thy vain fancy to thy fame;
Contending in thy favourite's defence,
Against thy honour, reason, and thy sense.
If all I can affirm no faith can gain,
Believe thy wound, and listen to thy pain.
Hark how thy blood thy favourite commends!
   Mer. That very blood will prove her best of
    friends.
And only be, when you the reason know,
To your malicious hopes a mortal blow.
Jove in your shape deep on her soul imprest,
And strongly with the horror still possest.
The sight of you new terrors did awake,
She did your person for your shape mistake.
And that deceiv'd her to a crime so brave,
She aim'd at Jupiter the blow she gave;
You of his sufferings alone complain,
You have the wound, but Jupiter the pain.
A crime will to her endless fame redound.
   Dia. Gods! then I must reward her for my
    wound.
   Mer. You ought!—but how?—the virtue she
    has shown.
Not all the laurels in your woods can crown.

Dia. Happy the moment when my blood was
    spilt!
I'll now have altars to my victims built.
Their glory shall exceed their past disgrace.
Bring 'em in triumph here to my embrace!
                        [Exeunt Nymphs.
  Psе. Oh! Gods! this impious sentence who can
    bear,
This is a plot betwixt these gods and her,
Wholly to ruin virtue by degrees,
That they may love and revel as they please.
Nay, glory in it too, and make it prove
A virtue worthy high rewards to love.
And shortly all will chastity disclaim,
And to be virtuous will be thought a shame.
  Dia. Oh! most provoking!——
  Mer. Her reproach disclain.
Her sland'rous tongue shall quickly end its reign.
I'll fetch a sov'reign Judge shall quell her pride,
And this debate impartially decide.   *[Exit.*
  Jun. She names but half your villanous design,
You plot my glory too to undermine.
Ungrateful Jove, now weary of me grown,
Will place my rival in my bed and throne,
And it is plotted here among you all!
And my severe revenge on thee shall fall. *[To Dia.*
I'll kill thy Nymphs, thy reputation blast,
Throw down thy temples, lay thy forest waste.
Thy self from cave to cave with tempests chace,
And in the savage beasts an instinct place
To tell 'em who their murderess used to be,
And make 'em for revenge go hunt out thee.
  Dia. Oh! foolish rage! which will no reason
    hear!
Your fury against me I scorn to fear.
Alas! your anger at your equal flies;
But yet, perhaps, you may my Nymphs surprise:

I to their innocence the more incline,
Your honour to respect as well as mine.
But since you fight your own disgrace to prove:
I'll both defend 'em against you and Jove.

Enter CALISTO, NYPHE *veiled, brought
in by* NYMPHS.

Come Princesses! this posture is not due!
Truth has unveil'd itself, and so may you.
Your beauties are not brighter than your fame,
Falsehood and malice you have put to shame.
For the rewards of virtue now prepare,
And scorn the utmost which your foes can dare.
      Cal. Oh! What kind power has the truth
         reveal'd?
      Dia. One that has all our wounds entirely
         heal'd.
      Cal. And your wound too! For unless that be
         whole,
My honour may be well, but not my soul.
      Dia. So well, that I am better than before!
My courage greater, and my pleasure more!
If I have any pain, 'tis that which flows
From the excess of joy, your fame bestows:
The mark of which, upon my arm I bear;
The only jewel, I am proud to wear.
      Ny. Oh! Glorious news! Who proves the liar
         now?   [*To Pse.*
Great goddess some revenge to us allow. [*To Dia.*
The impious author there of all this evil,
Let's offer up a victim to the devil:
But she in mischief does so much excel,
Pluto, in fear, will keep her out of hell.
She'll be a greater plague than any there:
Furies themselves will be afraid of her.
      Pse. Did ever falsehood virtue so outbrave?

Great goddess, on my knees, revenge I crave.
[*To Juno.*

Jun. You fierce, tempestuous Spirits of the air,
Who late confin'd me, to my aid repair :

Enter SPIRITS, *the* NYMPHS *stand on their guard.*

The favour which you forfeited regain ;
The honour of your injur'd Queen maintain :
These bold rebellious Nymphs in pieces tear,
And throw their limbs in whirlwinds round the air.
   Dia. Approach who dares ! Nay, for permission
      pray
To blow out of my woods one leaf away.
   Ny. Oh ! Goddess ! let 'em come ! for I'm in pain
Till one of 'em at least by me is slain.

   As they are ready to encounter, Enter JUPITER
      and MERCURY.

   Jup. Must I my heav'n eternally forsake,
To quiet the disorders which you make ? [*To Jun.*
   Jun. Return'd again ?--Oh ! most tormenting
      sight !
There, I resign to you, your sole delight.
Make her your goddess in the room of me,
I'll bear no more the royal mockery,
Nor be a statue to adorn your throne.
   Jup. And are you weary then of empire grown ?
   Jun. I am, and of my life ! —— And to be free,
Desire no blessing like mortality ;
That my own hand might pour out with my blood
My sorrows and my life ! ——
   Jup. I wish you could ! ——
That both of us and all the world some ease
Might find of your eternal jealousies.
   Jun. Who is in fault ?
   Jup. Your folly is the cause,
For I will not be limited by laws ;

You but in part my kindness can enjoy,
My ocean must a thousand springs supply.
Once more I own this royal maid, I strove
To tempt by all the arts of threats, or love ;
But 'gainst her virtue did no more prevail,
Than the old giants when they heav'n did scale.
They piled up hills on hills my throne to seize,
I mountains heapt of golden promises ;
But found her virtue from my reach as far
As from my palace all their mountains were.
Like those fond fools when I was most sublime,
I did but in the reach of thunder climb.
Her soul shot down such lightning from her eyes,
Instead of spoiling, I ador'd my prize.
Once more embrace her then, and after this,
The least injurious thought of her dismiss.

       [Juno embraces Calisto.

And Mercury the wrong which you have done
That fair young Nymph, with low submissions own,
And to whatever suff'rings she thinks fit
To sentence you, with penitence submit.

 Mer. I gladly to her fair tribunal come,

       [Kneels to Nyphe.

And humbly on my knees attend her doom.

 Ny. I recompense enough from this receive,
Revenge and malice to your Nymph I leave.

        [To Mer.

 Jup. And those good virtues, which her gentle
  mind
So much adorn, she shall rewarded find.
Now you, who with such zeal the ruin sought

        [To Pse.

Of these fair Nymphs, shall to your doom be
  brought.
I hope my words they credit may afford,
And all for truth acknowledge ! ——

 Pse. Not a word.

Jup. Oh! Insolence! Charge me with falsehood
    too?
Pse. Falsehood, I hope, is false, though spoke
    by you.
Power gives not language the more truth or sense.
   Jup. Astonishing! drag her to torments hence.
   Cal. Spare her, for I my honour scorn to owe
To her acknowledgements.
   Ny. No, let her go,
For she has done, and let her suffer ill.
   Pse. Now I will stay to contradict your will.
The fondlings dandled upon fortune's knee
Were sav'd, 'tis true, from my conspiracy.
But to no merit have the least pretence,
Excepting pure insipid innocence.
   Dia. Your judgment, if you please, great Psecas!
    spare;
We, with your leave, of that sole judges are.
Oblige us now your reason to relate,
Why you pursued the Nymphs with so much
    hate.
   Pse. My hatred stoop to have concern for them?
You much mistake, the error I contemn.
Seeing what fondnesses abus'd your mind,
Having some kindness for you, I design'd
To disabuse you, set your judgment right,
And honour you with being your favourite.
But since you from your own good fortune go,
And have not wit enough desert to know,
I throw you wholly out of my esteem,
And no submission shall the loss redeem,
Though in deep sorrow at my feet you fall
For now I scorn you, nay, I scorn you all.
Gods, goddesses, and Nymphs, away I'll fly,
And keep no more such trifling company.
I'll hunt alone, and in my self delight,
And be my own most dear-lov'd favourite.

Dia. She is grown frantic!

          [Psecas offers to go, is stayed by Juno.

  Jun. Rather she is brave.

Stay gen'rous Psecas, I thy friendship crave,

Bury not all thy worth in a retreat;

Give me thy love, and I will make thee great.

  Jup. A most harmonious friendship this must

    prove!

The fates design'd 'em for each other's love.

For none love them, and they have love for none;

Their kindness centres on themselves alone.

And they are so exactly of a make,

Each may the other for her self mistake.

Now must the last and heaviest sentence fall

Upon my self the greatest criminal.

My wretched self, as to my crimes is due,

I doom to part eternally from you.   *[To Calisto.*

And to the pain of heav'nly joy to go;

But yet I must not leave you here below.

In pity to the world, I must remove

Those fatal eyes, out of the reach of love.

Love must not here those killing darts retain

To wound and torture gods, and murder men.

And yet to place you in my heav'n, would be

Not your reward, but my felicity.

Some middle region I must prepare,

Where all may with some ease your beauty bear.

I then entreat, you will, to end this war,

Accept the small dominion of a star.

There you and beauteous Nyphe may dispense

With cooler beams your light and influence.

On the great ceremony Hermes wait,

Let all the gods give their appearance straight.

These virgins' consecration nought debars,

I'll in a full assembly crown 'em stars.   *[Exit.*

Enter STREPHON, CORYDON, DAPHNE, SYLVIA, *Chorus of* SHEPHERDS, *as from the Temple.*

Chorus.	Happy lovers! happy live,
	And all the gods their blessings give.
Cor.	Lead along, and with delight,
	Let us hasten on the night.

Enter two AFRICAN WOMEN.

Stre. What vision's this is come to greet us?
Cor. See! the night is come to meet us.
1. *Afr.* Stay gentle swains be not afraid,
    To see our faces hid in shade.
    We, but lately were as fair,
    As your shepherdesses are.
    Did not a frantic youth of late
      O'erset the chariot of the sun?
Cor. He did, and his deserved fate
    He met when he had done.
2. *Afr.* It is he that hath undone us:
    He pour'd whole streams
      Of melting beams,
    Red, and glowing hot upon us.
And now we range the world around,
To see if our lost beauty can be found.

Enter a third AFRICAN WOMAN.

3. *Afr.* Rejoice, rejoice! our beauty's found,
    Our lovely white and red,
To two chaste Nymphs of Cynthia's train is fled,
    And they must stars be crown'd:
    And now instead of what we sought,
    Our black with us must fair be thought.
All ⎱ This happy fate, who could divine?
three. ⎰ Our beauty then in heav'n must shine.
1. *Afr.* No losers we shall prove,
    By parting with our red and white;

If black will serve the turn of love ;
　For beauty's made for love's delight.
3. *Afr.* See ! See ! the Nymphs are coming here.
Sylv.　　But oh ! what glorious apparition's near ?
　The clouds amazing glories gild :
　All the clouds with gods are fill'd,
　And all the gods appear.

CALISTO *and* NYPHE *enter under a canopy, supported by* AFRICANS ; *immediately upon their entrance, a heaven is discover'd filled with gods and goddesses.*

The whole concludes with an ENTRY *of* AFRICANS, *and this Song.*

　Daph. Must these be stars ? And to heaven remove,
Before they have tasted the pleasures of love.
That the gods so ill, such beauty should use !
What mighty cost must nature lose ?
　Sylv. I cannot so much beauty show,
But what I have, I'll better bestow,
Not upon gods, or glories above,
Or empty renown, but pleasure and love.
All pleasure but love from our hearts we'll be chasing,
We'll kindle our selves into stars with embracing :
We'll every moment our pleasures renew,
Our loves shall be flaming, and lasting and true.

EPILOGUE.

The EPILOGUE *spoken by* JUPITER, *who descended out
of the Heaven, and addressed himself to* CALISTO
and NYPHE.

The stars for your reception now prepare,
And the ambitious heav'ns expect you there;
But I will spoil their hopes, and break my vow,
For I've considered there are stars enow:
And this inferior world can scarce dispense
With the entire loss of so much excellence.
With each of you I can oblige a throne,
I'll keep you then to grace some fav'rite crown.
On that design you here shall still remain,
                           [Turning to the company.
And I'll dissolve into a Nymph again.
Which will no less this fair assembly please;
For Nymphs, in courts, have sway like deities.
You wits who think you gallantry display,
To laugh at ev'ry thing a god can say,
Will in good manners to a Nymph submit,
And own whatever beauty speaks for wit.
Perhaps the power of beauty to express,
We choose our language careless as our dress.
None should come hither to attend, but gaze;
Here beauty's charms not wits you ought to praise.
And 'tis your safest course, judge you of show,
Fine cloaths, and faces, tunes, and dances too;
For those are things which you may chance to know.
There is no doubt but you have ears and eyes,
Your understanding most in question lies.

But what do I here trifling thus with these !
There are the powers to whom we sacrifice,
                    [*To the King and Queen.*
In whose great presence I may well allow
To lay aside my useless godhead now.
You, sir, such blessings to the world dispense,
You are indeed a special providence.
And since your rule such joy to all procures,
All should contribute what they can to yours.
Wit by your smiles a lustre does maintain,
And beauty keeps a long and happy reign,
Your right in them is therefore so entire,
They, above all, your pleasure should conspire.

EPILOGUE

BY JOHN DRYDEN, ESQ., POET LAUREAT.

INTENDED TO HAVE BEEN SPOKEN BY THE LADY HEN. MAR.
WENTWORTH,

When Calisto was acted at Court in 1675.

As Jupiter I made my court in vain ;
I'll now assume my native shape again.
I'm weary to be so unkindly used,
And would not be a God, to be refused.
State grows uneasy when it hinders love ;
A glorious burden, which the wise remove.
Now, as a nymph, I need not sue, nor try
The force of any lightning but the eye.
Beauty and youth, more than a god command ;
No Jove could e'er the force of these withstand.
'Tis here that sovereign power admits dispute ;
Beauty sometimes is justly absolute.
Our sullen Cato's, whatsoe'er they say,
Even while they frown and dictate laws, obey.
You, mighty sir, our bonds more easy make,
And, gracefully, what all must suffer, take ;
Above those forms the grave affect to wear,
For 'tis not to be wise to be severe.
True wisdom may some gallantry admit,
And soften business with the charms of wit.
These peaceful triumphs with your cares you bought,
And from the midst of fighting nations brought.

You only hear it thunder from afar,*
And sit, in peace, the arbiter of war :
Peace, the loathed manna, which hot brains despise,
You knew its worth, and made it early prize ;
And in its happy leisure, sit and see
The promises of more felicity ;
Two glorious nymphs † of your own godlike line,
Whose morning rays, like noontide, strike and shine ;
Whom you to suppliant monarchs shall dispose,
To bind your friends, and to disarm your foes.

* The war between France and the Confederates was now raging on the Continent. SCOTT. Dryden's Works, 2nd Edition, Edinburgh, 1821. 8vo. Vol 10, p. 138.

† The glorious nymphs, afterwards Queens Ann and Mary, both lived to exclude their own father and his son from the throne. Derrick, I suppose, alluded to this circumstance when in the next line he read *supplant* for suppliant monarchs.— SCOTT, *ib.* Derrick was the previous editor of the poetical works of Dryden, and not improbably made the alteration purposely to show how little he respected the two usurping Queens, as he must have thought them.

NOTES OF THE PERFORMERS IN THE MASQUE.

The Lady HENRIETTA WENTWORTH was the only daughter of Thomas, eldest son of Thomas Lord Wentworth, who was created Earl of Cleveland by Charles I. He survived the restoration, and died 25th March 1667 at the advanced age of seventy-six. His son predeceased him, having died in the year 1664, leaving by his wife Philadelphia, daughter of Sir Frederick Carey Knight, Henrietta, who eventually became Baroness Wentworth, the title of Cleveland failing in the Wentworth family upon the death of her grandfather.

Grief for the execution of the Duke of Monmouth is believed to have been the cause of her premature demise. As his Grace was one of the Dancers in Calisto, whilst the Lady enacted the part of Jupiter, it is not unlikely that the Masque may have been the commencement of the intimacy which continued until put an end to by the violent death of the Duke. On the scaffold he spoke in vindication of her honour, although it was very well known that after leaving his wife, the heiress of Buccleugh, they had lived together as man and wife at Toddington, in the county of Bedford, where she died of a broken heart in 1686, and was buried under a costly monument. The barony devolved upon her Ladyship's aunt Anne, the wife of John Lord Lovelace, whose daughter Martha walked at the coronation of Queen Anne as Baroness Wentworth. Upon her death in 1745 the barony passed through the Noel and Milbank families, and is now, in right of his mother, inherited by the eldest son of the Earl of Lovelace, who made out his claim recently before a Committee of Privileges as son and heir of Ada, Countess of Lovelace, daughter of George Gordon Byron, Lord Byron.

Anne Palmer or Fitzroy, COUNTESS OF SUSSEX, had the honour of having been recognised by Charles as his daughter, although born previous to the separation of her mother Barbara. subsequently created Duchess of Cleveland, from her husband, Roger Palmer, Earl of Castlemain, afterwards embassadour by James II. to the Pope. Charles, who thought himself the father of the child, assigned her the Royal Arms with the Baton Sinister, married her to Thomas Lennard, Baron Dacre, and created him Earl of Sussex. He had a large estate, which he contrived to injure materially. The Barony of Dacre still exists, and, should the present noble Lord die without lawful issue, will pass to his brother, who presently holds the high position of Speaker of Her Majesty's House of Commons.

The LADY MARY MORDAUNT was the daughter and heiress of Henry, second Earl of Peterborough, by Penelope, daughter of Barnabas, Earl of Thomond, of the kingdom of Ireland. He was nominated ambassador to negotiate a marriage between a daughter of the house of Modena with the Duke of York, which he effected, and acted as proxy in the marriage ceremony, bringing the princess through France, and landing with her at Dover on the 21st November 1673. At the coronation of James II. he bore the sceptre with the cross, and on Sunday, 19th of April 1685, he was declared Groom of the Stole, and the golden key delivered to him. In June the same year he was made a Knight of the Garter, and duly installed the 22d July following. He died on the 19th day of June 1697.

The Earldom of Peterborough devolved on his nephew Charles, but his daughter succeeded to the barony of Mordaunt of Turvey, and a great portion of his estates. She married in 1677 Henry, seventh Duke of Norfolk, but unfortunately for her, whether from studying Ovid in his original tongue, or enjoying the poet through the medium of a translation, she forgot herself so far that her husband divorced her in April 1700. She married Sir John Germaine, and left him a large portion of the Peterborough estate.

Of Mrs JENNINGS. a very suitable representative of the envious Psecas, all that is necessary to say is that she subsequently became the wife of John Churchill, Duke of Marlborough, and for many years the confidante and adviser of the Princess Anne, both before and after her accession to the British crown.

Lord Hailes privately printed from her Grace's own manuscripts a selection of her sayings, which are well worthy of perusal. Pepys, in February 1665, tells a story about her Grace's elder sister Frances, afterwards Duchess of Tyrconnel, which is amusing enough : " What mad freaks the mayds of honor at court have : That Mrs Jennings, one of the Dutchesse's maids, the other day dressed herself like an orange wench and went up and down and cried oranges, 'till falling down, or by some accident, her fine shoes were discovered, and she put to a great deal of shame."

Frances Jennings died a Duchess, but only by a creation *after* the expulsion of James II. Her first husband was Sir George Hamilton, grandson of James, first Earl of Abercorn, and brother of Anthony, author of the Memoirs of Count Grammont. He was killed in the wars, and she became the wife of Richard Talbot, a bigoted papist, who was created Earl of Tyrconnel in 1686, and Duke of Tyrconnel in 1689. He died in August 1691. His lady, hurled from her high estate, was subsequently compelled to sell—certainly not oranges—but millinery, " in the new Exchange in the Strand,"* to support herself, and unwilling to be recognised, she wore a *white mask* and a white dress, and was known by the name of the White Widow.

She subsequently removed to Dublin, where she lived, to all outward appearance, in extreme misery, and where she died at the advanced age of eighty-two in the year 1730, whilst her sister Duchess was living perhaps more miserably, in pomp and splendour, in Blenheim and Pall Mall, a torment to herself and all around her.

The COUNTESS OF DERBY was Elizabeth Butler, daughter of Thomas, Earl of Ossory, eldest son of the first Duke of Ormond. She was the wife of William Richard George, ninth Earl of Derby, who died in 1702. Her only son and her youngest daughter Elizabeth died unmarried in the lifetime of her mother. Her eldest

* Life of Mrs Godolphin. Notes, p. 260.

1 22

daughter, Lady Henrietta Maria, married first John Annesley, fourth Earl of Anglesea, by whom she had an only daughter, the Lady Elizabeth Annesley, who died young and unmarried; and secondly, John, Lord Ashburnam, created Earl of Ashburnam in 1730, by whom she had one daughter, the Lady Henrietta Bridget, who died unmarried in 1732.

The amiable and charitable lady Derby died in 1717. Her will, dated the 23d of February 1714-15, was proved on the 26th of July 1717 by her executors, Charles, Earl of Arran, her brother, Francis Annesley, William Bromley, and Thomas Ashurst, Esq. It appears from the deed that her ladyship possessed considerable wealth, a portion of which she bequeathed for religious and benevolent purposes. Some of the bequests are interesting, such as " her brilliant diamond eare rings, given me by the late Queen Mary, and also one brilliant diamond locket, with the said late Queen Mary's hair in it," which were left to her executors for sale, with instructions to employ " one hundred and fifty pounds of the produce thereof in setting out poor boys and girles, not being charity children or in the charity schoole then of the parish of St James, Westminster, of equall number of each sex, apprentices at the discretion of my trustees;" a similar sum from the same source is destined for the boys of the parish of St Martin-in-the-Fields. One hundred pounds is devised to the Society for Propagating the Gospel in Foreign Parts, and the same sum for "redemption of poor Christian slaves out of the captivity of slavery of infidels." Whatever residue might remain of the produce of the sale of the diamond ear rings and locket was to be divided among her ladyship's servants in her houses in St James' Place and Kew. She was possessed also of considerable property in lottery tickets. These she ordered her trustees to sell and apply the produce for benevolent and charitable purposes, amongst which was a sum of fifty pounds for the relief of " poor distressed French Protestants." Similar sums are to be applied for relief of the poor prisoners in the Marshalsea Prison in Southwark, and in Chester and Lancaster jail. Judging of her character from the destination of her estate by will, Elizabeth, Countess of

Derby, was a " right noble lady," worthy of the illustrious and ancient race of which she came. One special legacy may be noted : " Item, I give the gold watch that was Queen Mary's to my sister the lady Grantham, if she be living at my death, and if she shall be then dead, then I doe give the same unto her daughter, the Lady Frances Nassau, if she shall be then living. As Lady Grantham did not die until 1724, the legacy had not lapsed, and the watch may yet be in existence and in possession of the heir of line, who had recently the Scotish barony of Dingwall and the English barony of Butler of Moore Park adjudged to him by a resolution of the House of Lords.*

Henrietta, COUNTESS of PEMBROKE and MONTGOMERY, was the youngest sister of the Duchess of Portsmouth, and at the date of her appearance in the Masque was a young bride. Philip, her husband, succeeded to the two earldoms upon the death of his half brother William on the 8th of July 1674, and on the 20th of May following was constituted Lord Lieutenant of the county of Wilts at the early age of twenty-two,† in honour of his alliance with a sister of the King's mistress.

Of this marriage there was only one daughter, Charlotte, who became the wife of John, the second Baron Jefferies of Wem, and brought him a daughter, Henrietta Louisa, who became the wife of the Earl of Pomfret. Upon the death of Lord Jefferies on the 9th of May 1702, his widow married Thomas, Lord Montjoy, but by him had no issue.

MISTRESS FRAZER, maid of honour to the Queen, was *Carey*, daughter of Alexander Frazer, a native of Scotland, of good descent, and medical attendant of Charles II. He was owner of the estate of Durris, commonly called Dores, in the county of Kincardine. In a letter dated St. Germans, Tuesday, 6th of August 1652, addressed by the future chancellor to Sir Richard Browne, Frazer is mentioned, and the following extract from Clarendon's State Papers quoted in a note : " I am glad you have so good a correspondent as Dr. Frayser, who is grown, God

* 15th August 1871.

† He was baptised 5th January 1652. Collins, by Brydges, vol. iii., p. 141. London, 1812. 8vo.

knows why, an absolute stranger with me : he is great
with Lord Gerard, and Mr Attorny, but he will speedily
leave us and go for England, which truly I am sorry for,
for the King's sake ; for no doubt he is good at his
business, otherwise the maddest fool alive."* This probably means that besides being an able physician, he
could, by his lively disposition, whilst curing his majesty's body, at the same time amuse his mind.

Upon the Restoration Frazer returned with Charles
and became his principal medical attendant. Evelyn,
8th May 1666, mentions that " Sir Alexander Fraser,
Prime Physician to his Majesty," dined with him. At this
date he was only a knight, but in 1673 he was created a
baronet of Nova Scotia, an honour now extinct, in consequence of failure of heirs male of his body.

His daughter was one of the beauties of the Court of
Charles, and on this account was selected to be an attendant nymph upon the goddess of Chastity. She subsequently became the first wife of Charles, the celebrated
Earl of Peterborough, who, previous to his succession to
that honour, had been created Earl of Monmouth, as the
lineal representative of Thomas Carey, second son of
Robert Carey, Earl of Monmouth, a title which had not
very long before become extinct in that family. By his
Countess, who died upon the 13th May 1709, his lordship had two sons, John and Henry, and a daughter,
Henrietta, married to Alexander, Duke of Gordon.

The second Countess was the celebrated singer Anas-
tasia Robinson, of whom an interesting account is given
by Dr Burney.† This lady was privately married to his
lordship, but the fact was not publicly acknowledged until
a brief period before his death. To prevent any question
as to its validity, in the event of his demise, and before
leaving this country for Lisbon, where he was ordered for
his health, " he found it necessary, not only to declare
his marriage to all his relations, but since the person
who married them was dead, to remarry her again in the
church of Bristol before witnesses. The warmth with
which he spoke on these subjects made me think him

* Evelyn's Diary and Correspondence. vol. iv., page 251.
2d Edition. London, 1854.
† History of Music, vol. iv.

much recovered, as well as his talking of his present state as a heaven to what was past."*

Every endeavour was made to prevent the Earl's voyage to Lisbon, but without effect, for he died on his voyage to that city on the 15th October 1735. His remains were brought back and interred in the family vault at Turvey.

"He was," said Lord Orford, "one of those men of careless and negligent grace who scatter a thousand bon-mots and idle verses which we painful compilers gather and hoard till the owners stare to find themselves authors. Such was this Lord. Of an advantageous figure, and enterprising spirit,—as gallant as Amadis, and as brave, but a little more expeditious in his journies: for he is said to have seen more kings and more postilions than any in Europe. His enmity to the Duke of Marlborough and his friendship with Pope," to whom he gave the watch, when *moribundus*, which he had received as a present from the King of Sardinia "will preserve his name, when his genius, too romantic to have laid a solid foundation for fame, and his politics, too disinterested for his age and country, shall be equally forgotten. He was a man, as his poet said, who would neither die nor live like other mortals."

The Countess survived his Lordship fifteen years, much respected and honoured. She resided at Bevis Mount near Southampton, sometimes at Fulham or Peterborough House. The former residence was the cherished abode of the Earl. In a letter to Pope, in which he prefers his "little Amoret to the stately Sacharissa at Stow," he observes, "I am sure the Farmeress at Bevis in her highest mortifications, in the middle of Lent, would feel emotions of vanity if she knew you gave her the character of a reasonable woman." Bishop Warburton in a note informs the public, that the "Farmeress meant the Countess of Peterborough, a Roman Catholic."†

At a later date Bevis Mount "again became the abode of the muses," having been purchased by the poet

---

* Pope to Martha Blount, August 25, 1735. Bowles' Pope, vol. x., p. 19; London, 1806, 8vo.
† Bowles' Pope, vol. viii. p. 262.

Sotheby, whose great merits at the present date are but little known.

Through the marriage of Lady Henrietta Mordaunt to Alexander, Duke of Gordon, the estate of Durris, or Dores, ultimately passed, upon the death of Sir Peter Frazer without issue, to the Gordon family. It was sold some few years since, in virtue of an Act of Parliament, and the price invested in the purchase of other lands more contiguous to the large estates of the ducal race of Gordon, now belonging to the Duke of Richmond and Lenox, the heir of line of the family.

Grammont gives the following description of the DUKE OF MONMOUTH :* "His figure and the external graces of his person were such that nature perhaps never formed anything more complete : his face was extremely handsome, and yet it was a manly face, neither inanimate nor effeminate, each feature having its peculiar beauty and delicacy. He had a wonderful genius for every sort of exercise, an engaging aspect, and an air of Grandeur : in a word, he possessed every personal advantage ; but in proportion to the greatness of his personal was the deficiency of his mental accomplishments. He had no opinions, but such as he derived from others ; and those who first insinuated themselves into his friendship, took care to inspire him with none, but such as were pernicious. The astonishing beauty of his outward form excited universal admiration ; those who before were looked upon as handsome were now forgotten at Court, and all the gay and beautiful of the fair sex were at his devotion. He was particularly beloved by the King ; but the universal terror of husbands and lovers. This did not long continue ; for nature not having endowed him with qualifications to secure the possession of the heart, the fair sex soon perceived the defect."

His father's love created great jealousy in the Duchess of Cleveland, whose children by Charles " were like so many little puppets compared to this new Adonis." To disguise this feeling, this most unscrupulous woman pretended a deep affection to Monmouth, which did not nevertheless impose upon the King, who, perfectly cognisant of the extreme liberality of the moral principles of

* P. 163.

the Duchess, deemed it more prudent at once to get him
a wife whilst a comparative youth than expose him to
the fascinations of a female so particularly meretricious.
Hence it was that there was selected from the house of
Buccleugh, Anne Scott, the daughter and heir of Francis,
Earl of Buccleugh, with a large estate—still possessed by
their descendants. " Her person was full of charms, and
her mind possessed all those perfections in which the
handsome Monmouth was so defective."* By letters patent
they were created, 20th April 1673, Duke and Duchess
of Buccleuch, and Earl and Countess of Dalkeith, &c. &c.,
in Scotland, a circumstance that saved the Buccleuch
honours from forfeiture, as the attainder of the husband
did not affect the separate honours in the person of the
wife.

Whether the Masque of Calisto brought the Lady
Henrietta Wentworth and the Duke for the first time
together is not known, but it is possible that the
elegance displayed by the Adonis of the Court in that
most graceful of all dances—a minuet—now laid aside
for a very different species of Terpsichorean exhibition—
was not without leading subsequently to that intimacy
and affection which Monmouth carried with him to the
scaffold, and caused the untimely death of the Lady
Henrietta. Monmouth was born at Rotterdam on the
9th of April 1649, and beheaded, in the thirty-sixth
year of his age, on Tower-hill, 15th July 1685. When
the final separation from the Duchess occurred is not
certain, but there were several children of the marriage,
the youngest of whom, Lord Francis, born in 1678, died
an infant. His youngest daughter, the Lady Anne, born
on February 17, 1675, was with her father in the Tower,
and was so much affected by his execution that she died
of grief soon after, and was buried in Westminster Abbey
on the 31st of August following.†

The Duchess married in May 1688 Charles, Lord
Cornwallis, whom she survived, and died upon the 6th
of February 1731-2, in the eighty-first year of her age.
She was succeeded in the Dukedom by her grandson

* Grammont, p. 166.
† Collins' Peerage by Brydges, vol. iii., p. 538. London,
1812, 8vo.

Francis, who was, upon the 23d March 1742-3, restored
by Act of Parliament to the title of Earl of Doncaster,
which had been forfeited by his grandfather.

From some letters written by her Grace to the Earl of
Leven and Melville,* it is plain that she took good care of
her means and estate, and was well versed, not in political but domestic economy, as most high-born dames of
that period were. In the conclusion of one of her letters
from London dated in June, but without the year of our
Lord, she says, " I shall bring a new chair to go in the
streets of Edinburgh, and an old one to cross the Court
of Dalkeith. I do most heartily long to be amongst you.
I wrett to you yesterday, you will never forgive thes two
letters coming so soon together. You will think me
extravagant in marble, but it is *to show you I do not
dispyse my old Castle.*† Her Grace was not very care-
ful in her spelling, for she has weding for wedding, mar-
age for marriage, &c. She sends the Earl a list of
articles she requires for her kitchen, to see if they can
be got in Scotland, if not, she will bring them with her
in " the shipe whair my goods are."

In another letter her Grace is anxious to be advised
what articles of dress could be procured in the north :
" The Duchess of Queensberry‡ told my daughter Dalkeith that the Ladys sent to England for their clothes,
and that there was no silk stuffs fit to be worn ther.
Pray ask your Lady if this be so, for if it is, we will
furnish ourselves here, but if it be not so, wee will buy
as wee want when wee com thair, and be drest like
other good Ladys and break non of your acts of Parliament."§

There is among the letters one of some interest, as
shewing her anxiety to have the mercy of the Crown

* The original letters were formerly in the hands of the late C.
K. Sharpe, Esq., who kindly permitted transcripts to be taken.
† Of Dalkeith, which formerly belonged to a branch of the
turbulent race of Douglas.
‡ Anne Hyde, daughter of the Earl of Clarendon, the
patroness of Gay, the author of the Beggar's Opera.
§ Sumptuary laws as to dress, to which the Scotch Parliament paid particular attention. A reference indicating the
etter was written previous to the Union.

extended to a poor Highlander called Hugh Maclane, who having been induced to drink a seditious toast in a state of intoxication, was informed upon, tried by court martial, and ordered for execution. This occurred in December 1701. She says, " I know not which way to endever the presarvation of this poor man, but if it can be done, if you could give me derection or help in this. Do not laugh at me, I am no soldieur, but a poor merciful woman."* It is to be hoped that her intercession was successful.

The Bishop of Oxford has not been exactly correct as to the nobleman who, at the date of the performance of Calisto, had the title of VISCOUNT DUNBLAINE. Sir Thomas Osborne was created Baron of Kiveton and Viscount Latimer in 1673. In the following year he was advanced to the Earldom of Danby on the 27th June. The Masque is distinctly mentioned by Evelyn to have been performed in December 1674. It was not printed and published until the year following. Thus Sir Thomas was, at the time of the representation, Earl of Danby and Viscount Latimer, and the title of courtesy of his eldest son was properly speaking Viscount Latimer.

Now the Bishop erroneously asserts that the Earl, "*after* the representation but before the publication, was created Viscount Dunblaine in Scotland, which dignity was assumed as a title of courtesy by his son Lord Latimer." The fact is otherwise, for the Scotish Viscounty *preceded* the English Viscounty and Earldom. It is evident that the Viscount Dunblaine mentioned was Peregrine the second son, and afterwards second Duke of Leeds, a dignity which the Earl of Danby subsequently attained after many risks, and an imprisonment of five years in the Tower. In the edition of Collins by Sir Egerton Brydges,† it is asserted that " Peregrine was in his father's lifetime created Viscount Dunblaine in Scotland on *the surrender* of his father's patent." In England very little is known of the usages of Scotland in Peerage

* The Earl of Leven was Governor of Edinburgh Castle. In the reign of Anne he was a General and Commander-in-Chief of all her Majesty's Forces in Scotland. He died in June 1728.

† Vol. i., p. 258.

matters, and mistakes are consequently by no means
uncommon. The " surrender" means "*resignation*," a
legal form by which a peer of Scotland could, before the
Union, resign in the hands of the Crown his honours for
a *new* grant, and Lord Danby, having attained a higher
dignity than that of a Scotish Viscounty, took this
method of obtaining the authority of the King to transfer
his northern Viscounty to his younger son, who at a
subsequent date, 19th March 1689-90, was called up by
writ to the English House of Peers as Lord Osborne of
Kiveton.

By the death of his brother Edward, Lord Latimer, in
January 1688, whose two sons died infants, Peregrine
eventually succeeded to the Dukedom of Leeds, Marquisate of Carmarthen, Earldom of Danby, and Viscounty of Latimer. He died on the 25th June 1729
in the seventy-first year of his age. The period of
his death establishes the Viscount to have been about
sixteen when he appeared in the Masque. It is
singular, that after the lapse of not very many years,
the representation of the Godolphins should devolve
on the Osbornes, and that the heir of line of Margaret Blagge should be the heir of line of her fellow-
performer Peregrine, Viscount Osborne of Dunblain.
His father was one of the prominent political characters
of the reign of Charles the Second, and had the satisfaction of being more hated than any other man in
the kingdom, if we may trust Burnet's History of his
own times. There seems no reason for doubting this
general detestation, for the following verses of a pasquil
or lampoon, extracted from a contemporary MS. which
was in the library of the late Charles Kirkpatrick Sharpe,
Esq., certainly support the Bishop's assertion :—

ON THOMAS, EARL OF DANBY,

LATE LORD HIGH TREASURER OF ENGLAND 1678-9.

TUNE *Peggy Benson.*

Zounds, what means the Parliament,
Sure they are drunk with Brandy
When they went to circumvent
      Thomas Earl of Danby.

But this ungrateful will appear
As any thing that can be,
For they received Fiddlers' fare
        From Thomas Earl of Danby.

Sir John Coplestone* did invite
All those he thought would bandy
For any thing, be't wrong or right,
        For Thomas Earl of Danby.

Shaftesbury did lie and lurk,
That little Jack-a-Dandy,
And all his engines sat on work
        'Gainst Thomas Earl of Danby.

Now whether he will stay or go
I think 'tis handy dandy †
If he stays, he'll be hang'd,‡ I trow,
        Poor Thomas Earl of Danby.

Of subjects, I did ne'er hear tell,
Nor can any in this land be
That deserves a halter half as well
        As Thomas Earl of Danby.

With what colour couldst thou say,
Since Lombard Street can brand thee,
That thou th' Exchequer debts didst pay,
        Fye ! Thomas Earl of Danby.

He was bid say so by his wife
That he'd be still a grandee,
For he ne'er told a lie in his life,
        True ! Thomas Earl of Danby.

Then Commons trust him not a whit,
If you do, you'll trapann'd be,
There's not so false a Jesuit
        As Thomas Earl of Danby.§

* Sir John Copleston was a cadet of the old family of that name in Devonshire. He lived at Pynes, near Exeter, an estate he inherited from his grandfather. Although the Coplestones were royalists, he engaged in the service of the Parliament. He was sheriff of Devonshire in 1655. He was knighted by the Protector at Whitehall June 1, 1658, for his services at the time of Penruddoch's revolt.

† A Child's Play, mentioned in the Vision of Piers Ploughman, and King Lear, and still existing. See Halliwell's "Archaic Dictionary," vol. i., p. 432.

‡ He was certainly not hanged, but he got five years' imprisonment in the Tower of London.

§ There are several more verses which, from their disgusting attack upon the ladies of the family, are unfit for publication.

The Lord DAINCOURT was Robert, eldest son of Nicholas Leake, Earl of Scarsdale, in the county of Derby, who succeeded to the Earldom upon the death of his father in 1680. Dying without lawful issue in 1707, his brother Richard became the next Earl, and his son Nicolas never having married, both the Earldom and Barony became extinct upon his demise in 1736.

Mr TREVOR was John, eldest son of Sir John Trevor, Secretary of State in 1672. His mother was Ruth, daughter of John Hampden, and great-niece of Oliver Cromwell. His younger brother, Thomas, was Chief Justice of the Common Pleas, and was created Baron Trevor in 1726.

It is probable that the Mr Lane mentioned as taking a part in the Masque was one of the Lanes of Bentley who had so materially aided Charles in his escape after the battle of Worcester, when, by the aid of Mistress Jane Lane, the King was safely removed from the place where he had been concealed, and ultimately enabled to reach the Continent.* Had David Leslie, afterwards Lord Newark, acted as he should have done, the result of the battle might have ended very differently from what it did.

Of the other person of quality, Mr Harpe, we have found no particulars.

In one of the stanzas *Edward*, who predeceased his father, is called Lord Latimer, proving thus that this was the title by courtesy, at that date, of the eldest son of the Earl of Danby.

* See the interesting volume called " The Boscobel Tracts," edited by J. Hughes, Esq., Edinburgh, 1830, 8vo. ; and the account of the King's escape, from his own recollection, by Lord Hailes. It is to the credit of Charles that he never forgot or failed to reward any single individual, however humble, that aided his escape.

PROLOGUE TO HORACE.

Spoken at Court

1668-9.

In a rare little book having the title of "Covent Garden Drollery," there is printed "Prologue to Horace, spoken by the *Dutchess* of Munmouth at Court." In the Biographia Dramatica it is mentioned that Horace, as translated from Corneille by the matchless Orinda, otherwise Katherine Phillips,* with a fifth act, supplied by Sir John Denham, was presented at Court by persons of quality, the prologue being spoken by the *Duke* of Monmouth.

Upon turning to Evelyn, it appears there is this entry in his Diary, 4th February 1667-8: "I saw the tragedy of Horace written by the virtuous Mrs Phillips, acted before their Majesties. Betwixt each act a masque and antique dance. The excessive gallantry of the ladies was infinite, those especially on that . . . Castle-maine, esteemed at £40,000 and more, far out-shining the Queen." On the 27th February the following year, the tragedy was again performed and witnessed by Evelyn.

There can be no doubt that this was the performance referred to in the "Covent Garden Drollery," and the only question is who spoke the prologue. The Peerage of Monmouth, according to Collins, was created upon the 14th February 1662-63, and the Scotish Dukedom not until April 20th 1673, after the marriage of the parties. The Play acted at Court was thus represented before the creation of the Buccleuch Dukedom.

As the Prologue is really good, and the little book from which it is extracted very scarce, it may be no unsuitable conclusion to finish the present volume with it.

* She died of the Small-pox, 22d June 1664.

PROLOGUE TO HORACE,

Spoken by the Dutchess of Monmouth
at Court.

WHEN Honour flourish'd ere for price 'twas sold,
When *Rome* was poor, and undebauch'd with gold,
That vertue which should to the world give Law
First under Kings, its Infant breath did draw :
And *Horace*, who, his Sovereign's Champion fought,
Its first example to republiques taught.
Honour and Love, the Poets' dear delight,
The field in which all Modern *Muses* fight ;
Where gravely Rhyme debates what's just and fit,
And seeming contradictions pass for wit ;
Here in their native Purity first grew,
Ere they th' Adulterate arts of Stages knew.
This Martial story, which through *France* did come,
And there was wrought in great *Cornelia's* Tomb,
Orinda's matchless Muse to *Britain* brought,
And foreign verse, our *English* accents taught ;
So soft that to our shame, we understand,
They could not fall, but from a Lady's hand.
Thus while a Woman *Horace* did translate,
Horace did rise above a Roman Fate.
And by our Ladies he mounts higher yet,
While he is spoke above, what he is writ ;
But yet triumphant Honours are to come,
When, mighty Prince he must receive your Doom :
From all besides our Actors have no fear.
Censure, and Wit, are beauty's vassals here,
And should they with Rebellion, tempt their rage,
Our Basilisks could shout 'em from the Stage.
But that their Fate would be two great to die
By bright *Sabina's*, or *Camilla's* Eye.

TURNBULL AND SPEARS, PRINTERS, EDINBURGH.